Stars Ascending

Heather Smith

Also by Heather Smith

Fated Darkness Series

Shadow of Twilight

Dusk to Dawn

Dawn of Light

Stars Ascending Series

Stars Ascending

Damon Salvatore. For showing us that the morally grey characters are in fact the most interesting and the right one to choose.

Chapter 1

Club Divine looked like something out of a serial killer documentary.

The sign was barely hanging on the wall and was chipped, with broad sections of it missing. Whether that was from the weather or intentional was yet to be determined. But that wasn't what drew her eye. It was the door painted a royal purple and guarded by a large, hulking bouncer.

Carolynn could feel her stomach twisting in knots, secretly wishing this wasn't some kind of murderer's anonymous club. Which, in her defense, would be just the type of situation she would find herself in. It didn't matter that it was her eighteenth birthday and her first time stepping into a club. Finding herself in a crowd of serial killers would be just her luck.

She glanced at her friend sitting in the driver's seat beside her.

Beth, her best friend and partner in crime, sat there with the broadest grin, kohl-lined golden-brown eyes alight with excitement and anticipation.

They had spent weeks preparing for this night. The night where they were both able to enter a club legally and dance the night away. Their outfits had been hand-selected from Beth's closet. Carolynn even curled her auburn hair instead of throwing it into its usual high ponytail. She tugged at the ends of her black mesh shirt that did nothing to hide the golden skin beneath or the cleavage shown off by the push-up bra Beth insisted she wear. Her outfit was nothing like what she normally wore, which usually consisted of leggings and tank tops. She felt utterly exposed and uncomfortable.

Beth swatted at her hands, which were still fidgeting with the material of her shirt. "Will you leave yourself alone? You look hot."

Carolynn's lip curled up, her cheeks heating. "I should have brought a jacket."

"No way!" Beth scoffed. "If I had a body like yours, I'd walk around naked all day."

Carolynn eyed her best friend skeptically, raising a brow. "That would be rather dangerous, given that we live in central Florida and you'd quickly resemble a lobster."

"You know what I mean," Beth said flippantly, gesturing toward her curves. "You have the body of an athletic model most girls starve for. I've seen you eat an entire tray of brownies. It's not fair."

Carolynn frowned down at herself and then at Beth. Her friend had curves most would envy, with an hourglass silhouette, yet it had always been one of her insecurities. She had somehow managed to find the perfect emerald green dress that accentuated those curves and had her breasts nearly falling out.

Carolynn still wasn't sure how she was able to move, let alone keep herself in it.

"Can we not compare our bodies and just enjoy the night? I promise I will try not to hide, if you promise never to compare me to a model again," Carolynn said plainly.

Models were tall and willowy, elegant and graceful, while she was awkward and spent way too much time with horses to be considered any kind of sociable. Large crowds made her nervous and uncomfortable. It was hard to control herself, and her mind, when there were so many around.

Tonight would be the ultimate test.

"Deal!" Beth beamed, nearly bouncing out of the car and her dress. "I promise!"

Skinny bitch.

"I heard that," Carolynn rolled her eyes, looking pointedly at the girl beside her.

Beth blew her a kiss just as she got out of the car and slammed the door shut behind her.

Carolynn pushed the door open and stepped out into the balmy summer air. The humidity instantly kissed her skin and felt as though she were breathing underwater. She glanced hopelessly at her hair, knowing full well she'd be lucky if the curls she painstakingly worked on only an hour ago were still in place by the time they reached the door.

Club Divine was more of a dive bar than an actual club, but it was the local hangout for teens their age, and the bartender was notorious for failing to check ID.

The girls approached the entrance. The clacking of their heels echoed off the gravel parking lot. The arch of her heels was already screaming in protest, and Carolynn instantly regretted not opting for the ankle-high boots she knew were buried in her closet, but Beth had insisted on the heels.

Carolynn and Beth each gave the man at the door their cover charge and stepped through the cracked door frame.

Carolynn blinked her eyes as they adjusted to the pulsing strobe lights and dim lighting, but what she found inside pleasantly surprised her.

While the outside looked like an abandoned building straight from *Dateline*, the inside was clean, with crisp lines of black and gold. Tasteful furniture was neatly adorned around the room, with satin curtains hanging from the wall as décor. A bar with black quartz countertops ran the length of the left side of the club.

The dance floor sat at the back of the club, littered with grinding bodies. The smell of body odor, cigarette smoke, and heavy perfume attacked the senses the moment they passed the threshold.

Both girls tried desperately not to choke or gag. Carolynn suppressed a cough that clawed at her throat, making her eyes water, but she inhaled, pushing past the feeling of her lungs constricting.

Carolynn felt her hand being seized by Beth, before being pulled through the crowd. She squeezed her friend's hand firmly so as not to lose her and lifted her head to see over the dozens of heads bent close together. The bar was getting closer as they made their way towards a specific individual leaning against the stone top.

Brian lounged back against the bar, oozing arrogance and lust. The tilt of his head, the purse of his lips, the way he held his chin above everyone else as though he were better. Carolynn couldn't wait for an excuse to smack that smug look off his face, but instead, she smiled for Beth's sake, trying not to truly vomit over the way his shit brown eyes took in Beth as though she were dinner. That look in his narrowed eyes, the look of dominance and ownership as they raked up and down her friend's body, left her feeling as though a bucket of slime had been poured over her head.

He reminded her of an '80s rocker who had a thing for motorbikes. His brown hair was gelled into a short mohawk, and he wore an oil-stained t-shirt, leather jacket, and dark jeans that also contained fluids she'd rather not inspect. Never mind that he worked in an auto body shop.

Beth pulled her hand from her grip as they drew closer.

Carolynn reluctantly let her go, even though every instinct was screaming at her to hold on, to not let him touch her. A part of her itched to reach out and peek behind the wall she kept tightly secured around her mind and peer into his, but she held herself back and strengthened that wall to keep temptation out.

The quartz bar was cool beneath her already heated skin. The club was warm thanks to the amount of people occupying the space, and the countertop was a refreshing kiss of coolness on her flesh. She signaled to the handsome-looking bartender, who looked barely old enough to be working behind the bar, but the corner of his lip pulled up into a wry smile at the sight of her.

Carolynn forced a smile, pursing her lips and feeling like an absolute fool as he walked towards her, flipping a towel over his shoulder.

Either the bartender didn't notice her lame attempt at seduction or he didn't care; he smiled at her all the same. Blue eyes were glued to her exposed chest beneath the mesh top. She couldn't help the hopeless feeling she felt as she took advantage of the distraction and ordered two shots of tequila.

This would either be the worst or best decision of the night.

Carolynn quickly tipped the glass back, trying not to flinch as the alcohol burned its way down her throat. Her eyes watered at the sensation until it hit her stomach, making her skin flush with warmth.

Beth suddenly appeared beside her, throwing her shot back.

"Well, that burns like the fires of hell," Beth yelled over the thrumming music, making a sour face as she laughed.

Carolynn couldn't help but smile at her friend's carefree giggle. That was until Brian came up behind Beth, wrapping his arms around her waist and hauling her back into his tall, lanky frame. Beth tilted her head back, eyebrows raised in surprise as he leaned in, planting kisses along her neck.

Carolynn looked away immediately, feeling awkward enough to order another shot and throw it back before the glass could touch the bar. She glanced over out of the corner of her eye and no longer found him sucking on her neck, no. Now there were tongue and hands, and moaning that would haunt her for the rest of her days.

She grimaced at the sight. "Okay, well, you two have fun with that; I'll just be over there," she said, gesturing towards the dance floor. Not like Beth was even paying attention, for that matter.

Carolynn turned her back to them and thrust herself into the buzzing horde.

Mingling with the dancers, she moved her hips with the beat of the house music and felt it take control of her body. It pulsed through her until her heart matched the tempo. Her hips rocked harder, her fingers gripped the roots of her hair, raising them in the air and back down her chest, settling on her hips. She could feel the pressure of the bodies around her, their energy, their minds. Most of them were pleasantly numb from alcohol, while others enjoyed the thrill of the chase and the music. She moved her hips in a circular motion, fingers tapping against her hipbone with the rise and fall of the pulsing base.

The music continued.

It could have been minutes. It could have been hours. All she knew was she couldn't stop, allowing the music to take complete control, filling her veins and fueling her body.

The music began to slow down, turning into a soft sultry sound. The air in her lungs felt like knives, scraping at the soft tissue. Her throat was dry. But she'd never felt so alive.

Carolynn looked around towards the bar where she'd left Beth, searching for her friend, but they were gone. Opening her senses and searching for that familiar imprint she could recognize anywhere, she finally spotted her with Brian in the back of the club, blending in with the shadows of the alcoves, cut into the wall to provide for moments exactly like the one they were sharing.

Trying desperately to remove the deeply sickening thoughts she could hear churning in her friend's mind, she felt her body gravitate farther down the wall into the darkest part of the club, where not even the strobe lights seemed to reach.

A tall man with wide shoulders and eyes the color of silver blue moonlight that seemed to glow out of the darkness leaned against the wall. Darkness clung to him, haunting the space he occupied as if the light wouldn't dare go near the shade. But those eyes. She had never seen anything so pale, so piercing, and they were looking right at her. Her legs trembled, fighting against her will to hold firm, but they wanted to move, to go to him. She widened her stance just slightly, planting her feet firmly where she was.

Carolynn reached out. Her mind spanned out over the club. Most of the occupants were buzzed with alcohol and weed, their thoughts simple and focused on either music or sex, easy to pick out, but as she reached the far corner of the room she hit a solid, ancient wall. For the first time in her life, she couldn't get inside someone's mind; only a fleeting glimpse of an emotion she could almost taste on the back of her tongue.

Brushing against his conscience, she could recognize anxiety and eagerness, bitter and tart.

Curiosity urged her to push harder, and dive deeper, which scared her in a way. She had never been so enthralled by someone as to go against her own conscience and morals and violate someone's mind. Before she had a chance to make up her mind, she caught movement along the wall as the man began to move, and he was heading straight for her.

He stepped away from the wall, and the light began to fill in his features and add dimension. She was finally able to make out his face, with high cheekbones and a strong, chiseled jaw with slight shadowing. His hair was dark and brushed back, almost iridescent like a raven's feathers, reflecting the flashing neon lights, casting his hair in pinks, blues, and purples. From what she could see, he wore nothing but black, formal and tailor-made, with a charcoal dress shirt fitted to his body, accentuating the curves and dips of his biceps and chest. The two top buttons were undone, revealing a patch of cool, creamy skin.

The corners of his thin lips twitched, as though he was fighting back a smirk.

She could feel her heart flutter erratically inside her chest. The closer he got, the more she was able to understand just how tall he was, clearing her height by at least a foot. Heat rushed to her face as he finally reached her on the dancefloor, standing but a few feet away.

Carolynn could feel those piercing blue eyes wandering over the length of her body, almost the same as she was doing to him. She felt slightly self-conscious, only imagining how sweaty and tangled her hair must look, but she forced her arms to stay at her side instead of messing with the knotted locks, like her fingers itched to do. She tilted her head back as his gaze met hers, forcing her to acknowledge that even with heels, he still towered over her.

Minutes felt like hours as they stood entranced with one another. The sultry tempo of the music around them shifted from one song to the next.

Mesmerized by his savage beauty, she had barely noticed he had moved until she felt a large, calloused hand seizing her own. Electricity raced up her arm and throughout every inch of her body, raising the hair along her flesh and alerting her to every move and breath he took. His eyes widened slightly, and his breath hitched for just a moment.

Could he feel it too?

He pulled her in closer until her body was completely flush with his. She didn't stop to think about the fact that she wasn't resisting, or how bizarre this might be; that would be something she could ponder later. Right now, all she wanted was to drown in the man that wrapped his arm around her waist, pressing his warm hand into the small of her back, thumb brushing over the exposed skin, which erupted in gooseflesh. She could feel the rise and fall of his chest, and her heart picked up speed as their bodies began to sway to the music.

Carolynn rested one hand on his arm. A hard muscle flexed under the buttery soft fabric, expanding and contracting as he guided her body with his own, allowing the music to take control. She couldn't keep her eyes from his, afraid to look away and break whatever spell they were under.

The air around them felt charged and electrified. Their breathing was deep and heavy as their bodies moved, and the way she was responding to every press of his fingers, the pressure of his legs against hers as he led them in the dance, stole the breath from her. The beating of her heart matched the quickening tempo of the music as the DJ moved on to something with a more Latin flavor.

He dipped her body backward, balancing her weight perfectly as her hair grazed the ground, until he brought her back up in a slow arch, their chests touching once more. Her hair fell around her, covering her shoulders, back, and both of their chests, sticking to the perspiration gathered around her temples. She looked into his eyes, silently willing her heart to slow, positive he could hear it even above the music. His inner iris looked to be made of thousands of diamond facets reflecting every shade of blue possible.

"Who are you?" she asked, finally finding her voice. The music was so loud she was certain he hadn't heard.

His long thick lashes fluttered as though startled by the sound of her voice, but she found her eyes roaming to his thin lips as they pulled into a devilish smirk. "Donnie." His voice was like silk, deep and smooth as though speaking to a lover.

Carolynn played the name on repeat, rolling it around in her mind, wishing to taste the way it felt on her lips. She grabbed a fistful of his shirt and pulled him down. He could have resisted, could have not given an inch, but he didn't. He leaned in closer until her cheek rested against his. The feel of his breath on the back of her neck sent shivers dripping down her spine. He smelled warm and cold, fresh yet ancient.

She whispered, just loud enough to be heard over the music with her lips brushing against his ear. "It was nice to meet you, Donnie."

Donnie shuddered, his skin vibrating against hers as she pulled back, untangling herself from his arms.

Carolynn turned her back to him, almost afraid to look over her shoulder and find him not really there, but she knew he was. The same way she knew his eyes had not left her, watching as she wove in and out of the dancers and out the club's front door.

The air outside was almost a relief as the balmy air settled on her skin that felt as though it was on fire. The faintest hint of salt coated her tongue from the nearby beach, which seemed to soothe her frazzled nerves as the adrenaline began to wear off. She gasped it in, knowing full well by the spasming of her pulse and the shakiness of her hands that hyperventilating was a very real possibility. She could still feel his touch on her skin. Every single cell he touched along her arms and back.

Despite herself, she giggled, glancing back towards the club door where Donnie stood just on the other side. She couldn't believe the way she acted, how bold and confident she had been. It was bizarre and odd, but felt so good. She had never been so enthralled by a guy, and it was intoxicating.

Correction — he was intoxicating.

A branch breaking rattled across the parking lot that was void of life. She flinched at the sound but instantly relaxed as she saw an overly large black wolf trotting in her direction.

"Shadow, you nearly scared me to death." Carolynn breathed out heavily, clutching at her chest.

Are you okay? The wolf's voice rang clear in her mind.

Carolynn frowned at the wolf eye level with her waist. "Why wouldn't I be?"

Her wolf seemed to shake her head, scanning the parking lot and the bouncer eyeing them curiously at the door. *It's nothing, pup. You know I didn't like the idea of you going out tonight.*

Carolynn snorted, hugging her arms as a cold chill worked its way through her. "Sometimes I think you need a life. Like a real wolfie life, but then I know you'll say —"

You are my life, pup, Shadow finished for her.

Carolynn gave her a pointed look, lips pursed. "Exactly."

"Carolynn!"

She and Shadow both spun around toward the club to find Beth stumbling with her heels in one hand, swinging them precariously in front of her.

"Where have you been?" Beth hollered, words slurring.

How much had she been drinking?

"I saw you come outside, and when you didn't come back in, I got worried." Beth pouted as she finally reached them and leaned on her shoulder. "I saw you dancing with some sexy man. Who was he? Have you been holding out on me? We're best friends; you're supposed to tell me everything. I know about your powers, you psychic bitch. Why do you shine? It's so pretty."

"Okay, Beth. I think you've had enough fun for one night. Let's get you home." Carolynn wrapped her arm around her friend's waist to support her weight.

"I don't want to go home," Beth whined, suddenly sagging in her arms. "Let's go to your house."

"Okay, fine," Carolynn grunted, nearly carrying Beth towards the teal Mustang.

She tried her best to be gentle with the drunk girl, but given her best efforts, Beth still managed to hit her head on the roof of the car getting into the passenger seat.

"Shit, I'm sorry," Carolynn apologized profusely, shutting the door and walking to the driver's side. Before getting in, she remembered the large wolf following at her heels. "You coming with us or meeting us there?"

I prefer to walk. That metal death trap is not the way I'd choose to die.

Carolynn narrowed her eyes at the wolf. "I'm going to try and not take offense to that."

Shadow didn't bother replying before she turned around and disappeared in the brush, effectively blending in with the night.

She watched her go before sliding into the cracked leather seat and bringing the car to life. The engine roared beneath her feet as she put it in drive and left the club in the rearview mirror.

Chapter 2

Thunder and lightning shook the earth and brightened the sky. Metal against metal rang in the air. The beating of something loud and soft echoed in the sky above. The earth was dead with no one and nothing in sight for miles. She was completely and utterly alone. Taking a step forward, her feet felt wet. Glancing down, she found herself standing in something dark and red.

Burnt coffee wafted up her nose. Carolynn sniffed the air gingerly as she opened her sleep-filled eyes.

The night felt like a dream. That is, until she tried to move her feet, kicking the comforter off, and the arches of her feet screamed in protest. She knew she should have rejected the heels.

She reached for the old flip phone on the nightstand beside her bed and found it to be only seven in the morning. She whimpered at the time on the screen, wishing desperately to escape back into the dreamscape, but instead, she got out from under the blankets and stood to stretch when a noise startled her. Turning back towards the bed, she found Beth snoring, face down in a pillow.

For a brief moment, Carolynn wondered if she should move her friend's face.

Are you going to make sure she isn't suffocating?

Carolynn turned toward the mound of black fur at her feet and found Shadow's silvery grey eyes watching her friend sleeping heavily on the bed. Beth's snoring grew louder.

"If she couldn't breathe, she wouldn't be so loud," Carolynn stated. She had definitely seen her friend sleep in more awkward and unforgiving positions than this.

Shadow huffed air out through her nose as though she was snorting at the comment.

"Come on, I'll let you out," she said, gesturing for the she-wolf to follow.

The stained carpet beneath her bare feet was rough in some spots as she walked across the small space and out of the bedroom into the even smaller living room. The old sofa held stains better left undiscovered but contained so many memories that her mother refused to get rid of it. The room was split in half by a long, singular counter, where she found her mom standing in the middle of their kitchen stirring creamer into a mug with a plastic spoon.

"Morning," she said, announcing her presence, which her mom hadn't seemed to notice.

Blonde, silvered hair fell back from her face as she glanced up, blue eyes wide with surprise. "Carolynn, honey. You're up early. I figured you'd be sleeping in until noon."

Carolynn bit her tongue, trying hard to keep from saying something snarky. She didn't quite have the energy for an argument this early. As though her mother didn't know she'd been working every day this summer to save for college in the fall. Not to mention the last time she'd even slept in. Between school and work the last several years, she couldn't afford to waste her time sleeping.

"Nope, just letting out Shadow," Carolynn said instead, forcing a smile before moving towards the front door.

She pressed her shoulder into the old door, pushing it out of the swollen frame and swinging it open. She walked down the splintered porch steps and sat on a chair that had seen better days in the front overgrown lawn.

Shadow instantly meandered into the reeds, nose to the ground as she found a spot suitable to do her business.

Carolynn ran her fingers through her knotted bedhead and began to work some of the tangles out as the wolf came back. College was only a month away, and soon Beth and her would be living on campus. The idea alone made her giddy and excited. Not just to learn and try new things, but to get out of this house and finally be on her own. She loved her mother, who had done her best to raise her, but ever since her father died two years ago, nothing was ever the same, and her mom had retreated farther and farther away.

They were practically strangers.

What's bothering you, pup?

Carolynn lifted her eyes to where Shadow sat. She settled her hands in her lap, leaving her hair as a project for later.

"It's nothing," Carolynn said with a shake of her head.

The wolf cocked her head to the side, not buying her answer. *Carolynn.*

Carolynn rolled her eyes, sighing deeply. "I don't know," she breathed out, glancing back at the open front door, where she could see her mother finishing what was probably her third cup of coffee, completely oblivious.

Shadow followed her line of sight to the silver blonde inside, gathering her bag for the day. *You know she loves you.*

"I know," Carolynn sighed once again, running her fingers through her tangled mess of hair, only to have it snag on a knot. She made a noise of frustration as she threw her hands back in her lap.

Footsteps approached, the floor creaking beneath a weight.

Carolynn quickly plastered a smile on her face as her mother stood looming behind her, placing a soft hand on her shoulder.

"Okay, cupcake, I'm headed out. I'll be home late. Helen called out last minute, so I'll be working another double tonight."

Carolynn nodded her head. Ramen noodles for dinner it was. "Okay, Mom."

"Love you!" her mother shouted over her shoulder as she strode past them towards the beat-up car that was one too many years past its expiration date.

The car started with a sputter, creating a plume of black smoke as she pulled out of their dirt driveway and down the road.

Carolynn watched the tin can disappeared from view. She loved her mom and appreciated how hard she worked to support the two of them, but sometimes, she just wished she'd pay attention more; to actually get to know her.

"Do you think my birth parents know where I am?" she asked passively, not even sure if she really wanted the answer. Her fingers automatically went to the necklace around her neck and the two intertwined stars hanging on the end of the gold chain.

It was no secret that she had been adopted. Her parents had told her the circumstances of her adoption at an early age, providing her with the only information they had — she was abandoned at birth and surrendered to a police station. She tried not to think of them, since it usually brought up feelings of abandonment, anger, and never-ending questions. Like, who were they? Did they have powers similar to hers, or was she an anomaly? A freak?

The necklace was the only thing that had been left with her. Well, that and a tattered old blanket that looked as if it had been homespun. It was shoved somewhere in her closet.

Why do you ask? Shadow questioned, resting her head in her lap.

Carolynn absently ran her fingers through the she-wolf's thick, soft fur, scratching behind the ears. "I just wonder if they ever cared. I mean, obviously they didn't. They abandoned me."

I don't think it's that simple, pup. There are many reasons why they couldn't raise you themselves.

"It doesn't matter. I don't know why I asked." Carolyn pushed off her knees and stood up just as she heard rustling from inside the house.

"Carolynn?"

Carolynn walked up the weathered steps and back into the house with Shadow at her heels, slamming the door rather forcefully behind her.

"I'm here, Beth. Was just outside with Shadow," she called out, heading back into her bedroom.

Beth was now sitting up with blankets strewn around her. Her brown, curly hair looked as though birds had nested in it throughout the night, and eyeliner was smudged around her eyes.

Carolynn tried not to laugh at the state of her friend. "How are you feeling?"

"Like Death came a-knocking and I told him to fuck off," Beth grumbled, pressing her palm to her forehead.

Carolynn frowned at the expression, not quite sure how that made sense.

"What happened last night?" Beth asked.

Carolynn hesitated, unsure which part of the night she would be referring too. Should she tell her about the guy she met?

Donnie.

Just thinking his name set her skin on fire. She swore she could still feel his hand pressed into her back, holding her, guiding her, and she had let him.

"Well, before you took off with Brian to the back of the club, you had a shot with me at the bar," Carolynn said, offering her a piece of the night.

"While I commend you for drinking, you pious bitch, I was referring to the tall, sexy man I saw you dancing with."

Carolynn tried to hide the smirk that began to spread across her face without her permission. Butterflies battered her stomach as her blood raced.

So, Beth had seen.

Beth straightened, perking up. "I don't think I've ever seen you smile over a guy, let alone blush. Who was he?"

"I don't know," Carolynn said.

"Look, this is not the fourth-grade Jameson debacle on repeat. I promise he is all yours," Beth swore, making an X across her chest.

"Hey, I told you we were going to get married, and then I saw you kiss him. That really hurt."

Beth waved her off as though it hadn't caused a big fight between the two of them and a long week of the silent treatment. "Water under the bridge. But seriously, who is he?"

"I honestly don't know. I've never seen him before."

Her friend chewed on her bottom lip, her thinking face making a rare appearance. "Maybe he's here visiting from out of town. He's definitely not from around here. Those clothes, that body. We would have spotted him by now."

Code for Beth would have already thrown herself at him if he had been local.

"I don't know," Carolynn repeated herself again. "We didn't talk."

Beth's mouth flew open at the assumption she was coming to, but Carolynn stopped her before the twenty questions started. She could already hear the dirty, sweaty thoughts wiggling around in her brain.

"Before you even start, no, we did not kiss, or anything of what you're thinking," Carolynn said, effectively earning her a disappointed look. "All we did was dance."

His hands had curled around her waist, calloused fingers brushed down the length of her arm as he had guided her to wrap it around his neck. The brush of his hair against her forearm. The way he had manipulated her body, coaxed her to step, sway, and move. It was as though they had been perfectly in sync.

"It's not fair you get to read minds, and I can't. I'm dying to know what you're thinking of right now to cause that deep of a blush," Beth said, pointing at her face.

Carolynn's hand came up to touch her cheek and sure enough, it was feverish.

"It's just, the dance was intense. Intimate," Carolynn tried to explain, but words failed her. "All I got from him was a name. Donnie."

"Donnie," Beth said, as though tasting it. Picking it apart one syllable at a time. "I bet you he's great in bed."

Carolynn whipped a pillow at her face, and it hit true, just like she knew it would. Beth look stunned, until she started laughing — a holding her stomach, cramping kind of laughing.

"You should see your face," Beth said, gasping for air.

"Well, it doesn't really matter now, does it? It's not like I'm going to see him again." Carolynn hated how her voice sounded pitiful, whiny almost, but she would be lying if she said she wasn't disappointed. Beth was right; she should have at least asked for his number, something.

"Never say never, babe," Beth smirked as she picked up her smartphone from the end table and checked the time, instantly cursing under her breath. "Shit, I have to get home. I didn't tell Mom and Dad I was spending the night, although I'm sure they assumed, but even still. Don't want them sending the police out looking for me."

"You should probably brush your hair first," Carolynn suggested, pointing to the nest atop her head.

Beth placed one hand on her head and grimaced. "Fuck me."

Chapter 3

arolynn and Shadow walked through the streets of town, weaving in and out of various shops. Most of the people walking along the sidewalk kept their distance, wary of the wolf. It wasn't normal for a wolf to be casually strolling through the town, but most of the regulars were used to seeing the odd pair.

Shadow was as tame as a Labrador, as long as no one tried to pull her tail, that is. She was surprisingly tolerant of being petted by people other than her, especially if they found her sweet spot just behind her right ear. Whether Shadow wanted to admit it or not, she was exceptionally good with kids. Children weren't normally afraid of her and had the habit of running right up, fascinated by her size and shiny midnight coat. The wolf enjoyed the tiny humans' energy and fascination, letting one even hug her one time — much to the parent's fright.

A hot and sticky wind blew through the city, coating her with even more perspiration. She felt sticky and in need of a shower more than anything, but they continued on. What she wouldn't give to live in an area that actually experienced all four seasons, but no, she had to live in the one state where they celebrated Thanksgiving and Christmas outside in the pool due to the oppressive heat. Florida was hotter than Satan's ball sack.

The sun was exceptionally bright today, not a cloud in the sky. She was glad she had opted for a black tank top, her shoulders and upper back absorbing the warmth of the sun, giving her olive skin a golden hue. The same tattered Converse sneakers she always wore skipped over an uneven crack in the pavement. Her long auburn hair streaked with black—a trend Beth thought would look good on her—was woven into a tight fishtail braid draped over one side. Not even the short shorts she chose, frayed and old, was helping to stave off the heat.

The bookshop was just ahead across the street. It was the newest addition in town and she had been eager to visit, to see what kind of selection it offered, but time had gotten away from her. It was her birthday weekend, which meant her boss had given her time off. One of the only times of year she actually accepted. Now seemed like the perfect opportunity to go inside.

Beth had promised to meet up with her for ice cream at the creamery down the road, but she had time to kill until then.

Carolynn looked both ways checking for oncoming traffic, before sprinting across the road, Shadow keeping pace beside her. The shop looked cute from the outside, where she could see neat rows of bookshelves containing hundreds, if not thousands of books. The front windows of the shop had some decorative writing advertising the newest release of books.

Eagerly, she opened the door, causing a bell to ring throughout the store, alerting the workers to her presence.

Shadow stuck to her side like glue, sniffing the air, keeping pace as the door closed behind them.

Carolynn approached the first set of bookcases, scanning the titles for something that might interest her. She picked out a handful of books that looked promising, quickly scanning the synopsis when she turned the corner into the next aisle and bumped into something. Stumbling back and dropping the books in her arms, she glanced up from the pile that had been in her hands.

Not something, but someone.

Carolynn found herself staring at a tall, slender woman in business casual attire, glasses skewed.

"I am so sorry! I wasn't paying attention to where I was going," Carolynn apologized, quickly ducking down, picking up the books scattered on the floor. Some hers, and others not.

The woman bent down as well, picking up the titles that must have been of her own selection. "It's fine." She breathed a laugh, as though the situation was somehow amusing. "I wasn't looking either."

Carolynn straightened, her books stacked and snuggled against her chest. She glanced down to find Shadow simply sitting back on her heels, watching the entire interaction with boredom.

Thanks for warning me, Carolynn mentally linked the wolf.

Oh, now I'm supposed to be your eyes and ears? The wolf scoffed.

Carolynn somehow resisted rolling her eyes at the wolf and instead found herself staring at the woman in front of her. She was beautiful. Her hair was a reddish brown, pin straight and cut to her shoulders in a pixie cut, with eyes that surely were cut from the finest emeralds. She had never seen anything so green before.

Her flesh grew warm as embarrassment settled over her. She knew she was raised better than to stare, but some part of her couldn't help it. Her hand twitched as if it wanted to reach out and touch her, but she gripped the books harder against her chest.

"Are you new to town?" Carolynn couldn't help but ask. "I haven't seen you around."

"I am, actually. I just opened this shop a few weeks ago." The woman smiled, revealing perfectly white teeth. Her voice was soft and melodic, deserving to be heard in operas, not a small-town bookshop.

"This is your store?" Carolynn asked, surprise obvious in her tone. She looked so young to be a business owner. She couldn't be more than a few years older than she was. "It's very impressive. I love your selection."

"Thank you." The store owner glanced at the titles Carolynn cradled in her arms, and her grin grew. "You have great taste. Mythology interests you?"

"Yes, it does. I'm actually going to be going to college to study it," Carolynn boasted, feeling her own grin spread.

"College?" the bookstore owner asked, brow raised. "That's impressive. Your family must be so proud."

Carolynn's smile faltered, shifting on her feet as she regripped the books in her arms. She could feel Shadow pressing her warm, heavy body into her thigh. The wolf's way of offering comfort.

The stranger's eyes finally dipped down to the wolf at her side, and she smiled brightly. "And who is this?"

"Shadow," Carolynn said, surprised by the woman's demeanor. She didn't seem frightened or put off by the fact that there was a rather large wolf in her establishment. "I hope it's okay that she's in here."

"Oh, of course." The store owner waved her hand as though to say it was no big deal. She headed for the front of the store and stepped behind the front counter, placing her own books down.

Carolynn followed, setting her own handful of books on the counter to check out. The woman took the books and began ringing them up one by one. Once the total showed up on the screen, Carolynn pulled a few bills out of her back pocket and handed them over.

"Thank you so much for coming by today," the woman said, placing each of her newly purchased books into a cotton tote with the store's logo printed on the front. She reached under the counter and pulled out a book the size of a Bible and placed it on the counter in front of her. "This is my gift to you, for being a fellow mythology lover and giving my store a chance."

Carolynn pulled the book a bit closer to examine it and was blown away by the cover alone. It was beautifully illustrated with expertly hand-drawn images. So lifelike, so realistic. It contained multiple images of Angels, creatures, and a few solitary men and women, their clothes soft and wispy. The title was written in precise and flawless calligraphy, *Aros: Mythology of the Gods*. She had never heard of it.

Carolynn pushed the book back on the counter towards the woman, afraid her dirty hands might soil its beauty. "No, I can't. This is too much. I appreciate the gesture, but I could never afford a book like this."

"Well, it's a good thing "m giving it to you as a gift. I won't take no for an answer," the woman insisted, picking up the book and placing it inside of Carolynn's bag among the purchased books.

Carolynn couldn't speak, she was blown away by the generosity of a stranger. "Thank you," she finally stuttered. "Thank you so much."

"You're welcome." The woman smiled, offering the handles to the bag.

Carolynn took the bag, slinging it over her shoulder, and made to turn away but stopped. "My name is Carolynn."

The least she could do was offer the woman her name.

The woman smiled even brighter, if that was possible. It was warm and inviting, and Carolynn basked in it. "It's so nice to meet you, Carolynn," she said genuinely, and even a tad sad. "My name is Neila."

"Neila." Carolynn smiled softly. "That's a pretty name."

Neila laughed softly. "I'm sure I'll see you again."

"You can count on it."

Carolynn left the bookstore, ready to head towards the creamery, when a buzzing went off in her pocket. She fished out the phone and flipped it open, reading the new text.

Shocker, Beth was canceling.

She flipped the phone shut rather forcefully and shoved the small device back into its pocket. Beth was going to get an earful the next time she saw her.

Walking south through town, in the direction of the trailer park she called home, she noticed Shadow's ear perked towards the distant woods.

Carolynn recognized the signs before she heard the wolf's stomach growl.

"Go ahead; go hunt," Carolynn urged the wolf.

Are you okay to get home? the she-wolf asked.

Carolynn tried not to take offense to the wolf's lack of trust. "Yes, I think I know the way after only living here my entire life," she said, her words clipped.

Try not to trip over your ego, pup. And with that said, the wolf took off, sprinting across the pavement and into the dense woods.

Carolynn gave the wolf a vulgar gesture as she lost sight of her and continued on down the road. The farther away she walked from the hustle and bustle of downtown life, the more desolate the streets became. The buildings grew further and further apart, looking more and more dilapidated and run-down. The city would rather put its funds towards the tourist scenes and not the poor folks barely scraping by.

There was a vacant lot on the corner. A store she used to visit almost daily with her parents. It used to be owned by an old Italian couple, selling baked goods and the best deli sandwiches money could buy. Her dad used to take her there, where they would share a container of rainbow cookies, soft and buttery, covered in chocolate with a raspberry jam filling, decorated in the colors of the Italian flag. They were her favorite and her father used to surprise her with them often.

The sun was high in the sky, beating down on her exposed skin. At this time of day, shadows were nearly extinct.

Carolynn squinted carefully at the vacant building when she noticed movement along the side. Even though the bare walls should be lit with the afternoon light, the western wall was a shroud of darkness with something lurking in the shadows. She stopped at the corner of the street, just in front of the building. Its windows were smashed in, and graffiti desecrated the walls. Carolynn couldn't help but feel a deep sense of loss at the state of the old bakery.

Movement along the side of the building caught her eye again. Someone was standing there, watching her.

Unable to help herself, she headed straight for the shadows, walking across the cracked parking lot. Whatever or whomever it was turned away, disappearing behind the building and into a series of alleys that connected to an old abandoned shopping outlet.

Carolynn kept her back along the wall, the cement blocks catching on her top. Whatever it was, it was fast. She quickened her pace, following it along the side of the building, around the back, and down an empty street.

Nestled between two abandoned shops, the alley thinned. She felt as though the walls were pressing in and confining her. It was a dead end.

No creepy shadow, no darkness of any kind. What in the world made her think to follow it? Whatever *it* was. A chill crept down her spine, the hairs along her arms spiking.

Someone was here.

"Are you looking for me?"

Carolynn spun around on her heels, eyes wide with shock and disbelief. It couldn't be.

"Donnie?"

Chapter 4

"**A**re you following me?"

Donnie stood in front of her; the same man as the night before that had held her and danced with her, manipulating her body in ways she'd never experienced. She could have sworn he was even wearing the same clothes.

Odd.

In the daylight, he was even more striking than she remembered. Everything about him was crisp, clean lines. Not a single wrinkle to be seen in his impeccable clothing. The man certainly looked good in dark colors—black slacks, and a charcoal gray dress shirt. Those top two buttons were still open to reveal that creamy, unblemished skin. His raven black hair seemed to now reflect shades of green, purple, and blue when the light touched it just right, making his ice-blue eyes stand out even more.

Carolynn fumbled for words, unsure if she was hallucinating him or not.

What was he doing out here in the middle of nowhere?

"I—I was just... but you were..." Carolynn stuttered, looking like the fool she knew she was. "What are you doing here?"

"You mean, like, existentially or in the literal sense?" Donnie asked, flicking an invisible fleck of dust from the arm of his shirt.

Carolynn raised a brow at the movement. She was certain there was nothing dirtying that shirt.,

His face was carved from stone, unyielding, not a trace of

emotion, yet she could tell he was teasing her. Her face pinched, and she sighed heavily with annoyance. His posture was stiff and formal, not at all like the way he had held her not twenty-four hours ago.

"If you're having an existential crisis, that's your problem. What are you doing here, literally? This isn't exactly the friendliest side of town."

"If it's not the friendliest part, then why are you here? A young woman, out alone. I'm sure horror movies have worse plotlines."

Carolynn scrunched her brow at him, crossing her arms over her chest. "You have a problem with answering questions, don't you?"

Donnie shrugged his shoulders.

Not really an answer.

"How did you find me?" Carolynn tried again, her gaze fixed on him, analyzing every movement, every twitch. He gave nothing away, as if he didn't have a care in the world.

"Who said I was looking for you?" Donnie narrowed his eyes, arching a brow, almost daring her to do something. What, she wasn't sure of.

Carolynn felt a slight shiver dripping down her spine, finding his words—the even, flat tone he was using—unnerving.

Two could play that game. She took a step closer, holding his gaze with her unsettling silver-grey eyes, piercing into his blue ones.

The rubber soles of her shoes tapped softly on the paved street as she continued to close the distance. Even though it was the middle of the day with the sun directly overhead, he was still shrouded in darkness, as though the sun's rays didn't dare to touch him. Shadows clung to him as though he was made of darkness, wrapping around him like a cocoon.

"You didn't want to see me again?" Carolynn breathed, her voice low, barely above a whisper, seductive as though speaking to a lover.

As close as she was, she now had to tip her head back to continue holding his gaze.

"Maybe I did," he confessed, a smirk tugging at the corner of his lips, enjoying their little game. "Maybe I was supposed to find you. You didn't even tell me your name."

"Carolynn." She didn't even hesitate.

"Carolynn," he repeated, as if trying the name out for himself.

She couldn't help the way her body reacted to how he said her name. Like nectar exploding on her taste buds. A warmth enveloped her in its safe embrace. A cool breeze on a stifling summer day.

It sounded perfect coming from his lips.

"How did you find me?" she asked him again for the second time.

"I didn't. I was exploring the town when I saw you walking this way," Donnie answered easily enough.

Lie.

Carolynn didn't have to read his mind to feel the pins and needles in her skin and know he was lying.

"Okay." Carolynn sidestepped, walking around him, leaving the way she came.

"Where are you going?"

"Home."

A warm, calloused hand slipped into hers, intertwining their fingers and pulling her back, turning her around to face him. The contact with his skin sent a current of electricity racing up her arm and straight to her chest. She took in a quick, unsteady breath, filling her lungs almost too quickly, shocked by the instant current she felt passing between them.

Was she crazy?

She saw a hint of emotion pass over his face for the first time since their meeting. His dangerously beautiful ice-blue eyes were wide, darting back and forth, searching her own for answers.

She wasn't crazy. Whatever it was, he felt it too.

"What?" Carolynn spoke, her voice losing all its confidence, uneven and more self-conscious than ever at the fact that his hand still clung to hers. It was rough and riddled with small scars, but strong and warm.

"I don't want you to go."

Carolynn raised a brow at him, eyes widening. No pins and needles. He wasn't lying.

That answer was not at all what she was expecting. His face was still hard, detached even, but his eyes were like windows to his soul, and she could see down to his very depths.

Donnie suddenly pulled his hand from hers. A brief look of fear passed over his features before quickly returning to what she now discerned as his mask. The moment was so fleeting, she questioned herself on whether or not it was even truly fear she saw.

The sudden removal of skin contact left her cold. Even in the hot, humid climate, she felt as if he had taken all of the warmth from her body when he pulled away, leaving her a frozen husk. She wanted the warmth back, the instant security his touch had afforded, but instead she pulled her now empty hand behind her back.

Carolynn.

Shadow's voice in her head was a shock to her system, almost comparable to jumping into a freezing spring on a blistering day. She tried to control her expression in front of him, trying not to appear phased or disturbed.

I'm here. Carolynn called out to her wolf, sending her a visual of where she was.

She could sense the wolf was worried for her. For what reason, she didn't know.

They didn't have much time left before the wolf arrived, and Carolynn wasn't so sure she was ready for the two of them to meet just yet.

"Phone," she said, holding out her hand.

Donnie was startled, actually taken aback. "Excuse me?"

"Let me see your phone," she repeated, slowly, like one would to a child.

That, he didn't seem to appreciate, his features hardening even more, if that was even possible. But he complied nonetheless, reaching into his back pocket and placing the phone gently in her waiting hand.

Carolynn almost rolled her eyes at the device. Of course, he would have a brand-new iPhone, dressed the way he was, the air of authority and nobility he carried himself with. Of course he came from money.

She swiped along the phone's screen. Not even a passcode. Cocky much? Tapping her finger quickly, she turned it off and handed it back to him.

Donnie raised a brow, curious as to what she was doing.

"My number. Call me sometime."

Without even bothering to wait for a response, she turned

from him, only to find Shadow standing at the entrance of the alley, her gray eyes fixed on the man behind her.

"Come on, Shadow," Carolynn called to her wolf, exiting the alley and leaving Donnie behind.

Who was that? Shadow asked, keeping pace beside her.

"A guy I met at the club last night," Carolynn said absently, walking back onto the main road that would take her straight to the entrance of the trailer park.

He seemed above average for a human.

Carolynn snorted. Never before had she heard Shadow ever make a comment concerning human physical standards.

Who's above average?

Carolynn glanced up towards the sky to find a beautiful barn owl, his masterly crafted wings expanded, floating in mid-air just over her head. He gliding down towards her, and Carolynn moved her hair to the side, raising her arm until it was parallel with the ground. The owl reached out, claws extended, landing carefully on her vulnerable skin.

"Spot!" Carolynn squealed, surprised to see him in broad daylight. Normally, the owl preferred privacy and seclusion in the forest. "What are you doing here?"

I came to see my favorite girl. Didn't feel right to miss your birthday yesterday, Spot said, ruffling his feathers against a brief breeze.

The owl had gray spots on his faded brown wings and on his head with a very distinct heart-shaped face, eyes completely black, and the feathers on his chest, neck, and face were snow white.

Carolynn couldn't help but reach out, stroking his downy soft chest with the backs of her knuckles. Spot normally didn't appreciate being pet, but every now and then he would allow it.

Today must be one of those days.

"I did miss you," she confessed.

The owl had been a staple in her life since before she could remember, always watching over her. Spot was different from other animals and birds. Animals typically spoke very simple speech. Most were unable to use words and instead forced to use images, but never Spot. Even Shadow had only used images to communicate when they first met. It took years of being around her and other humans for the wolf to develop her own complex dialect and thoughts.

Carolynn had wondered if Spot had known someone else who was telepathic and if that was how he had learned speech, but he would never confirm it. No matter how persistent or relentless she had been, she would get nothing from the owl. All she wanted to know was whether she was truly alone or if there were others out there like her.

I'm sorry for not being around. Something came up.

"Yeah? Like what? Couldn't catch enough mice for dinner?" Carolynn chuckled.

There was a predator detected around my nest. I was helping my mate by trying to find it, the owl said, his words tense and clipped.

Carolynn drew her eyebrows together, steps slowing as worry gnawed at her. Spot didn't talk about his nest that often, let alone his mate. He hated to think that there were creatures out there seeking to hurt him.

So, who were we saying was above average? Spot asked, his voice growing lighter.

A man. Shadow informed him, padding softly beside her.

Do I even want to know? The owl sounded disturbed by the prospect of a possible man in her life.

"Are you jealous, Spot?" Carolynn asked, teasing him. "'Cause you know you'll always be my best man."

I am not jealous, Spot grumbled, flapping his wings in annoyance.

"The fact that you just winged me, says you are," Carolynn pointed out. Winging for owls was claiming dominance, staking a claim on another to ward off predators or other suitors. It wasn't just singular to mates, but their chicks as well. "There's nothing to be jealous about anyways. I don't even know him. We only just met last night."

Do you want to get to know him? Spot asked. His heart-shaped face tilted to the side.

It always unnerved her when he looked at her like that. It was almost too human.

"I don't know; maybe," she confessed softly. To her own ears, she sounded unsure even with her heart racing at the thought of seeing him again.

Would he use the number she saved in his phone?

They entered the trailer park, passing the faded and chipped welcome sign marking the entrance. She passed houses with varying levels of maintenance. Some took care of their homes—cutting the lawn, a fresh coat of paint, and even lawn ornaments—while others, not so much. Her house was located in the very back, more isolated than the rest, nestled against the thick forest.

If you like him, you should try.

Shadow grumbled beside her, as though she didn't agree with the owl.

"I don't know; we'll see," Carolynn said, leaving it at that. She didn't want to dwell on it too much and risk getting her hopes up. She thought back on their meeting in the ally. The way the shadows enveloped him, reacting to his every breath.

Why do you sound so hesitant?

"Why are you being so persistent?"

Maybe because I've never heard you mention a man, let alone hear Shadow comment about one.

Carolynn frowned, exhaling loudly. How could she even explain the bizarre man?

"I don't know how to explain it. It's like there's a wall around his mind. I can't get any kind of read on him, and that's never happened before. And he has these shadows that seem to surround him, it's odd."

Shadows? Spot asked, feathers bristling. *Does he have a name?*

"Donnie," Carolynn said, the name sounding better and better the more she said it.

Without another word, Spot took flight, jumping from her arm before extending his wings and beating them hard as he gained height.

"Seriously? Give a girl some warning next time!" Carolynn yelled at him as he took off over the trailer park, disappearing behind the trees. "Stupid buzzard. You know he has the attention span of a gnat, right?"

Go home and stay there until I get back, Shadow told her, before also leaving her in the middle of the road and disappearing in the greenery as a squirrel darted up a tree.

"What the hell is with you forest freaks?" Carolynn yelled out at the two wild animals. "Well, that's just great," she mumbled, walking herself home.

Carolynn tossed the bag of books onto the bed as she fell back on the soft mattress, sighing dramatically. She had no work today, and Beth already canceled on her. Free time wasn't normally a luxury she had in surplus.

Glancing at the sack beside her, she pulled out its contents and sifted through the books she bought, but stopped on the one the shop owner gave to her.

It really was a stunning book, she admired as she ran her fingers along the hardcover, tracing over the images painted there. The Angels and their silvery wings were stunning.

What she knew of Angels was fairly limited. All she knew was Angels were typically errand boys for the Gods. What kind of errands they ran, well, those varied, but no matter which mythology one looks into, their roles are typically the same.

There was also a beautiful bird, with expansive wings in colors of gold, red, and orange, each little feather containing its own iridescent rainbow. A Phoenix, rising from the ashes.

After inspecting the introductory page, Carolynn quickly realized this was an entirely new mythology to her. She had never heard of some of the terms or Gods already named. Excitement quickly had her burrowing into the bed and finding a more comfortable position to sit in.

Flipping through the pages, each mythological creature seemed to have its own detailed drawing, even more so than the cover. She stopped on the Phoenix, transfixed by its meticulous detail, from the head with its sharp beak and soulful eyes, to the plume of feathers down its chest and across those magnificent wings. She envied the artist. To capture something so lifelike, was truly a talent. The book described the Phoenix as one of the rarest and most coveted of all creatures in Creation.

"A Phoenix isn't born, it's made," Carolynn read aloud, pondering what the words could possibly imply.

Continuing on, she finally reached the Gods. Like the creatures, each God had its own image. Each one perfectly rendered, from their hair, to their body type, to the type of clothes they preferred. The first one she stopped on was a man. His head was full with long black hair, sporting a thick beard. His eyes were dark and settled deep in his face, with bushy brows, and he seemed to have a permanent scowl on his face. While he certainly seemed a bit softer than she imagined a God to look, there was definitely something menacing and unforgiving about him. Oddly enough, he reminded her of the Vikings of Old.

Matias, God of Enchantments and Creation, Father of the Angels, King of the Gods, Ruler of Aros. His power is enchantment, the ability to influence emotions, desires, and even thoughts. Matias used his power to rise as King and establish his throne. He is known to be intolerable, violent, and full of greed.

Carolynn skipped the rest about the power-hungry God and moved on.

The next page showed a man almost completely swallowed by a tattered cloak, riddled with holes and burn marks. Judging by the silhouette, he was reed thin but very tall. All that really showed was his face. The left half was almost beautiful, like something from Renaissance art, but the right half was ruined with burns and scars.

Oriel, God of Death and the Undead, dominion over Demons, Ruler of the Underworld, and brother to King Matias. Oriel is charged with protecting the realm of the Underworld, keeping the dead from the living. The God of Death is regarded as cunning, patient, and without mercy. Although he is supposed to remain impartial, history has proven, if the price is right, he will send his pet, the black snake (name unknown) as his personal assassin.

Goosebumps covered her skin as she glanced back at his picture. He certainly looked like Death.

She continued reading through the names and duties of the other Gods, and a few stuck out to her.

Sarena, an ancient Adalonian Goddess. She is the Goddess of Protection and Woman. Sarena is said to be the most beautiful of the Gods. The Goddess is notorious for her feats in battle and believes in justice and vengeance for all wronged women. She is also an advocate for peace and surrender.

The passage went into more of her exploits, but the image of the Goddess drew her attention. Sarena's hair was a deep russet red, long, and naturally wavy. So long it extended past the end of the picture. Her face looked as though it had been constructed from a master sculpture with high cheekbones, a delicate nose, stubborn chin, and brilliant emerald green eyes.

She flipped to the next page, the paper soft and silky as she took in the next God.

Dominius, God of Light, Wild Animals, and Prophecy, also known as the Truthteller. Dominius is the elder brother of Matias and Oriel. The God has the gift of truth and prophecy. It is said, Dominius is the oracle spoken of in thousands of tales, and in religions all over Creation. He can shapeshift into any creature, plant, or tree, and commune with them as well. Dominius delivered the prophecy, The Child of Demis.

Without even taking a moment to observe his image, she flipped straight to the back of the book and found the Table of Contents, where she located the exact page number dedicated to The Child of Demis.

Skipping to the page, she read the prophecy.

The Child of Demis – Prophesized by Dominius

Two children of the Gods shall destroy all laws of Aros, and create a child. The child will be born on the night of the Blood Moon. The child alone will possess more power than the Gods themselves. During the child's eighteenth year, the Demis child will ascend, overthrowing the King and creating a new order of peace. The child is the guiding light of hope.

"No pressure at all," Carolynn said softly to herself.

The idea of that much responsibility and expectation made her nauseous.

In one of the final chapters, skipping past the history of Aros, she came to the section dedicated to Angels.

"Angels are beautiful, immortal beings, created by Matias, King of the Gods. Matias created the Angels for purely selfish reasons as an army that would help keep him in power—spies, messengers, and assassins. Unlike humans, Angels are not granted the freedom of will or choice. They were not granted certain liberties and freedoms. Instead, they are forced to do as commanded by their maker, binding them to him by blood."

"That sounds like an interesting story."

Carolynn leaped off the bed, or at least tried to, but ended up getting tangled in the comforter and fell back into her pillows. "Holy shit! A little warning would have been nice!"

"I'm sorry, honey. I thought you heard the door shut," her mother tried to contain her laughter but was unsuccessful.

"It's not funny," she grumbled, closing the book still in her hands and setting it down on the nightstand. "You nearly gave me a heart attack."

"I really am sorry," her mother straightened against the doorway, composing herself. "I just popped in really quick for a change of clothes before my second shift. Wanted to see if you needed anything."

"No, I'm good," Carolynn said, trying to offer a reassuring smile.

"Try not to stay up too late. If you go anywhere, make sure you are with Beth or Shadow," her mother counseled.

Carolynn pursed her lips together, nodding her head. "Yup, promise."

As though she wasn't left on her own most nights.

"Have a good night," her mother said on her way back out the door.

Carolynn didn't bother with a response as she glanced back at the book on her nightstand.

Chapter 5

The gravel road created plumes of dust that kicked up with every step.

Shadow had yet to return, and Beth was still incognito, but that didn't mean Carolynn had to stay inside. She still had daylight left, and she was technically an adult now. An adult without a car, but still, she could walk to the diner by herself. She had twenty bucks to her name, and a good ole fashioned cheeseburger sounded perfect.

Carolynn stepped off the road into a grassy ditch just as a pickup truck sped by. She could hear the passenger's thoughts for the briefest of moments. They were on their way to meet with friends at the movies. One of them had a stash of pot with them. She quickly rebuilt the walls of her mind, effectively blocking them out. She hadn't realized they had been down.

Being a telepath wasn't all it was cracked up to be. It never made sense to her why people would wish for such a curse. She'd been hearing voices in her head since she was four years old. Fourteen years later, she had mastered control mostly because she had to, but it was important to learn where and when to use her power. Slipping into someone's unsuspecting mind was easier than breathing, and that could be dangerous.

Though she rarely used it, it did come in handy every once in a while. Especially during her chemistry final, senior year. If she wanted to graduate with her class, she had no choice.

Although, she did consider herself lucky that her telepathy

wasn't solely limited to humans. She could communicate with almost every animal. Usually the smaller the animal, the more limited the communication, but it didn't stop her from trying.

After her mother had left the house for the start of her second shift, she spent the next few hours reading that book. Some of the entries she found to be quite disturbing, and here she thought Zeus's exploits and crimes were deplorable.

Carolynn hadn't even made it to the diner yet, and she could only imagine what she must look like. The Florida sun, blinding and suffocating, did nothing to help her appearance, as it burned the air she breathed, wrapping her in a sticky cloud of moisture. Thankfully, she had enough common sense before leaving the house to throw her auburn hair up into a messy bun, lessening the chances of arriving looking like a drowned rat, and exchanged her black tank top for a black racerback. She fidgeted with the stud pierced through her nose as she wiped the sweat off her brow.

Pushing through the diner door, she was met with a refreshing blast of ice-cold air, an instant relief against her scorched skin. The smell of burnt coffee and maple syrup washed over her.

Looking out over the diner's occupants, Carolynn searched to ensure her usual table was unoccupied, and luckily it was. Tucked away in the back corner was her booth, where she slipped into the leather seat that still contained hers and Beth's signatures from freshman year.

One of the waitresses immediately came up to her table, pen and pad at the ready. "Carolynn, nice to see you without that mutt of yours for a change," Margie said, one brow raised.

Carolynn smiled up at her brightly. "Oh, Marg, don't act like you don't have a soft spot for Shadow. I see you slipping her pancakes when we walk out."

Margie pursed her lips, an undeniable smirk spreading. "What can I get you, darlin'?"

"Coke and a cheeseburger please, no mustard or pickles," Carolynn said without even bothering to glance at the menu.

"You got it." Marg didn't even bother writing it down since it was the typical thing she ordered almost every time she came in. Marg glanced back over her shoulder before subtly leaning in, lowering her voice. "There's a man just over there who keeps looking at you. Do you want me to get rid of him?"

Carolynn leaned back in her seat, looking around Margie to the other side of the diner, only to find those familiar ice-blue eyes staring right at her. Suddenly, her pulse began to race, and lightness bloomed in her chest.

"Thanks, Marg. I got this. You can bring my food to his table," she said slipping out from the booth.

Margie gave her a wink, tucking the pen back into her bun. "You got it, darlin'."

Carolynn walked across the diner, shoes sticking to the linoleum floor as she approached his table. He watched her every step of the way, tracking her until she stood directly before him.

"Are you following me?" Carolynn asked, cocking her head to the side.

"I believe I was here first," Donnie said, picking up his coffee cup and toasting her before taking a deep drink.

"Hmm, well, I do believe this is my diner."

"I don't see your name anywhere."

"Actually, there's a booth back there with my name on it."

"I'll have to remember that for next time." Donnie narrowed his eyes, holding her steely gaze.

"What are you doing here?" Carolynn questioned him. She couldn't remember if that was the second or third time asking him since they met.

"Enjoying this delicious cup of coffee," Donnie smirked.

"Please, everyone knows this place has shit coffee."

"Careful, Carolynn. I'm starting to get the impression that it's you following me."

He was teasing her. She knew he was teasing her, and it was infuriating. She flexed her fingers at her side and instead of stomping her foot like she wanted to, she slid into the booth across from him, folding her hands on the table. She leaned back into the cool, cracked leather, taking note of his apparel.

"Do you ever wear anything that isn't fifty shades of black?"

Donnie glanced down at his attire and furrowed his brow. "I thought I looked good in black."

Carolynn snorted. Of course he would think that. Not that he was wrong. It looked striking on him against his creamy skin.

Made his dazzling blue eyes really pop, especially with the onyx hair. But she didn't need to tell him that.

"Why are you here?" she found herself asking yet again.

"Would you be disappointed if I said I was here for you?"

Carolynn's heart faltered in her chest. There were no pins and needles in her hands, so he wasn't necessarily lying, but she didn't buy it either. She pushed down her brick wall and tried to peer into his mind, but all she met was a steal wall.

"I'd call you a liar," Carolynn stated coolly.

"Ouch." Donnie feigned hurt, hand going to his chest where his heart should be, but that devilish grin made its appearance again, revealing a dimple in his left cheek.

Heat flushed her face, but she was saved from further embarrassment when Margie showed up with her burger, sliding it on the table in front of her.

The food smelled greasy and horrible in all the best ways. Donnie eyed the heart attack in waiting, brow raised, almost questioning if she was indeed going to eat that.

Carolynn picked up the burger and bit into it, allowing the American cheese and meat to melt into her mouth.

His smile seemed to widen as she chewed her food.

He was an odd one.

"So, Donnie, how old are you?" Carolynn asked in between bites.

Donnie looked utterly unimpressed with a flat expression. "Twenty-four."

Pins and needles in her hands almost had her dropping the burger in her lap. She set it down easily on the plate before wiping her hands on a napkin.

Lie.

It's not that he didn't look twenty-four, he really did look to be in his mid-twenties, but still, he was lying.

She let it go, seeing as how she was eighteen now and his age didn't really matter. It's not like he was a teenager. None of the boys in her high school even held a candle to him. But it also peeved her that this was now the second time he had lied to her.

"Is there a particular reason you lie about your age?" Carolynn asked, biting into a fry.

Donnie had the mug to his lips, ready to sip the hot liquid, when he suddenly sputtered, choking on the drink.

Carolynn couldn't help the wide grin that spread across her face, holding her chin high, taking a deep satisfaction from his reaction. "I don't think you're supposed to inhale the liquid."

Donnie reached for a napkin, dapping at his chin and shirt where the liquid had spattered. He set the mug down, a bit harder than necessary, in her opinion. His nostrils were flaring, and his lips were pressed into a thin line.

"I've upset you," Carolynn said, observing his body language, and sat up straighter in her chair. She instantly felt a tightness in her chest as guilt set in.

Why did she always have to open her mouth?

Donnie's features hardened once again, face going taut and expressionless. Except for his eyes; those eyes held hers as though they were a lifeline.

"Hardly. You just caught me off guard. Which, I have to admit, doesn't happen very often," Donnie confessed.

Truth, as no pins and needles stabbed her palms.

Carolynn took some odd sense of pride in that small fact.

"No matter how old you are, just thought I'd let you know, I'm eighteen. In case you were wondering," Carolynn said.

In case he was wondering if she was underage or not.

That small smirk came back out to play, hinting at that perfect dimple. "Good to know."

Carolynn's phone buzzed loudly from her back pocket. She frowned at the vibration as she pulled it out and flipped it open reading the text. It was Beth letting her know she was on her way. She quickly texted her back letting her know where she was.

"Anyone important?" Donnie asked, watching her type away on the small ancient flip phone.

"My friend, Beth," Carolynn answered him before putting the phone back in her pocket.

"The curly haired girl you arrived with at the club?"

Carolynn tilted her head to the side, blinking slowly, as she paused to examine him. Should she be weirded out that he was watching her?

Probably, and yet for some unexplainable reason, she wasn't.

She was actually flattered. Out of everyone at that club, and there were certainly a ton of women there, he had singled her out.

"Aren't you mighty observant," Carolynn said, sipping on her soda. "Some might find that creepy."

"But not you," Donnie stated rather than asking.

She took yet another moment to look at him. This man was a total stranger. She had no idea who he was, where he came from, or what his past was, and yet, there was not a single cell in her body telling her to be careful. If anything, her hormones were daring her to push him more. See how far she could press him. She wondered what his lips tasted like.

"Apparently not. Not sure if that's a good thing," Carolynn admitted.

"Oh, most definitely bad," Donnie said, just before getting out of the booth and throwing a twenty-dollar bill onto the table.

"Leaving already?" Carolynn asked, trying desperately to keep the disappointment from her voice. They had barely talked.

"I have an appointment I should be getting to, and I'm sure you'll want some alone time with your friend," Donnie said, pushing his hands into his pockets. "We'll see each other again."

Carolynn chortled, pursing her lips. "I guess we'll have to see if you actually use that number I gave you."

"You can count on it."

Donnie's gaze burned into her, into her soul, and left an imprint she was sure she could never be rid of. They could have been like that for minutes, an unmeasurable amount of time, until his gaze flicked up, breaking their spell. That stony complexion snapped back into place as the half smile came out once again.

"Afternoon," he said to someone standing behind her, just as he turned to leave out the side entrance.

Carolynn watched him turn away. Observed the way he carried himself, the way his muscles rippled beneath the satin shirt, and that ass—

"Not a bad view."

Beth's voice startled her, almost causing her to leap out of the booth. She hadn't even heard her approach, or notice the fact that she was now sitting directly in front of her, where he had sat just moments before.

"Now I know my drunk memory hadn't done him any justice. That man is divine." Beth groaned out that last part, which Carolynn could have done without. "I gotta say, if I had never seen him with my own eyes and you tried to explain him to me, I would swear to the Almighty Himself you were lying."

"Thank you so much for the trust," Carolynn said, drinking from her soda.

"Have you guys kissed yet?" Beth asked, leaning forward on her hands.

"We literally just met."

"So? What is stopping you? Do you not like him?"

"I don't know him."

"What's to know? He's a perfect specimen of a man."

Carolynn could have sworn there was drool coming out of her friend's mouth. She ground her teeth as her body tensed, palms heating, and pressure gathered in her head, Beth's comments grating on her. "Can you stop, please?"

Maybe it was the tone in her voice, but Beth straightened, her smile completely gone. "Care, your hands."

The tension instantly released as she jerked back from the table, only to find two burn marks in the perfect shape of her hands. The wood was scorched, charred black, and cracking. She inspected her palms and found nothing, no blistering, no evidence at all that she had been burned.

"There must be a loose wire around here," Carolynn said, covering the burns with her napkin. She pulled the twenty-dollar bill out of her pocket and tossed it beside the one Donnie had left, leaving the booth.

"Carolynn, wait," Beth called to her as she all but ran from the diner.

Pushing through the doors, she was instantly greeted with the evening's musty humidity and the sun setting in the west, painting the sky in beautiful purples and pinks. She breathed in deeply, filling her lungs with the water-logged oxygen, and took some kind of comfort from its drowning weight. She knew Beth stood beside her, waiting.

A hand slipped in hers and Carolynn automatically flinched, trying to pull her hand free, but Beth clung to her as though she were drowning in the sea and that hand was her only salvation. Clutching her hand to her chest, she could feel her friend's steady heart beating, calm and reassuring.

"I got you," Beth said, her voice steadfast.

Was she having a panic attack? Is that what this was?

Carolynn simply nodded her head, continuing to breathe in and out in deep, slow breaths.

"Mom totaled her car today."

Carolynn whipped her head to the side, frowning at Beth. "What?"

"That's why I couldn't meet up with you for ice cream earlier. Apparently, Mom was at the mall, forgot to put the car in park and it rolled backward off the retention wall."

Carolynn narrowed her eyes, sure she was kidding, but Beth looked as serious as ever, and she started laughing. Her sides cramped, and her breath caught in her throat as she struggled for air between fits of giggles.

"I'm sorry; it's really not that funny," Carolynn said, struggling to regain control of herself, eyes watering. "Is she okay?"

"Sure, she is. She was too busy trying on dresses for the charity ball they have this weekend," Beth said, smiling, "Feeling better?"

Carolynn straightened, squeezing the hand Beth still held. "Yes, thank you."

"What was that in there?"

Carolynn glanced back at the diner, where the table they had sat at only moments before was now permanently marked with her hands prints, scorched into the wood.

"I have no clue."

Chapter 6

The Mustang pulled in front of the dilapidated double-wide trailer Carolynn called home. The lights were off, making it look more like an abandoned foreclosure, than an actual home. She most likely wouldn't see her mother again until morning.

"Hey, by the way: Dad hired some new guy to help at the barn."

Carolynn's brow furrowed, confusion plain on her face. "Why? He didn't say we needed help."

"I think he assumes with you going off to college in a few months, he'd need more help with the basic chores. Better to break him in now while he can learn from you, than have to do it himself when you're gone." Beth shrugged her shoulders.

"I'll be back every weekend and holiday. I'm only going to be an hour south," Carolynn said, suddenly feeling uneasy about leaving.

She didn't want to have to leave the barn and everything she had accomplished there. Didn't want life to move on without her, but that was part of growing up, wasn't it? Or at least that's what she'd been telling herself as the growing pit of anxiety continued to build with each passing day.

"He'll be in bright and early tomorrow for you to get him started," Beth informed her. "Dad said he's from up north. Not sure he knows about anything to do with farms or horses, so that should be interesting."

"And I'm sure you will do absolutely nothing to help me," Carolynn looked at her pointedly.

"Help you, yes. Help the new guy, absolutely not. I love watching you break 'em in," Beth smirked wickedly, causing Carolynn to chuckle.

She got a kick out of breaking in new recruits for unknown reasons. It was kind of like horses. With the right amount of pressure, they will either surpass expectations or fail. There is no middle ground.

"I will see you tomorrow then," Carolynn said, opening the passenger door.

A hand grabbed her, stopping her from exiting the vehicle. She turned back to find Beth gripping her, knuckles bone white. Her mouth was open as though she wished to say something, but she closed it tightly into a thin line.

Carolynn peered into her friend's mind, as easily as flipping on a light switch, and was instantly bombarded with concern that tasted of lemon. She read her thoughts, deciphering the more immediate ones, and smiled gently at her.

Not for a second did she sense or feel fear.

"I'm okay; you don't have to worry about me," Carolynn said, squeezing her friend's hand.

"Do you want me to stay over? I can, if you need me."

Carolynn knew that.

Beth's loyalty and dedication to their friendship had never been a question. Not since the first day of third grade when she pushed a girl for picking on her. Right then, Carolynn chose her, and Beth did the same. It had always been them against the world, the foundation she clung to when the world and her own mind threatened to rip her apart.

Aside from her parents, mostly her dad, Beth was the only one in the world who knew all of her secrets and had never looked at her differently. While Beth was the party girl, the wild child, she was her sister first.

"I promise I'm okay. Shadow should be home soon, if she isn't already. I won't be alone," Carolynn said with a smile.

Her words seemed to comfort her friend, as her shoulders relaxed and her eyebrows no longer cut into her forehead.

Carolynn leaned across the console, and hugged Beth, giving her shoulders a tight squeeze.

"I'll see you in the morning," Carolynn said before pulling away and getting out of the Mustang.

The window rolled down. Beth was cranking the handle, almost entirely leaning in the passenger seat. "Love you, bitch!"

Carolynn chuckled, walking up the porch steps as she shouted over her shoulder the exact same sentiment.

Something dark and long caught her eye as it slithered across the edge of the deck and down into the bushes. Shivers racked down her spine at the sight of the snake. Must have been soaking in the last bit of heat the wood had retained from the day's blistering rays.

She could hear the sports car back out of the drive and take off down the road as she got her key into the door, and threw her shoulder into the splintered wood, trying to unstick the door. It opened with a sickening pop as she stumbled inside, fumbling for the lights.

One of these days that door would be the death of them. Either someone would kick it in, which honestly wouldn't take much force, or they would be trapped inside or out. Neither scenario was ideal.

The inside of the house looked as if it had been untouched in the last few hours. Definitely no Mom, as the coffee pot still contained this morning's brew. She grabbed a water bottle from the fridge, one of the few remaining unexpired items, and twisted it open.

Carolynn headed for her bedroom, turned on the light, and found a large wolf sprawled out across her bed.

Shadow cracked open an eye, the same silver-grey as her own, and stared at her coolly.

I was sleeping, the wolf grumbled.

"I apologize, Your Highness," Carolynn said, voice dripping with sarcasm as she shut the bedroom door behind her.

You were gone when I got home, the wolf commented, barely lifting her head off the bed, *Where were you?*

"I went to the diner for dinner," Carolynn said, gathering her night clothes to change into after a much-needed shower. She could still feel the humidity clinging to her skin, as though the sticky heat was glued to her.

By yourself? Shadow cracked open an eye, watching her.

"I was with Beth."

It wasn't a complete lie. Though, why she felt the need to

exclude Donnie from the conversation, she didn't understand.

Maybe a small part of her wanted to keep him all to herself. She wasn't ready to share, especially since they were still on uneven footing. It could be she was imagining all the mixed signals he had been throwing her way. Maybe he really was a stalker who showed up in random places she frequented. But for some inexplicable reason, she didn't believe that for one second.

Carolynn made quick work of her shower, scrubbing at her skin until the residue of the day washed down the drain.

Her hair was still wet as she climbed into bed, braiding the length behind her. Pulling the covers up, Shadow shifted to the side to allow her room. She laid back on the pillows and stared up at the ceiling. Glow in the dark stars still clung to the roof, giving off a barely visible neon green glow. Her and Beth had stuck them up there the summer before sixth grade, and there they stayed.

Even against her will, her mind wandered to the diner and the marks burned into the table. She raised her hands to her face, inspecting the vulnerable flesh of her palm, the deep grooves that ran the length of her hand. There were no blemishes, no marks, nothing indicating anything out of the ordinary had happened, and she could barely remember the incident. It happened so quickly she didn't realize what had occurred until it was too late. Only when she saw the look of concern and alarm on Beth's face, did she know something was truly wrong.

And it had been her. She did that. She burned the table with her bare hands, leaving it permanently charred and branded. It had never happened before. She had never been able to do anything other than read minds and talk to animals. What if it happened when she was working with the horses, or riding in a car, or around people?

Her stomach churned, and her head became light and foggy.

Is everything okay?

Carolynn's eyes snapped to Shadow in the dark room. The only thing she could make out of the wolf was her eyes and the one diamond shade of white on her chest.

"I'm fine," Carolynn told her wolf, somehow sounding sure of those two words.

She took one last look at the palm of her hands. Hands that

seared and scorched.

Everything's fine.

Thunder rumbled, and lightning flashed. Metal clanged in the distance and a steady pounding reverberated through the air.

Carolynn stood in an empty field, grass dead and lifeless for miles and miles, as far as she could see. Glancing down at her feet, there were two bodies, broken and contorted beyond repair.

She cried out for help. Screamed for someone to come. Anyone. But she was met with a terrible silence. She could feel the wetness streaking down her face, when movement caught her attention out of the corner of her eye.

A dark figure stirred on the horizon, moving in her direction. A long stick dragged in the dirt at its side.

It opened its mouth as though to speak, but nothing came out as a loud buzzing sound filled her ears and drowned out the world.

Carolynn jolted awake as a heavy weight lay on her chest. She pushed out her arms, hands meeting soft fur and an overly large wolf. She shoved the wolf off as she tried to blink her eyes open, her vision blurry and unwilling to focus as though she was still stuck in that wasteland.

She glanced over to the window and found the morning's first rays streaming in through her sheer curtains.

You were dreaming, Shadow said, her voice edged with concern. *You cried.*

Her fingers brushed against her cheek and sure enough, moisture was gathered in her eyelashes and down her face. She rubbed the rest of the wetness away with the back of her hand, scrubbing away the evidence of the nightmare that was already fading.

"Sorry I woke you," Carolynn said, sniffling her stuffed nose.

What's going on, pup?

"Knock, knock."

Both Carolynn and Shadow sat up, alert and wide-eyed as her mother pushed open the door, not bothering to actually knock and instead made a knocking gesture in the air as she stepped into the room.

"Good morning, beauties," her mother said, chipper and happier than anyone had a right to be this early in the morning.

"Morning, Mom," Carolynn said, erasing the last bit of sleep from her eyes. "Did you just get home?"

"Yes." Her mother sighed dramatically, sitting on the corner of the bed. "I am exhausted, but I wanted to see you before I slept for the rest of the day and you left for work."

"Oh, okay," Carolynn said awkwardly, undoing her braid and working out the snag with her fingers.

Her mother scooted closer to her on the bed, hands folded in her lap. Carolynn eyed her suspiciously. She didn't even have to read her mind to know something strange was going to come out of her mouth.

"I missed your birthday," her mother started, "and it dawned on me as I was driving home that I hadn't even realized. I forgot my own daughter's birthday."

There it was.

"Mom—"

"No, let me talk," her mother cut her off. "I know I've been a shit parent since your dad died. I retreated into my work and tried to stay busy, but I think I lost sight of the most important thing in my life—in mine and your father's life—and that's you, my star."

Her mother reached out and held the pendant around her neck between her fingers. "You know this came from your birth parents?"

Carolynn swallowed with some difficulty, ignoring the stinging in the back of her eyes, and nodded.

"I was always slightly jealous of it. That they had left it for you. But it never seemed right to take it off. That's why we called you Star."

Carolynn knew all of this. Had heard the stories enough times, about how she had been found wrapped in blankets with nothing but the necklace.

"You were our greatest gift," her mother sniffled, stubbornly refusing to lift her eyes from the pendant. "I know we've had our difficulties. Sometimes I think you and I are a lot more alike than either of us would care to admit, but I promise I will try and be better."

"I know you try your best," Carolynn said, finally finding her voice. "I know Dad's death was really hard for you."

Leukemia had finally claimed his life after the worst six months of their lives. Two days before her junior year, she had said goodbye to him as he passed peacefully in his sleep, worn down and nothing more than skin and bones.

"But I hadn't just lost a husband; you lost your dad," her mom said, meeting her gaze, blue eyes shining. "He was so proud of you."

Emotion choked her, clogging her throat and weighing down her chest as though an elephant had sat down. Not in a million years had she expected this heart-to-heart. She had fully expected her and her mother to carry on as they were, becoming more and more estranged as she left for college.

Carolynn reached out and took her mother's hand. It was wrinkled and thin. When had she lost so much weight? She brushed away a tear that had betrayed her and rolled down her cheek.

"Thank you," Carolynn said with a sad smile.

The front door banged open, rattling the two of them. Carolynn almost bolted upright, but the sound of a familiar voice stopped her.

"Mom! Care!" Beth's head poked through the bedroom door only to find the two of them still holding hands, with tear-filled eyes. "Am I interrupting something? Did someone die?"

"Elizabeth," Carolynn warned, using her friend's full name.

Did she not understand what a filter was?

"That was insensitive, wasn't it?" Beth grimaced before sitting beside her mother, wrapping an arm around her shoulders. "Susana, Momma, what's wrong?"

Carolynn watched the two of them. Beth was always so much better at showing her emotions and reacting appropriately. Maybe she should have hugged her mother, but instead, she pulled her hand back into her lap and shifted uncomfortably.

Susana, her mother, didn't seem to notice or take offense as she patted Beth's knee, leaning into the half hug. "It's nothing, just realizing what a terrible mother I've been."

Beth's eyes widened meeting hers. *Did you say something?*

Carolynn subtly shook her head once. She was just as surprised as Beth was to hear the confession.

"Well, there's always room for improvement," Beth offered,

giving her an awkward shrug.

Susana threw her hands up in the air as if shocked by Beth's lack of defense, almost affirming her suspicions. "Well, would you two at least care for some breakfast?"

"Unless you count bottled water and ketchup as breakfast," Carolynn said, pressing her lips into a thin line.

Susana frowned, pinching the bridge of her nose. "Right. Grocery shopping it is."

"You don't have to; I know you're exhausted." Carolynn tried to give her mother an out but was stopped by a raised hand.

"I can sleep after. I want us to have dinner together. Beth, of course, you're invited," Susana glanced at her friend.

"I don't have any plans," Beth said with a shrug. Their usual buffer.

"Perfect. I'll make lasagna," Susana beamed.

"That sounds delicious." Beth matched her energy, glancing towards Carolynn, who sat there, stone-faced as ever. She shifted on the bed before standing, adjusting the length of her dress. "I am actually here this early for a reason. I have to get this young lady here to work."

Carolynn stared at the finger directed at her and internally sighed getting off the bed. "Let me get dressed."

"Is it Monday already?" Susana asked, glancing at the watch on her wrist as though the old analogue watch would provide her with the date.

"It sure is," Carolynn heard Beth say as she closed the bathroom door behind her.

She stared at herself in the mirror and saw eyes rimmed red from the crap sleep she got, her increasingly long hair hanging in wavy locks from the braid she slept in. Her roots had grown out, leaving a gap between her head and the black dyed streaks. She still couldn't decide if she should let Beth touch them up or get rid of them entirely. The silver diamond stud in her nose was slightly sticking out, which she pushed back down. Her ears were rimmed with various piercings, her small way of rebelling as she got older. Although, why she ever trusted Beth with a needle was beyond her.

While she appreciated her mother trying, or at least acknowledging her shortcomings over the last two years, some part of her just couldn't trust her to follow through. It was her dad that was always the consistent one. The one who always knew where she set down the car keys, reminded her of appointments, and did the grocery shopping. Her mother would forget her head if it wasn't already attached.

She went through the small dresser contained in her closet and pulled out a fresh pair of tan riding breeches and a tank top. She stripped out of her night clothes, replacing them with the pants and top, along with a pair of black leather, knee-high riding boots. Quickly running a brush through her hair and replaiting it, she tossed her hair back over her shoulder before adding a layer of mascara to her lashes and a touch of foundation to cover the dark circles that were already rearing their ugly head.

Leaving the bathroom, she was adjusting her top when she heard her mother and Beth out in the kitchen. Slipping her phone into her back pocket and exiting the room, Shadow silently at her heels as though she were indeed her own personal shadow, she found her mother laughing at something Beth had said.

Susana turned towards her at the sound of her approach, smile still broad and light. "Star, did you hear about Beth's mom and her car?"

"Yeah."

Susana didn't seem fazed by her monotone response and instead turned back to her friend, laughing into a steaming mug of coffee. "Thomas must be livid."

"Dad is certainly not happy about two cars in two years. He's been on the phone with insurance since last night," Beth admitted, sipping on the bottled water in her hand.

Carolynn opened the fridge and extracted her own bottle, twisting open the lid. "Beth, we should be going. I want to get there before the new guy arrives."

"What new guy?" Susana asked, blue eyes sparked with curiosity over the rim of her mug.

"Just some new help Dad hired. Carolynn's going to train him up, get him ready for when we go to college," Beth said, rocking back on her heels with excitement.

College was barely two months away, and both of them were beyond excited. They already picked out an apartment off campus they would be sharing. Beth's dad had refused to allow them to live in the dorms, claiming something about predators and how vulnerable two young girls would be, and insisted on the apartment in a gated community. While Carolynn appreciated him and everything he did for her, she still insisted on paying him back in some way. She wasn't sure how, but she knew she'd figure something out.

Susana frowned, looking to her daughter, brows furrowed. "I thought you were coming back on weekends and holidays?"

"I am," Carolynn said. "But he's still going to need the additional help during the week to keep the training consistent."

"Did he even consult you on hiring this kid?"

Beth seemed to back away, leaving her mother's ire directed solely at her. Her mother was never someone who reacted well to change, and this new hire meant she was really leaving in less than two months' time.

"No, but I'm sure he has the stable's best interest in mind. If he hadn't hired this new person, I would have suggested the same thing."

"Have you ever met him? How do you know he'll be even halfway decent?"

"We don't—"

"And if he isn't," Beth interjected, wrapping her arm around Carolynn's shoulder, offering her support, "Carolynn will kick him to the curb faster than he can push a wheelbarrow."

"We really should be going," Carolynn said, leaning towards the front door that felt a mile away.

Susana nodded her head, blinking a few times before a smile tugged at her lips. "Of course. You girls have a good day. I'll see you later tonight."

Carolynn didn't dismiss the opportunity as she grabbed Beth and all but fled the house. Nearly running down the porch steps, they both got into the Mustang. Shadow didn't even protest as she jumped into the backseat. Beth revved the engine to life, and they peeled out of the driveway.

"Well, that was intense," Beth said, glancing back in her rearview mirror as though she expected her mother to be chasing after them.

"You have no idea."

Chapter 7

The Mustang pulled onto a long winding driveway, large weeping trees lining the path. The paved drive led to a grand two-story Victorian house. It was a brilliant white color with a wrap-around porch that circled the entire first floor. The second story had two balconies that could be seen from the front. The right one led directly up to Beth's bedroom, with a vine-covered lattice running down the length of it.

The memories of climbing up and down flashed in her mind every time she looked at it.

Off to the left, farther back on the forty-acre property, the driveway extended past the main house and out to the stable, which looked like an even larger, more industrial version of the home.

The stable, or better named Equine Facility, was a twenty-stall stable. It was a white building in the shape of an L with green shutters and a shingle roof. In the curve of the building was a large arena with jumps of various sizes, wooden barrels, and red traffic cones. Beyond the stable was the remainder of the property, sectioned off into assorted sized fields to allow the horses to graze and enjoy the sticky humidity.

Beth bypassed the main house and parked directly in front of the stable.

Carolynn opened the door wide enough for Shadow to jump out, shaking out her fur. She could already hear her wolf friend complain about the stink of the metal deathtrap that was Beth's muscle car, which she intended to fully ignore.

The smell of hay, manure, and horse immediately flooded her senses. She breathed it in deeply, basking in the comfort of the nearby horses.

The wolf took off around the stable, disappearing from sight. Most likely to antagonize the stallion they kept out back. They had a love-hate relationship.

Inside the stable, Carolynn stepped through the first door on her right. The stable's office was hers—Thomas effectively handed it over before the start of her junior year, before her life fell apart. This stable kept her from drowning in her loss, and kept her floating and anchored. The room had been cleared out just for her. He even added fake potted plants, scattered randomly throughout the room.

"For a feminine flare," he had said.

The room had been painted a soft yellow, cleared of every cobweb and dust bunny. He'd even been generous enough to get her a new desk.

She tossed her phone onto the large oak desk before leaving the stack of paperwork calling her name behind.

The stalls greeted her with loud nickers and neighs. Large heads poked out over the stall doors, bobbing in greeting. Carolynn tried to block most of them out of her head as they all tried to welcome her back all at once. It was always like this after a weekend away, and it never ceased to make her smile.

Carolynn greeted each horse by name, treating them all to a sugar cube. She stopped at a stall, the fifth one on the left with a bronze nameplate engraved, *Tempest.* Inside the stall stood a beautiful Andalusian mare, her coat a pale translucent grey, with her mane and tail a long, wispy silvery-white.

She stroked Tempest along the side of her neck, feeling the coarse hair scratch at her skin. Beneath her hand, she could feel the horse's tendons and muscles thick and rigid beneath the skin. The power that resided in the large horse was magnificent to witness, but even better to feel when they rode together.

A sugar cube lay in the palm of her hand as she held it out to the mare. Tempest took it gingerly, the whiskers on her chin tickling her skin. The horse stamped her hoof on the dirt-packed stall, waiting to be taken out and saddled.

"Easy, girl," Carolynn cooed, patting the mare's neck.

It has been a long two days without you, Tempest said, bumping her head against her shoulder.

Carolynn couldn't help but lean into the mare, resting her head against the thick skull of the horse. They stood like that for a moment, just enjoying the presence of each other, the peace and quiet she reveled in every time she was with her companion.

"I missed you too," Carolynn said, her voice barely above a whisper.

"You know, it always amazes me how comfortable you are with horses, but humans you get weird with," Beth said, interrupting their moment.

Towed behind her on a lead was a black Friesian mare, hooves clopping on the smooth pavement of the hall. The horse Maria was a true black beauty, coat sleek and glossy, a beautiful obsidian color. The hair on her mane and tail was long and thick with a slight natural wave, almost as if they had taken the time to crimp the hair. Her body was elegant and sleek-looking, with a long-arched neck and short-eared head.

"Hello, Maria," Carolynn said, offering the moody mare a sugar cube, which she took, lips tickling her palm.

More treats? Maria asked, nudging her hand.

"Later," Carolynn promised, petting down the mare's neck as Beth led her further down the aisle toward the saddle station.

Not bothering with a lead, she opened the stall door, allowing Tempest to walk out on her own. Tempest followed her down the hall, stopping just in front of the tack room. Carolynn went inside, taking in the smell of worn leather and shoe polish, and gathered her saddle, reins, and other items she'd need. Setting them down on a wooden fixture, ensuring nothing was touching the floor, she gathered a bucket near the tack room door that held an assortment of brushes and hoof picks.

Rubbing Tempest down, loosening the dirt and hair and cleaning her hooves was a mindless task, and Carolynn and the mare enjoyed going through the motions of it all. The repetitive movements relaxed her shoulders and number her mind, but she couldn't shake a lingering anxiety that had been creeping up on her since she awoke.

As she was gearing Tempest up for their ride, strapping on the saddle and tightening the halter, movement towards the end of the stable caught her attention, and a middle-aged man walked towards them. He was at least a head taller than her, making her tilt her head back and squinting her eyes against the harsh sunlight at his back. His dark brown hair was thinning and combed over.

Beth's dad, Thomas, took notice of both girls readying their horses and smiled approvingly.

"Hey, Dad," Beth said, with her back to her father.

"Beth, Carolynn," he said, acknowledging them both, his voice deep and rough.

"Thomas," Carolynn said by way of greeting.

Thomas frowned at her use of his name but moved on quickly. "Carolynn, I'm sure Beth told you about the new kid coming in today. He should be here in about an hour. Show him the ropes and give him the grand tour. You already know what we expect of him and the basic duties he'll be performing." Carolynn nodded her head in understanding as he offered Tempest a peppermint, which she was more than happy to take. "You're still responsible for the horses and training. That won't change until the day you come to me and tell me you're moving on from this place."

Carolynn tilted her head at the man who had been like a second father to her, giving him a look of annoyance. "We've had this discussion. Why would I want to go anywhere else?"

"Even so," Thomas said, all but ignoring her. He pulled a folded sheet of paper from his back pocket and handed it to her. "Here's his application. Look it over, throw it away. Whatever you want."

"Yes, sir." Carolynn nodded, hand outstretched to receive the paper, but Beth all but pushed her out of the way to snatch the resume and began reading it immediately.

"Jason from New Jersey," Beth said, reading aloud. "Do you think he knows Snookie?"

Carolynn pursed her lips at her friend to keep from laughing. Thomas eyed his daughter with that look that told her he didn't believe she took anything seriously. Granted, he wasn't wrong, but she knew Beth better than that. She just knew how to make light of situations and how to have fun. It wasn't a bad thing, but her father definitely wished she had taken more of an interest in the family business. He had always been generous, sometimes too generous to Carolynn. Tempest was a prime example, gifted to her on her thirteenth birthday, but she'd read his mind enough times to know he wished it was Beth that ran the stables.

Thomas waved at them as he left, disappearing in the sun's glare.

Carolynn ducked under the large horse, reaching for the thick piece of leather that secured the saddle to the back of the horse, wrapping around her belly, and pulling it through the saddle loops. She buckled it tightly against the horse, securing it properly. That one piece of leather could make or break a rider. Literally.

Tempest was saddled and ready to ride when Carolynn noticed Beth was having difficulty with Maria's girth. She left Tempest to stand alone, recognizing Beth needed help as her white mare shifted on her feet as though she could already feel the wind racing past them.

"Easy, girl. A few more minutes," Carolynn said to her mare as she headed for Beth.

By the way Maria's stomach was expanded, Carolynn smirked, catching on to the problem. She motioned for Beth to stand aside and took the worn girth from her friend's hand. Beth stood there, hands on her hips, watching. She looked ready to stomp her feet at the mare, which made the situation all the more laughable. Carolynn took two of her fingers and jabbed the mare in the ribs, forcing the horse to release the air she'd been holding, blowing out her nostrils loudly. She secured the girth, pulling up on it until she couldn't anymore, and buckled it in.

"She's a brat," Beth said, sticking her tongue out at the young mare.

"She matches your personality beautifully," Carolynn said, smirking as she patted the horse's neck. "Don't be a turd," she told the horse.

It's so easy to mess with her, the black beauty said, her amusement evident by her tone.

Carolynn couldn't help but laugh aloud. "She's just bored and having a laugh at your expense."

"She's learned it from you," Beth accused her, pulling on her riding gloves and helmet. She put one foot in the stir-up and hoisted herself up onto Maria's back.

Carolynn grinned as she put on her own riding gear and pulled herself up onto Tempest's tall, wide frame. She gripped the reins in her hands, flexing her fingers around the worn leather, and clicked her tongue at Tempest, urging her forward. Tempest followed behind Maria, who was already two paces ahead, out of the stable and toward the open field around back.

Shadow was sitting near the start of the field, waiting patiently for the two riders and their horses, watching them as they got closer. Maria neighed anxiously at the wolf, but Tempest ignored her entirely.

The open field was wide and vast, nearly five acres of cleared land with enough room for them to safely canter on short, stocky grass. As soon as they entered the field, Carolynn dipped forward in her saddle, holding her body over the horse's neck. Tempest needed no further communication and took off into a canter. Carolynn tightened her knees against the mare's sides as she held the reins loosely in her hands and clutched tightly to the mane. The wind whipped past her, stinging her cheeks and tossing her braid, a respite from the heat and humidity as they passed Maria and Beth galloping. She loved the feel of Tempest's muscles pumping beneath her, propelling them both forward in a rush of speed and strength.

Time spent on the back of Tempest, running free through the open field, was the surest way to reach perfect clarity. Her mind was an open canvas as colors of green grass, blue sky, and orange warmth filled her vision whisking by in a blur. The impact of hooves meeting the earth could barely be felt as she slid along the saddle, the horse's gait smooth and effortless as though they were flying.

Carolynn couldn't help but laugh. Beth and Maria were a horse-length behind them, keeping up but unable to pass. Beth was enjoying the ride almost as much as she was, giggling just as loud, her face a simple expression of joy. It wasn't often Beth joined her on her daily rides, as the girl typically preferred going back to bed and sleeping till noon, but days like these were priceless.

Riding was her escape, her release from life when the pressures of the outside world became too much. Riding gave her something to focus on, exhausting her mind and body in one swoop.

Carolynn's bottom glided in the saddle, leading Tempest into a trot and a walk with only the pressure of her legs, allowing the horse a quick respite before Tempest felt the urge to run once more. Nearing the end of the second lap, Carolynn noticed a man leaning against a fence post of their enclosure, watching them.

Carolynn pulled back gently on her reins, bringing Tempest to a halt and allowing Beth and Maria to move in at their side. Both girls and horses were winded, taking in gulps of air. Tempest's sides rose and fell heavily, shuddering beneath her as she breathed loudly.

"Look," Carolynn said, nodding towards the figure in the distance. "You think that's him?"

"Jersey Shore guy?" Beth squinted her eyes, and a wicked smile spread across her face.

Carolynn knew that look, knew her friend all too well. That face spelled trouble.

"Let's go say hi," Beth said, nudging Maria into a canter, racing ahead of Carolynn.

Chapter 8

Tempest was able to catch up with Maria even if she did have a head start. Both mares raced towards the entrance, but Carolynn pulled back on the reigns, slowing her horse down as they got closer. They transitioned into a trot, bouncing up and down controlled by her knees and heels, until the horse transitioned into a walk. Carolynn allowed her hips to fall into motion, rolling back and forth as Tempest sauntered forward, Beth and Maria at her side.

No biting. Let's try and be nice, Carolynn projected to her horse and Beth's, not daring to speak the words aloud in front of a stranger.

I'm always nice, Tempest retorted back, swishing her tail at her, flicking her arm with its ends.

That was unnecessary.

She found Shadow still sunbathing near the gate, but her ears were perked straight up, eyes open, tracking the newcomer.

How has he been? Carolynn asked, speaking to the wolf.

He hasn't spoken a word. Only watched. Shadow said, but something about her tone was off.

Carolynn halted the mare as she finally got close enough to make out his features. Swinging her leg over the horse, she slipped out of the saddle, landing on the dry grass and kicking up a small plume of dust. She left the reins over Tempest's neck, not bothering to hold them as she stepped forward. He was much taller than her, with pale shaggy blonde hair that hung past the tips of his ears and into his sapphire blue eyes. She noticed his ear lobes were gauged with black plugs.

Looking him up and down, she took in his attire. From the zip-up hoodie to the designer jeans and shoes that did not belong in a barn, Carolynn's lips pressed into a thin line. She resisted the urge to rub at her forehead as she tried to decipher what in the world he was thinking of dressing like that in a place like this.

"You are going to regret wearing those Jordans," Beth said, still atop her horse, apparently inspecting him just as she was.

Carolynn and Jason both looked more closely at his shoes as he rocked back on his heels. All he had to offer either of them as an explanation was one simple shrug.

Okay, then.

"You must be Jason," Carolynn said, stepping forward and offering the man her hand. "I'm Carolynn."

Jason took it, the hand in hers was soft and unblemished. "Nice to meet you, Carolynn."

Carolynn felt a slight shudder ripple through her as their skin touched but it disappeared as quickly as it arrived as she pulled her hand back. "Likewise. This is Beth, Thomas's daughter," she said, gesturing toward Beth just as the girl was sliding out of her saddle, walking up to stand beside her.

Maria's reigns were in her hand as she offered Jason her free one, shaking it as well.

The man didn't smile or frown as he shook their hands, but simply wore a stony and blank expression.

Off to a great start.

Beth pulled the slip of paper she had folded into a tiny square from her pocket and began to read aloud. "It says here you graduated high school last year and just recently moved here. Why Florida?"

Carolynn peeked over her friend's shoulder, taking in some of the information. He was nineteen and said he had worked at a ranch up north. Judging by his attire, she highly doubted that.

"Work."

Both Carolynn and Beth allowed him another moment to expand, but he didn't. He just stood there shifting from foot to foot looking as though he'd rather be anywhere else.

Fantastic.

Carolynn tried to smile at him, to offer him some sort of warm welcome, but she was finding it difficult, as annoyance already began to seep in. "Right. Well, there are other things to do here as well. We have a lot of rivers and lakes to cool off in and relax."

What was she doing trying to impress him? He was here for a job. He was supposed to impress her.

"Did you go to college? I hear the schools up north are really nice." She still wasn't sure why she was bothering. His stiff posture and raised brow were giving her all the signs of a boy who was not interested in chit-chat.

"Does it really matter? College experience wasn't a requirement."

Carolynn bit the inside of her cheek to keep from saying something she couldn't take back. "No, it's not."

Apparently, it didn't require a brain or decent work attire either. He'd soon realize his mistake, and she didn't even need to help him along with that fact. Just basic chores would soon ruin those jeans and shoes.

For some odd reason, she looked forward to that inevitability.

Jason seemed to be looking around as though expecting someone else to show. "Do you know who I'm supposed to report to? I was told there was some chick that ran this place."

Carolynn could hear the colorful language coming from her friend's mind as clear as the blue sky. Maybe she should take offense at his dismissive tone and the obvious sexism he was displaying, but she didn't.

"I don't think I introduced myself properly, then," Carolynn said, somewhat hoping to start this entire interaction over. "My name is Carolynn. I'm the chick."

Finally, she got the appropriate response she was looking for. He seemed startled by her revelation, his eyes wide, taking her in as though seeing her for the first time.

That kind of hurt.

"What are you, barely out of high school? How are you in charge of a multi-million dollar stable?"

His lack of confidence in her capabilities again wasn't surprising. She looked forward to educating him. Beth was bristling beside her. If she was a cat, the fur down her spine would be standing straight up, back arched, and hissing. The image of it almost had her laughing out loud. Her friend's mind was screaming at the guy before them. Always ready to pick a fight and defend her honor. It was cute.

Easy, Beth. Carolynn said, trying to calm her down. *Let's give him a chance.*

Come on! Let me rip him a new one. Dude is being a total d—

Carolynn cut the link between their minds as her friend continued to curse him out.

"Come on. I'll show you around the stable," Carolynn said, gesturing for him to follow as Beth gathered both horses' reins and followed closely behind.

Shadow sat up, somehow startling Jason as though he hadn't noticed the extra-large wolf sleeping on the ground.

"Is she yours?" Jason asked.

Carolynn didn't appreciate the disgust in his tone. It grated her nerves. "She is," Carolynn said, claiming full ownership of her wolf. "She bites people who don't like her."

It wasn't necessarily the truth, but she didn't want Jason getting any ideas, ill or otherwise.

"I'll do my best to get on her good side," Jason said, but still kept a healthy distance from the she-wolf as Shadow took up her usual position at her heels.

Not likely, Shadow commented.

Jason fell in step beside her as he tucked his hands in his front jacket pockets. How he wasn't sweating beneath that hoodie would forever be a mystery to her. She could feel the cotton tank top already acting as a second skin against her hot flesh and couldn't wait for the relief of a cold shower.

Beth led both of the horses to their station in the halls, where they awaited to be relieved of their tack and brushed down before being released to graze out in the fields.

Do we like him? Tempest asked, her black eyes following Jason at her side.

Not sure.

The mare tossed her head, butting her chest as she did. Carolynn raised her hand and scratched down the front of her face up into her mane between the eyes. Reaching the itches, she knew resided behind the ears.

Carolynn glanced at Jason to find him still standing at her side, as though waiting for something to happen. He was eyeing her, eyes lingering too long. She ignored his staring as she unbuckled the straps on the side of the halter and slid it off the mare's head.

"Beth, stand aside. Jason, go ahead and relieve Maria of her tack," Carolynn said, instructing him with a nod of her head towards the black beauty.

Jason didn't hesitate, didn't refuse, but instead walked towards the mare, one hand out as he approached her rear, and ran his fingers along her sweat-soaked coat.

Carolynn went through the motions of disassembling the saddle and halter from Tempest while keeping an eye on Jason as he worked to unsaddle Maria. Surprisingly, Maria was being a model mare, standing patiently for him and allowing him to remove the tack, receiving pets and encouragement along the way.

Maybe he was better with horses than people. She could relate.

Beth came around, watching Jason working with her horse. Her arms were crossed over her chest, and she looked as close to pouting as Beth would get.

"He's kind of hot in that troubled boy sort of way, but I still wish you'd let me yell at him," Beth whispered to Carolynn as she lifted the saddle from Tempest's back.

"Just your type then?" Carolynn said, voice dripping with sarcasm as she carried the saddle into the tack room and put it back on the shelf.

Carolynn came out of the room to find Jason's arms brimming with tack and gear, awaiting her direction on putting it away. She gestured for him to follow her back inside the tack room and directed him to each place the tack was to be put back, while also showing him other gear he would need in the future.

When they were done, they found both mares still standing in the hall of the stable, hides sleek with sweat and waiting to be released. Shadow was once again sprawled out on the stable floor, head resting on her paws, watching.

"Go," Carolynn instructed, patting Tempest on the rear as both mares trotted out of the stable and disappeared around the corner. She knew full well both horses would go directly back to the pasture they had just been running in.

"Wait, should we brush them first? Won't they take off? How will we catch them?" he asked, arms flailing, looking at her as though she truly were stupid.

Carolynn tried not to take offense. From the outside, she could see how it would look to let two horses go and expect them to do anything but what they're told. Maybe she should have played it safe and walked the both of them to the pasture. How would she explain her control to an outsider, when that would only lead to more questions?

"First of all, there is no sense in brushing them right now, since they are only going to go out and roll in the dirt. We will take care of that when we bring them in for the night. Second, I've trained my horses very well. If you walk outside this barn right this minute, you will find the two of them already back out in the pasture, grazing to their heart's content. We don't need to catch them. All you gotta do is shake a bucket of feed, and they will come running," Carolynn informed him.

He still didn't seem to believe her as he stomped his expensive shoes out of the barn and disappeared after the horses, only to see him walk back, a bit slower than he left, hands back in his pockets.

Guess he had to see it to believe it.

"Why don't you go back out there and shut the gate, so they stay in the pasture and then we will go through the rest of the stable, and I'll introduce you to the rest of the horses."

Jason nodded his head in silent acceptance and turned back around on his heels.

"This is why you're in charge," Beth said, coming up to stand beside her once more. "You have way more patience than I do."

Sometimes, that was true. Beth was normally the hothead, prone to outbursts, but Carolynn wasn't immune; she just had more to lose.

Carolynn spent the remainder of the day showing him the ins and outs of the stable and each stall, the dietary requirements of every horse, the feed storage, the tack room, and the schedule each horse was on for feed, breeding, and training. She had personally introduced him to every one of their horses by name, pointing out the ones to steer clear of, particularly the stallions.

A ringing sound echoed through the stable.

Her phone.

Carolynn left him at the stall of one of their breeders. "Just give me a minute; I have to go answer that."

Jason nodded, preoccupied with the pretty Andalusian before him, pockets full of peppermints and sugar cubes.

Didn't think it would hurt to bribe the horses into liking him.

Carolynn ran for the office, hoping to make it before the last ring, when she snatched it off the desk and flipped it open.

"Hello?" she answered, voice sounding slightly winded.

"Am I catching you at a bad time?"

The hairs on her arms rose at the sound of that deep, melodic voice. Carolynn froze mid-step as she headed out of the stable towards better reception.

"Donnie," she breathed, slightly bewildered and surprised. Her heart raced in her chest, and her hands began to sweat, the phone slipping in her grip.

"Didn't think I'd call?" She could hear the teasing in his voice and could almost imagine that stupid grin. Maybe even that dimple would be on display.

Her brain was floundering, searching for something to say. "No, I... just that, well, you. Ugh, crap."

She dug the palm of her hand into her forehead, mentally cursing herself.

What the hell was wrong with her?

Donnie chuckled through the phone. The sound was pleasant. "I'm sure you look cute flustered."

"I am n-not flustered," she said, slightly stuttering. "You just surprised me, is all. I didn't think you would have the courage to call."

Is something wrong? Shadow suddenly appeared at her side with no warning, seemingly out of thin air, making Carolynn jump.

"Shush," she said, hissing down at the wolf by her side.

"Did you just shush me?" he asked her.

Carolynn could imagine him laughing at her. She was acting like a crazy person, and she knew it. Of course, he wouldn't know she was speaking to her wolf.

"No, I'm sorry, I wasn't talking to you," she said in a rush.

"So you *are* busy."

"I'm just at work right now."

"Where do you work?"

"Morgan Stables." As soon as the words left her mouth, she questioned herself.

Why was she telling him this? She barely knew the man.

"So you like horses? That's interesting."

"I don't know why I'm even telling you any of this," she said, shaking her head.

"Why, are you trying to hide things from me?"

"I barely know you."

"We can change that."

Carolynn's brow rose, lips pursed as she tried to puzzle together his meaning.

"I guess I will just have to make it up to you when I see you next."

"What—" Before she had a chance to finish her question, the call ended. "What the fuck?"

Chapter 9

After her disastrous, unexpected call, she continued working with Jason and spent the remainder of the afternoon attending to the stack of paperwork left for her on the desk. She was currently taking a break as her eyes started to go cross-eyed staring at numbers, and instead decided to watch Jason muck out the stalls and ruin his expensive shoes. Although she had to give him credit, he wasn't complaining.

She left him to his work and stepped outside, taking in the vast blue sky. The sun was beginning its descent in the west, radiating colors of violet, orange, and yellows with a few wisps of clouds.

She hadn't realized it had gotten so late. Mom was probably waiting on them for dinner, but then again, it's not like she had gotten a call from her either. A part of her knew she should be the bigger person, go home, and have a nice dinner with her mother, but some small sliver of her was almost afraid of what she would find when she walked into that house.

In the field, she spotted Tempest grazing near the edge of the property line. A familiar weight leaned against her leg, instantly warming her through her breeches. Glancing down, she found Shadow and scratched behind her ears. The fur was soft and dusty from sprawling out in the stable all day.

She closed her eyes as a breeze picked up and brushed against her face. The few strands of hair that had escaped her braid throughout the day whisked past her ears, picked up by the flow of air. She could taste the nearby sea, salt permeating the air.

Carolynn went to call to the horses lounging in the field but stopped herself as Jason came out of the barn, bucket in hand, and began shaking the feed, bouncing it off the plastic walls. Each of the horses instantly lifted their heads, stood up from their nap, or ceased chasing one another and began to head for the barn at full tilt.

She walked back into the barn and found each of the stall doors already open, ready to receive their occupants. She smiled, glad to know he was paying attention during her instructions.

Each of the horses entered the stable and headed directly for their stalls, awaiting their dinner. Jason went through the aisle, shutting each of their stalls as all of the horses made their way inside and began devouring the feed She went back into her office, grabbed her phone and turned off the lights. She sent a quick text to Beth, letting her know she was ready when she felt someone watching her.

Jason leaned against one of the stalls, those blue eyes skimming over her body. She met his gaze, challenging him, letting him know she knew he was watching her, but it didn't seem to deter him.

"Do you have a question?" she asked, breaking the silence.

"I'm still trying to figure out how someone as young as you is responsible for running a place like this," he said plainly.

Given that he was barely older than her, she ignored the first part, but Carolynn had to give him credit, he was brave.

"When you've been in and out of this stable since you were eight and worked the last six years for a man he trusts you," she said with a shrug.

Jason grunted as though he didn't believe her, but what other answer was he looking for? She had nothing else to give.

"You can go ahead and head home. You did well today, but I do have one piece of advice," Carolynn said, glancing down at his muck-stained shoes. "Try wearing better shoes tomorrow."

Jason glanced down as well, frowning at the ruined sneakers. "I will try and remember that."

He gave her a half wave as he exited the stable. She wasn't far behind, but first, she had to find a certain she-wolf that had disappeared over an hour ago.

Walking down the aisle of the barn, the horses chewed noisily around her. Some lifted their head in greeting, others were too busy with their nose in the buckets. She stopped at Tempest's stall, noticing her coat wasn't as dusty as the rest.

"Did someone brush you?" Carolynn asked, brow furrowed.

Tempest raised her head, lips smacking as she ground down her feed. *That new boy came out to the field earlier and gave me a good brushing. He got all my good spots.*

Carolynn gnawed on her lower lip as she considered what the mare had said. He must have gone out while she was in the office.

Well, that was unexpected of him.

"Thanks, Tempie. I'll see you tomorrow."

Leaving the horses behind, she stepped outside the stable and around the back, exactly where she knew she'd find the wolf.

Shadow lay in a flat part of the yard, sprawled out half asleep, her belly looking a bit larger than it was earlier.

"Find yourself a good meal?" Carolynn asked, interrupting her nap.

Shadow cracked an eye, but didn't bother to get up. *The fields here are rich with game. Lots of rabbits.*

Carolynn tried not to look disgusted even though her stomach rolled at the thought. She had to admit she was starving. The sandwich Beth had brought her hours earlier barely put a dent in her hunger, and now her stomach was gnawing at her.

"Beth is going to be here any minute to take us home. Are you coming?"

Shadow side-eyed her for a long moment before dramatically pulling herself up off the ground and stretching both her front and back end. Carolynn rolled her eyes at the wolf.

"You are so dramatic."

You are one to talk, the wolf retorted, walking with her as they headed towards the front of the barn and the house beyond.

Carolynn scoffed. She was not dramatic. Beth was always the drama queen between the two of them. She was the peacekeeper.

As they headed for the big house, a flicker of movement caught her eye. She glanced towards the edge of the stable wall, the last few feet of the building they needed to walk past, and spotted a six-foot black snake. She nearly jumped over Shadow, standing on the other side of the wolf so that Shadow was between her and the danger noodle.

Like I said, dramatic.

"I hate snakes," Carolynn hissed. It didn't matter that she knew it was a garden snake and it couldn't really do any permanent damage, they still creeped her out.

They walked the rest of the way a bit quicker and found Beth sitting in a rocking chair on the front porch.

Carolynn took the steps two at a time and sat in the chair beside Beth's. Shadow stayed at the foot of the stairs, ears perked as though listening for something. She sighed in relief as she sank back into the chair and undid her hair, fingers running through the long strands, undoing any tangles they found.

"How was your day?" Carolynn asked Beth, who seemed to be smirking at something on the phone glued to her hand.

"Very good," Beth said, eyebrows wiggling.

Carolynn did not have to read her mind to know what she had been up to most of the afternoon. She could smell Brian's cheap cologne from where she sat.

"Gross," Carolynn said, gagging for effect. She wasn't quiet about her dislike for the guy her friend had been seeing for over a year. There was just something about him that told her he wasn't a good person. He was going to end up hurting Beth one way or another.

Beth chuckled. "How did it go with the new guy? There's something about him that just grates on my nerves."

"He actually did pretty well, I have to admit. He's a bit standoff-ish but he worked pretty hard," Carolynn said, rocking back in her chair on the wood deck.

"Well, that's something at least. I didn't like the attitude he was giving you earlier."

"I noticed."

"And his clothes! Who comes to work at a barn dressed like that?"

Carolynn raised a brow at her friend as her voice rose steadily higher. "Tell me how you really feel."

"He's some spoiled rich kid, an entitled ass," Beth spat.

"And you're one to talk about being spoiled?" Carolynn gestured towards the house and land surrounding them. Beth never knew what it was like to shop at the thrift store or eat ramen for weeks on end.

Beth shot her a warning look that told her she had gone too far. "Whose side are you on?"

Carolynn straightened, taking her tone seriously. Something was off. "Yours. I'm always on your side, you know that," Carolynn said, and this time she really did dive into her friend's mind. Beth was a liar. She hadn't been romping in the sheets all afternoon, or at all today, but rather fighting with Brian over God knew what. Carolynn had the sudden urge to knee him in the dick. She could hear the things he called her rattling off in her mind, and no one deserved to be talked to in that way. "Are you okay?"

Maybe it was how her tone had changed or that she had stopped rocking, but Beth instantly avoided her gaze. "It's nothing."

"Beth."

"Not now, Care. I know you know, but not right now," Beth sighed and did what she does best. Changed the subject. "You ready to go home and have the big dinner?"

"I'm actually kind of dreading it," Carolynn admitted aloud. She would drop the issues with Brian for now, but they would revisit the topic.

Beth's lips pressed into a thin line. She knew the struggle Carolynn had with her mother. The relationship had always been rocky and unstable, but when her dad passed, her mom kind of gave up, and maybe she did too. She grew tired of fighting for someone who couldn't remember to pick her up from school.

"I know, but I'll be there. Maybe it won't be so bad," Beth tried.

Carolynn simply shrugged, unsure what to say or how to feel over any of it. Instead, she opted for her own distraction.

"Donnie called me."

"Club guy?"

"The very one."

Beth bolted upright, nearly falling out of her chair. She clutched the armrest, stabilizing herself as her jaw met the floor.

"Close your mouth, or you'll catch mosquitos," Carolynn warned her.

"And you're just telling me now?" Beth shrieked.

Shadow's head whipped toward them, fur down her back

raised, ears alert.

Carolynn shushed her loudly and explained the short two-minute conversation she had with the guy.

"What? That's it?" Beth asked, sounding slightly disappointed.

"That's it," Carolynn said, leaning back into her chair, rocking once again as Shadow ignored both girls.

"But he did say he'd see you again?"

"Yes," Carolynn sighed, remembering how flustered she was with him on the phone. The way he had caught her off guard and how she sounded like a stuttering fool. Idiot.

Carolynn caught Beth staring. Those big brown eyes searched her face, mouth pulling into a teasing smirk. Her brow rose in response, glaring at her friend.

"What are you staring at?"

"You," Beth chuckled. "You like this guy."

"Please. I barely know him."

"Sometimes, that doesn't matter."

"I've only spoken to him like three times," Carolynn said, holding up her fingers for emphasis.

"It's not always necessary to know someone for there to be a connection," Beth said with a shrug.

Carolynn internally rolled her eyes and stood up from her chair, feeling oddly unsettled by the turn of conversation. "We need to get going. Who knows if there is even dinner waiting for us at home."

Beth did in fact roll her eyes as she stood and gave her a mocking bow. "As Your Highness commands."

The drive to her house was a quiet one. Neither of them spoke, seemingly stuck in their own heads. She didn't intrude on Beth's thoughts, leaving her be, but that didn't mean she wanted to be in her own. Beth's words had stirred ideas better left undiscovered.

They pulled up to her trailer and the lights were actually on inside.

Carolynn opened her door wide for Shadow to jump out first, hearing Beth's slam shut only a moment before hers. She noticed her mother's beat-up car parked on the side of the house. She was definitely here.

"Well, it doesn't look to be on fire," Beth said, sounding as though it was something she had expected. "Shall we?"

Carolynn inhaled deeply before walking up the weathered porch steps and forcefully pushing open the front door.

The room was a grey haze, making her eyes sting and burning her nostrils. Both girls instantly started coughing, waving their hands in front of their faces trying to clear the smoke.

What the fuck?

Panic began to build in her chest as tears gathered in her eyes from the smoke. Had something happened? Was the house actually on fire?

As they moved farther into the house, they finally reached the kitchen and found her mother, nicely dressed, waving a towel in the air as though that would clear the smoke that was currently inhabiting their house. On the top of the stove was an overly crispy lasagna.

"Mom, what happened?" Carolynn yelled, garnering her attention.

Susana whipped around, not realizing someone else was in the house. "Girls! How does Chinese sound?"

Chapter 10

By the time the Chinese food had arrived, every window and door had been opened to air out the house. Carolynn was certain the smell was there to stay as she sat at their makeshift dinner table to eat. She could swear her hair and clothes reeked of smoke.

"Thanks, Mom," Carolynn said in between bites of her beef and broccoli. She was pleasantly surprised that her mother had remembered her favorite dish.

Beth mumbled something similar in between shovels of her fried rice, but Susana had barely touched the General Tso in front of her. Carolynn felt as though she wanted to speak, had something on her mind she needed to purge, but even with her ability would she never dare to step foot into her mother's mind. Not only because her mother was an adult who had done things with her father that no child should ever hear about, let alone see a memory of, but she was almost afraid to see what her mother thought of her, how she thought of dad.

"Is something wrong?" Carolynn asked, sitting up in her chair a bit straighter.

Beth paused with the fork halfway to her mouth, blinking between the two of them.

"Wrong?" Susana repeated, as though she hadn't heard correctly. "Why would something be wrong?"

"You haven't touched your food," Carolynn pointed to the

untouched takeout before her as proof. She hadn't even removed the lid.

Susana glanced down at the meal, almost surprised to see it there. Carolynn and Beth both watched her carefully. She was certainly acting weird.

"I think it's finally hitting me that you're leaving," Susana said, her voice low and strained as though she was on the verge of tears.

Carolynn shifted uncomfortably in her seat, unsure what to do or say. "I'll only be in the city. I'll be back. It's just college."

"Yeah, I'll bring her back every weekend," Beth said with an empathetic nod.

"I know," Susana said, still keeping her gaze down on the fried chicken. Her arm moved from out of her lap as she placed an envelope on the table. "I was going through some of your dad's things today while you were gone, and I found these."

Carolynn reached for the manila envelope and hesitated before opening it. Was it a letter from her dead father talking about all of the things he would miss out on in her life? Was it a will bequeathing her his bare minimum personal effects? She already had his favorite football sweatshirt tucked away safely in her closet next to her own baby blanket.

She opened the envelope and pulled out its contents, examining them carefully.

At first, she was confused. Had it been meant for all of them or just her? Was it a joke, or was she actually expected to read this? Her eyes widened as her fingers tried not to crumple the paper.

"I don't get it," Carolynn finally said, glancing up at her mother.

"Your father had been doing his own research, and he found some information he had hoped to give to you himself, but, well, the cancer ..." her voice trailed off, unable to finish, but Carolynn knew what she was about to say.

The cancer took him faster than any of the doctors predicted.

Carolynn glanced back down at the papers. There were over twenty documents, all with random cases and occurrences.

"Now, your father of course had no concrete proof, just ideas and theories, but he thought you might want to have it just in case," Susana said, a small smile splayed on her face.

Beth scooted closer, her chair scraping against the linoleum floor as she peered over Carolynn's shoulder and read the papers. Her brow furrowed, lips moving as her brain processed what she was reading.

"You guys think Carolynn is an alien?" Beth asked, sounding almost defensive.

"God, no," Susana half laughed, as though the idea was ridiculous. Not like it hadn't crossed all of their minds at some time or other. "We don't think you're an alien, but we do know there is something different about you. I've never met anyone who can do what you do. Your father just thought you might want some more information before you went out into the real world. On your own."

Carolynn flipped through some of the pages, scanning the titles and noticing some lines were highlighted. "Manifested into adulthood," she read out loud. "What does that mean?"

"It means your father believed, based on some of his research, that your powers may grow, evolve when you reach adulthood," Susana explained.

Carolynn forced herself not to look at Beth, not to remember the scorched handprints. "You mean turning eighteen could somehow spark a growth spurt?"

"Exactly." Susana almost sighed with relief, as though any of this information was a good thing.

All it did was confirm how different she truly was.

"Is that supposed to be a good thing?" Carolynn asked, her voice slightly raised and agitated. "Am I supposed to be proud that I'm not human? That I struggled to master my telepathy powers and now may have more?"

"Star, it's not just about your powers." Susana leaned forward against the table, eyes bright. "You've never been sick. You heal faster than humanly possible. You don't burn after being in the sun for twelve straight hours with no sunscreen. I just want you to be careful."

She quickly buried down the impulse to yell, to lash out, and accuse her mother of something, but of what she wasn't sure. Wasn't she doing what any good parent would do? Prepare their child for the big bad world. Unfortunately, in her case, if the world caught wind of what she could do, she could end up as someone's science experiment and locked away in *Area 51*.

"I know," she said, sighing, setting the papers on the table. She rubbed at her forehead, at the headache that was forming there.

"I also got you something for your birthday," Susana said cheerily, as though she hadn't just dropped a bomb, and lifted a small brown bag from beside her chair and into her lap. "Happy Birthday."

Carolynn stared at the brown bag, almost afraid to open it. Hadn't there been enough surprises for one night? But she reached for the bag, opened it, and pulled out something hard and ceramic.

"Isn't it cute?" Susana nearly squealed.

Beth snorted at her side and went back to eating her dinner.

It was an ornately painted barn owl in all shades of the rainbow. While the bird's shape resembled Spot, it showed none of the majestic and stunning colorings that made barn owls so special. It looked like something from a tourist shop near the beach.

"It reminded me of your little owl friend. I thought you'd like it," Susana said, finally opening her dinner and stabbing her fork into one of the soggy pieces of chicken.

"Thanks, Mom."

The rest of the evening was thankfully uneventful as it became apparent her mother hadn't gotten a wink of sleep, nearly falling into her food at least twice. Carolynn and Beth finally sent her off to bed.

"You can stay the night if you want," Carolynn offered her best friend, not really wanting to be alone.

Beth gnawed on her bottom lip which was answer enough in itself. "I would, but I think I'm actually going to head over to Brian's and have a chat with him."

"Of course," Carolynn nodded, tapping her foot on the ground, shifting on both feet when she thought of something. "Would you mind dropping me off in town? I'd like to go to the bookstore before they close."

"Sure. You okay to get back home on your own?" Beth asked, gathering her keys and purse from the couch

"Yeah. I can walk home; it's not far." She ducked into her bedroom for a quick moment, grabbed the last bit of spending cash she had left, and met Beth at the door.

Outside, Shadow was sleeping on the gravel drive. She had been unwilling to step inside with all of the smoke and chose to stay out in the fresh air. Not that Carolynn blamed her. The wolf lifted her head as they bounced down the steps and made their way to the Mustang.

Where are we going? Shadow asked, standing up from her nap.

"Beth is going to drop me off in town. I'd like to go back to the bookstore, but you can stay here." Carolynn offered her the out.

Shadow shook the dust from her hair before trotting to the car, ready to jump in the back. *Where you go, I go, pup.*

The drive into town was quick, taking no more than ten minutes, but the silence made it drag. She wasn't sure how to feel, how to process the documents her father had left her, and it's not like Beth offered stimulating conversation either. She could hear her friends thoughts like they were her own, rattling off ways to talk to Brian without causing another explosion. She was afraid that anything she would say would set him off.

Carolynn hated Brian all over again.

Beth pulled the Mustang up to the front of the bookshop. The lights were still on inside. Glancing around, she noticed the streets were bare, with very minimal foot traffic.

"Thanks for driving me," Carolynn smiled before pulling on the door handle, when Beth grabbed her hand on the armrest.

"You are not an alien," Beth said with a completely serious tone and face. "But even if you were, I'd still love you."

Carolynn snorted, rolling her eyes. Well, she was almost serious. "Thanks, bestie," Carolyn made to leave the car but thought better of it for a moment longer. "And Beth... He doesn't deserve you. You deserve to be treated with kindness and compassion, and I don't think Brian will be able to give you that."

It was a hard truth, but it was the truth. Even if her friend didn't heed her advice, she at least deserved to know her worth.

Beth smiled sadly. "Thanks, babe."

Carolynn knew full well Beth would stay with the pathetic excuse for a man, but she couldn't let her go, not with all the troubling thoughts cycling in her head, not without at least saying something.

"Text me when you get home," Beth said as Carolynn stepped out of the car, letting Shadow out behind her.

"Same," Carolynn told her, slamming the door shut.

She watched as the car disappeared from view.

You're not an alien, Shadow said, sitting at her side, watching a couple walk with ice cream cones dripping onto the pavement.

"You don't even know what an alien is," Carolynn retorted.

I know you are not one, Shadow said once again.

Carolynn noted an odd tone to her voice, as though she was one hundred percent certain, but she brushed it off and headed inside.

The bell rang above her head, alerting the occupants to her arrival. There was no one at the checkout counter, so she walked towards the book stacks, perusing the shelves. She found the section she had been looking for, pulled one of the books out, and began flipping through the pages. Some of the pictures were obscured and ridiculous, while others were downright disturbing.

"Reading up on aliens?" a voice startled her, nearly causing the book to slip from her hands as she jumped slightly. "I'm sorry. I didn't mean to sneak up on you."

Carolynn glanced around, annoyed with herself that she hadn't heard the store owner's approach. She was usually much more observant.

"Neila, right?"

"You remembered." The woman smiled, genuinely surprised.

"Of course I did," Carolynn said. How could she not remember her; she was beautiful and had given her a book. Best impression ever.

"How did you like that book I gave you?"

"It was very informative, very detailed, which I appreciate," Carolynn said. "It even gave me a nightmare."

"Really?" Neila frowned. "How odd."

Carolynn simply nodded.

"So, you're interested in aliens?" Neila asked again, pointing to the book in her hands.

Carolynn glanced down at the open page and slammed it shut, putting it back on the shelf. "No, not really. Just curious."

"You know, they say aliens aren't just from other worlds, but can also come from other dimensions."

"Other dimensions?"

"Like parallel planes. They exist in the same space as ours, just different places and time," Neila tried to explain.

Carolynn somewhat understood what she was saying. She'd seen enough superhero movies to get the gist, but that still didn't explain where she came from.

"Was that your boyfriend who dropped you off?" Neila asked.

Carolynn glanced at the front door where Beth had so clearly pulled up and smiled, trying not to laugh. "Um, no. That was my best friend, Beth. I don't have a car, so she gets to be my personal driver."

"Well, that's nice of her," Neila said, perking up. "Not about the not having a car part, I'm sure that sucks, but having such a good friend is rare these days."

Carolynn couldn't help but nod in agreement. It was why she and Beth were so close. Reliable friends weren't easy to come by, and when you have one like Beth, why trust more people to be able to hurt you?

She glanced at Neila, who held a spiraled notebook in her hand that looked like it had been through the ringer. The corners were creased, spiral was bent out of shape, and the cover had coffee stains, but what drew her eye was the large diamond on her ring finger.

"Are you married?"

Neila glanced down at the ring, splaying her hand, allowing the diamond facets to catch the light and sparkle. She smiled sweetly at the sight of it. "No, I'm not married."

"That's an awfully large diamond for not being married," Carolynn commented, raising a brow.

Neila chuckled. "You're not wrong. Marriage just isn't in the cards for us. I'm already his."

Carolynn couldn't help but smile, thinking how nice that must be. No one really needs a piece of paper to declare their love. There are other ways.

"That sounds nice," Carolynn admitted out loud.

"Do you have anyone special in your life?" Neila asked, looking genuinely interested, leaning a bit forward.

This time it was Carolynn chuckling. "No, not really."

"Oh, come on, a girl like you. You're stunning; you must have boys lining up."

"No, not really. I don't really have time for it. Between work and getting ready for college, it doesn't really leave a lot of time for dating." No sense in mentioning Donnie. Who knew where that would lead. She glanced at the time on her phone and realized the store should have closed five minutes ago. "Crap, I'm sorry to have kept you late. I should be getting home. I have work in the morning."

"Let me give you a ride. I'd hate for you to walk home," Neila offered, walking towards the front desk, assumingly to grab keys.

"Oh, no, thank you. Really, it's a short walk home. I enjoy the fresh air." Carolynn put her hands up, waving them no. The last thing she wanted to be was more indebted to this woman.

"Well, then at least take this," Neila said, as she was scribbling something down on a piece of paper before handing it to her.

Carolynn took the slip, curiosity getting the best of her, and found ten digits written elegantly. "Your number?" she asked stupidly. Of course it was her phone number, but she couldn't very well be rude and ask why.

"Yeah, in case you ever wanna chat or grab some tea. Sorry, I'm not a coffee drinker." Neila laughed at herself.

"Neither am I. I can't stand the taste, but tea sounds nice," Carolynn smiled, appreciating the gesture, and tucked the number into her pocket. "Thank you."

Sleep had been a distant thought that she continued chasing and seeking until finally darkness consumed her.

Thunder rolled across the land as lightning struck granite rock. Metal clanged in the distance as swords sparked off of one another. There was a steady beat, pounding through the air, like hundreds, if not thousands, of bird taking flight all at once.

Carolynn stood in a field, the ground dead beneath her feet. Glancing down, she spotted two bodies, the one with curly brown hair she recognized immediately. She knelt down in the dirt, tears streaming down her soot-streaked face. She brushed the hair back from Beth's face, her eyes closed as though she was simply sleeping, but her chest didn't rise and her lips were blue with death. She had a shallow cut across one of her cheeks, and blood pooled at the corner of her mouth.

She screamed for help, for someone, anyone, to come, but no one answered. A figure moved off in the distance towards her, a sword in his hand dragging through the earth. Its mouth opened, and crows flew out, feathers dropping to the ground as black as night.

Chapter 11

Work was exhausting. Her shoulders were stiff, and she had a crick in her neck.

Shadow was off prancing through the woods or doing whatever it was wolves do and had been gone all day. Something about her pack that resided in the forest along the edge of town. She'd be back sooner or later.

Carolynn was in the office, going over feed schedules and trying to figure out where they would be ordering their next shipment of hay. The lack of rain in the area was creating a shortage and forcing prices to skyrocket. It was giving her a migraine.

The rumbling of a car engine distracted her, and she raised her head from the sheets of paper she had been staring at the last thirty minutes. She glanced at her flip phone on the desk, noting the time. It was barely four o'clock.

Beth was up at the house, and even she wasn't lazy enough to drive the Mustang down to the barn. She hated getting her car dirty and wouldn't risk getting horse muck on the car floor.

Carolynn got up from the desk and poked her head out into the aisle, where she saw Jason do the same farther down out of one of the stalls he was cleaning.

"Are you expecting someone?" Jason asked, face smeared with God knows what and a shovel in hand raised above his head.

What he expected to do with that shovel, she honestly didn't know, but it made her smile.

"Not that I know of," Carolynn chuckled. "Put the shovel down, Sparky. I'll go check."

Carolynn left the new guy alone in the barn as she headed out into the blinding sunlight. She covered her eyes with one hand as she squinted and found herself face to face with a sleek black classic convertible, something straight off a lot from the sixties, in pristine condition.

She couldn't make out who was in the driver's seat as the reflected rays off the windshield obstructed her view, but she didn't have to wonder for long. The driver's door opened.

It was the hair that she recognized first. She knew of no one else's hair that could reflect such colors as his did. How he managed to fit in the compact car was a mystery to her, but he stood up, unfolding himself to his full height so that she had to tip her head back in order to see him properly.

Those glaringly beautiful icy eyes found hers, and that devilish smirk splayed across his face until that stupid dimple made an appearance.

He was here. At her work, standing in the dirt, no doubt ruining his leather boots and pants. No, not pants, black jeans. He was wearing jeans. If she thought he was impressive in black slacks, seeing him in jeans did something else to her. A tightness coiled deep in her belly as she skimmed down his body, from the dark Henley that hugged his chest and arms perfectly to the denim that clung to his hips and thighs, not to mention the leather boots that were probably still too expensive for this place, but still better than sneakers.

She walked up to him slowly, almost afraid he would disappear in a cloud of smoke. He leaned back against the car, running a hand through his silky hair as he watched her.

"You have a habit of just showing up uninvited, don't you?" Carolynn couldn't help the word vomit. The question had been ringing in her head from the moment she realized it was him.

Donnie didn't seem offended or put off by the question, but merely shrugged, "It's a curse."

"On you or me?" Carolynn half laughed, nerves buzzing in her stomach as she stood in front of him.

"Of that, I am not sure," Donnie admitted. "Right now, the

jury is out."

"Ah," Carolynn said, unsure of what to do or say. What was this between them? Were they flirting, courting, is that what all of this was, or was it just hanging out? Were they friends, or were they more? Did she even want more? She was leaving for college soon. Would that make this a summer fling?

Questions buzzed through her mind faster than she could process, and she hadn't noticed him move off the car and close the distance between them. She wasn't used to being caught off guard or someone else taking the lead. Hell, she wasn't accustomed to any of this. The last boy she kissed was in ninth-grade gym class, Aaron Randall. He tried sticking his tongue down her throat before she'd been ready, which earned him a black eye for his efforts. He told the class he'd fallen on the bleachers and clipped the railing.

Since then she had sworn off boys. She got close a few times, but it just never felt right.

Calloused fingers gripped her chin, raising her head, forcing her eyes to meet his. God, he was tall. Tall and so damn beautiful she was sure a marble statue had been carved of him at some point. Maybe an angel painting with his likeness resided somewhere.

"Where did you go?" he asked, thick brows furrowing, pinched together. "You got quiet."

"My head was being loud," she admitted in a whisper. She wasn't even sure why she was whispering, but looking into those swimming blue eyes that held every color in the sky was like experiencing inner peace and war all at once. She wasn't even sure why she was confessing, but it didn't seem as though she had much control of her faculties around him.

His hand moved from her chin and settled on her shoulder, thumb brushing her neck. She felt her flesh warm at his touch, her heart pounding in her chest, and nerves fluttered beneath her skin.

A throat cleared nearby. Donnie sighed with annoyance, clenching his jaw as his head swiveled.

Carolynn turned as well but knew very well who was trying to get their attention. Why he felt the need to interrupt was beyond her, but she was almost too preoccupied with the fact that Donnie's hand was still on her shoulder and he hadn't pulled away.

Jason stood at the entrance of the stable, leaning against the handle of the shovel he still carried with him. "Hey Carolynn, the horses have been fed and watered and are shut in for the evening. I'm going to head out."

Carolynn pulled her phone out of her back pocket and sure enough, it was dinner time. "Oh, thanks, Jason. I'll see you tomorrow."

Jason kept his eye on Donnie a moment longer, before turning back to the stable to return the shovel and head out. Carolynn turned back to Donnie and found his own gaze still lingering where Jason has disappeared to, face pinched and eyes narrowed.

"A friend of yours?" Donnie asked, sounding more annoyed than she'd ever heard him.

"Barely." Carolynn almost laughed. "The owner just hired him the other day."

Donnie made a non-verbal guttural noise that she couldn't quite decipher. He was still turned away, as though waiting for Jason to reemerge. She didn't know what had possessed him or why he was suddenly so distracted, so she reached up, her fingers grazing his smooth cheek, thumb brushing along his jawline. Her touch seemed to shock him as he turned, eyes wide, sucking in a quick breath.

"Well, don't you two look cozy."

Carolynn almost cursed up a storm, but instead opted for releasing a struggled exhale as she dropped her hand and turned to where Beth now walked down the drive from the big house.

"Beth," Carolynn said, almost in warning. Her friend would certainly hear about this later. Whatever 'this' was.

Donnie pivoted, his hand shifting from her shoulder to rest against the small of her back. Carolynn forced herself not to lean into him, not to show how much his touch was affecting her.

Now she really wished Beth would go away.

Carolynn glanced up to find him smiling at Beth, but no dimple. She took too much pleasure in that simple fact.

"Donnie, this is Beth. Beth, Donnie," Carolynn said making introductions.

Beth stopped in front of them, eyes darting to the arm that was now around her back, and arched a brow before holding her hand out to him. "Hello, I'm the best friend I'm sure Carolynn has told you all about."

"There has been some mention of a friend," Donnie said, voice teasing as he took her hand and shook it.

"I am so glad you're here," Beth ignored his passive comment and rocked back on her heels. "Would you mind bringing our sweet Carolynn home for me? I was going to, but since you're here . . ."

Nice. Way to make it sound like she was some charity case to pawn off onto the next person, but Carolynn could see what her friend was up to. She was setting them up, forcing his hand.

Carolynn shook her head. "It's fine. You don't have to."

"I'd be honored," Donnie said, his fingers splaying against her spine, thumb brushing bare skin where her tank top had risen.

"Perfect!" Beth squealed, clapping her hands. "You two try not to have too much fun without me. I'm off to Brian's."

Carolynn frowned, finally taking notice of her friend's clothing. It was a bit more dressed up than her normal attire, definitely exposing more skin than normal, as her cleavage nearly spilled out of her strapless top. Most nights, Brian's house consisted of endless parties and drink-a-thons. She never liked Beth going to them, let alone go without her.

"I can come —" Carolynn tried, but was cut off.

"Absolutely, not," Beth said, not so subtly eyeing Donnie, eyes widening.

This is your perfect opportunity to spend some time with him. Get to know him if you must, and then tell me all about him in bed, 'cause I bet you he is fire, Beth said, almost yelling into her brain.

You are shameless. Carolynn projected back, unable to help the small roll of her eyes.

"Please be careful and call me if you need anything," Carolynn said aloud, giving her friend the most serious look she could muster.

"Yes, Mom," Beth drawled mockingly before turning on her four-inch heels and heading back up to the house where her car resided.

"You really don't have to take me home; I can get there by myself," Carolynn said, trying to give him an out.

"How would you get there?"

Carolynn paused, unsure she heard him right. "What?"

"If I didn't bring you home, and it looks like your friend

certainly won't be tonight, how would you get home?" Donnie asked again, brow raised.

He had cornered her. He had backed her into a corner, and she hadn't even realized it until now.

"I would walk home," she admitted, holding his gaze.

"How far is home?"

"Seven miles."

"Absolutely not."

Carolynn's teeth clenched over the absurdity in his voice. Did he not think her capable? "It wouldn't be the first time. I'm used to walking."

"That was before me," Donnie said, as though that was final.

"You think just because we met a few days ago, my life has suddenly been altered?" Carolynn scoffed.

"It has," Donnie said flatly.

He didn't blink, didn't waver. She finally sighed heavily, glaring at him as though that would do anything. "Fine, have it your way."

"I usually do." He smirked, moving out of her way, still keeping his hand on her back, and beckoning her towards the car.

"My dad always warned me not to get into cars with strangers," Carolynn commented as she stared at the car, almost too afraid to even look at the classic, let alone touch it.

"Sound advice," Donnie said, not at all put off as he opened the passenger door for her.

"But my mother would tell me to jump feet first," Carolynn also mumbled, still wondering how her parents, being such complete opposites, ever made it work.

Donnie seemed to find that humorous as he chuckled, watching her slide into the leather seat of his car and buckle in. "I think I'd like your mother."

Carolynn glanced up at him like some towering God and gave him her best glare. "Oh, she'd love you."

Donnie snorted, rolling his eyes before shutting the door. She watched as his tall, lean yet muscular figure strode around the car and somehow fit so comfortably behind the wheel. As they backed out of the driveway, Carolynn could have sworn she caught sight of Jason, looking out from the stable, and watching them leave together. She couldn't shake the odd chill that raced along her skin as the stable faded from view.

"Where too?" Donnie asked, staring out at the two-lane road leading away from Beth's.

"You can just take me home," Carolynn suggested.

"That's too easy," Donnie insisted, tapping his fingers on the steering wheel. "Where is somewhere you like to go?"

Carolynn glanced down at her horse-riding clothes and instantly felt like trash in his very classic, very expensive car. "All I can think of is showering right now," she admitted. "I stink of horse."

Donnie glanced over as though only now realizing she was indeed covered in dirt and horse hair, but he shrugged, not seeming to care in the slightest. "Where's a decent lake around here?"

"You want to go swimming?" Carolynn asked, unsure she heard him correctly.

"You afraid?" he challenged.

"Never," she said, a bit too fast. "I just don't have any extra clothes with me."

"I have some extra clothes in the back." He noticed the suspicious brow she rose. "You never know when they might come in handy."

She couldn't deny the practicality of it.

While swimming hadn't exactly been on her list of things to do today, she did like the idea of swimming. Being able to wash away the smell and dirt and just relax in the crystal clear waters that would be sure to zap any remnants of the sticky humidity the day had coated her with.

"You're on," Carolynn agreed to his somewhat random idea. "Only if you promise to feed me after."

Donnie smirked, that stupid dimple showing up. "Deal."

Chapter 12

Carolynn directed him out of town.

The spring she enjoyed was off the beaten path and just outside the border of her city. In all her time visiting it, she had never seen another soul there.

She couldn't help watching him from the corner of her eye. The way he seemed so relaxed in the driver's seat and how effortless his driving was. Did he drive for work? Maybe some street racing? He looked like the sort to do off-the-books work or even unsavory jobs that law enforcement might frown upon.

"What do you do for a living?"

Donnie frowned, hands regripping the steering wheel. "What?"

"What do you do for work? I'm assuming you have a job," Carolynn asked again.

Donnie's lips pressed into a thin line, and his shoulders tensed. "I work. I guess you could say I'm a freelancer."

"What kind of jobs do you do?" Carolynn pressed.

"What is this, the Inquisition?" Donnie asked, brow raised, side-eyeing her.

"No, this is me trying to get to know you. How else am I to do that without asking you questions?"

"By watching someone, by paying attention to the little things," Donnie answered her. "Like how you bite your lip when you're nervous, or you fidget with your shirt."

Carolynn forced her hands still in her lap and clamped her

mouth shut.

"Or how you were nervous for your friend back there going to that party on her own," Donnie explained, smirking as he took note that he had hit the nail on the head. "Who is this guy? Brian? Is he bad?"

"Yes," Carolynn said without a moment's hesitation, knowing deep in her bones he was a shit person and an even shittier boyfriend. "But Beth can handle herself."

God, she hoped that was true.

"Great job of deflecting by the way," Carolynn noted, almost as an afterthought. He was a little too good at distracting her.

"Was I wrong?" Donnie challenged, that stupid dimple was as distracting as ever.

"I really don't think that's the point," Carolynn pointed out. "You still haven't answered my question."

"To answer your question," Donnie repeated, "I do whatever I'm hired to do. Odds and ends sort of things."

"So, like a handyman?" Carolynn asked, unsure what he meant by any of what he just said.

"Sometimes."

Not the best of answers, well, not really an answer at all, seeing as how she still had no clue what he actually did for work, but she let it go. For now.

"What about you?" Donnie asked. "What made you want to work with horses?"

Carolynn froze, unsure how to answer that. "Well, I don't know." She sighed, brushing a loose strand of hair behind her ear. "I don't think anyone's ever asked me that."

"I'm assuming you like them," Donnie smiled, teasing evident in his voice.

"Of course I like them, but working with them was just kind of right place, right time," she told him. "Being friends with Beth, we were always down at the stables growing up. Her dad taught me how to ride, and then how to train, and then how to run the place, and it just kind of progressed from there. I think he always hoped Beth would take an interest when she saw me doing everything, but it's not Beth's path. She's too wild to settle for farm life."

"And you're not?"

"Not what?"

"Wild?"

Carolynn's mouth hung open, words failing her as she sat there, unable to answer him. While she wasn't a thrill-seeker like Beth was, reckless and sometimes a danger to herself, Carolynn wasn't a picnic either. She could feel his eye on her, noticing every hitch in her breath, every move she made.

Did he think she was wild?

"Turn left," she called out, as they were just about to pass the turn-off.

The car bumped down a dirt road lined thickly with trees. As she bounced in her seat, she instantly regretted taking him here, risking his priceless car, but that smile, that smile that stole the breath right from her as they bounced down the road, told her enough. He didn't care one way or another.

"This is definitely off the beaten path," Donnie noted, as the road ended into a small trail taking them farther into the woods. The sun was still high in the sky and offered the perfect lighting that filtered through the leaves, casting the scenery in sparkling greens.

"I promise I am not taking you off to murder you," Carolynn teased, offering him a stiff salute.

Donnie cocked his head, leaning into her as that devilish smirk came out to play. "It's not me I'm worried about."

Carolynn wet her lips, her mouth suddenly very dry as her chest and neck flushed hot. His eyes traced the movement of her tongue, and she wondered what it would be like to be kissed by him.

"We should get going before we lose the sun." Carolynn cleared her throat, before pushing open the door and stepping out of the car.

The grass was a bit dry beneath her boots, making a slight crunching sound, but that didn't worry her. While most of the lakes and ponds would be nearly dried up, her spring was fed by an underwater lake, constantly feeding it crystal clear water year-round.

She heard his door slam shut as she walked towards the path and glanced back over her shoulder. "It's not far from here."

"Lead the way," Donnie gestured her forward, and she took the lead.

Not even a dozen yards in, they came upon a spring that stretched across the length of an Olympic-size swimming pool.

Its water was a turquoise blue and clear enough to see the rocks at the bottom, nearly thirty feet down. The spring was bubbling as it moved with its own current along the rocks that encompassed it. She peered back at Donnie to measure his reaction and smiled as he looked genuinely mesmerized.

"I call it my oasis," Carolynn told him. "Not entirely original, I'll admit, but it fits."

"That it does," Donnie admitted, bobbing his head.

Carolynn grinned, internally jumping up and down that he liked it almost as much as she did. She had never taken anyone here. Only Beth one time, but after sticking one foot in the frigid water, she demanded they return home. Spot had shown her the area when she was thirteen, barely a mile from her house.

"You want to go in?" Carolynn could feel the day's heat sticking to her skin and tank top.

Donnie eyed the spring, and something sparkled in those eyes nearly as clear and deep as the water. "Absolutely."

He pulled off his leather jacket and hung it on a low-lying branch of one of the nearby trees. He peeled off his leather boots and socks, setting them at the base of the same tree.

Carolynn could feel his eyes on her as she unzipped her thigh-high boots, pulling them off and stuffing the socks inside. She undid the button of her breeches and pulled them off, revealing black lace underwear. She knew she should turn, maybe hide the partial nudity, but she didn't move, didn't budge. Instead, she stood there and let him look as she watched him pull his shirt over his head.

She was staring. They both knew she was staring, but just as she hadn't turned away, neither had he.

He was glorious. His body was as imperfect as it was beautiful. She could make out faint scars along his chest, abdomen, and arms. They were long faded, barely visible, but she could see them. Her fingers twitched, wanting to reach out and trace them. Anger burned in her, boiling her blood. She wanted to hurt whoever had hurt him. But the scars only added to his strength, his resilience, almost as much as the cut abs and defined pectorals told her he either knew his way around a gym or he was a hired bodyguard. Most likely both.

Carolynn left her tank on, not quite willing to bare her pink bra to him, and walked over towards the side of the spring, where the ground was more elevated. She stood on a rock that sat on the edge of the spring about five feet above the water, where she knew the bottom to be deep enough she didn't fear hitting the rocks below. She put her arms over her head and dived smoothly into the crystal-clear water.

The cold temperature shocked her body, immediately erasing any memory of heat and sweat. She broke the surface and looked for Donnie. He stood two feet away from the water's edge.

She swam over to a rock ledge that was the perfect height to sit on without drowning. She leaned back against the cool rock, closing her eyes, allowing her body to bask in the rays of the remaining daylight while the water washed away the day's filth. She heard a splash somewhere off to the side, but she didn't bother opening her eyes, as she could tell by the ripples in the water, he was swimming towards her. When she felt the movement cease, she finally cracked an eye open and found Donnie floating in front of her. His raven black hair was sticking out every which way, water dripping like diamonds from the ends. She scooted over to make room for him.

Donnie shook his head, scattering water droplets around them. "I thought we were swimming."

Carolynn grinned and pushed herself off the wall, shooting past him. She could feel him chasing after her, only an arm's length away. She dived down to the bottom of the spring, her ears popping from the pressure, lungs straining for oxygen, but she forced the feelings down as she touched the bottom, rocks smooth beneath her feet.

She opened her eyes and didn't see him. He hadn't followed her down and she couldn't make out his figure above her at the surface. Something brushed against her ankle, wrapping around her foot. She looked down and found herself caught in roots along the bottom of the spring. She reached down, trying not to panic as she pulled on the vines, but nothing. They didn't budge, only tightening and seemingly entangling her even more.

Her air was running out as the pressure built in her head, screaming at her that her time was up. She pulled on the roots again and again, but they didn't budge or break. Air bubbles escaped her mouth as she opened it to scream, but that was her mistake. Water quickly filled her mouth and lungs. Black spots swam in her vision.

Was the sun setting already?

Chapter 13

She was floating. Suspended with no tether, no tie to this plane. Pain radiated in her chest as something hard thumped her. Fire ignited in her lungs, her throat, and her mouth as she coughed, her body forcing all of the liquid out. She sputtered for a few moments, taking in gulps of air, inhaling deeply even through the trail of pain blazing down her throat. She was lifted up and sat down on a warm, hard body, held tightly as though afraid she might slip away.

Carolynn wheezed as she struggled to breathe, coughing one last time, before she finally opened her eyes, blinking away the wetness gathered there. His hair was plastered to his face, his own breathing labored and quick. His hand reached out, brushing the wet hair back from her face, running his hands along her arms, her face, almost as though he wanted to assure himself she was okay, she was alive.

And she was alive, because of him. He saved her. She was drowning—no, she *had* drowned—and he had pulled up from the bottom of the spring and brought her back to life.

His hands lingered on her face, cupping her cheeks, thumb rubbing along her jaw tilting her head up.

"Are you okay?" he asked, eyes searching hers.

"Yes," she said, her voice raspy and hoarse. "Thank you."

"Don't thank me." Donnie shook his head. "I didn't—"

"You saved my life," Carolynn said. This time she reached out, cupping his face in her hand, and forced him to meet her eye.

Carolynn felt as if they were frozen in time. She was sitting in his lap on the water's edge, curled into his body, warm and solid and firm beneath her, and she had never felt so safe. She traced her finger along his jaw, to his chin, and down his throat, where she rested her hand on his chest above his racing heart before she slid her hand back up and around his neck until the wisps of hair brushed along her fingers. It was smoother and softer than she had imagined, even if it was sopping wet.

The heat radiating from his body kept the chill off her skin. Even in the dead of summer, with the near-death experience and taking in half of the springs freezing water, her body temperature was dangerously low. His arm was wrapped around her waist, hand resting comfortably on her hip as his thumb drew small circles into her flesh. Did he know he was doing that?

An embarrassing rumbling emanated from her stomach, snapping them both out of whatever moment they were having. Carolynn pulled her hand away, glancing down at her belly, flushing red.

Donnie for the briefest moment cracked a smile, a rough laugh escaping him. "I did promise you food."

Carolynn offered him a small smile, mouth parched and throat still burning. She made to get up out of his lap, determined to stand on her own two feet, but her limbs felt heavy and useless.

"Let me help," Donnie offered, cradling her to his chest and standing up with her in his arms as though she weighed nothing more than a sack of feathers.

He carried her away from the water back to their clothes and placed her feet gently on the ground, keeping his arms around her until they were both sure she wouldn't topple over. He stepped away to grab their clothes, taking all the heat with him. Her mouth instantly began chattering, teeth clacking together.

Donnie's thick brows furrowed together, eyes narrowed as her body began to tremble. "You're freezing," he said, as though not fully understanding the word.

"I think my body is in a bit of shock," Carolynn guessed. It probably wasn't far from the truth. The truth was, he had taken the sun with him when his touch left her, but she certainly wasn't going to say that out loud.

Donnie unfolded his shirt in his arms and held it over her. "Arms in," he instructed, and for once she didn't protest, desperate for heat, any heat.

She put her arms through the holes before he shimmied it down her body. It was loose around her neck and the bottom of the shirt reached her mid-thigh. It looked like she was wearing a dress, not a shirt. But even with the Henley, she still shook beneath the thin cotton. He pulled his leather jacket off the branch and wrapped it around her shoulders. With the cover of the thick leather and heavy weight, her tremors almost immediately disappeared. She was able to breathe through her mouth again as she inhaled slowly, taking controlled breaths. She pushed her arms through the jacket holes. She wasn't sure if it was the jacket or a lingering effect from the man before her, but the jacket cocooned her in a warmth of its own.

"Let's get you back to the car," Donnie said, leaning in as though to pick her up again.

"I think I can make it there," Carolynn said, not wanting to feel like an invalid.

"I wouldn't want you falling on a branch and hurting yourself," Donnie raised a brow.

For once, she wasn't sure if he was teasing her or not, but she had to admit, he wasn't wrong. Even though she was somewhat standing on her own, barely even swaying, moving was an entirely different beast.

Donnie pushed his feet into his boots before gathering her items left on the ground and handing them to her. She took them in her arms just before he slid an arm beneath her knees and swept her up. She swallowed hard as he walked into the small stretch of woods from the spring to the car. She was oddly surprised by how effortlessly he moved, cradling her against him. She felt stiff in his arms, even though all she wanted to do was lay her head on his chest. Even through the jacket and shirt over her wet clothes, his bare skin was like the surface of the sun, radiating warmth.

A loud screech ran through the trees. Carolynn glanced up and recognized the tan wings and heart-shaped face of an owl circling overhead. Spot swooped low enough to graze the tops of the trees, but she averted his gaze. For some reason she could feel strong emotions coming from him, none of them warm or pleasant.

She would have to table that conversation for later.

They made it out of the woods and back to the car, heading straight for the trunk. Once again, he gently set her down on her feet, making sure she was able to stand on her own before releasing her. She tried not to take his care of her too seriously, too personally, even if her stomach was fluttering, and not just from hunger pains.

He bent forward, digging in the trunk looking for something, and she watched as his muscles rippled beneath his creamy white skin. He turned slightly away from her, reaching for something farther in the trunk, when she noticed two long ridges down his shoulder blades. Had he been injured there?

Donnie stood up with a fresh shirt in hand, a playful smirk tugging at his lips. "For a rainy day."

His jeans looked like they were already drying in the oppressive Florida heat as he pulled the shirt over his head, once again covering his perfectly sculpted body. She almost sighed audibly. Almost.

She was standing there in nothing but her underwear, shirt, and jacket. She should at least try to be decent and put back on her breeches, but the idea of trying to wiggle those dirt-stained pants up her body did not entice her. She felt stable enough to walk towards the passenger door, leaning a bit more than she'd like against the steel frame. A firm hand pressed into her lower back. She glanced up into his worry-filled eyes as he opened the door for her. She hated the way her heart stuttered under his gaze, the way her skin heated and blushed, or how her stomach was doing summersaults over the most basic of gestures, but it was, all at once.

Carolynn ducked into the car, molding herself into the seat, and relaxing her head back against the headrest when the car door shut. It didn't take long for him to get behind the wheel and the car to start, already backing them out the way they came and driving down the road into town.

The purring of the engine was like white noise in the background as her eyes fluttered closed, feeling exhausted. Her hand was suddenly seized by one much larger. Her eyes flashed open, almost unable to comprehend that he was, in fact, holding her hand. She had to see it to believe it.

Sure enough, his hand, nearly double the size of hers, entwined their fingers. His grip on her was firm, the callouses on the pads of his fingers and palm were rough, but she didn't mind it. Tingles raced up her arm, making her chest warm and fuzzy. Now she certainly wasn't going to fall asleep, not while he was touching her.

"Where are we getting that cheeseburger I promised you?" Donnie asked, his lip pulling into a smirk, from what she could see of his profile.

Carolynn couldn't control her own lips from spreading into a smile in response. She directed him to the local drive-thru where she ordered a double cheeseburger with fries, and a soda. Donnie ordered the same.

Sitting in the parking lot, in a car that belonged in some magazine, they ate together in comfortable silence. Carolynn nearly inhaled her food, unaware of how truly hungry she had been. Maybe it was the near-death experience, but she downed that cheeseburger as though it was her last meal.

She told him the general direction of her house, the sun already setting, the light quickly fading. For some reason, she felt oddly nervous about him seeing her house. Would he judge her for living in a dilapidated trailer? Did he care about such things? He obviously came from money, but would he mind if she didn't?

His grip tightened on hers, his thumb brushing against her hand in soothing circles. Could he sense her anxiety?

She instructed him on the last turn, lights brightening her dark, empty home. Her mother's car was nowhere to be seen, but there was a large-looking wolf sitting on her porch, awaiting her arrival.

Donnie put the car in reverse, cutting the engine. She didn't know if it was the food or his presence, but she felt like herself again, fully capable of opening her door and getting out on her own. She stepped out into the darkness. Dead grass crunched beneath her feet as she held her breeches and boots against her chest. He came around the car, automatically resting a hand against her lower back.

Was he doing that because he was afraid she was a fall risk or because he wanted to?

"Thank you for bringing me home, and for the food," Carolynn said. "And for saving me."

"You don't have to thank me," Donnie said, rubbing the back of his neck and ducking his head.

Carolynn approached the steps towards Shadow, whose large head lifted in the air, nose twitching as she sniffed. She didn't even get to lift her foot before the wolf was in front of her, sniffing her up and down, ears pinned back.

What happened? Where are your clothes? Why do you smell like death? the questions raced in her mind all at once, causing her head to spin.

The hand at her back tightened.

"I'm fine," Carolynn said, placing her hand on the wolf's head, rubbing between her ears. "I'm okay."

Shadow backed out of reach, growling at Donnie, lips pulled back and teeth bared. *I will kill him for hurting you.*

Carolynn froze at the hostility and violence that rolled off her wolf. Donnie nearly stepped in front of her, arm out in front of her chest, pushing her back. The light from the car seemed to dim a bit. Maybe she wasn't feeling as well as she thought as she watched the shadows shifting and gathering, slinking across the dead floor.

"Shadow, enough," Carolynn commanded, her voice resonating between the two of them. *I will explain everything later, but that is enough.*

Shadow's mouth closed, lips pulling back over those sharp teeth, but she still didn't take her eyes off Donnie.

I don't trust him, was all she said, before moving around the man and sitting at her heels, fur pressed against her bare leg.

Carolynn gently placed her hand on top of the arm in front of her, barring her, protecting her. He complied, turning back to face her.

"I'm sorry," he apologized.

For what, she didn't know. Her wolf acting out wasn't his fault. She meant to tell him so, when a loud ringing nearly startled her into dropping the load in her arms. It was her phone. She dug through the pockets of her breeches, finally fishing the phone out on its last ring, and flipped it open.

"Hello?" Loud music pounded in the background. She frowned at the phone, noticing Beth's number. "Beth?"

"Carolynn," the voice said softly, "I need you to come get me."

"Where are you?" Carolynn yelled into the phone, hoping Beth could hear her above the music. She held her hand over her other ear, hoping to hear her better.

Donnie was watching, brows furrowed, eyes narrowed.

"I'm at Brian's," Beth said a bit louder. "Can you come get me?"

This time, Carolynn could hear her friend's voice breaking. Her heart hammered in her chest as adrenaline flooded through her. Something was wrong. She glanced up at Donnie, but she didn't even have to ask, he simply nodded his head once, already directing them back to the car.

"I'll be right there," she promised Beth.

"Hurry," she said, panicked, before the line went dead.

Carolynn nearly flung herself in the car, Donnie made to shut the door for her, but a black furball got in the way.

I'm coming, Shadow said, standing between the door and its metal frame.

"Stay," Carolynn said. They really didn't have time for this.

I'm coming, Shadow repeated. Without warning, she somehow managed to climb into her lap and get into the small back row of the car.

Carolynn looked up at Donnie, eyes wide. "I'm sorry; she's being an overprotective ass," she growled, throwing a glare back at the wolf, who seemed to ignore her altogether.

"Don't worry about it," Donnie shrugged, shutting the door.

You better not scratch this car, or I will make you sleep outside for a month, Carolynn threatened the wolf, but in vain, it seemed, as she continued to ignore her.

They peeled out of the driveway. Carolynn gave him directions to Brian's house in a rush. Luckily, he lived not far away, so the drive was quick, and yet it felt like forever. She jammed her feet back into her riding boots, unwilling to walk barefoot into his house. Lord only knows what had touched Brian's floors.

"You said this guy she's seeing," Donnie started, "he's bad?"

"Yes," Carolynn said, fidgeting with his shirt she still wore.

"Do you think he—"

"For his sake, I sure hope not," Carolynn said, trying to ignore the lump in her throat and the burning in the back of her eyes.

Sure, Beth and Brian had had some fights in the past, but never before had Beth called like this, nearly begging to be picked up. Never. Beth would rather walk home in shame than ask for help.

Something was wrong. She just knew it.

Faster than she could have imagined, the car came to a jarring halt in front of a two-story house. The street was jam-packed with cars, the house booming with music so loud she could visibly see the windows rattling in their frames.

Carolynn glanced at Donnie, noticing they were double parked beside an old Honda, but he cut the engine off, clearly not giving a damn. She didn't quite care either. They both exited the car, Carolynn holding her door for Shadow, who also insisted on coming. She was actually comforted by the wolf's presence but also worried for her safety as well. Who knew if some lunatic inside had a gun.

Carolynn was already walking up the path to the front door, pavement cracked with weeds. She could feel Donnie at her back, his presence dark and looming. A sharp thrill went through her to know he was here with her. Shadow kept up with her pace on her heels, sticking to her like glue. She pushed open the door, black paint flaking off in her hands. The first thing to hit her senses was the overwhelming smell of weed, body sweat, and liquor-sweet vomit. The house was packed with people varying in age. The first floor was flooded with bodies dancing.

Carolynn pushed her way inside, most backing away wisely at the sight of Shadow, others shirking from Donnie's sheer size at her back, but none of that mattered. She spotted the stairs down the hall, knowing exactly where she knew she would find her best friend. She moved for the stairs, the people parting for them like the red sea. She took the stairs two at a time, Shadow raced ahead of her, past a lip-locked couple, and stepping over a passed-out drunk.

At the top of the stairs, she saw Shadow running into the first bedroom on the right. Inside, the room was dark with black painted walls and a king-size bed with all black covers and comforter. The only light in the room was a dimly lit lamp on a nightstand beside the bed, Carolynn flipped on the ceiling fan's light, illuminating the room. Donnie stayed in the doorway as Carolynn walked around the bed and found a crumpled Beth, almost in the fetal position, huddled in the corner.

Shadow lay down in front of her, head resting on Beth's shoes, licking her hand.

Carolynn knelt down beside her, placing a hand gently on one of Beth's knees. She reached out to her telepathically, brushed against her mind, reassuring her, letting her know she was safe.

Beth peered out from underneath her arm. Her right eye was swollen into a thin slit, black and blue bruising already visible and dark beneath the skin.

Carolynn sucked in a sharp breath, choking back bile, filled with a different sort of horror and fury. Beth's face was streaked with mascara, her other eye swollen from crying, nose running with snot. Carolynn gently tugged on her, pulling her friend into her arms as Beth released the last bit of tears she had left. She stroked her curly, knotted hair, assuring her everything was going to be okay.

She looked to Donnie, who still stood in the doorway as though barring anyone from entering, and looked into those eyes, now the color of cool darkness.

Carolynn gripped Beth by the arms and hauled the both of them up, standing together. She turned Beth this way and that, examining for any other injuries.

"I'm okay," Beth said, as though trying to reassure her.

Carolynn froze, looking her friend dead in the eye. "You are not okay," she said firmly. "This is not okay."

"I know," Beth whispered, eyes cast down to the carpet.

"We should call the cops."

"No!" Beth shouted, before remembering where she was and lowered her voice. "I just want to go home. Better yet, can we go to your house?"

"Beth, he should be put in jail for this," Carolynn tried to reason with her, but Beth just shook her head, curls falling down her face.

"I don't want to deal with all of that," Beth pleaded. "Please, just get me out of here. I swear, he and I are done."

Carolynn's heart shattered as more tears flowed down her friend's swollen face. She turned around, looking for backup, but found the doorway empty. She could hear shouts from downstairs, as the music cut off abruptly and bottles were knocked over as glass shattered. She gripped Beth by the arm, pulling her out of that room and back down the stairs. Shadow followed at the rear.

They found Donnie at the base of the stairs, pinning Brian against the wall, his feet dangling nearly a foot off the ground as his fist gripped into the front of his leather jacket. Donnie's face was a mask of fury and vengeance, beautiful and deadly. He wanted to hurt Brian, she could see it in the darkness of his eyes, muscles rippling with the itch to break every single one of his bones.

Brian just hung there, feet kicking against the wall. His eyes were bloodshot due to the fact that he was piss drunk and high. His face was a mixture of anger and fear.

"Do you feel like a man when you hit a woman?" Donnie snarled in his face, voice deep, promising violence.

"Donnie," Carolynn called to him. The last thing she wanted was to get him involved—worst case in trouble with the law if Brian decided to press charges.

Donnie's grip seemed to loosen at the sound of her voice. He tossed Brian aside as if he weighed no more than a rag doll, landing with a thump on the wooden floor. Before Brian could even move to get up, Shadow was suddenly there, paw on his chest, forcing him back to the floor. She growled in his face, teeth bared, saliva dripping on his shirt. She snapped her jaw once. Brian squealed in fright, which seemed to be enough for the wolf. Shadow backed off, moving back to stand at the girl's side.

I think he pissed himself, Shadow noted, sniffing the air.

Donnie swept Beth into his arms, cradling her against his chest, similar to how he had held Carolynn not even a few hours ago, and made to walk for the door, expecting for Carolynn to follow, but she still stared at Brian.

He had hurt her friend. The one person who meant the world to her, who had always had her back through thick and thin. Someone who was caring and honest, and good, and he hurt her.

Carolynn knelt beside the pathetic trash on the floor and looked deep into his cold black eyes. He flinched back under her unsettling stare.

"I'm only going to say this once, Brian, so listen up. If you ever come near Beth again, even pick up the phone to call her, I'll know," Carolynn vowed. "If you so much as think about her, I will personally find you and beat you with your own tire iron I know you keep in the back of your truck." Her voice echoed in the room so silent the flickering of a candle could be heard. The stench of fear was eminent.

Carolynn stood back up slowly, keeping eye contact the entire time, until she turned her back on him to find Donnie still holding Beth with Shadow patiently waiting, all three staring at her, each with their own separate emotions she couldn't pick apart to tell which belonged to whom. She could hear Brian clumsily pulling himself upright as she took a step toward her friend, when she heard him speak.

"The stupid bitch deserved it."

Donnie's face went white as a sheet, eyes wide and almost instantly black. Beth curled into herself, burying further against Donnie as though the words had physically struck her.

Carolynn spun around on her heels before Donnie had the chance to drop Beth where he stood, and closed the remaining distance between them in one stride.

Rage and adrenaline pumped through her, fueling every muscle in her body. Just as she had practiced a thousand times, her right hand closed tightly into a fist, and she swung her arm with the full weight of her body. Her fist collided with his face. Cartilage snapped and the sound of bone breaking echoed off the stained walls. Brian dropped to the ground, clutching his nose, blood streaming down his face as he cried.

Carolynn stepped on the side of his left leg, applying near-breaking pressure to the tibia. She could feel the bone straining beneath her weight, and a small smile crept on her face. "Next time, it'll be worse."

She straightened out her jacket, releasing her foot from his leg, and turned back to Donnie, Beth, and Shadow.

Beth's one good eye was wide open in shock and awe. Donnie wore the devilish smirk with a stupid dimple, and all she could feel from Shadow was pride.

"Now we can go."

Chapter 14

Carolynn drove the Mustang back to her house, Donnie's lights reflecting in her rearview mirror. He was following them home. Even when she tried to tell him she could get them home on her own, he still insisted on following them back. Shadow was in the back seat, head resting on the center console, where Beth was rubbing between her ears.

Beth had been quiet most of the way, staring solemnly out the window as the street lights passed by in a blur.

"I can't believe you punched him."

Carolynn glanced at her friend out of the corner of her eye. Her knuckles were still stinging, but she flexed her hand around the wheel, ignoring the pain.

"He deserved worse," Carolynn nearly growled, anger still hot in her blood.

Carolynn pulled the Mustang in front of her still-dark house, her mother nowhere to be seen. Donnie pulled in behind her, cutting the engine at the same time she did. She opened the driver's door, letting Shadow out behind her as Donnie came directly for her. He took her hand in his, inspecting the fist that had just broken someone's nose, twisting and turning it. The skin had split on initial contact, blood was still smeared on her skin. The wounds were already healed but the flesh beneath was still tender.

"Are you okay? Most people break their hand after a punch like that," Donnie asked, her hand still in his grasp.

Carolynn looked up to meet his gaze, eyes back to the color of frozen arctic ice. "I'm not like most people."

She had never spoken truer words.

Beth came around the side, arms wrapped around herself. "Thank you for coming for me," Beth said, words soft and choked with emotion. "Both of you."

Donnie nodded, no, not nodded, bowed his head, as though somehow honored. Carolynn offered her friend a smile, rubbing her arm.

Beth looked at Carolynn, really looked at her, as though seeing her for the first time, and her eyes widened as she took in her clothes, lack of pants, and riding boots. "What the hell have you two been up to tonight, and where are your clothes?"

Carolynn glanced down at herself, entirely forgetting that she was, in fact, wearing only underwear and a tank top beneath Donnie's oversized shirt and jacket. She pulled down on the ends of the Henley, knowing full well she was covered, but feeling exposed beneath her friend's gaze.

"Well, we were swimming, and then I got wet..." Carolynn rambled.

"Getting wets the best part," Beth said, brow raised suggestively.

Carolynn's face flushed hot, biting on her lower lip to keep from saying anything else.

The last thing she was going to do was tell her friend she'd nearly drowned. Not after everything she'd just been through.

"Okay, then, let's get you inside and cleaned up, shall we?" Carolynn lightly pushed Beth towards the door, where Shadow already waited.

"Wait." Donnie held his hand out, stopping the two of them from advancing. He dug into his pocket and pulled out a small metal tin, offering it to Beth. "It's a salve. Use it on your bruises, you'll feel much better."

Beth took the tin from him, eyebrow raised. "You just so happen to have this in your pocket?" she asked.

Carolynn wanted to scold her. She should be grateful, but Donnie responded before she had the chance.

"I hurt my hand yesterday and have been using it myself," he answered her with zero hesitation.

Beth leaned in as though to whisper a secret and said, "Did you punch someone too?"

All Donnie did was smirk, giving her a small wink that left Beth chuckling, holding the tin to her chest. "Thank you, again. I'll just be inside."

Carolynn watched as Beth walked up the steps and helped herself to the spare key under the matt. Not very original, but no one ever bothered with their end of the trailer park. She forced the door open with her shoulder. Shadow glanced back at her, as though she wanted to stay and supervise.

Go inside with Beth, please. I'll be just a moment, Carolynn told her wolf.

You have two minutes, and then I'm coming out here and biting him, Shadow promised, slipping inside after Beth before the door closed.

Carolynn turned back to Donnie and just as she did, his hand came up, fingers brushing back the hair from her face and tucking it behind her ear. Sparks set off across her skin, lighting her up inside.

"You should use that salve on your hand. It'll help with the soreness," Donnie said, his voice low and intimate, breath fanning her face.

Carolynn inhaled sharply, almost afraid to breathe, as his hand curled around the back of her neck. His other hand came up to rest on her arm. She tried to reach out with her mind for the first time since they met and brushed against his consciousness. While she couldn't breach the wall, she could feel some kind of emotion from him—desire, need, and regret. He wanted to touch her, no, needed to be touching her, like two magnets unable to be separated.

That was how this felt.

"Thank you," Carolynn said, voice thick and heavy with the day's events. "Thank you for saving me. For helping with Beth—"

"Beth was all you," Donnie interrupted. "I just followed your lead."

"Either way, thank you for being there with me," Carolynn repeated. "For having my back."

"Always," Donnie promised, thumb brushing along the bottom lip he had been staring at.

Kiss him!

Carolynn's eyes widened, head snapping towards her bedroom

window, where she could plainly see both Beth and Shadow. Their faces might as well be plastered to the glass. Her face turned hot as she chuckled, trying to brush off the embarrassment.

Donnie's hands dropped from her reluctantly, hesitating as though he didn't want to let go, but he did anyway. Carolynn started to shrug out of his jacket but he stopped her, grabbing the leather lapels and pulling them back up around her neck.

"Keep it. It looks better on you," Donnie said, flashing her that smile with the dimple that left her knees weak.

Carolynn couldn't help the smile that spread across her face as she pulled the leather jacket tighter around her. It smelled just like him and still contained his warmth.

"I'll see you tomorrow," Donnie added before backing away.

Their eyes remained locked as he made it back to his car. She gnawed on her lower lip as she continued to smile like some giddy schoolgirl, but she couldn't help it.

Only when his car pulled out of the driveway and the lights faded off in the distance did she finally go inside to find a disappointed Beth and an annoyed Shadow waiting for her in her bedroom.

"Why didn't you kiss him?" Beth shrieked, hands thrown up in the air as though the fact that her and Donnie hadn't kissed was their biggest problem of the night.

"Maybe because I could hear you practically shouting in my head. You damn creep; this isn't a soap opera." Carolynn pulled off the leather jacket, hanging it on the hook on the back of her door. She glanced down at herself and noticed she was still wearing his shirt and her boots.

"Sure looked like one." Beth smiled, wincing as it tugged at her swollen eye. "What happened to you today? Where are your clothes?"

"Shit, I left my pants in his car," Carolynn remembered, annoyed with herself.

It wasn't like she didn't have a dozen more, but they were her favorite. Maybe she could get them back tomorrow. If he really did come around tomorrow.

"Carolynn, you're avoiding," Beth noticed, staring at her pointedly with her one good eye.

"*I'm* avoiding?" Carolynn scoffed. "Do you want to tell me what caused that?" she asked, pointing at her bruised face.

"Brian's an asshole," Beth stated, as though that explained everything. "I said something he didn't like, he was drunk and high, so he punched me."

Carolynn's hand balled into fists at her side. She was about three seconds away from getting back in Beth's Mustang and running that slime ball down with the car. He deserved worse than a broken nose.

I should have bitten him, Shadow said.

"Did you see him piss himself, though?" Beth started to laugh. A deep belly laugh that brought on cramps. "Oh my god, that was priceless."

Carolynn laughed slightly, but she kept a wary eye on her friend.

"Or how about you storming through that house in nothing but boots and a shirt. You looked like a firecracker on speed, all small and fiery like some warrior goddess there to defend my honor," Beth continued to laugh. "You broke his fucking nose. It was amazing."

Carolynn grinned, pressing her lips into a thin line. Waiting.

"Donnie was so nice to bring you to me. I wasn't sure how you were going to get there, but I knew you wouldn't leave me," Beth said, starting to come down from the adrenaline. "I mean, he fucking hit me. He—he actually hit me."

Carolynn stepped closer, arms out.

"How could he? I've done nothing but take his shit, and put up with his drinking, and for what?" Beth asked, pointing to her bruised eye. "For this?"

"I know," Carolynn spoke to her softly, moving in.

"I gave him everything," Beth cried, tears now streaming down her face.

"I know," Carolynn repeated, closing the last bit of distance between them and wrapping her arms around her best friend. Together they crumpled on the bed, as Carolynn held her.

They lay like that for a while. Beth switching between fits of crying, yelling about what an ass he was, and back to crying. Her friend was grieving. Grieving over the relationship she thought they had, what she dreamed they could be, and then the reality of it all. Carolynn helped her apply the salve Donnie had given her, trying her best to be gentle as Beth winced beneath nearly every touch. Her face was even more swollen with the added crying, nearly the entire right side of her face was puffy. But Beth finally fell asleep, curled in a ball in the middle of her bed.

Carolynn sat up from the mattress, stretching out the kinks in her back as she padded to the bathroom, Shadow following closely behind. She could sense the wolf still had every intention of finishing their earlier conversation. It was the last thing Carolynn wanted to do.

She pulled the door closed, leaving it cracked open, before flipping on the shower, steam almost instantly filling the room.

Are you going to finally tell me what happened? Shadow asked, tail bristling on the floor.

"What's there to tell? We went swimming," Carolynn said, looking at herself in the mirror. Her hair was an absolute catastrophe. It was definitely going to take more conditioner than normal to get all of the tangles out.

Do not lie to me, pup. What happened while you were swimming? Shadow growled in her mind.

Carolynn flashed her a look. She was exhausted, mentally and physically drained. Why was the wolf attacking her? "I stayed under the water too long and took some water in. It's not a big deal. I'm fine."

She didn't know why she didn't explain the whole truth. Couldn't explain why she was holding back on Shadow, her companion and confidant, the thorn in her side she had grown so used to over the years. The animal she could never imagine her life without. But she was.

I don't believe you, Shadow finally admitted, almost shaking her massive head in disappointment,

"I'm sorry, Shadow," Carolynn said, not sure exactly which part she was apologizing for. "I'm really tired. It's been a long day. Can we talk more tomorrow?"

Shadow didn't say another word and slipped out of the bathroom, leaving her in silence.

Carolynn felt like shit. Felt guilty for hiding what really happened and felt like a crap best friend for allowing Beth to go to that party without her. Even with her powers, she couldn't have stopped what happened tonight. What happened in her spring, her oasis, the one place she had always felt safe. She had nearly drowned in its waters. If not for Donnie, she would have.

The ghost of his touch still lingered on her skin, her neck, her hair, and arm. As though he was still with her, brushing his thumb along her lip, securing the jacket around her body, holding her against him as he carried her to his car. All of it.

Flustered, she pulled off his shirt, laying it gently on the counter and peeled off the sticky, muddy boots, and stepped into her steaming hot shower. It felt like heaven against her skin, working out the kinks and knots.

She cut the shower shorter than she would have liked, but exhaustion began to take its toll, as washing her hair became almost painful, keeping her arms up. She got out, quickly dried off, and changed into an oversized t-shirt. She crawled into bed beside Beth, pulling the comforter over the both of them, and glanced down at Shadow.

She didn't like that they were in such a weird place. It left a knot in her stomach.

Shadow, she called to her. he wolf lifted her head in answer. *Can you come lay with me?*

Shadow cocked her head at her human, but got up off the floor, stepped up onto the bed, and curled in on her side, back pressed into her belly. Carolynn dug her hand into the wolf's warm fur, feeling her heart beat against her ribs, closed her eyes, and fell asleep.

Thunder rolled across the land as lightning struck granite rock. Metal clanged in the distance as swords sparked off of one another. There was a steady beat, pounding through the air, like hundreds, if not thousands, of birds taking flight all at once.

Carolynn stood in a field, the ground dead beneath her feet. Glancing down, she spotted two bodies. The one with curly brown hair she recognized immediately. She knelt down in the dirt, tears streaming down her soot-streaked face. She brushed the hair back from Beth's face, her eyes closed as though she was simply sleeping, but her chest didn't rise, and her lips were blue with death. She had a shallow cut across one of her cheeks, and blood pooled at the corner of her mouth.

She screamed for help, for someone, anyone, to come, but no one answered. A figure moved off in the distance towards her. A sword in his hand dragging through the earth. His mouth opened and crows flew out, feathers dropping to the ground as black as night.

Chapter 15

A rough, wet tongue grazed her cheek, jolting her awake. Carolynn swatted at Shadow, bouncing her hand off the wolf's warm nose. "I already took a shower," she grumbled, still half asleep.

You had a dream again, Shadow said, not caring that she was still exhausted.

"I know," Carolynn sighed, forcing her eyes open and staring blurringly at the ceiling. The sun was just barely rising, as her room was cast in pastel pinks from her curtains.

"Why are we awake?" Beth groaned, rolling over and throwing a pillow over her head.

"Because Shadow likes to torture us," Carolynn said sarcastically, eyeing the wolf.

Shadow huffed loudly through her nose. *I could start howling.*

"Oh, no, please don't," Carolynn pleaded, repeating aloud what the wolf had said to Beth.

Beth bolted upright, glaring harshly at the wolf. "I will skin you for a rug," she threatened, clearly remembering the last time Shadow had howled, causing the entire pack in the neighboring woods to join in. It lasted for over twenty minutes and resulted in the police being called.

It was a nightmare.

Shadow stepped off the bed, stretching as she went, shaking out her fur. *You humans are violent.*

Carolyn frowned, unable to fight that logic.

Beth leaned over her, grabbed her phone on the nightstand, and checked the time, immediately swearing enough to make a sailor blush.

"What's wrong?" Carolynn asked, finally sitting up in bed. She had an annoying crick in her neck that she began trying to stretch out to no avail.

"I've already got missed calls from both of my parents." Beth jumped out of bed, pushing her feet back into her heels from the night prior. "I don't even know why they panic. It's not like they don't know I spend most nights here."

"Except for when you're not here," Carolynn pointed out. There were plenty of times Beth had told her parents she was spending the night, when in fact she was at Brian's. She had been caught and grounded on two separate occasions.

"Not anymore. That boy is dead to me. His number is deleted and blocked from my phone." Beth smiled proudly. That is, until she frowned.

"What's wrong?" Carolynn asked, standing up.

Beth's hands went to her face. Her perfectly normal face. No more bruising, no more swollen eye. It was as though it had never happened.

"My face, it doesn't hurt." Beth smiled, running into the bathroom, squealing at the sight of her no longer bruised eye. "Holy shit, what was in that salve? It's a freaking miracle worker. Now I don't even have to try to lie to my parents."

Carolynn rolled her eyes, as though that would ever stop her.

"I have to get going," Beth said, already halfway out the door, "I'll see you at the stable."

"Of course you will," Carolynn half waved at her back, the front door already slamming shut.

Carolynn half stumbled towards the bathroom and her closet, where she got changed into a fresh set of clothes for the day. Plaiting her hair into a clean braid down the center of her back, she heard the door slam open. She stuck her head out of her bathroom, eyeing her wolf on the floor, who seemed equally puzzled, staring at the bedroom door.

Had Beth forgotten something? Maybe it was her mother

finally arriving home.

"Carolynn!" Susana yelled from the living room.

Carolynn rolled her eyes, sighing loudly. What was it now? Did she have another flat tire? Was there no more coffee? She threw open her door to find her mother standing in the frame of the front door, still wide open and letting in the humidity. She made to scold her—A/C was expensive enough—that is, until she noticed her wide eyes, filled with fear, pointing at something on the floor.

Shadow growled beside her, teeth bared, inching in front of her body, protecting her front.

Carolynn froze as she took in the black snake stretched out on the carpet floor of their living room, head raised off the ground. It was staring at her mother; until Shadow started growling. The snake whipped its head in her direction and stared right at her. Its scaly black skin glistened in the sunlight streaming through the open door, its coal black eyes watching her.

"Carolynn, get back," Susana called to her, trying to move around the snake, when it twisted on her, hissing, tongue snaking out. Susana stopped, rooted where she was.

The snake turned back to Carolynn, rising about a foot off the ground, coiling around itself, as though readying to spring forward.

Carolynn stared at the snake. She could speak to horses, wolves, dogs, and cats. While she had never tried communicating with snakes, loathing their very existence, she refused to back down. She looked into the snake's solid black eyes and peered deep into its mind. Blackness swept over her, coating her in a thick, oily feeling that left her weighed down and exhausted. She almost stumbled back, losing her footing, but she shook her head, trying to clear the cobwebs.

The snake was made of pure darkness. The darkest parts of humanity—greed, hate, jealousy, and fear.

He wasn't a garden snake.

Why are you here? Carolynn projected to him, pressing her will to his, forcing herself into his mind.

The snake hissed, baring extremely long, curved fangs. Shadow growled even louder in challenge, snapping her jaws in front of him, but the snake paid her no mind, not even registering her as a potential threat or even her existence. It was just Carolynn and the snake.

The snake reared up, nearly reaching her eye level. She had severely underestimated its length, as its tongue slithered out of its mouth, tasting the air in front of her. She could hear her mother whimper where she stood, but she didn't move, barely breathed.

Carolynn wouldn't let the snake hurt her mom or Shadow, or herself. A calm settled over her as she inhaled slowly and deeply. It didn't matter what she was, or where she came from, she would not back down. Her arms and legs tingled, her head feeling light and dizzy. The sun seemed to have fully risen, as light filled the room. The snake shrank back, hissing as though the light was painful.

Leave, she commanded, forcing her will on the creature.

The snake recoiled as if it had been struck down by an invisible force. It twisted in on itself into a tighter ball, withering and hissing in pain. It turned, slithering out the door, past her mother, and out of sight. Susana finally moved, slamming the door shut. The blinding light ceased as the door closed, and Carolynn sagged back into the wall behind her, her breathing labored as though she had just come in from running.

"Are you okay?" Carolynn asked her mother. For some reason the sound of her own voice shocked her, sounding steady and calm, the complete opposite to how she was feeling.

"I'm okay," Susana moved in closer, pulling her into a stiff hug. "How did you do that?"

Carolynn pulled back, frowning. "Do what? You've seen me talk to animals before."

Did it hurt you? Did it touch you? Shadow asked, sniffing her legs, arms, and chest.

Carolynn rubbed the wolf's head, scratching behind the ears. "It didn't touch me."

"You weren't just talking to it, Star," Susana said with a shake of her head. "You were glowing."

"I was what?" Carolynn asked, positive she hadn't heard her right.

"Your hair, your skin, it was coming out of your hands. You were this brilliant white light," Susana explained with her hands, but Carolynn just shook her head.

There was no way.

It's true, pup. I've never seen anything like it, Shadow confirmed.

"But that's not one of my powers," Carolynn said lamely, still not able to process any of what was happening.

"Maybe it is now," Susana offered, speaking aloud what they all seemed to be thinking. "Has anything else happened lately? Any other new powers pop up?"

As though she was simply shopping for milk.

"No," Carolynn lied through her teeth. No way was she telling her mother.

Why are you lying? What has happened that you haven't told me? Shadow asked, nudging her hand with her warm nose.

I may have burned a table with my hands, Carolynn silently confessed and almost instantly blocked out the wolf's immediate scolding.

"How do you think it got in?" Susana asked, still staring at the spot where the snake had been only minutes before.

"Beth left not long ago, she must have left the door cracked open," Carolynn surmised with a shrug.

"The door was locked when I got home."

"Well, this house *is* kind of falling apart, maybe there's a hole somewhere we don't know about," Carolynn offered, mostly trying to comfort herself.

She really hated snakes.

Susana seemed to finally take notice of her state of dress, riding boots already zipped and hair braided. "Oh, honey, do you need a ride to work? I was going to catch some sleep, but I can drive you first."

Carolynn waved her off. "No, it's okay. I was going to walk. I could use the fresh air. You get some sleep."

"Are you sure?" Susana asked again, but Carolynn could hear it in her voice, she was doing her motherly duty by asking, but really was dead on her feet.

"Positive. I'll see you later," Carolynn smiled, running back into her room and grabbing her phone and keys before leaving the house.

Carolynn scanned the yard for a scaly black nope rope but found nothing out of the ordinary. Shadow was by her side as they took off down the road, away from the trailer. She could feel the wolf pressing against her mind, wanting to talk, but Carolynn kept her mind shut. She wasn't ready for a lecture.

They hadn't even made it to the end of the road before Carolynn was attacked by a rush of feathers, wings slapping her in the face. She held her hands up protecting herself, yelling at him to stop.

Spot landed on the rail of the nearby fence, his feathers prickly and puffed out with fury.

What were you thinking taking that boy to the spring? Swimming with him half-naked? I watched you nearly drown! Spot shouted in her mind.

Drown? Shadow's voice rose sharply. Finally, the missing piece clicked in place for her, and the wolf was angry. Angry and disappointed.

Carolynn's cheeks stung where Spot had slapped her with his wings and now burned with shame.

"I didn't drown, exactly," Carolynn tried to defend herself but was failing miserably. "Look, I'm fine. I'm okay."

How could you be so reckless? You don't even know that man. What if he hadn't pulled you out? Spot asked, black eyes glaring at her.

"Then I guess I'd be dead," Carolynn shrugged. As though Donnie would really just leave her beneath the water to die.

Carolynn! Shadow scolded.

"What?" Carolynn asked. "It's a stupid question. Same as the comment about swimming half-naked. What do you think a two-piece is? Bra and underwear, almost the same thing, except I distinctly remember keeping my shirt on, you peeping tom!"

Her voice was rising along with her own anger. Who did he think he was?

All I want is to keep you safe, Spot said, tone finally lowering. *What if something had happened to you?*

There was a snake in the house today, Shadow informed him. *It almost bit her, but she blasted it away with white light.*

Carolynn glared sharp, pointy daggers at the wolf. Now was not the time for sharing.

You did what? The owl's head swiveled unnervingly towards her. *Anything else I should know about?*

She burned a table with her hands, Shadow added.

"Shadow," Carolynn hissed, instantly feeling the sting of

betrayal.

How am I just hearing about this? What else haven't you told us? Spot accused.

Carolynn was losing her patience and her sanity. "It's not like you've been around all that much lately, so excuse me for not sending a letter to wherever the hell it is you sleep at night. And last I checked, what I do is none of your business. *Either* of your businesses. What do you care about me or my powers or who I chose to spend time with, naked or not? You are not my father!"

Carolynn froze, instantly regretting the words as they left her mouth.

"Spot," she started.

You're right, Spot said and took off, wings flapping hard as he caught the current and soared high over their heads, disappearing into the sun's rays.

There was nothing but silence in her head as emotions warred within her. She was a terrible friend for the things she said, but there was also untold pent-up anger and aggression flooding through her veins. She wanted to yell, wanted to scream, wanted to break something. Energy coursed down her arms, as a concussion erupted from her hands, the air rippling in front of her as a blast of energy left her body and slammed into the fence where Spot had perched only seconds ago. Wood splintered in the air, exploding in every direction.

Carolynn and Shadow both ducked, turning their backs, sheltering their bodies from the debris. Once the ringing in her ears began to lessen and she no longer felt shards of wood pelt her body, she slowly stood, turning back around to find the once pretty picket fence now blasted to pieces in six feet in diameter.

Her mouth gaped open as she stared down at her hands. The pent-up energy she had felt was now gone, clearly expelled somehow, but how? She quickly tucked her hands in her pockets. The third power in as many days. That couldn't be good.

Carolynn glanced guiltily at Shadow, pieces of fence, or rather mulch, riddled throughout her coat. She knelt down beside her wolf and brushed the bits of wood from her fur.

"I'm sorry. I'm so sorry," she said, her voice silently breaking as a solitary tear slipped free.

What was going on? What was wrong with her?

It's okay. Let's just go for a little walk and clear our heads. I'm sorry too for saying something to Spot. I was out of line, the wolf apologized, surprising Carolynn.

Carolynn wrapped her arms around Shadow's neck, burying her face in her fur and breathing in her musky, wild smell. Shadow pulled back, licking the salt from her face before she stood up. She wiped at her cheek, rubbing the slobber off on her pants.

"Gross."

Chapter 16

Their walk took them clear across town. The farther they walked, the less people they saw on the streets. She was actively avoiding the touristy scenes and shops at all costs, not even in the mood to visit the bookstore. She had somehow wandered into the ritzy part of town. The part of town she could never dream of feeling a part of, with her run-down trailer being far from the perfect scene of the suburbs.

The community of cookie-cutter, two-story homes came in various shapes and sizes. The homes were adorned with perfectly green, neatly trimmed lawns and tailored flower bushes of all breeds and colors.

She stopped at a pale-yellow two-story home, with shutters a vintage blue. It was quite a bit larger than the surrounding homes, a pure show of wealth and privilege. The front porch was decorated with peace hybrid tea roses. Their sweet and fruity smell flooded her senses as the wind blew in her face. Shadow sneezed twice at her side, back to back. She inhaled deeply, savoring the beautiful smell.

The front door swung open, and Neila walked out of the house, picking the morning paper off the porch.

Carolynn froze at the sight of the bookstore owner. Their gazes met, and Neila's emerald green eyes grew wide as saucers. She stepped down the front porch steps, her face lighting up as a smile graced her face.

"Carolynn, what a surprise. What are you doing here?"

"You live here?" Carolynn asked in shock. She wasn't quite sure what she had expected Neila's house to look like, but it certainly wasn't this. Although, it's not like she ever really thought about it at all, and why would she?

"I do." Neila nodded. "How did you find me?"

Neila bent down and petted Shadow on the head. Carolynn didn't feel the need to warn her off as Shadow gave her a lick in greeting, something she never did with anyone other than her. Even Beth had a fifty-fifty shot of getting nipped, and Beth had been around Shadow since she was a pup.

"I didn't mean to," Carolynn said, sounding distracted. "We were just out for a walk when I noticed your rose bushes. They're beautiful."

"Thank you," Neila stood, straightening out her knee-length, short-sleeved dress, showing off her figure perfectly. She had black ballet flats on, which seemed like an odd pairing with such an elegant dress, but all in all, she was the definition of a wealthy businesswoman, which left Carolynn feeling odd and out of place in her riding clothes. "Would you like to come in? I just pulled some wild berry muffins out of the oven."

Carolynn's stomach growled loudly at the sound of food. Breakfast hadn't been a priority given the way her day started, and all of the walking had left her starving. She knew Neila heard it by the way she was trying hard not to outright laugh, with one hand covering her mouth.

"Yes, I would like that, thank you," Carolynn followed after Neila, entering the house with Shadow still at her side. "I'm sorry; is it okay if she comes in?"

"Of course," Neila answered, as though that wasn't a silly question.

Neila shut the door behind them, quietly and effortlessly, which was pleasant compared to her own home's front door. The house was styled in a classy and elegant fashion. The front door opened straight into a grand foyer with a white marble staircase leading up to the second floor. A crystal chandelier hung from the ceiling, illuminating every corner of the room.

Neila led them into a sitting room to the left. It was ordinary compared to the grand entrance they had come through. The room held a beige suede reclining couch and loveseat. Hanging on the wall was a sixty-inch flatscreen television, adorned with a surround sound home theater system with five speakers scattered throughout the room.

"Sit, make yourself comfortable. I'll just go grab the muffins," Neila said, gesturing towards the couch.

She watched as Neila left through a door off to the side, which must have connected to the kitchen. The minute the door opened, an overwhelming smell of freshly baked treats engulfed her. Her stomach protested for food loudly as she sat down on the couch, cursing her body to be silent. Shadow sat down beside the couch, nails tapping against the hardwood, leaning against her legs.

"What are we doing here?" Carolyn whispered, half asking herself, half asking the wolf.

Quiet. She's coming, Shadow instructed.

Neila came back with a tray containing a basket of muffins, two tall glasses of milk, napkins, and ornate porcelain dishes. There was also a bowl of raw ground beef she set on the floor before Shadow. Carolynn's eyes widened as Shadow instantly went for the food, not questioning any of it for a second. She set the tray down on a walnut coffee table directly before her and placed two muffins on a plate, each the size of her palm, handing a plate to Carolynn.

Carolynn didn't hesitate, the smell making her mouth water and her stomach grumble painfully. She peeled back the paper liner and bit into the carb-filled goodness, berries instantly exploding on her taste buds. The muffins practically melted in her mouth, still warm, and the fresh berries delightfully sweet. She almost moaned in pleasure, but caught herself, refusing to cause further embarrassment.

"These are amazing," Carolynn complimented her between bites. She took a long drink from one of the glasses, the ice-cold milk helping to wash it down. "Berry muffins are my favorite."

"Really? Mine too," Neila smiled, picking at her muffin. "Did you get a chance to read any of that book I gave you?"

Carolynn set her empty plate down on the tray, dabbing at her mouth with a napkin. She leaned back against the couch, folding her hands in her lap to keep from reaching for another. "I did. I have to say, it's nothing like any mythology I've read before."

"No, it's not."

"It's interesting, though. The way some of the aspects of the different tales and people are similar to the ones we already know, yet they're different, more brutal, and beautiful in a way. Somehow more realistic, if that makes any sense. Or at least as realistic as ancient Gods and Angels can be."

Neila laughed. "Well, I'm glad you liked it."

Carolynn nodded, reaching up to fidget with her necklace. She could feel Neila watching her, her gaze lingering on the stars around her neck.

"Are you okay?" Neila asked, as though she could sense her anxiety.

Was she that transparent?

"I'm fine," Carolynn said, lying miserably.

You are a terrible liar, Shadow confirmed.

Carolynn kept herself from visibly rolling her eyes. She looked around the room, taking in all the little baubles, little rocks carved into various animals. They were adorable.

"Are you from here? Did you grow up here, I mean?" Neila asked, breaking the silence.

"Um, yes," Carolynn said, sounding unsure to her own ears.

"You're not sure?" Neila asked, brow raised.

"I'm adopted, so I honestly don't know where I was born," Carolynn informed her. "But I was raised here, if that's what you meant."

"Adopted," Neila repeated. "That has to be hard."

Carolynn shrugged, pressing her lips together. "It's all I've ever known. My parents are great. We didn't have much, but we got by. My dad died of cancer two years ago, so it's just me and my mom."

"I'm sorry for your loss," Neila said automatically, eyes saddening. "And you said there's no guy in your life? I find that hard to believe of a beautiful woman such as yourself."

Carolynn's eyes slightly widened in surprise. That was the first time someone had ever referred to her as a woman and not a girl. Granted, she was barely legal, but it felt good, like some sort of recognition she didn't know she needed or even wanted.

Her face reddened as a half grin tugged at the corner of her lips. Would she see him again today? No doubt she'd be spending the entire day waiting to see if he'd show up.

"I know that look," Neila teased, eyes brightening. "Who is he?"

"Just a guy I met a few days ago. I really kind of like him," Carolynn admitted to the stranger in front of her. As soon as the words left her mouth, she knew them to be true. She hadn't even thought the words before speaking them and yet, it felt right. "I will say it's been an odd couple of days. Ever since my birthday, it's been a whirlwind."

Neila swallowed audibly as she set her plate down, rubbing her hands along the length of her dress.

She almost looked as though she was going to say something, when a loud bang coming from the kitchen startled them both. The walls shook around them, causing Carolynn to flinch in response and look to Neila, who was already giving her an apologetic look.

"That stubborn, impossible child!" A tall slender man came charging into the sitting room. His face was red with fury, lips pinched into a fine line. His eyes were a dark brown, but they looked to be lightening by the second. His dark hair was sticking out every which way like he got into a fight with a tree. He and Neila both looked to be about the same age, in their mid to late twenties.

Neila quickly stood up from the couch. "Darling, we have a guest."

The man halted hard in his tracks, looking from Carolynn to Neila and back again. Shock swept across his face.

Carolynn frowned, staring at the strange man.

"Carolynn, this is Sam; Sam, Carolynn," Neila said, introducing them.

Sam stood frozen in place. His jaw looked as if it might unhinge itself and drop onto the wooden floor. Carolynn stood up from the couch, Shadow following suit at her side.

"I'm sorry to intrude, but I really should be going. I have to get to work." She started for the foyer, Shadow's nails clacking against the wood floors.

"Carolynn." Neila followed quickly behind her, her face apologetic.

"It's okay. I have to get going anyways. Thank you so much for the muffin, it was delicious."

"At least let me drive you."

Neila smiled sweetly, but the stubborn set of her jaw told her enough. She wasn't going to be able to say no, and given how far she had walked out of town, she wasn't going to make it to Beth's until lunch.

"That would be great, thank you."

"Let me just grab my keys." Neila ducked out of the room before she could get a word out.

Carolynn could hear the jingle of keys and then hushed, angry voices.

"What are you doing?" she heard Sam ask in a low growl.

"Taking her home," Neila snapped back.

"You know that's not what I mean."

Neila came back into the foyer with a silver sequined clutch in one hand and a set of keys in another. "Ready?"

"Yes."

Neila took them through a door just to the right of the front entrance, leading into a three-car garage. Sitting in the middle of the garage was a silver Audi R8 GT. Carolynn's mouth dropped to the floor, eyes blown wide open. She looked from Neila to the car, and back again. She had to have been born into money. No small-town bookstore brought in enough to afford a car like this.

"This is yours?"

"I know, it's a bit much," Neila said, frowning at the car.

Carolynn nearly snorted in agreement but decided against it. Glancing down at Shadow, she raised a brow.

I'll see you at the stable, Shadow said, sprinting out of the garage as the door automatically lifted, disappearing from view.

"She didn't have to go," Neila said, sounding a bit sad.

Carolynn took one look at the interior of the car and nodded once. "Yes, she did."

Neila slid into the driver's seat as Carolynn cautiously set herself into the passenger seat. She was afraid to touch anything for fear that she might break something or scratch the leather. The closest she ever got to an expensive car was Beth's dad's Tundra. Then again, Donnie's classic car was priceless, didn't that count?

Neila started the engine. It made a quiet purring sound, humming in her ears. She drove out of the garage and peeled off down the street, avoiding the main parts of town by taking back roads only.

"Where do you work?" Neila asked, making conversation during their quiet drive.

"Morgan Ranch," Carolynn informed her. "Just on the outskirts of town."

"I've heard of it. Gorgeous property. They breed horses, right? Real pretty ones too," Neila smiled.

"Yes. We breed and train Andalusians and Friesians. They are beautiful creatures." Carolynn nodded.

"You know some cultures believe that horses are the ferriers between worlds."

"Probably something to do with Pegasus," Carolynn surmised. "Sometimes it does feel like I'm flying when I'm on the back of a horse. Or as close as I'll ever get."

Neila chuckled as the ranch came into view. She pulled the Audi up to the front of Beth's house, where Carolynn could see Beth standing on the porch, hands on her hips, mouth gaping open, gawking at the car parked in her driveway. Carolynn couldn't help the smile that tugged at her lips over her friend's obvious jealousy.

"Thank you for driving me. I really do appreciate it," Carolynn said, grasping the handle of the door.

"Anytime," Neila said, offer sincere. "Call me if you need anything."

Carolynn felt puzzled by the last comment as she got out of the Audi. She watched Neila pull out of the driveway and off the property.

"Who the hell was that?" Beth stamped her feet down the porch steps, crossing the distance between them quickly.

"Neila."

"Who the hell is Neila?"

"She's the owner of the new bookstore in town," Carolynn informed her friend as they both walked down towards the stables. Beth's brown curls bounced with each step, streaming behind her in the humid breeze.

"And you're just hanging out with her?" Beth asked. "Who owns a bookstore and drives a two hundred thousand dollar car? You know who? Drug dealers."

Carolynn snorted until she realized Beth was stone cold serious, chin stubbornly set, eyes wide. "She is not a drug dealer." At least she didn't think she was.

"Or an assassin," Beth said dryly.

Jason stepped out of the stable, pushing a wheelbarrow full of manure, flies circling the foul smell. He swatted at the flies as they began to move on him. Carolynn noticed he was wearing ripped Levi jeans and a white t-shirt. He was already soaked with sweat, making the thin material cling to every part of his chest, back, and arms. She couldn't help but notice the lean muscle on his body and instantly blushed, turning away.

"You're here early," Beth said, speaking aloud Carolynn's own thoughts.

"Yeah, I just wanted to get a head start on things."

Carolynn glanced at him still pushing the wheelbarrow. "The manure goes out—"

"—to the back of the stable. I know," he said, finishing her sentence.

"Right," Carolynn nodded in confirmation.

Jason took the manure around the side of the stable, out of view. She glanced at Beth, whom she noticed staring a bit longer than necessary, seeing as how he was already gone. She elbowed her friend playfully in the ribs, which caused Beth to elbow her as well. It wasn't hard enough to yell about but it left a dull, smarting pain. In response, she tapped Beth behind her knees with her boot, forcing Beth's legs to buckle, her kneecaps meeting the dirt, hands splaying out to catch herself.

Carolynn ran for the stable, away from the angry gremlin now covered in dust and dirt. She could hear colorful expletives coming from her friend, and all she could do was laugh until her sides cramped.

"Carolynn! That was not funny!" Beth yelled as she chased after her.

Chapter 17

Carolynn was in the stable office, looking over the next order she had to place for feed. Ledgers and paperwork were scattered across the surface of her desk, notes from various vendors, and the diets of each of the horses. Picky beasts.

Hairs rose on the back of her neck when she felt someone watching her. Glancing up, she found Jason leaning against the office doorway. She put her pen down, meeting his gaze. He wasn't doing anything in particular, wasn't ogling her, but the way he stared unnerved her. Gooseflesh spread across her arms and down her back.

"Can I help you?"

"I was just coming to see if I could do anything for you. Anything to help," Jason offered, arms crossed over his chest.

Carolynn leaned back in her chair, eyebrow raised. "Bored already?"

"Not at all," Jason smirked. "I just figured a little ass-kissing never hurts."

Carolynn snorted. Was this guy for real? She leaned forward with her elbows on the desk and eyed him. "What exactly are your intentions with said ass-kissing?"

"I figured it can't hurt to stay on your good side," Jason said flatly.

Not a lie but not exactly the truth either. Her skin prickled along her hands. He was hiding something; she just didn't know what. Her upbringing held her back from diving into his mind and uncovering what he truly wanted. She resisted the temptation.

"You can go ahead and get Tempest for me. I'd like to take her out for a ride. Gather my tack, I'll saddle her," Carolynn instructed.

A good rider always saddled their own horse. It was just common sense.

"Absolutely," Jason nodded, a slight twinkle in his eye as he turned on his boots and left her office.

Carolynn's phone went off beside her, dinging loudly. Who could possibly be texting her? Beth went back to the house for a nap, still exhausted from the prior night's activities. Unless it was her mother.

Picking up the phone, she flipped it open, and her heart instantly began to race as his name lit up her phone. A smile spread across her face as she opened the message and read it.

What time do you get off?

Carolynn smirked, texting him back that she would be done around three.

He almost immediately wrote her back. *See you soon.*

Carolynn gnawed on her lower lip, trying to keep from jumping up and down, fainting, or doing something else stupid, love-struck girls do. Instead, she stood up from her desk, placed her phone down, and went to saddle her horse. Maybe riding would help cool her blood and level her head. She needed to get a grip.

She left her office and found Tempest standing at the end of the aisle, her tack all laid out for her to ready the horse. Carolynn pulled the bridle over Tempest's head, securing the bit in her mouth and strapping the buckles along the side of her head. Tempest butted her shoulder, nudging her back.

Where is your head at? You seem distracted, Tempest reached out, head-butting her again.

Carolynn rubbed down the front of her face with her hand, pushing the horse's large head away. "It's nothing."

Try saying that without smiling.

Carolynn chuckled, a grin spreading even further. She couldn't stop thinking about him. About how close they had gotten. The feel of his hands, his touch, his body against hers. How he dominated the space around them, and yet she was still able to maintain her own sense of self, and he encouraged it. Most guys would have charged head-first into last night's situation, insisting on playing the hero, but he didn't. He stood back and watched her take charge. And damn did that not turn her on even more.

Tempest's nostrils flared, blowing hotly on her hip. *You smell like a mare in heat.*

Carolynn swatted at the mare's nose, dodging beneath her head and around to the side, throwing the saddle pad up on her back. "Will you stop that, I'm fine."

"Who's fine?"

Carolynn whirled around to find Jason lingering in the tack room. How long had he been standing there? Watching her talk to herself, or rather the horse.

"Me, I'm fine," Carolynn said, then shook her head. "Not fine, like, I think I'm fine, just, I'm feeling fine." Kill her now.

Jason raised a brow, lips pulling into a teasing smile. "Right."

The sound of breaks squealing interrupted their awkward exchange and Carolynn almost sighed in relief.

"Perfect timing. That'll be the hay delivery. Why don't you go ahead and give them a hand with that? You know where it all goes and how we like it stacked. I'm just going to go for a quick ride," Carolynn pointed down towards the end of the hall, where she was sure a large truck was already backing up to the stable entrance.

"Yes, ma'am. Holler if you need anything," Jason said, tipping his head.

She watched him go, cocking her head to the side.

Is that the boy you'd like to mate with?

Carolynn straightened faster than a hairpin. Giving herself whiplash, she twisted on the mare. "What?"

You are inspecting that boy. Is he the one you are wanting to mate with? Tempest repeated herself again.

"Oh my god, no," Carolynn choked out, nearly gagging out loud. She lifted the saddle over her head and began to strap it on with the girth, tightening as much as she could. "Will you stop with this mating crap? That's not how we say it, and I don't want to mate, I mean, be with anyone, least of all Jason."

So there is a man, Tempest neighed, stomping her foot on the ground. *You deserve someone who makes you happy.*

Carolynn gave one final tug on the girth and buckled it in, before pulling down her stirrups. She smiled at her mare, giving her a pat on the neck. "Thank you."

Carolynn and Tempest walked out of the stable before she put one foot in the stirrup and pulled herself onto the horse's back. She steered Tempest around the back of the stable when she saw Shadow's black form walking up to them.

"Where have you been all day, traitor?" Carolynn asked, cocking her head to the side.

Traitor? Tempest asked.

Shadow glared at her human. *It doesn't take five minutes to get here, pup. That woman's house was miles away, and you made me walk.*

Carolynn did feel guilty leaving Shadow like that. She hadn't realized just how far it would be for the wolf to travel. "I'm sorry, Shadow, I hadn't realized."

It's fine, Shadow grumbled, as she walked past them to the water trough near the edge of the pasture, lapping up the water as though she had been trapped in a desert.

Carolynn's guilt grew as she watched her wolf drink greedily. She was being a real ass, and she knew it. She nudged Tempest with her heel, urging her forward into the pasture. She brought the mare to a trot, warming the both of them up. The humidity quickly left a sheen of sweat along her skin, her tank top quickly stuck to her body.

She nudged her heels into the horse's abdomen, bringing Tempest into a canter. Her body immediately fell into rhythm in her saddle as her mare took off, fast and sure-footed. As they reached top speed, Carolynn noticed something was off with her movements, her legs becoming unstable around the horse as the saddle became loose, sliding along Tempest's back.

Carolynn made to call out, to shout, or yell, but Tempest was already taking a turn along the pasture's edge. She felt time slow as she was thrown from the horse. She was light and weightless as the speed they were going flung her through the air fast and hard. She saw the ground beneath her as nothing more than a green blur and curled herself into a tight ball, leaning into the fall.

The impact could have been worse as her body rolled on the rough earth, but some how she managed to pop up and land on her feet, stumbling backwards until she was sure she wouldn't fall back on her ass. She bent forward, inhaling deeply as panic began to set in, adrenaline coursing through her. What the hell had just happened? Her lungs and chest felt tight, like an elephant was sitting on her.

Tempest galloped over, prancing around her in circles. She could hear Shadow yipping, paws pounding into the earth to reach her.

Carolynn, are you alright? Tempest asked, frantic and worried.

Carolynn held her hand up, as though to say she was okay, but was she? How had she managed to land a fall like that? She should have easily broken something. She twisted her arms around, looking at them each way. Other than a few scrapes and cuts along the backs of her arms, she was unharmed.

Shadow finally made it to her from the far end of the field, tongue hanging out and panting, but she jumped up on her hind legs, paws settling on Carolynn's shoulders as her long snout sniffed over her face and in her hair.

What happened? Are you okay? I smell blood, where are you hurt? Shadow landed back on all fours, circling her and inspecting every inch of her body. She stopped at the marks on her arms. They were already trying to heal, but unsuccessfully due to the dirt and debris still in the wounds. *We need to get these cleaned up before you get an infection.*

"I don't get sick," Carolynn reminded her, the adrenaline already wearing off. Her arms were aching badly.

You say that now, Shadow retorted.

Carolynn half walked, half stumbled over to Tempest, who still shifted on her hooves waiting. The saddle hung loosely on the mare's back, shifting and sliding with each of the horse's movements. She lifted the stirrup and slid her hand between the girth and the horse, pulling. There was at least four inches worth of slack. She should only have enough room for two fingers to fit between, no more, no less. She walked around the horse, checking the other side of the girth, and found a large tear in the leather near the top towards the buckle straps. Only half an inch of leather was holding the piece together. It was a wonder it hadn't snapped entirely. It was a new piece of tack, too. She had never seen anything like it.

She knew she had tightened and secured it before riding. She knew she did.

We need to get you back to the stable and clean you up, Shadow instructed, nudging her in the butt to get moving.

There was no way Carolynn could get back in the saddle with the condition of the girth. Her legs were cramping and sore, her back felt like she'd been dragged across asphalt, not to mention the pain in her arms was growing by the second. She needed to clean them up so they could heal properly.

The walk back was slow and arduous, and she leaned on Tempest more and more as they drew closer to the fence line. Shadow kept close to her side the entire way. She wasn't sure if the wolf expected her to pass out or what, but she appreciated the sentiment.

As soon as they reached the fence line, Carolynn yelled out for Jason. The guy poked his head out the barn door, saw her limping, and ran over.

"Are you okay?" he asked, brows pinched.

"Just decided on flying lessons today," Carolynn laughed, which caused a spasm to rake down her back. "Can you take Tempest for me and get her cleaned up? I'm just going to go into my office."

"Yeah, of course," Jason nodded, taking the mare's reigns and guiding her towards the stables.

Carolynn glanced down at Shadow, trying to give her a brave smile, even though all she wanted to do was lie down on the dirt floor. She noticed smudges of red on her yellow tank top. She glanced over her shoulder at the back of her arm and noticed the cuts were weeping, leaking onto her shirt.

Great, the one day she didn't bring an extra top.

Beth, Carolynn reached out with her mind, hoping her friend wasn't still sleeping.

This was one of those days she was grateful to be a telepath.

God, it's so weird when you do that. What if I was showering, or peeing, or drinking, and I choked?

Carolynn ignored her banter and began to move slowly toward her office on the other side of the stable. *Can you bring me a new shirt, please?*

Sure. What did you do, fall in a muck pile? 'Cause I would totally not laugh at you for that.

Just bring the shirt, please.

Fine, whatever; be down in a few minutes.

Carolynn closed her mind off as her friend continued to grumble. She finally made it back to the office and shuffled across the room to the wash basin in the corner. She opened the cupboard beneath the sink and began to pull out the peroxide and bandages. Once she got the debris out of her wounds, she knew her body would heal rather quickly, but until then, she had to do this the old-fashioned way.

Turning the water on, she let the basin fill up, squirting a couple pumps of hand soap into the warm liquid. Mixing it with her finger to get suds formed along the top, she plunged one arm at a time under the water. The wound burned as though someone had stuck a lit match beneath her skin. She hissed through clenched teeth as she rubbed her fingers along the cuts, trying to rub out the dirt and debris buried beneath the skin, agitating the wounds and reopening them. The water began to turn pink, but she kept at it. She had to get all of it out if she wanted them to heal.

Once the skin felt smooth and no longer rigid, she repeated the process with the other arm. It sucked and left her swearing like a trucker. Shadow lay at her feet, patiently waiting and avoiding the water spewing onto the floor. She grabbed a clean towel from the cabinet and patted her arms dry. She checked on the cuts again. They were deeper than she'd thought, as though she had rolled on jagged rocks and not dirt and grass. She poured peroxide onto the towel and reached around herself to pat the antiseptic on when she heard footsteps.

"Thanks, Beth, you can just toss it on the desk," Carolynn said, glancing in the mirror. But she didn't find Beth. She froze, body going rigid as Donnie stood in her office doorway, staring at the cuts and scrapes down both her arms. "Donnie."

Donnie moved faster than she expected. One minute he was frozen in her doorway, eyes darkening by the second, and the next he was at her side, hands cradling her injured arms, inspecting them closely, but with the gentlest touch.

"What happened?" Donnie asked, voice low and deep. It sent shivers down her spine, and not in a bad way.

"I'm okay; I just fell off my horse," Carolynn said, keeping the oddity with the girth to herself.

"Does it hurt?" he asked, rubbing his thumb along the top of her hand.

"A little," she said, voice soft, "but I heal fast. I just need to clean them."

Donnie took the peroxide-soaked towel from her and began dabbing gently along the cuts. They still stung, but the pain was less, or maybe she was just distracted by the fact that he was here, taking care of her yet again. Not that she minded.

Once both of her arms were clean, he picked up the gauze bandages and began to wrap each of them carefully.

"You're lucky I have an endless supply of clothes and that we are roughly the same size, except for your boobs, which are smaller than mine," Beth rambled as she walked into the office, finding Donnie bandaging her arms. "What the hell happened?"

Carolynn winced at the loud voice Beth used. "I fell off Tempest."

"What do you mean, you fell?" Beth scrunched her face in disbelief. "I don't think I've ever seen you fall off, not once. Now, me, I take falls almost weekly, and I've been riding longer than you."

While she had a point, Carolynn didn't much feel like getting into it. "I don't know; I think there was something wrong with my girth," she said, brushing it off, hoping that would be the end of the conversation.

"Do you need me to take you home?" Beth asked, noticing the wince she made as she turned towards them.

"I'll take her home," Donnie said, keeping one arm around her waist, the other holding her hand. While her balance was fine, her body was sore. She didn't think she needed the extra support, but she wasn't going to tell him that.

Carolynn could hear it in his tone, he was leaving no room for argument. Her and Beth exchanged a look. Carolynn couldn't help the light giddiness she felt with him here, helping her, taking care of her.

Are you OK with that? she heard Beth ask, not wanting to speak out loud.

Carolynn subtly nodded once, with a thankful smile. She took the shirt still in Beth's hands. Her arms were already starting to feel better, the burning and pain already receding. It was her body that ached. She wasn't sure if it was from nearly flying across half the field, tucking and rolling the way she did, or the overdose of adrenaline, but every inch of her hurt.

"Thank you," she said to Beth, squeezing her hand. "Can you guys give me a minute while I change? I don't want to go home covered in blood, in case my mom's home."

"Of course." Beth squeezed her back before leaving the room.

"I'll be right outside," Donnie said from just behind her, his hand grazing her elbow as he walked past, shutting the door as he went.

Carolynn carefully pulled her soiled shirt off, trying desperately to avoid the bandages and aggravating the healing wounds. Once she pulled it off, she found Beth had brought her one of her tank tops that had a built-in push-up bra that read, *Bite me.* She silently cursed her friend as she put it on, adjusting it around herself. While she didn't have breasts like Beth's, which would have definitely filled out the bra more, it did push hers up, accentuating what she did have.

She opened the door to find both Beth and Donnie waiting in the hall. She glared at Beth, glancing down at her own breasts and back to her friend. "Why do you hate me?"

Beth pressed her lips together to keep from laughing outright, but a hysterical giggle managed to escape. "It's not like you told me you were hurt."

Carolynn shook her head. She honestly should have known better.

"Is Jason lurking around here?" Beth asked, looking down the end of the aisle.

"He's at the other end of the stable putting Tempest away for me," Carolynn said, pulling on the ends of the tank top. She felt ridiculous in the stupid thing.

"Your stable hand is here?" Donnie asked, voice questioning.

"Of course he is; he works here." Carolynn almost laughed but stopped when she saw his stony expression. Those ice-blue eyes were darting to the other end of the stable where she knew Jason to be, as though he could see through the walls.

"Are you ready to go?" Donnie asked her, eyes roaming over her body, brow raising as he read the saying on her shirt. "Interesting."

Carolynn shot her friend another look that promised revenge. Beth held her hands up in surrender as she backed out of the stable slowly.

"You two kids have fun," Beth said, not at all subtle. "Donnie, don't break my girl here; she's precious."

"I already know that," Donnie said, taking a step closer towards her, brushing a stray hair back from her face and tucking it behind her ear.

An electrical current raced along her skin at the contact as bats beat in her stomach. A bump against her leg jolted her. She glanced down to find Shadow with her wallet and phone in her mouth.

"Thank you." Carolynn patted her head before taking the items and stuffing them into her back pockets. "Jason!"

Jason's head peered out from around the corner, as though he had been standing on the other side of the wall the entire time. "Yes?"

"I'm leaving early. Can you handle feeding the horses by yourself tonight?"

Jason's sapphire eyes darted from her to Donnie and back again, face one of confusion, before he gave her a small smirk. "Of course. I'll see you later."

Chapter 18

The car ride was a quick one as Donnie sped through the backroads. He pulled the car into the driveway of her house, and Carolynn noticed her mother's junker in its usual spot.

Crap, she was really hoping not to have to deal with her mother.

The one time I need her not to be home, and she is, Carolynn complained to Shadow in the backseat of the car. There was no way she was going to let her walk again, not after this morning.

She'll be worried at first, but then she'll forget, Shadow commented.

That fact should make her sad, maybe even a bit angry, but it didn't. It was just the simple truth of her mother. It wasn't like her mother forgot about her, she just spaces out and tends to gloss over details.

Carolynn glanced over at Donnie, who had been silent the whole way. She had noticed his jaw flexing, teeth grinding, as though he was disturbed or thinking really hard about something, but he had held her hand the entire way, their fingers interlaced on the center console.

"Do you want to come in?" Carolynn offered, glancing at her front door.

Donnie seemed to be staring off in the distance. She wasn't sure if he heard her or not. She gave his hand a light squeeze, brushing her thumb along the top of his hand. His eyes snapped to their hands, the ice thawing in his eyes.

"I'm sorry, what?"

"Do you want to come inside?" she asked him again. She wouldn't push it if he didn't want to, but boy did she want him to.

Donnie's eyes locked on her front door, staring at the faded paint and chipped swollen wood. She could sense his hesitation, his reluctance.

"Sure, if you don't mind introducing me to your mother." Donnie side-eyed her, giving her that smirk she was really starting to adore.

"I think you might come to regret that optimism," Carolynn warned him. "My mom can be a bit much."

"Moms love me," Donnie told her, the dimple making its star appearance.

"I think you mean women love you," Carolynn corrected.

"You think?"

"You're kind of pretty."

Donnie chuckled, the sound deep and resonating from his chest. She made to open her door but found he was already outside the car, opening it for her. She got out, the movement slow and steady. While the stiffness was fading, it wasn't fast enough. She knew enough that by tonight she'd be right as rain. It was just until then that really sucked.

Carolynn walked up to the steps, silently cursing the stairs as she stepped up them. Shadow raced ahead, waiting patiently at the foot of the door.

I can hear your mom getting ready inside. Sounds like she's leaving, Shadow said, ears perked.

That was a bit of relief.

Carolynn pushed her key into the lock, unlocking the door, and tried to put her body weight into opening it, but the stupid thing didn't budge. She glanced up at the sky and noticed dark clouds gathering on the horizon. Rain was coming, which meant extra moisture in the air, which meant the old, rotted wood was swollen in the frame.

"Fucking door," Carolynn groaned, mumbling under her breath. She did not have the energy for this.

Donnie came up from behind her. She could feel the heat of his body at her back, barely brushing against her but making her super aware of his every breath, every movement. He stretched his arm over her head, placing his hand on the door. Carolynn made to push again, Shadow also leaned into the door, and with a groaning sound, the door unstuck, swinging open.

"Thanks," Carolynn half laughed, slightly embarrassed by her dilapidated house. "It's really time for a new door."

"I've been saying that for years, but with your father not around, it's not as easy getting things done." Her mother rounded the corner out of her bedroom, head almost buried in her large purse, digging something out of the bottom. "Hey, honey, how was—what happened?"

She really wished people would stop asking her that, or that random occurrences resulting in injury would stop happening. Either would be fine.

"She fell off her horse," Donnie informed her mother, still standing at her back.

"You never fall off your horse," Susana said, tossing her bag on the couch. She came over to inspect her, turning her every which way, and looked over the white bandages still wrapped around her arms.

"Mom, I'm sore," Carolynn told her as her mother kept poking and moving her around.

"Sorry, Star," Susana apologized, stepping back. "It's just after that snake this morning and now this, it's like the world's gone topsy-turvy."

"Snake?" Donnie asked, voice turning grave and confused. "What snake?"

"We had a snake in the house this morning," Susana told him. Though why she was telling him anything blew her mind. "My shining brave Star got him out."

Carolynn's eyes went wide as she stared at her mother, mouthing at her to stop, which Susana completely ignored.

"I'm sorry my daughter is so rude. I'm Susana. Who might you be?"

"Donnie."

Carolynn couldn't help the small smile that spread across her face. Susana glanced from the man at her, back to her, and back again, trying to puzzle out how he fit into her daughter's life. She noticed the way her mother was eyeing him, acknowledging just how good-looking he was but also the fact that she had never heard of or seen him before.

"Are you new to town, Donnie?" Susana asked him, arms crossing over her chest.

Carolynn nearly rolled her eyes right then and there. Now she wanted to start acting like a mom?

"Just recently moved," Donnie confirmed.

"What brings you here?"

"Work."

"What kind of work do you do?"

"I'm a hired contractor." His responses were clipped and short, leaving her nerves frazzled.

"Alright, well, this has been fun," Carolynn said, interrupting whatever it was they were doing. "Mom, are you going to the hospital?"

"I am, one of the girls called out, and they asked me to pick up an extra shift," Susana said, picking her purse up off the couch. "I won't be home until tomorrow. You going to be okay? There's a big storm coming in off the coast."

"I'll be fine," Carolynn nodded, giving her mother a reassuring smile.

"No sleepovers other than Beth," her mother warned, brow raised as she glanced between the two of them. "I mean it."

Carolynn's eyes nearly bulged out of her head, and she choked on the air in her throat. "Jesus, Mom."

"You two kids have fun." Susana smiled evilly as she walked around them, slamming the door shut behind her.

"I am so sorry," Carolynn apologized, turning towards him.

Donnie chuckled, the sound vibrating from his chest. "It's fine. I'd be worried if she didn't assume I'd have my way with her daughter."

Carolynn blushed hard, her cheeks warming and chest flushed. She glanced down at her clothes, at the saying on her shirt and the grass stains on her pants, and frowned. "I'm going to get changed really quick. Make yourself at home. There's water in the fridge."

Carolynn left him alone in the middle of her living room and went straight for her bathroom. Shutting the door firmly behind her, she looked at herself in the mirror. Her hair was a mess, with random strands hanging around her face and half of her braid undone. She had dirt streaks along her chest and arms where she hadn't scrubbed her skin. The breeches were most definitely ruined, riddled with rips, but not deep enough to reach the skin. She undid whatever was left of her braid, brushing out the hair until it was free of tangles. Carefully undoing the bandages, she removed the gauze wrappings. Her arms and shoulders were still a bit stiff as she unwrapped the thin material. Turning so she could see the backs of her arms properly, she noticed the cuts were now no more than thin, red lines down her arms, already scabbed over. In the next few hours, they would be completely gone, not even a scar to show.

She pulled the ridiculous-looking tank top off, throwing it into her dirty pile, seriously considering burning the damn thing. She unzipped her boots and threw them in her closet, before shimmying out of her breeches. Her legs and ass were crampy, most likely from her not-so-stellar landing, but all in all, there were no bruising or blemishes on her skin.

Stepping into her closet, she found a clean pair of black leggings and a tank top, carefully putting them on so as to not reopen the healing scabs. She didn't want to leave Donnie out there on his own too long, so a shower was out of the question. The next best thing was deodorant and body spray.

After one last glance in the mirror and somewhat satisfied with the woman looking back, she turned off the light and left the bathroom. Sitting in the middle of the room was Shadow, patiently waiting. She instantly grew anxious. Shadow had made it clear she wasn't a fan of Donnie's, for whatever reason. Would she give her a hard time? Threaten to bite him again?

I will stay in here until he leaves, Shadow informed her, before curling up on the ground. *But if he does anything you don't want, I will eat his stomach.*

Carolynn frowned, trying to work out the logistics of what the wolf had said. "You'll bite his stomach?"

No, I mean I will attack him, rip out his jugular and then make a meal out of his entrails.

Carolynn nearly gagged at the image painted for her. "That was too much. Way too much. I think you need to stop watching horror movies with Beth. Immediately."

They are very informative. Humans are worse than animals.

Well, she wasn't wrong.

Carolynn left Shadow alone to her dark thoughts and headed back out to the living room, but Donnie wasn't where she had left him. She glanced around and found a tall, hard man in her kitchen, standing in front of her stove. She curiously walked around the counter. He had his back to her, and something amazing permeated the air filled with Cajun spices.

He was cooking, in her kitchen. Actually cooking a meal. She couldn't remember the last time someone had used their kitchen for something other than coffee and cereal. Other than the botched lasagna the night before. It was definitely before her dad had gotten sick. She didn't even know they had smoked sausage in the fridge, or that there was anything even mildly edible in there.

Donnie glanced at her over his shoulders, dark strands of hair falling in his eyes as he eyed her attire, gaze instantly going to her unbandaged arms. "How are you feeling?"

"Still a bit sore, but otherwise okay." She walked over to him and found him cooking one of her favorite comfort meals, Jambalaya. She gnawed on her bottom lip as she tried to keep from grinning stupidly.

"Is something wrong? I hope it's okay. I just figured you'd be hungry after everything today," Donnie asked, motioning to her with a wooden spoon in one hand.

"No, it's perfect." She smiled before jumping up on the counter and leaning back against the cabinets.

Donnie stirred the food a final time before turning the heat down and putting the lid on. They had at least twenty more minutes until the food would be done cooking.

He stepped closer to her, running his hands down the backs of her arms, carefully brushing against the healing cuts. She didn't move, didn't flinch, didn't wince. His touch was like a cool breeze on a hot summer day, refreshing and a breath of relief. Sparks danced along her skin as his hands moved down her arms and back up again. Even sitting on the counter, he was still a head taller than her. His uneven breathing fanned her face as she sat still, allowing his hands to roam and explore. His gaze was filled with lust and wonder as he brushed along her shoulders and neck. One of his hands stopped as it wound its way into her hair at the base of her neck, tilting her head back.

Hunger and desire hung between them, his lips slightly parted as he stared down at her lips. She couldn't stop looking at his eyes, his lips, his face, taking in every twitch, movement, and change of expression. His other hand grazed along the side of her body, down her ribs, and settled on her hips, his fingers digging into her flesh as though he was trying to contain himself.

"I don't want you to regret this," Donnie said, voice rough and deep, exposed and brutally honest.

What was there to regret? How could she possibly not want this? Want him?

She may not have been sure of anything in her life, but this, him, she was certain of, and she wanted it all.

She wouldn't tell him. She would show him.

Carolynn moved. Her hands wrapped themselves in the front of his shirt and pulled him closer, closing the distance between them. His lips pressed against hers, and she could have sworn her heart stuttered, as though a shock had rocked through her. His hand tightened in her hair, tipping her head back further; the other one gripped her waist, dragging her closer. Her knees automatically opened in response, allowing him to step between them as she locked her feet behind him, tightening her thighs on his waist. She opened her mouth for him, tasting him as their tongues met. He tasted like thick honey, sweet and smoky. She pressed her chest against his, breasts tingling from the sensation.

A deep growl emanated from him, causing his chest to rumble against hers. Her lower stomach coiled and tightened uncomfortably. She moved her hands up his chest, wrapping them around his neck and into his hair where she tugged on the roots, causing him to moan. She took it in, devouring his noises, his taste, his mouth.

He moved his lips down her neck, sucking on her flesh, peppering her with kisses, and running his tongue down her collarbone. Carolynn arched back, head meeting the cabinets as he kissed along the top of her breasts. Her skin sizzled where he touched, desire and need coursed through her, demanding more. She called his name, moaned it more like, and he moved back up her neck in response, slipping his tongue between her teeth. His hands were in her hair, on her face, running down her arms, up her sides, and around her back. Permanently branding her with his touch, his taste.

Donnie pulled away, putting distance between them, leaving them both gasping for air. Carolynn stared at him, wide-eyed, pressing her legs together to relieve some of the pressure already building at the apex of her sex. His eyes darted to her knees clamped together and those ice-blue eyes darkened, pupils dilating.

"Don't do that," he said. No, he growled the words, like a predator staring at his next meal.

She arched her back, leaning her head against the cabinets as she rubbed her legs together again. A jolt of pleasure forced her to release a breath of air. She watched as his Adam's apple bobbed in his throat. Had she been reading it all wrong? Did he not want to take it further with her? She wasn't experienced in any of it, but of all the times she imagined going further with a guy, this seemed like the perfect time.

Donnie stepped forward, flipping off the burner, and moved the pan onto a hot plate. He backed up a step once again, his gaze moving down her body slowly and back up again. She couldn't stop it, couldn't stop this need inside her. She'd never felt anything so strongly before, and she had to get it out, or she'd erupt. Her hand moved over her hip to the front of her leggings. Before she could even rub against the thin cotton and offer herself some sort of release, he moved faster than she could track, hand shooting out and pinning hers above her head on the wooden cabinets.

"Don't do that," Donnie repeated, eyes now wholly black and bottomless.

It should frighten her—she'd never seen anyone's eyes change and shift the way his were right now—but it didn't. Excitement buzzed through her like a drug, making her bold and fearless.

"Or what?"

Donnie tilted his head ever so slightly and eyed her curiously, taking the bait. "Only I will be the one touching your pussy," he said, words final and commanding. She had never heard that word used and been turned on, not like she was now. Her skin grew tight and hot, breasts swelling beneath her tank as she bit on her bottom lip. "Do you understand?"

Carolynn nodded, keeping that lip firmly between her teeth, where his stare lingered as he moved back. She wanted to whimper, to beg him to touch her, to offer her release.

"Stand up, kitten."

Her heart rate picked up at the control in his voice. She pushed off the counter and stood on wobbly knees she locked tight, steeling her spine.

Donnie stepped forward, closing any distance between them, his hands resting on her hips, thumbs pushing beneath her waistband.

This was really happening.

"Do you want this?" Donnie asked her.

He wasn't commanding or demanding anything from her. He was asking for her consent.

"Yes," she said, breathy and panting.

"Do you want me?"

The sadness in that question was almost enough to shatter her heart. She wanted to bring him to her chest and hold him, but she didn't think he'd appreciate that, so she said the first thing that came to mind. "Always."

Donnie snickered, those perfect lips pulling into his devilish grin. "Don't make promises you can't keep, kitten."

Before she could protest and tell him just how wrong he was, he hooked her pants and underwear with both thumbs and pulled them all the way down to her ankles. Cool air brushed across her sex, making her shiver where she stood. He tapped her ankle, a silent request for her to step out of her leggings, which she obeyed. His hands slid up along her legs, one on the outside, the other traveling along the inside. He was on his knees before her, his tall figure leaning in, kissing his way up her thigh until he reached the bundle of nerves swollen and begging for release.

He kissed the bundle, lips warm, breath hot. She inhaled sharply at the contact, bright lights flashing behind her eyes as she gripped onto the counter. He breathed her in, taking in her scent. A deep growl emanated from him. The vibrations against her clit sent her head rolling back. He had barely even touched her, and already she was writhing.

"So sweet," Donnie purred against her sensitive flesh. He

glanced up at her from between her thighs, mouth hovering just above the one spot she'd wish he would touch and taste. Those hooded, black eyes took her in, seeming to breathe in deeply, as something or someone else entirely took over and those lips spread into a smile. "Hold on, kitten, if you can."

That was the only warning she'd get as he dove forward, tongue and lips sucking her in his mouth, flicking against her bud. Carolynn threw her head back. An indecent breathy moan slipped past her lips. She gripped onto the counter, the cabinets, anything she could grab. His hands came up and gripped her by the waist, not allowing her to escape, to get relief from the pressure, the tongue lashing as a sensation built deep within her.

She glanced down and saw his dark hair against her bare flesh, his fingers digging into her hips, mouth sucking and teasing, drinking from her, when suddenly phantom hands gripped her thighs and placed her on the counter, spreading her legs even further as her feet gained purchase on the counter to keep from falling. His hands were still on her hips and hadn't moved, yet something else held her thighs wide open as he buried his face in her pussy. She couldn't think about it, couldn't process it. All she could do was hold on and ride her pleasure as he built and built her into a crescendo.

Her hands ended up in his hair as she pushed his face farther into her sex, grinding on him. He moaned against her, as though he was deriving pleasure from her own, which sent a different type of thrill through her. Something was reaching its peak deep inside of her. She felt feverish and faint, as though she was boiling from the inside out.

Donnie teased and nipped, using teeth and tongue, dragging her pleasure out of her. Her breathing grew ragged and rough. She didn't think she could hold it much longer.

"Cum for me, kitten," Donnie urged, instructing her. "Cum for me now."

And cum she did. Fireworks exploded behind her eyes, her hand tightened in his hair, as he sucked and drank from her, taking in all of her pleasure, wringing every last drop from her. She came and came until she was sure she would lose consciousness and slumped back against the cabinets, panting and strung out. The hands from her thighs and hips finally released her, slowly lowering her legs back down to the ground.

In a daze, he helped her get back into her underwear and leggings, even going as far as to pull them up her legs, securing them around her waist.

Thunder rumbled in the distance, rolling across the earth, deep and boisterous.

Donnie leaned in and kissed her softly, lips gentle and coaxing. She could taste herself on his tongue, sweet and salty. This wasn't as fevered and aggressive as their earlier kiss had been. It was sweet and gentle, tender and warm. His hand came up and brushed a strand of hair back over her shoulder, cupping her face as his thumb brushed along her bottom lip.

"You're too good for me," Donnie finally spoke, his voice low and reserved, eyes locked on her lips.

Carolynn looked up into his eyes, the blue coming back slowly as the pupils constricted.

"You don't know me as well as you think you do," Carolynn said, her voice returning. She rested her hand on his chest and felt a chasm within him, deep and wide. It had been there for some time, maybe longer than he ever realized, and he was constantly towing that line, trying to see how far he could push himself before he finally fell in, lost to the darkness.

She threw him a line. She would catch him before he fell.

"I should get going."

Her heart bottomed out in her stomach as confusion settled in. She swallowed hard, her mouth suddenly dry. Had she done something wrong? Had she made it too easy? She suddenly felt extremely self-conscious, crossing her arms over her chest and backing away a step, but he wouldn't let her, instead gripping tighter to her waist and face, pulling her back in.

"It's not you—"

"If this is you telling me 'it's not you, it's me' bullshit, I swear on all that is holy I will feed you your testicles," Carolynn swore, giving him the hardest glare she had ever delivered.

Donnie's lips rose into a smirk, as though he found the idea intriguing. "So violent. I like it," he purred, making her insides melt all over again. "What I was going to say was, it's not you, it's the storm and your mother. She specifically told me I cannot spend the night, and it sounds like it's about to monsoon outside."

Carolynn felt irritated. While all of that was perfectly reasonable, she didn't want him to leave, didn't want this moment to end. "But we haven't eaten yet."

"I just ate," he said with a raised brow, licking his lips as though tasting her all over again.

Carolynn bit her lower lip again, causing his eyes to darken once more.

"Kitten, if you keep that up, I'll never leave, and you won't be able to walk straight for a week," Donnie made her a promise.

"I don't think I would mind that," she found herself saying, surprising the both of them. When had she become so lusty?

Donnie chuckled, his lips brushing against the crown of her head. "I'll see you later."

Carolynn's bottom lip stuck out in a pout, but she quickly sucked it back in before he noticed. No way was she going to whine or beg him to stay. He made her no promises.

"Don't forget to eat," Donnie said, giving her a stern look. "Actual food."

"Yes, sir."

Donnie froze as he made to turn and leave, instead glancing back at her over his shoulder. "I don't think you understand what you do to me."

Chapter 19

Donnie was driving down the back roads, speeding through twists and turns with ease. Thunder rattled his windshield as the storm chased him and pushed him forward. What had he been thinking? What was he doing?

It was almost as though he couldn't help himself when he was around her. Like something inside of him craved her, needed to touch her like he needed air in his lungs to breathe. He could still feel her on his tongue, in his mouth, and all over his skin. And all he wanted was more. He wanted to spread those sweet lips until she squirted again in his mouth. He wanted to bend her over and fuck that sweet ass from behind. But most of all, he wanted to hold her close and protect her from the world. From his world.

He had been so distracted by his hard cock rubbing against the seam of his pants, he hadn't noticed the hooded figure stepping out into the middle of the road. Donnie slammed on the brakes, swerving onto the shoulder of the road. The hooded figure walked in front of his car and into the headlights before stepping beneath the trees that lined the roads.

Donnie got out of his car, slamming the door shut behind him. The wind whipped through his hair, picking it up and tossing it in his eyes. Raindrops began to splatter on the hood of his car, sizzling from the retained heat, but he didn't care. He put his hand on the figure's shoulders, spinning him around and ripping the hood back.

Donnie grabbed Jason by the front of his shirt and lifted him off the ground, slamming his back into the nearest tree.

"What the hell do you think you're doing?" Donnie hissed, grinding his teeth together. Lightning flashed above them, illuminating the road for the briefest of moments.

"I'm just curious as to what my father might think about his favorite toy making nice with the girl he was sent to kill. Or did you forget your orders?" Jason asked coolly, his mouth pulled into a shit-eating grin.

Donnie almost laughed at the child, at the arrogance and stupidly placed bravery. It would get him killed one day. But his words chilled him. He put the boy down, taking a step back and getting the full measure of the boy before him. He crossed his arms across his chest and grinned, raising a brow at him. "He sent you down to kill Carolynn?"

"He sent me down as backup in case you couldn't finish the job yourself. They felt a shift in you not long after you got here. His fears were confirmed when you started making excuses as to why it wasn't done yet." Jason laughed, thunder rattling the trees. "Now I know why. Tell me, was she a good lay? Was she worth it?"

Fury pounded through his dead heart, and he nearly exploded on the child, decimating him until he was no more than specks of dirt littering this diseased earth, but he held himself back. He hadn't gotten this far due to lack of control, and he wouldn't start now. He had to play this smart.

"The fact that you think you could kill her, gives me a good chuckle. For you to think you could ever best me at anything makes you a fool, a *child*." He spat the word. "You are nothing compared to me. I have three thousand years on you, boy. Don't forget that," Donnie said, towering over Jason until the kid took the tiniest step back.

It was all he needed.

"If you're still going to kill her, how do you plan on doing it?" Jason asked.

"She trusts me. I have her right where I want her," Donnie said with a smirk, making to turn away before he thought of one last thing, just as the rain began to pelt down. "Oh, and don't ever jump in front of my car again. If it has so much as a scratch, you will find out what I am truly capable of."

Chapter 20

Carolynn sat on her bed, digging into her bowl of Jambalaya as some drama played on her old television. Shadow had left shortly after Donnie, something about storms and her pack, and hadn't been back yet.

She glanced at the book Neila had given her still lying on her nightstand. She picked it up, brushing some of Shadow's stray hair off the cover, and leaned back against her bed. She flipped through the book, bypassing the Gods, and found the section on Angels.

"The Angel of Death goes by many names. Some include Abaddon, Azrael, and Sammael," she read aloud. "Some have correlated the Angel of Death to Lucifer, but the Angel of Death was not a Prince of Hell or a fallen angel. He is the servant of Oriel, God of Death, the last creation of Matias, and the Angel of Death. The Angel was first created for the purpose of assisting Oriel with ferrying souls between worlds and keeping the demon population manageable. But this Angel was different in comparison to his brothers and sisters. Being surrounded by death night and day, made the Angel crave death, destruction, and mayhem."

Carolynn looked at the image that was supposed to be the angel in question, but all it depicted was a lone figure, wrapped in shadows and darkness. The only thing that was identifiable were long, beautiful raven wings.

"Some say this change in the Angel of Death was due to Matias becoming complacent and inconsistent when it came to the task of creating new Angels. Others believe it could be the Angels were given souls with the ability of free will. The Angel of Death was the last known angel to be created. The Angel is responsible for countless wars, famines, diseases, extinction of civilizations, and assassinations. Angels do not feel, they do not love or hate, that is until the Angel of Death and his thirst for darkness."

Rolling thunder rattled her windows and walls, shaking the fragile foundation of the house and startling her from her book. A flash of lightning illuminated her room, causing the television to flicker. They would most likely lose power soon. They always did during storms such as this one. The wind was whipping against her house, sounding like a tornado was just outside her window. She wondered how many trees would be toppled over on the roads tomorrow.

Closing the book and setting it back on the nightstand, she worried for Shadow. She didn't like her being out in the woods during storms like this. She didn't care that she was a wolf and mostly wild, she still much preferred her being home and safe, well, safe-ish. This storm seemed excessively violent.

She pulled her phone out of her pocket and noticed it was nearly nine o'clock. She felt exhausted after the events of the day and was ready to curl up in bed and fall asleep, but this storm would most likely squash those dreams.

At least she didn't have to worry about her mother driving home in this storm. It was good she was at the hospital instead of stuck at home, where she would do nothing but pace until it passed.

Carolynn left her bedroom, placed her empty dish on the kitchen counter, and walked through the family room to the front door. She opened it with a yank and stuck her head outside. The wind was blowing with a vengeance, threatening to rip the door from her straining grip, whipping her hair around her face and head. The trees surrounding her house were being bent back and forth like wildflowers in a spring breeze. She scanned the yard for any sight of her wolf, but all she could see was what the too frequent lightning strikes allowed her to see, which wasn't much.

"Shadow!" she yelled, but her words were caught by the wind and thrown away. It was useless to stand out there when Shadow would come home when it was safe. She could hear the rain pelting the ground and moving fast toward her. She slammed the door shut just as it poured down on her house, locking the door for good measure, for some reason reassured by the clicking of the deadbolt.

The light fixtures on the ceiling flickered. Then the house went completely dark. She couldn't see five inches in front of her. At least, not until a flash of lightning brightened the room for half a second. Carolynn took her phone back out of her pocket and flipped it open, using the screen as a guide as she went into the kitchen and found the flashlight under the sink.

"It's not like this isn't creepy or anything," she said aloud to herself, her words echoing in the house. She always hated it when she was left home alone during a storm.

Her phone lit up from an incoming call. She glanced at the number and didn't recognize it but answered anyway. "Hello?"

"Carolynn? It's Neila. I just wanted to make sure you were okay. They were saying some parts of town are without power."

"Yeah, I'm okay. My power's out, but I have a flashlight," Carolynn said, glancing out her back-sliding glass door.

A flash of lightning lit up her backyard. Something moved. She blinked a few times. It must have been a trick of the light, but she could have sworn she'd seen a silhouette of a man amongst the trees of the woods.

"Carolynn?" Neila called, full of concern as she stood in silence.

"Um, yeah, I'm here," Carolynn said, voice empty. She turned her back on the sliding glass door and glanced out the double-paned window beside her front door. This time, she definitely saw someone standing outside, now on her porch.

In a panic, she dropped down to the floor, hiding behind the kitchen counter, and clicked off her flashlight. She was out of sight of both the front and back doors. Her breathing intensified, and she willed herself to calm down. Panicking wouldn't do herself any good if the person got inside. What had the past ten years of karate lessons taught her if not for this moment? Silently she thanked her dead father for forcing her into those classes as a child.

This was how people died in scary movies. She could just be seeing things, maybe it was a trick of the light, the storm messing with her mind, but deep down she knew it wasn't that. Someone was outside.

"Carolynn, what's going on?" Neila asked, voice rising.

"Someone's here, outside the house," Carolynn whispered into the phone.

The phone went silent. She pulled the device away from her face and checked the screen to see if the call had been dropped. It hadn't.

"Can you get out?" Neila asked, voice steady.

Carolynn could have sworn she heard an engine starting in the background. "No. I don't know if there's more than one," she said, praying to whatever Gods listened that there was only one.

The creaking of her front door could be heard from where she was as it opened. Rain slamming into the house became louder, making it harder to hear her intruder. Her heart raced rapidly, pounding in her chest. "He's in the house," she croaked, trying desperately to keep her voice down.

"Carolynn, keep the phone on. Don't hang up. I'm on my way." Tires screeching on wet pavement could be heard through the phone speakers as she set it down on the linoleum floor.

Carolynn held onto the flashlight tightly, clinging to it, ready to use it as a weapon if need be. She heard footsteps getting closer, and the squishing sound of wet shoes on the carpet.

Suddenly she felt an intense burning pain coming from the back of her head as her body was lifted up off the floor by her hair, and she saw a gloved hand wrapped around her long auburn ponytail. The hand was attached to a tall hooded figure, telling by its build and stance, it was a man. The way he held himself, his posture seemed eerily familiar. She could hear a terrible, sickening scream, tearing through the air, louder than the pounding in her ears from the intense pain of her hair being ripped from her head, and realized it was coming from her. She closed her mouth and tried to push through the pain, still clinging to the flashlight.

She regripped the plastic light in her hand and smashed her attacker across the face with it. The stranger lost his grip on her hair with a grunt and let go, stumbling back. Carolynn fell to the floor in a heap, her head burning fiercely. She got to her feet, one hand gripping her head and the other out in front of her, feeling her way out. She could hear the man behind her lunge in her direction. She ducked down on the ground and felt a slight breeze as his body soared over hers. She could make out his shape as he tucked and rolled on the floor, landing smoothly on his feet.

Carolynn got up and dashed for the front door. If she could just get outside, maybe she could yell for help. She could feel him closing the distance, his feet pounding on the floor, when her scalp flared in pain again. Her vision blurred. All she could see were patches of black and white framing her vision.

Was it the lightning or was she losing consciousness? She tried to quickly clear her head and think past the pulsing pain. She spun towards the intruder and saw a flash of metal in his hand. She thrust her palm up into his nose. She could feel the cartilage snapping beneath the impact. He released her hair once again as she felt a slight stinging sensation near her right hip.

She wasn't going to run, not again, not in her house. Stepping into her fighting stance, her feet spread apart, left foot in front of the other. She raised her fists to protect her face and was ready to block his next attempt at her hair. The intruder swung his right arm, aiming for her face.

Carolynn ducked out of the way, keeping her balance on the balls of her feet. She came up with an uppercut, her fist slammed up into his face, rattling his teeth. Before he had time to recover, Carolynn spun around and kicked out. The ball and heel of her foot collided with his midsection with such force that he was blown back, crashing through the sliding glass door and out onto the back deck.

She stood there a few moments, anxiously waiting for him to rush back inside, to come at her again, but instead, she could see his dark form pushing himself up off the ground and running for the cover of the woods.

Chapter 21

Neila sped up to Carolynn's house, coming to a screeching halt, tires skidding in the wet gravel. She peered out the windshield through the racing wipers and noticed the house was void of all light and life. The power was still out, but she saw no movement from inside. Her heart was pounding, fear threatening to drown her. She grabbed her industrial flashlight before getting out of the Audi and slowly walked to the front porch.

The hairs on the back of her neck were standing straight, ears straining to catch a sound, any sound, but she could hear nothing coming from outside. The storm had moved on, lightning still illuminating the sky above. Perspiration clung to her skin as the humidity settled heavily in the air.

Her heart was pumping in her ears as bile rose to the back of her throat. What if something had happened to her?

Neila saw the front door was wide open, carpet soaked and mud-stained. She put her hand up against the splintered door frame and clicked her flashlight on. Directing the light inside the pitch-black house, she illuminated the interior, and what she saw had her stomach bottom out. Furniture was upturned, a coffee table was shattered into pieces, and muddy footprints stained the floor. She froze when she saw a statue-like figure standing in the middle of the room. Carolynn was still, standing in her fighting stance, eyes fixed on the shattered sliding glass door.

The electricity flickered on, the sound of an A/C running

started, and the overhead lights lit up the whole house. In proper lighting, she was able to see Carolynn fully. Her hair was knotted near her scalp, small chunks hanging free. Her knuckles were bruised and bloody, split open and blood freely dripped down her hand. But the girl froze where she stood, unfazed by the lights, by the beeping of the oven clock, all of it.

Neila carefully approached her and walked around to stand in front, slowly coming into her peripheral. The girl was in shock.

Neila stretched out a hand, placing it on her shoulder. "Carolynn."

The sound of her voice and the light touch seemed to bring the girl back to the present, as Carolynn stopped staring out the back door and regained focus, looking into her eyes. That coloring and the cool expression nearly knocked her on her ass as a serious sense of déjà vu overwhelmed her.

"Mom?" Carolynn asked, confused and disoriented.

Neila's heart stuttered, her mouth dry like sandpaper. "It's Neila, Carolynn. Are you alright?"

"How did you know where I live?" Carolynn asked, voice quiet and questioning, not yet processing the events of the night.

"Are you okay?" Neila asked, ignoring the question. "Are you hurt?"

Carolynn blinked a few times, lips moving slowly as she tried to process it all. "I don't think so," she said, but her hand rose to the top of her head and she closed her eyes, wincing and flinching at the touch. "My head."

"What happened?"

"He got me by my hair," she started, glancing around the room as the puzzle pieces began to fit together. "I hit him with my flashlight. I tried to run, but he grabbed me. I think I broke his nose, then I kicked him." She pointed to where there should have been a sliding glass door. The back door was completely shattered and caved in, as though a great force had blown out of the house.

"You kicked him through the door?" Neila asked, eyebrow raised, lips pursed. She was impressed.

"Yes," Carolynn said, lowering her hand to her side, where she winced and hissed in pain.

"Let me take a look," Neila offered, taking a step forward, but

Carolynn automatically retreated.

She held her hands up, backing up a step. "I won't touch you. I just want to help. This has been a traumatizing night, and if you're hurt, we need to get you checked out."

"No hospitals," Carolynn said panicked, eyes widening, the first hint of fear she'd seen from her all night.

"No hospitals," Neila repeated. It wasn't exactly what she meant anyways.

"I'm just sore," Carolynn said, still not sounding all that present. "And rattled."

"Of course, that's totally understandable." Neila nodded. "At least come and stay at my house, just for the night. I can't leave you here alone, not after what happened."

"I can't. The house..."

"Don't worry about the house. It'll be fixed before your mom gets home in the morning. I promise."

"I couldn't ask that of you."

"Good thing you're not asking," Neila said with a small smile.

"Okay," Carolynn said hesitantly, glancing around the wreckage of her house. "Let me just grab some clothes."

"I'll wait here."

Carolynn went into her bedroom, closing the door behind her. Her head burned as though she had been scalped. Well, she nearly had been. Her head pounded with fury, and her right hip stung as though someone had poured liquid fire on her. She clasped her hand over her side and pulled her hand away wet and sticky with blood. She glanced down at herself. She was wearing black, and it had done almost too good of a job concealing her injury.

She walked into the bathroom and pulled the tank top over her head, leaving her in nothing but a bra and leggings. She had finger bruises on her arms and shoulders. She couldn't even remember him gripping her, let alone hard enough to bruise, but it was the swollen red, three-inch-long cut along her hip that caused her to pause. It was slowly weeping, but it looked angry and jagged, as though the knife hadn't been sharp enough to slice cleanly through.

Carolynn opened one of the counter drawers and pulled out a washcloth. She held it under the sink as she turned on the facet, letting it soak up the warmth from the water. She dabbed at the cut, hoping to clean it, but the second the fabric touched the wound, a white-hot searing pain shot up along her ribs and up her neck. She bit her tongue to keep from yelling out as her body spasmed from the shock. She held her breath and leaned against the counter for fear of fainting.

Glancing down at the shallow wound, her eyes were wide with surprise. It was only a small cut. It would heal on its own, and everything would be fine. She was lucky it was only her hip and he hadn't gutted her. It would heal; she just had to give it some time.

Carolynn rummaged under her sink and found a long thick bandage and tape. She secured it over the wound and quickly changed into a clean pair of sweatpants and a tank top carefully as to not aggravate the wound and cause a fresh flare-up. She grabbed a bag off the closet floor and stuffed it full of clothes for the next day. She strained to pick up her boots she'd chucked in the corner, wincing as she did, and put them in the bag as well.

Glancing back at herself one last time in the mirror, she looked sadly at her hair. It was knotted and matted on the top of her head, and she could already see some thinning spots. The fucker had got her good. She wanted to kick him through a wall again. As carefully as possible, she attempted to brush out the mess, but ended up giving up as her scalp was just too tender and instead put it up into a high ponytail.

Carrying the bag half open, glancing around the room to see what else she might need, her eye fell on the jacket hanging off the edge of her bed. She slipped her arms into Donnie's leather jacket, breathing in his smell that instantly settled over her like a warm blanket. She grabbed a few toiletries off her dresser and met Neila back out in what was left of her living room.

"I'm ready," Carolynn said, slinging the backpack over her shoulder, careful not to hit her hip, and offered the woman a smile.

"Great," she said, pushing a cell phone into her back pocket. "I've already made arrangements for someone to come and clean this up and replace the back door before the sun rises."

"I don't have the money."

"I know you don't know me very well," Neila said, stopping her from talking any further, "but money is not an issue. Let me help you."

Carolynn hesitated. What was this stranger's stake in any of this? Was she really just doing this out of the goodness of her heart or was there something else? But she couldn't turn down the offer. Her mother would have a heart attack if she saw the state of the house. If she learned that someone had attacked her while she wasn't home, she would never forgive herself.

"Thank you," Carolynn finally said. "My mom would lose whatever marbles she has left if she found out."

"Are you sure you don't want to call her?" Neila asked.

"No way," Carolynn said, glancing at the shattered back door and the blood droplets on the floor. "It's better if she doesn't know."

"Okay." Neila nodded once. "Let's go."

The drive to Neila's house was a short one, definitely not as long as walking. Neila didn't stop for lights or stop signs, nor did they come upon any cops, which was odd, but not entirely surprising given the storm and the damage some people may have experienced. They probably had better things to worry about.

Neila pulled the Audi into the garage, closing the door behind them. Carolynn got out of the car and gripped the door for support as she stood, the world spinning around her.

Neila was at her side immediately, a hand under her arm to steady her. "Are you alright?"

"Just tired. I think the adrenaline is finally fading," Carolynn said warily.

"Let's get you up to your room," Neila offered an arm for her to lean on, slinging Carolynn's pack over her own shoulder. She led her inside and up a flight of stairs.

Carolynn couldn't remember the exact way she led her through the house, but before she knew it, her head was resting on a soft feathered pillow. She could feel Neila slipping off her shoes and pulling the comforter up over her shoulders. The last thing she heard before slipping into unconsciousness was heavy steps pounding up the staircase.

Thunder rumbled loudly. Lightning struck granite rock. Sparks sprang to life, igniting the nearby brush, spreading fast as lightning stretched across the horizon. Metal clanged as swords were struck together. Wings beat against the wind as men and women, as well as horses with wings, flew through the air. Carolynn stood in the middle of a war, filled with beautiful and horrible-looking creatures. Men and women battling each other.

Carolynn looked down at her feet and found two bodies dead and broken. She knelt down beside them, tears streaming down her soot-soaked face. She noticed Beth, her eyes closed, flesh riddled with scratches and cuts. She looked as though she was sleeping peacefully but her skin was milk-white and her lips blue with death. Silver-blonde hair covered the other face, which she brushed back and gasped, falling back on her rear, hand covering her mouth to keep the scream in. Her mother's blue eyes were glazed over with death, staring up into the blood-filled sky.

She looked up at the scene unfolding around her, struggling through tear-filled eyes, when she spotted Donnie among the endless sea of fighting bodies. Blood and soot streaked across his face and body. He was shirtless and wearing no shoes; his pants were riddled with holes from swords biting into his flesh. His face was tear-streaked as he mouthed something to her, but she couldn't hear him over the raging battle.

Chapter 22

arolynn jolted awake as a heavy weight lay on her chest. She bolted upright, her vision blurry from unshed tears. She rubbed at them, trying to clear her vision. Her breathing came in short and quick starts, her mouth cotton dry and hoarse as though she had been screaming. Sunlight filtered in through curtains she didn't recognize, and found herself in a room she'd never been in before. But the hulking wolf standing on top of her, that was real. She pushed her off as she felt suffocated, the walls closing in.

"Shadow?" she half-sobbed. Last night's events came rushing at her, and she suddenly felt extremely small.

Shadow inched closer to her until they were face to face. The wolf gave her a hard lick from jaw to hairline, erasing the salty tears already flowing. *I am so sorry I wasn't there for you, pup. I don't know what I would have done if something happened to you.*

"I don't know why any of this is happening," she cried, burying her face in the wolf's thick fur, running her hand along the wolf's back, soothing herself more than anything.

Were you hurt? Are you okay?

Carolynn was getting tired of being asked that. She was tired of there being a need to ask that. She tried to push herself up into a sitting position when pain ignited up her side. Gasping, she fell back on the bed clutching her hip.

Why did it still hurt? It should have healed by now.

What's wrong? What is it? Shadow asked, pressing her nose into her chest, her arms.

"It's nothing; it's just a scratch," she sniffled.

Let me see, Shadow said, nudging the hand covering her hip with her wet nose.

Carolynn reluctantly obeyed and raised her shirt to reveal the cut. She heard the wolf growl, low and menacing. She glanced down at the cut and found it to be worse than last night. The cut had bled through the bandage she applied and dark spider web veins were stretching out from the edges of the bandage, spreading up her side. The sight of the cut had her taken aback. She pulled her shirt back down.

How could it have gotten so much worse overnight?

That is not nothing. We need to tell—

"No one," Carolynn hissed, cutting her off, wiping away the remaining wetness from her face. "We are not telling anyone. I have never been sick or hurt, and I'm not about to start now."

Carolynn carefully sat up off the bed, careful to avoid stretching, or moving, or even breathing, for that matter. "How did you even get here? How did you know where I was?"

I went back to the house after the storm and found the front door wide open and the house a wreck. I could smell blood on the floor, but then I recognized Neila's scent and figured you were with her, so I ran here.

Carolynn couldn't help but feel a bit sad and guilty, leaving Shadow to find their house in that state, but she was glad to have her back.

Sliding out of bed, she pulled her clothes out of the bag waiting for her on the nightstand beside the bed. She quickly changed into her riding clothes, trying to ignore the stabbing pain she experienced with every movement. She found the bedroom she was staying in had a connecting bathroom and sighed with relief. Inside the restroom, she did her business and tried to work out the knots in her hair. It wasn't as painful as last night, but the scalp was still tender as hell, like someone had taken a meat tenderizer to her brain. She did the best she could, wincing with each stroke of the brush, and quickly braided her hair back. She brushed her teeth quickly and shoved her items back into the bag.

She could feel Shadow watching her, sense her eyes tracking her every move. She tried not to show pain, tried not to wince with every step she took, even though it sent a fiery lance along the entire right side of her body. She was slightly limping, and she knew it, but it was better than crying on the floor.

Carolynn left the bedroom and slowly made her way down the stairs with Shadow at her heels. The smell of French toast wafting from the kitchen made her stomach turn sour and nausea roll through her. She pushed open the swinging door and found Neila standing over the stove with a tall slender man with black hair standing intimately close behind her, his face buried in the crook of her neck, their backs to her. She cleared her throat loud enough to be heard over the pecking noises.

Neila and the man spun around quickly. Neila's cheeks were flushed with color, her emerald green eyes wide. The man felt oddly familiar though different, with eyes similar to her own, only a touch darker.

"Carolynn, we didn't hear you," Neila said, interrupting her thoughts. "You remember Sam."

Carolynn caught herself staring at him and coughed to hide her embarrassment. "Yes, vaguely."

"I was just making breakfast. Are you hungry?" Neila nudged Sam lightly with her elbow, snapping him out of his stupor.

"I hope you don't mind; French toast is my favorite," Sam said, taking a seat at the kitchen island.

Carolynn couldn't help but smile in return. "Mine too," she said, before looking back to Neila apologetically. "I would love some, but I need to be getting to work. Would you mind giving me a ride?"

"Oh, of course," Neila said, laying her spatula down and untying the apron at her waist, setting it down on the marble counters. Food forgotten.

Carolynn waved at Sam as she followed Neila out to the garage and into the Audi. Neila made no protest when Shadow climbed in after her, lying across the back seat, so Carolynn said nothing.

"That wolf really loves you. I'm not sure how you didn't wake up last night with all her howling. She nearly woke up the whole neighborhood trying to get our attention last night on our porch," Neila informed her as she backed out of the driveway.

Carolynn glanced over her shoulder, frowning at the wolf. Shadow's only response was blowing out air loudly through her nose.

"I'm sorry if she was a nuisance."

"Not at all. I think it's great you have such a loyal friend."

Carolynn was surprised by Neila's choice of words. Most people wouldn't consider a wolf a friend. Hell, most would have called animal control on Shadow for pulling a stunt like that in a ritzy neighborhood. The fact that she referred to Shadow as her friend and not a pet was validation she didn't know she needed.

"How are you feeling?" Neila asked, glancing at her out of the corner of her eye.

She was getting tired of that question.

"I'm okay," Carolynn said, staring out the window as the world whizzed past.

Shadow whimpered softly in the backseat, her grey eyes drooping. Carolynn ignored the wolf, and Neila pretended as if not to have heard it.

"Here we are," Neila announced, pulling the Audi in front of the stables. "Call me if you need anything."

"I will. Thank you for everything," Carolynn said before opening her door and stepping out of the vehicle.

She only made it a few yards away from the car before she realized that Shadow wasn't with her. Glancing back, she could have sworn she saw Neila talking with Shadow, but the wolf jumped out of the car before she could even consider walking back. The wolf pushed the car door shut with the side of her body and trotted up to her side, staring out over the fields, sulking.

"Were you just talking to Neila?" Carolynn asked, glancing between the wolf and the car backing away.

That's absurd, Shadow scoffed. *You know I can't talk to anyone but you.*

"But I saw—"

Saw me what? Shadow asked, before turning tail and heading into the stables.

Carolynn blew air out her nose loudly, feeling a headache coming on. She looked up into the cloudless sky, the sun beating down so early in the day. Her skin already felt hot.

She headed inside the stable and into her office, where she didn't find Shadow but Beth, sitting behind her large oak desk.

"Carolynn, finally. I've been waiting forever. Jason's not coming in today," Beth said, anxiously.

Carolynn waved her hand at Beth, motioning for her to get out of the chair. Beth obeyed with a sigh of protest and proceeded to sit on top of the desk instead.

Carolynn carefully sat back in the chair, positioning herself to sit more on her left hip.

"What do you mean, he's not coming?" Carolynn asked, setting her bag on the floor.

"He said he's not feeling well," Beth said, carefully, eyes roaming over her. "Where did you just come from? Did you walk here?"

"Neila dropped me off. Someone broke into my house last night," Carolynn said biting on her nails and swiveling on the chair. "They attacked me."

"Fuck, seriously?" Beth stood up from the desk. "Are you okay? Did they hurt you?"

"I have a cut on my hip," she told her friend, lifting her shirt to show Beth. She didn't bother looking at it. Judging by how the wound seemed to contain its own heartbeat and Beth's sharp intake of breath, she could only imagine how it looked.

"Carolynn, you need to go to the doctor," Beth gasped. She placed the back of her hand on her forehead. "Fuck, you're burning up."

Carolynn tried to ignore the slight panic in her friend's voice, ignore the concern and anxiety that tasted sour in the back of her throat. She knew this was freaking her friend out. Beth had never seen her sick, never seen her injured, and it was scaring the crap out of the both of them.

"No, no doctor." Carolynn shook her head. "There's a reason my mom always took care of my medical stuff. We don't know what's in my blood, what it could reveal about me. No doctors."

"Then we need to call your mom," Beth insisted.

Susana had been an ER nurse for the last twenty years. She had never trusted medical facilities and had done all of Carolynn's own physicals and medical exams since she was a baby. Given her powers and abilities, they didn't trust the system to keep her safe.

But Carolynn shook her head. "No, it'll be fine. I just need rest, and it'll heal," Carolynn said stubbornly. She felt drunk, and lightheaded, and an odd tingling sensation ran down her spine, making her skin crawl.

"Why don't you go lay down in my room," Beth offered, her forehead creased with worry.

"No, can you just take me home? Call Matt in and have him do the chores around the stable?" Carolynn asked. Matt was Beth's cousin, who helped out on the weekends or her days off, though she rarely ever took one, but now would be the perfect opportunity. All she wanted was her bed. "I need to check on my mom and the house."

"Okay, sure." Beth nodded. "And if you feel better, there's a party happening tonight down on the beach. That might be fun."

Beth was trying to offer her a distraction, and nothing screamed distraction quite like a beach party.

"Sure," Carolynn said absently. A party was the last place she wanted to be, but maybe fresh air would do her good. "I'll invite Donnie. I'm sure after a nap, I'll be good as new."

Carolynn tried to stand but could barely feel her legs, let alone stand upright. Beth slung her arm over her shoulder and half carried, half dragged her out.

Shadow, we're leaving, Carolynn reached out telepathically to her wolf.

Shadow came running around the back end of the barn, tongue lolling out of her mouth. *Already? What's happened?*

"I'm tired," Carolynn said out loud, but she could tell by Shadow's thoughts and feelings coming off of her in waves that her wolf wasn't buying what she was selling.

Carolynn didn't remember getting into the car or Beth driving her home.

All she remembered was rocking forward as the Mustang came to a bracing halt, opening her eyes, and finding herself back at her house. Beth came around to the side and helped her out of the car and into the house. The first thing Carolynn noticed when walking through the front door, was how clean it was. No more muddy footprints, bloody puddles, or wood splinters to worry about. The back-sliding glass door was completely replaced.

It was like last night had never happened. Like it was all a bad dream.

If only.

Beth helped her into her bed and placed the covers up to her chin as chills began to rack through her. "I don't want to leave you."

"I'll be fine," Carolynn said through chattering teeth. "Just need to sleep this crap off, and then we can go party tonight."

Beth didn't look so convinced, brows furrowing and eyes filled with worry. "I'll be back in a few hours. Call me if you need anything."

Carolynn drowsily nodded her head. "Promise."

She heard Beth closing the front door and the roar of the Mustang's engine growing fainter as it drove farther away. She settled down into her bed, burrowing further under the covers. She rolled over onto her side as the mattress dipped, shifting beneath her. Shadow curled into her, offering her body heat.

You have a fever.

"I'll be fine," Carolynn repeated for the twentieth time that day.

She closed her eyes listening to the steady rhythm of Shadow's breathing. Her mind felt heavy as she drifted into a dreamless sleep.

Chapter 23

Carolynn bolted upright out of bed, jolting Shadow beside her, as her phone rang somewhere near her head. She searched around for it blindly until her hand met the cold plastic of the phone. She blinked several times, trying to clear away the sleep and gain focus. Without bothering to check who was calling, she flipped it open.

"Hello?"

"Hey, hun, how are you feeling?" Beth's voice came through the phone.

Carolynn glanced around, trying to remember where she was and how she got here. She was back in her bedroom, and from the purples and pinks painting the sky outside her window, she had slept the entire day away. She sat up and felt her head, her chest. No more fever, no more pain.

She knew she just needed sleep.

"I feel great actually."

"Thank God, I knew it was just a fluke. Nothing can take out my Carolynn." Beth's voice jumped up an octave and Carolynn could almost imagine her jumping up and down in her bedroom. "I'm on my way to pick you up for that party if you're still up for it?"

"Absolutely," Carolynn smirked, pushing the covers off and shifting on the bed around Shadow, who refused to move. "See you soon."

Beth had already hung up, and she noticed she had a missed

text from Donnie. He wanted to see her tonight.

She texted him the address where the local youth liked to gather on the weekends, asking him to meet her there, shut the phone, and threw it back on the bed. She went straight for her closet, shuffling through her limited clothes and decided on what was best to wear.

Are you sure you're okay? Shadow asked, still lying on the bed.

"I'm fine, really I am." She gave her wolf an encouraging smile before finally selecting her outfit and change. "But you are not coming to the party. I won't be out long."

The last thing she needed was to show up to a party with her wolf. She got enough weird looks.

Carolynn quickly changed into her outfit and strapped on a pair of black ankle booties. She walked over to her full-length mirror and gave herself a once over. She wore a green and black plaid corset top with black skinny jeans tucked into her boots. She took a quick glance at her hair and knew she could do better. Going back into the bathroom, she turned on the curling iron.

As she was adding the finishing touches to her makeup, Beth's Mustang roared as it pulled in front of her house. Her hair was a mess of long silky loose curls, and the only makeup she wore was a dab of black eye shadow on the outer corner of her eyes, black eyeliner, and mascara. Less was always more.

Carolynn's phone went off as she heard the front door open and close. She picked the small device up off the bed and recognized her mother's number.

"Hey, Mom," Carolynn answered the phone, stuffing a ChapStick in one of her front pockets.

"Hey, baby! I'm so sorry I didn't come home," Susana spoke loudly through the phone. "I fell asleep in one of the on-call rooms, and my next shift starts in thirty minutes. Are you okay at home by yourself?"

Carolynn smiled at Beth as she came in, gave her a once over, and smiled approvingly with two thumbs up. "Yeah, I'm fine. Don't worry about me."

"You're the best, Star. There's money in my sock drawer for pizza if you're hungry, but I'll definitely be home tomorrow night."

Carolynn took a good look at Beth, motioning for her to twirl.

She wore a skintight olive tube dress, black suede wedges, and a leather jacket. Her brown curls were pulled back from her face, pinned behind her ears but hung loosely around her shoulders. She mouthed the word *hot* to her friend.

"Tomorrow night, got it," Carolynn repeated, following Beth out of her house, waving bye to Shadow, and grabbing Donnie's jacket as she left.

"Love you, baby."

"Love you, too," Carolynn said, before hanging up the phone.

"Donnie meeting us there?" Beth asked, slipping into the driver's seat.

Carolynn checked her phone for another message from him and found his reply. "Yep, he's already there."

"Perfect." Beth turned the ignition, firing up the car. "Things seem to be going well for you two?"

Carolynn watched out the window as the sky darkened by the second. A smile bloomed on her face as she remembered last night in the kitchen before everything went to hell. Donnie's face between her thighs, how he had pinned her, and her face grew hot for an entirely different reason. "Very."

"I see that smirk," Beth said, calling her out.

Carolynn didn't say anything more as they neared the beach. The smell of salt in the air was heavy on her tongue. She could taste it, feel it clinging to her skin and eyelashes. As they pulled up, they found the parking lot was jam-packed with cars. They could see the glow of a large fire from where they parked. As they neared the site, bodies blocked the view of the ocean and music blared from a stereo nearby. She pulled the leather jacket on, tightening it around her neck. While it was still hot and humid out, even with the sun setting, the chill off the water rattled her bones.

There was a large bonfire in the center of the crowd. Most of the attendees were kids her own age. She recognized a majority of them from high school; the rest were townies. Some of them noticed her, waving and saying hi. She hadn't seen anyone from high school besides Beth since graduation day.

Carolynn felt a hand rest on her shoulder as she began to enter the throng of people. She was itching to dance and visit with her old classmates when she spun around and found Donnie standing behind her. He wore his usual black Henley, leather jacket, dark wash jeans, and boots. His hair was neatly brushed back, most likely with his fingers as only a single piece hung in his eyes. The only out-of-place thing about him was a thin cut under his eye.

"What happened?" she asked. She looked closer at his skin and could see patches of yellow, fading bruises lying just beneath the skin. They seemed to be healing remarkably fast, since it would take a normal person days for a bruise to fade down to yellow. Given that she just saw him last night very up close and personal with not a single mark on him, something must have happened after he left. He was not only bruised on his face but his arms as well, and that was only the skin she could see, not covered by clothes. She could only imagine what was hidden by the dark shirt.

Instinctively, she reached up and cupped his face, brushing her fingers softly along his cheekbone. He didn't flinch, didn't move, instead leaned into her touch, eyes fluttering closed.

"What happened?" she asked again, softer.

His eyes flashed open, going cold and distant as he pulled back from her touch. "Wrong place, wrong time."

Carolynn flinched, pulling her hand back, and hiding it in her jacket pocket. She swallowed with difficulty as she shifted on her feet. "You got into a fight?" Images of last night flashed through her mind. The attacker, her hair being ripped from her head, cartilage snapping beneath her fist, kicking him through the door.

He didn't answer her. He was holding something back.

"Was it you?" she asked, hating herself for sounding so small and weak, but the possibility had her feeling lightheaded and feverish all over again. It couldn't be him.

Donnie's brows pinched together. "Was what me?"

"Did you break into my house last night?"

"What?" he snarled, tone deep and menacing as darkness swept around him, around them.

"Did you break into my house and attack me last night?" she asked again, this time stronger.

"Did they hurt you?" Donnie's hands gripped her arms, dragging her towards him until their chests touched but that wasn't what shocked her. Shadows brushed back her hair, stroked her neck, grazed down her sides, touching all of her that it could, but he didn't seem to notice—or notice he was doing it at all. Those ice blue eyes only stared at her, wide and fearful. He was afraid for her.

Carolynn's eyes slightly widened, face alight with understanding and realization. "You're like me."

Donnie let her go, nearly dropping her on the ground. The shadows ceased almost immediately, retreating back to wrap at his feet. He scoffed, offering her a smirk that didn't reach his eyes. "What's that supposed to mean?"

"Your shadows, your darkness. I felt them just now, and last night in the kitchen, touching me," she knew she wasn't crazy, knew it was real and he had powers.

Donnie chuckled, eyes bright with laughter. "Did you hit your head?"

Carolynn's face fell, anger bubbling inside. Her skin felt like it was on fire, tight and stretched thin. "Don't do that. Don't make me sound crazy."

"Sorry, kitten, I have no idea what you're talking about," Donnie shrugged, shoving his hands in his pocket.

Her palms burned. He was lying. He was lying directly to her face.

"You asshole," she breathed, tears stinging her eyes. She held it in, kept it together. She would not give him the satisfaction of seeing her cry. "So it was you last night. You tried to kill me?"

Donnie's mask fell, and vengeance darkened his eyes. "I would never hurt you," he promised, and she believed him. Her palms didn't sting. It wasn't rational, it didn't make sense, but she believed him and that made his lie hurt all the more. "I would destroy anyone who touches you."

"Isn't that what they all say?"

Carolynn didn't wait for his reply. She backed away and slipped through the crowd. She could hear him calling to her, feel a slip of his shadows reach out and brush against her hand, but she stepped out of their reach. She felt as though all the oxygen was being sucked from the air.

The attack last night wasn't him. He said he wouldn't hurt her, and her lie detector didn't go off, but then who was it?

Donnie had powers of some kind, that he did lie about, but why? Did he not trust her? What did they really know about each other? While she had shared so much with him, he hadn't shared any of his background with her. She didn't know where he was from, who his family was, where he went to school, or what it actually was that he did for work.

She knew nothing.

Carolynn veered off away from the crowd, towards a small run-down shed in the sand on the outside of the party. She clutched at her stomach as she neared the shed and leaned against the chipped wood, lying her head back. An overwhelming wave of nausea racked her body. She laid her hand on her chest, her neck. Her skin was on fire. She was surprised she wasn't in actual flames. Her body was overheating. She glanced up at the sky and tried to concentrate on the stars hiding behind the wispy clouds as she tried to gain control of her breathing and force air in and out of her lungs.

"Hey, are you okay?"

Carolynn didn't bother to see who it was. She would know that voice anywhere.

Beth came up beside her and leaned against the shed as well. Carolynn refused to look away from the sky, the moon nearly full, beautiful and silver.

"I saw you talking with Donnie. It looked heated. Is everything okay with you two?" Beth turned to face her and froze at what she saw.

She noticed Beth taking in the chilling paleness of Carolynn's skin, and her hands gripping at her stomach, chest rising and falling, heavily and rapidly.

"What's wrong?" she asked, panicked.

Carolynn turned, and Beth's face went stark white. Her grey eyes were bloodshot and her lips were turning a dark shade of blue.

"I can't breathe," Carolynn gasped. Her knees buckled beneath her. She couldn't feel her legs or her arms. She heard a scream before darkness claimed her.

Chapter 24

"Help!"

Donnie's head rose over the crowd. The sound of panic and terror choked the air from his lungs. He knew that voice. Knew who it belonged to.

He ran in the direction of the cry for help, trying to force down the pit that was forming in his stomach as his feet slipped in the sand.

Gods, please don't let it be her.

A large crowd already began to gather near the shed, surrounding two people on the sand. He pushed his way through the crowd, his shadows helping and being a touch more forceful than was needed. In the sand, was Beth kneeling on the ground, tears running mascara down her face, and cradled in her lap was Carolynn. Skin as pale as fresh snow, lips blue, and she was unconscious.

Donnie could barely make out the rising and falling of her chest. He threw himself on the ground beside them and laid his hand against the side of Carolynn's cheek. Her skin was dangerously hot, as though she was burning from the inside. Those perfect lips were the shade of a deep blue due to the lack of oxygen her body was receiving, cracking from dehydration.

Something was killing her.

"What happened?" Donnie asked, panic rising as he pressed his fingers to the side of her throat, checking for a pulse.

She was still alive, but for how much longer?

"She said she couldn't breathe, and then she just collapsed. I don't know what happened," Beth said in between sobs.

Carolynn had said she was attacked last night, he remembered. "Was she hurt?"

"What?" Beth asked, unable to focus.

"Was she hurt? Has she been injured?" Donnie asked again, checking over her arms.

"A cut," Beth finally said. "She has a cut along her hip."

Donnie turned her on her side checking the left first. Nothing. Shifting her the other way he lifted the shirt up and found a bandage. He peeled it back, and the foul smell nearly had him spilling the contents of his stomach all over the sand floor. The wound was infected, but what was worse was the black spider veins dipping below the waist of her jeans and moving up toward her ribs.

Poison.

"Fuck," he growled, pulling her shirt back down.

Donnie slipped his arms beneath her body and lifted her, cradling her against his chest, instantly sweating from the amount of heat rippling off the body. Beth struggled to stand, losing her balance in the loose sand as she chased after him. The onlookers moved out of his way as he nearly ran for his car in the parking lot.

"Where are you taking her?" Beth asked running after him, tears streaming down her face.

"To someone who can help."

Donnie stood on the porch, Carolynn held tightly to his chest, with Beth at his side, looking around at the perfectly manicured lawns and expensive houses. With his fist, he banged on the door loudly. He was being courteous by not outright breaking the door down, but that didn't mean he had to be quiet.

The door opened quickly, and a small woman with dark auburn hair stood on the threshold, ready to give him a good lecture until she took notice of who stood on her doorstep, and the precious bundle in his arms. A tall man stood in the hall behind her, eyes identical to the woman in his arms, brows furrowed as he came to stand behind the woman.

"What the—" Neila started to say, but Donnie didn't give her a chance to finish her sentence as he barged through the front door and into the foyer.

Beth followed him in, eyes wide, taking in everything and everyone around her. He didn't have time to answer the questions he was sure would pour out of her.

"She collapsed," Donnie informed them, cradling Carolynn tightly to his chest. It was the only way he could be sure she was still breathing, her heart still beating.

"She said she couldn't breathe," Beth confirmed timidly beside him.

"I'll take her," Sam said stepping forward but Donnie shot him a glare, baring his teeth. There was no way he was letting her go, not to him.

Neila seemed to accept that he wouldn't be passing her off and gestured towards the stairs. "Let's get her upstairs."

Sam walked up first, taking two steps at a time as the rest followed quickly behind. Down the hall they went, into one of the bedrooms, where Donnie saw a king bed. He placed Carolynn down onto the soft mattress, her body limp and unresponsive as her head lolled to the side. He ran his hand down the side of her face, brushing the hair back. She was still too hot. There was no way her body could take much more.

His shadows demanded to come out, demanded to touch her, to help her, but he kept them back. There was a human in the room, and he couldn't put any of them at risk. When his shadows were involved, he could not contain his primal side, and right now he was already teetering on the edge towards madness.

"She's been poisoned," Donnie growled, low enough for only Sam and Neila to hear. They both whipped towards him, shock and despair plain. "A cut on the hip."

Neila stepped forward as though to look, but Donnie whipped his head towards her, barring his teeth.

"Donnie, we're here to help," Neila spoke softly and carefully, her hands out and open, showing him her pure intentions. "I only want to help."

Donnie swallowed hard, desperately trying to reign in his anger, his instincts. He backed away until his body hit the far wall, arms crossed over his chest so as not to do anything foolish.

Neila made to check her hip when he spoke.

"Right side."

Neila moved towards the right, rolling Carolynn carefully until the skin was exposed. As soon as she pulled back the bandage, the three of them flinched as the smell attacked their senses. Beth stood there, blissfully unaware of Death hanging in the room.

Sam cursed under his breath, his face sunken, shaking his head as though this wasn't really happening. Neila sucked in a sharp breath. Donnie could sense the emotions roiling between the two of them. The worst was before them, and the chances of her surviving—no, he wouldn't think like that. She would survive. It didn't matter what they had to do, he would not let her die.

"It's black venom. It's the only explanation." All eyes turned to him as he stood secured to the wall, his gaze wild and fierce.

"Beth, can you go down into the kitchen? Get some towels and a bowl of water," Neila instructed, trying to get the human out of the room.

Beth nodded, unable to tear her eyes from her friend, but she left room, shutting the door behind her.

"She was attacked last night, but she didn't tell me she'd been hurt," Neila said the moment the door clicked shut, glancing down at Carolynn.

"If that's true, then someone told them where she is and who she is," Sam said, glaring at him.

Donnie met his stare, ignoring the eerie fact that those eyes were twins to her. "They've known about her whereabouts for a while now. It was only a matter of when."

"How do we know it wasn't you who did this?" Sam asked, taking a daring step forward.

The man was brave. Stupid, but brave. He respected that, but the implication he was insinuating would not be tolerated.

"If it was me, she'd have been dead," Donnie said firmly, holding his stare. "I don't miss."

"So you don't deny it?" Sam asked, brow raised, taking yet another step forward. "You think we don't know who you are? What your purpose is? Do you take us for fools?"

"Do you take me for one?" Donnie asked, voice low and menacing. He could feel his eyes darkening as his shadows slipped out, wrapping around him. "As if I don't know who the two of you are?" He glared at both Neila and Sam, as though it wasn't obvious, and anyone with a trained eye could see it. "Now you want to play the concerned figures. Well, where were you when she actually needed you? Too busy preening?"

Sam's eyes widened. Donnie almost smirked. Did the man think he really didn't know?

"Death follows you wherever you go. It's who you are," Sam said, as though he needed a reminder. "Whether it was you or not, she is dead with you either way."

Donnie pushed off the wall, closing the distance between them until he towered over the man. It didn't matter that he technically outranked him. It didn't matter what his position was or his stakes in any of this; he would not tolerate the disrespect.

"Whatever my original purpose was is not my priority now," Donnie promised. "By my blood, my allegiance is to her and only her. Do you understand me?"

He'd done it. He drew a line in the sand that could never be taken back. A vow such as that could only be broken by death, and he saw by the widening of those grey eyes, Sam understood the seriousness of it. It didn't matter if this was his plan or if any of this was his intention. Even if he didn't want to accept it, this had been his path from the moment their eyes connected in that club.

His shadows swept out, curling around his arms, and reaching out for her, stroking her skin, looking to comfort. They needed her, craved her.

She was his. She was his star in a sea of darkness.

Sam almost seemed to relax, his shoulders dropping as he took a step back. Neila exhaled the breath she'd been holding, visibly relieved they hadn't torn each other apart.

"We need to hurry," Neila said, glancing down at Carolynn.

Fire ran through her veins, poisoning every cell in her body. Her skin itched as though there were a thousand fire ants crawling over every inch of her body. Her lungs burned with every small, insignificant breath she took. She was drowning in a sea of flames, desperately trying to escape the heat. She wanted to scream, to tear at her skin, to rip off her clothes, as the mere touch of them caused her searing pain, but she couldn't move. She was frozen, being tortured in her own mind. Frozen in a tundra of fire with no escape, except for the periodic moments of blissful oblivion.

The dream started out the same. Thunder shook the earth and lightning cracked, splitting across the blood-red sky. Terrifyingly beautiful men and women fought against each other with swords in hand. She saw an eerily familiar middle-aged man transform into a great lion, twice the size of one found on the plains of Africa, and lunge for another man wearing a long black cloak. A woman, more beautiful than she could ever imagine, stood in the midst of it all, fighting with men twice her size. A longbow was strapped across her back, and she carried a double edged sword in each hand. Her movements reminded her of dancing as she parried and struck.

There was another man off to the side, molding fire in the palm of his hands, giving it breath and shaping it to his will, firing arrows, hammers, and swords of pure living flame, cutting down everything within a ten-foot radius. She squinted her eyes as she recognized Neila amongst the fighters, fighting nearly as well as the beautiful woman with swords, but unlike the others, her body was covered in bruises and cuts, blood and sweat streaked across her skin.

Overhead, winged humans and creatures of all colors and sizes battled against each other, bodies, teeth, and steel colliding. Some swooped down to the earth, attacking those on land.

Carolynn felt compelled to do something, to help in some way. She tried to move, tried to step forward, but her feet hit something solid. She looked down and found her mother and Beth, dead. Their bodies were broken in irreparable angles. It looked as if something had shattered their bones. Their eyes were glassed over by death. She bent down on one knee and closed their eyes, water dripping onto their faces. She wiped her eyes with the back of her hand and found it wet.

She glanced up, away from her mother and best friend, and found Donnie standing just feet away from her. He wore no shirt and shoes. His chest was streaked with the blood of others and dirt from the chaos around them. He looked as broken as she felt, ice blue eyes heavy, and mouth set into a tight line. He carried a long sword at his side. It looked old, ancient even, with engravings in some foreign language she didn't recognize engraved down its center.

Donnie was yelling something at her, but she couldn't hear him over the battle that raged around them. She wanted to reach out, but a cold, piercing pain bloomed in her chest. Her mouth hung open, her mind not registering the events as an odd warmth trickled from her mouth. Was she drooling? Had she truly lost all control of her faculties? She glanced down at her chest in shock. The tip of a sword protruded from her center, straight through her heart.

Her eyes widened as the world around her darkened and black iridescence filled her vision.

Chapter 25

Something soft and spongy brushed against her skin. No longer did she see flames of deep reds and oranges, but tinges of blue were beginning to seep through. Someone was leaning over her with eyes the most exquisite green she had ever seen.

"Neila?" Carolynn asked, tilting her head to the side.

"No, my dear." The woman smiled sweetly.

Her hair was a rich auburn that was braided in intricate twists into a crown atop her head. Her face was thin, with prominent cheekbones and full cherry lips. She wore a white dress that clung to her body and swept to the floor. It reminded her of mist.

Propping herself up on her elbows, she found herself lying back on lush, spongy grass surrounded by what was in fact white mist.

"Am I dead?" Carolynn asked, her voice echoing into the white abyss.

"No," she said with a simple shake of her head. "Not yet."

Well, that was comforting. "Where am I?"

"I'm not sure you're ready for that."

She wasn't really sure she necessarily wanted the answer either. "What am I doing here?"

"I've brought you here to shield you from your pain. It will only lead to a quicker death if you were left in its clutches."

Carolynn breathed in heavily, digesting her words. She was dying. Somewhere, her body was dying.

"Who are you?" she asked, feeling slightly foolish to ask. She felt as though she should already know, but the answer was just out of reach.

"I think the real question here is who are you?" the woman asked, offering her hand.

Carolynn took it and stood on her own two feet. The hand in hers was soft and gentle, yet contained incredible strength.

"I'm Carolynn,' she said, confused, brows furrowed.

"Who are you really?"

She hesitated, not really sure where this was going. Instead of answering, she shrugged. She didn't even know who she was. Was she human or an alien? Were her powers a gift or a curse? Why did it seem the whole world was after her, when she'd done nothing but live her life and work on a farm? She never hurt anyone, never used her telepathy for bad. She only had one power, was that so wrong?

"You can do so much more."

Carolynn's eyes widened as she looked into her eyes, so bright and green, like the richest rainforest.

You can hear me? Carolynn asked, using only her mind.

Yes.

Carolynn was lost for words. Never before had she met someone who could do what she did, and yet here this woman was. She was stunned frozen, her lungs seizing as she stuttered.

"Listen to me carefully, dear, we don't have much time. Those dreams you've been having aren't just dreams. They are premonitions, visions of your future. Do not ignore them. Do you understand? Do *not* ignore them," the woman said, holding her gaze with severity. "There is a war coming, my child. The fate of our world, your world, is in your hands. Do not be afraid of your powers. Embrace them. Accept them. If you don't, all will be lost."

The words echoed in her ears and in her mind. Carolynn shook her head, sensory overload—information overload. She tried to fit everything the woman was saying together, her words puzzling. If what she was saying was true then that meant her mom and Beth—

"Wait, are you saying my mom and Beth are destined to die?" she asked, her voice breaking as emotion choked her.

"Nothing is written in stone. Events can change. Your actions and those of the people around you can change them, but you must ascend."

"Ascend? Ascend to what?"

"Your power and your destiny."

Carolynn stared deep into her brilliant green eyes when suddenly, it clicked into place. "Your name is Sarena!" she said, recalling the book that was still sitting on her nightstand. "I read a book about you, it had your picture, but—"

"Not all is as it seems," Sarena said, slipping her fingers underneath Carolynn's necklace, cradling the double star pendant in the palm of her hand. "You are our Star."

"Carolynn."

Donnie sat beside the bed, running his hand along her dull auburn hair. Her face was pale and covered in a thin sheen of sweat as her body battled the fever ravishing her system. He noticed how periodically she would scrunch her eyebrows or twitch her lips, mumbling something incoherent. He put his hand softly against her cheek and left it resting there, rubbing his thumb along her skin.

She was still alive. She was still here, with him.

Shadow lay on the bed beside Carolynn, letting out a low whine every now and then, head resting in her lap. The wolf gave him a curt nod, before taking watch.

Donnie got up and left the room, closing the door quietly behind him. Outside the door in the hallway stood Neila and Sam, pacing.

"Where's Beth?" Donnie asked, voice low.

"Sleeping in the next room," Neila jerked her head to the bedroom next to Carolynn's. "Poor thing is frightened to death but is refusing to leave. She has no idea what's going on."

"Nor should she," Donnie said, looking at the closed door that led to Carolynn's friend. She had no business in their world. She would never survive.

"How is she?" Neila asked, referring to Carolynn.

"Weak. Her fever grows stronger by the hour. She doesn't have much time left," Donnie said, stating the obvious. It was already a miracle she had lasted this long, but how much longer could her heart last or her brain from becoming scrambled eggs?

"What do we do? I've never heard of a cure. Have you?" she asked, clinging to some kind of hope.

"Why are you asking him? As if he would help," Sam snickered, glaring at him. "Your job all along was to kill her, and now is your perfect opportunity to let it happen."

Donnie bristled. He glared at the man, his hands tightening into fists at his side as his shadows reared back, but he let it go. Hurting him would only hurt Carolynn. He ignored the male and turned to Neila.

"There might be something, but it's a long shot. It requires me to go home, and if I do find it, it might mean bringing them to your doorstep. Are you prepared for that?" he asked her, laying out the possibilities.

"We can handle our own," Neila declared, standing straighter, reaching for the dagger that he knew was stashed in one of her pockets. "If there's a shot at saving her, we have to take it."

Donnie nodded. "I'll be back as soon as I can. Please keep her alive until I get back."

His heart, or what was left of the shriveled, dead thing inside of him, broke at the idea of leaving her. But he had to take the chance of never seeing her alive again in order to take the sliver of hope of keeping her breathing.

Donnie disappeared before their very eyes in a cloud of black smoke, dissipating with him. Sam glanced around, as though expecting the male to suddenly reappear.

"What if he doesn't come back?" Sam asked.

Neila whirled on the male beside her. Her partner, her lover, her mate, and she nearly knocked his teeth into next week. Instead, she glared daggers at him, threatening violence with her entire being. Thunder cracked outside, shaking the house.

"If you don't stop insulting him, you will have bigger problems than just the two of them being together," she said, eyes sparking. "Are you blind or just that stupid?"

"What are you talking about?" Sam asked.

Gods, he really was dense sometimes.

"Did you not see the way his shadows reacted to her? How his first instinct was to protect her and comfort her? He wouldn't even let you hold her," Neila pointed out, praying he would connect the dots on his own.

"So?"

Maybe not.

"When have you ever seen one of them acting primal?" Neila asked pointedly. "They're mated."

Sam shook his head in clear denial. "No."

"They may not have completed the bond just yet, but it's there," Neila broke the news. "And if you don't get your shit together and let go of your overbearing crap, we will lose her."

"What do you mean, I'm your Star?" Carolynn asked. It was the pet name her mother had always given her, and it sounded weird coming from a stranger who was apparently a Goddess. A real-life Goddess. She pulled back from the woman, letting her pendant fall back against her chest.

"All in good time," the woman said, her voice smooth and calming, like sitting beside a stream and hearing the water run along the rocks. Sarena glanced up towards the deep blue sky that hung above them, as though someone or something was calling to her. She looked down at her with a sad smile. "I must go. It was lovely to meet you, Carolynn. We will see each other again."

She watched as Sarena vanished into the mist. She was there one moment and gone the next. Carolynn twisted around, looking every which way, but there was no sign of the Goddess. A translucent white mist surrounded her completely in a vast, empty space that had no ending. She suddenly felt incredibly isolated and alone.

She wrapped her arms around her body as a cold shiver ran across her flesh At that moment, all she could think of was Donnie. Being wrapped in his arms, held against his warm, hard body, and the instant comfort she felt when she was with him.

Why did she have to be such an ass the last time she saw him? Yes, he had lied, but if that was her last moment with him, she would never forgive herself.

Sarena. She had been speaking to a literal freaking Goddess.

How was any of this happening? Was it all a hallucination? Some part of the fever she was clearly dying from. That stupid cut. She began running through what the Goddess had said and shook her head. If her dreams really were visions, glimpses into the future, then that would mean Beth and her mom were in danger. She had to get back, had to protect them.

Carolynn started to pick through the past week ever since the dreams started. That stupid book Neila had given her. Had Neila known? Did she know about her power, who she was? She had to have.

Then there was Donnie. He had made an appearance in her last dream, standing in a sea of bodies with that wicked-looking blade that looked like it belonged in some Viking movie. How did he fit into any of this? Or Neila, for that matter.

She needed to get back. Needed to speak to Donnie, to hold his hand, and be told everything was going to be okay. The gentle way he cradled her face and brushed her hair back. How amazing their first kiss had been, his lips crushing against hers as though there was no one else in the world but them. His heavenly smell that she longed for and dreaded. It was the first thing she noticed about him and the last of her senses to fade after he would leave.

Carolynn closed her eyes and took in a deep breath, imagining him right in front of her, close enough to touch.

Her eyelids drooped heavily, making it hard for her to open them. Her body felt as if weights were laid on top of her, keeping her from being able to move. Sand had been poured in her mouth, or at least that was how it felt, unbearably dry. She forced her eyes open, vision blurry and unfocused. There was barely any light where she was.

Someone was sitting beside her. She tried to say something, make a sound, but all that came out was a croak.

"Carolynn," someone breathed in relief.

Carolynn glanced over to find Neila sitting beside her, face pale and eyes red and swollen. Her hair was pulled up into a messy bun and her clothes were wrinkled with wear.

She tried to speak, but nothing came out. Neila's eyes widened in realization, grabbing a glass from the nightstand. She placed a hand under her head and lifted her up, tilting the cup to her mouth. Carolynn swallowed a bit, sputtering some as her throat seized up with the motion, but it was better than nothing.

"What happened?" she asked, her voice raspy.

"You were poisoned," Neila said, carefully, as though there was more, but unwilling to say.

Carolynn mulled that over in her head. Explained why her wound wouldn't heal, but why would someone want to poison her? Why had any of the events in the last week happened, was the better question.

"How did I end up here?" she found herself asking, glancing around at the room she spent the night in.

"Donnie brought you."

All that did was bring up more questions, but her body and head hurt too much to think, to process. How did Donnie even know where 'here' was? Did he know Neila?

"Where is Donnie?" Carolynn asked, searching the room as though he might step out of the shadows, but she saw no one.

"He'll be back," was all Neila said.

Carolynn looked into her eyes and smiled weakly. She felt winded and exhausted and just the thought of moving was enough to nearly send her into a coma, but somehow, she managed to move her arm and took Neila's hand in her own. It was warm and soft, but strong. Exhaustion settled heavily on her, but she fought it, or at least she was trying to.

"I'm dying, aren't I?"

Carolynn watched as Neila inhaled sharply, eyes sparkling. "I won't let that happen."

Carolynn tried to take in a solid breath but came up short, her body defying her. She looked up at the ceiling, missing her glow-in-the-dark stars as she tried to force the threatening sea of emotions from swallowing her whole. She could feel the heat within her body climbing. Panic flooded her.

"Donnie," she whispered, before her eyes rolled to the back of her head and her vision went dark.

Chapter 26

Donnie stared down the coast, his boots sinking in the crystal white sand, turquoise blue water lapping at the shore. He hated the beach. Hated the sand and how it got everywhere. Hated the sea and its endless horizon and unknown depths. Hated how the beach was the last place she had been thriving and alive. For all he knew she was already dead.

No. He refused to believe that. He would know if she was gone. He would know.

Pacing back and forth, he constantly checked the watch on his wrist and the cliffs above. In this part of the land, one never knew what might sneak up and try to take a bite.

He stopped pacing as he felt a shiver in the air. A slight rippling, a shift in the ether as she stepped out of a veil of mist and stood before him.

"Sarena."

"Donnie," the Goddess said as though she were surprised, but he knew she wasn't. "You're either very stupid or very brave for calling me at this time." Sarena cocked her head to the side as she examined him closely with those emerald green eyes that saw and heard too much. "But we both know your no fool. Why have you called me?"

"I need your help," Donnie said, biting back the bitter taste of asking a God for help, but he swallowed his pride. "I need to find—"

"Yes, I know all about it, and Carolynn," Sarena said, cutting him off. "But why come to me? You know I don't have the means of finding a cure; that is, if one even exists."

"But you know someone who does. If you could talk to him, get him to understand, then maybe he would help."

Sarena sighed deeply, chewing on her lip for a moment as she thought about his request. Donnie stood there tight-lipped, watching the Goddess with irritation. He wished she would stop doing that.

"I never thought I would see the day you would become a man. Or at least as close to a man as a creature like you could get. You knew the risk to yourself by coming here, and yet you did it anyway," Sarena noted. "All for a girl?"

Donnie almost growled at the Goddess, not caring about the repercussions as he stood straighter, squaring his shoulders. "She's not just a girl."

"I couldn't agree more," Sarena said with a nod. "I'll talk to him and try to convince him, but you're coming with me."

The Goddess extended her hand to him.

Donnie glared at the hand but took the small, fragile-looking appendage, knowing full well it was more lethal and deadlier than most. His eyes widened in surprise as her grip far exceeded his own. He closed his eyes as he felt the ground disappear beneath their feet only to be replaced by soft grass.

Looking around, he found that they were standing in a field of wildflowers. He took in his surroundings and saw that they were walled in on all sides by an endless forest.

A tall, lean man stood next to an oak that looked to be at least fifty feet tall and eight feet wide, his back resting against the ancient wood. They walked closer to him. The first thing that caught Donnie's eye was the piercing grey eyes. They had always made him feel uncomfortable, as though the God could see right through him, much like he experienced with Carolynn.

"Now, you know that I love a visit from you, my dear Sarena, but why have you brought him here?" he asked, without looking up from the blue butterfly perched on his finger, stretching out its delicate, paper-thin wings.

"We need your help, Dominius," Sarena said flatly, cutting to the chase.

She never was one for small talk.

Dominius watched as the butterfly flew out of his hand and disappeared into the green wood. "What can I do for you?"

"I need a cure for black venom," Donnie said, before the Goddess could speak.

"You need a cure? Aren't you usually the cause of pain and death?" Dominius asked, eyebrow raised.

"Not this time."

Dominius stared at him with a stony expression, unmoving and unyielding, before giving him a simple grunt. "Well, if that's the case, then whom might the cure be for?"

"Are you saying there is one?" Donnie asked, the tiniest spark of hope igniting.

"Answer my question first."

Donnie looked to Sarena for help, for some sort of assistance, but the Goddess merely stood there, waiting for his answer as well. Like she didn't already know. He couldn't find the words, couldn't explain his heart or put to words what she was to him.

Sarena sighed loudly. "Dom, it's her. She's been poisoned, and he's trying to save her life."

Dominius jerked upright, stark grey eyes wide. "Who attacked her?"

"We don't know. We've been a little busy trying to keep her alive," Donnie said, voice on the edge of violence. He already owed whoever dealt that cut an introduction to his sword.

Dominius approached him, circling him as though for inspection, looking him up and down like he was searching for something. "What has changed? Why are you now trying to save her life? Wasn't it you that was charged with ending it?" Dominius asked, curiosity peaked.

Donnie's shadows flared, sensing danger, and wrapped around him. They urged him, begged him to return to her, but he quieted them. He was doing this *for* her.

Dominius gasped, taking a step back, hand over his chest. "I have to say, even I never saw this coming."

Donnie ignored the outburst, not bothering to ask what it was the Prophet God saw. "Will you help us or not?"

"Of course." The God nodded, sitting down in the field of

flowers, laying back on the soft grass. "Let me see what I can find out."

Donnie watched as the God closed his eyes and seemingly fell asleep. He looked to Sarena, eyes wide and in a panic. "You have got to be fucking kidding."

Sarena wrapped her hand of steel around his arm and dragged him back with unparalleled strength, especially for someone of her size. Sometimes, looking at her, he forgot she was not only the Goddess of wisdom, but of war as well. He followed her lead, away from the now sleeping God.

"This is how he works; do not interrupt him."

"Does he not understand that we are a little short on time?"

"Believe me, he understands perfectly."

Green surrounded her on all sides. The canopy of dense leaves and branches overlapping above filtered in green light from the sun. Rich moss covered the tree trunks, and the earth was covered in a layer of thick, soft grass. She had never seen so much green in her life. Every which way she turned was an endless forest. Birds sang from their nests above, flitting from tree to tree. Insects flew past her ear, and she swatted at them in annoyance.

Among the variety of life and sounds, she felt calm and at peace. It was undeniably beautiful, untouched and unmolested by man, perfect in its organic setting. It reminded her of the times she used to venture out into the woods just behind her house. When Spot would accompany her as they explored, building forts and pretending enemy forces were trying to invade.

Carolynn felt a sharp pain in her chest as she recalled their last encounter. What if she never got the chance to tell him she was sorry. She never meant to get so heated and say the things she did. She never meant any of it.

She tried to push the thoughts of him to the back of her mind, refusing to let this be the end of her story. When she survived this, she would find him and tell him everything. The new powers that seemed to be multiplying, the attacks, Donnie, everything.

Carolynn began walking. She had no clue where she was or where she was heading, but that didn't seem to matter. She brushed her hand along the trunk of a large tree, wider than the width of her arms and taller than most buildings she saw in the big city.

Immediately she felt as though she had touched an exposed wire. She could feel everything about the tree as though it was an extension of her. From the creepy crawlers slithering over its roots as it took in nutrients from the earth, to the water being filtered through its trunk, to the branches that were homes to thousands of creatures and animals alike. and the leaves basking in the sun, absorbing its energy to be reused. She could feel it all.

It was overwhelming yet so beautiful.

She continued walking, her hands outstretched, brushing against everything she could. She began to pick up different vibrations, different voices from each tree, bush, and flower she touched. As though each had its own consciousness, its own heartbeat, and thoughts. Each and every one of them unique and precious. She felt more alive than she could ever remember feeling, which was ironic, considering the that she was, in fact, dying.

As she continued her stroll through the seemingly endless forest, she heard voices. Stopping where she was, her breathing slowed as she strained to hear, trying to tell where it was coming from. She turned her head slightly to the left. They were coming from that direction. The holly bush her hand was resting on told her so.

Donnie could feel his patience wearing thin but knew it was best to hold his tongue. He glanced at Sarena, the most bewitching Goddess in their realm, and watched as she stared peacefully into the Evergreen Forest. As he observed her, his heart pained him, being reminded of Carolynn. For all he knew, she was dead already and this was all for naught.

He refused to believe that. He would know if she was gone. He would feel it somehow.

He would save her no matter the cost.

A flicker of movement caught his eyes as Dominius sat up from the ground. His face was sullen as he pushed his long, thin fingers through his fine brown hair.

"Well?" Donnie asked impatiently.

"I found something." Dominius stood up and staggered forward a step.

Sarena was beside him in less time than it took a heart to beat. She put her arm around his waist, holding him up until he was steady on his own feet. She assisted him over to a large stump in the ground, worn down from eons of use.

Donnie tried to wait patiently as the God collected himself, but his shadows were nipping at his heels, urging him to leave, to get back to her. He wanted to scream at the God to hurry.

Dominius took in a deep breath, as though still processing whatever it was he saw. "There is a loophole to everything, even the black venom."

"What did you find?" Sarena asked, voice calm and ethereal.

Donnie was impressed with the Goddess's ability to hold herself together with quiet dignity and patience as she stood several feet away from him, her hands folded neatly in front of her. He understood her stake in all of this, well, at least some of it, and couldn't imagine the turmoil going through her. Her face hinted at no emotion except for her brilliant green eyes. They were troubled and fixed intently on the Prophet God.

"There is a way to cure the girl, but it is not a path to choose without consideration of its consequences. You must choose," the God said, directing his words strictly at him.

Donnie's heart warmed in his chest. There was a way after all.

"There is no choice to make. I won't let her die," Donnie stated facts. "What do I need to do?"

"Your blood is the key."

Donnie stilled, his body going slack, arms hanging loosely at his sides. He blinked slowly as though time had actually stopped, his mind processing what the Prophet God was implying.

His blood. Only his blood could save her.

He swiveled his head to the war Goddess, eyes accusing. "Did you know about this?"

Sarena's mouth hung slightly open. She licked her lips, teeth grazing along the bottom. "No," she breathed.

Her surprise was believable enough, but that didn't help the fact of the matter. Which was how utterly fucked he was.

Donnie rubbed at the back of his neck, fingers raking through his hair as he tried to think through all of the possible outcomes. Of all the things he thought of to save her, this was nowhere on the list of possibilities. He glanced back to the Goddess and found her watching him intently.

"Thank you for your help," Donnie said to the Prophet, trying to keep his voice from shaking as his nerves wrecked through him. He felt as though there was an earthquake happening internally, feeling unsteady and ready to crumble at any moment.

"I wish there was an easier way," Dominius said, sincerely.

Donnie slid the mask on, leaving his face expressionless, offering the two Gods a nod of respect.

He noticed a slight change in the Goddess's posture, eyes narrowing, glancing over his shoulder.

"Come, Dominius. We have a guest coming, and we shouldn't intrude." She looped her arm through Dominius, hoisting him up off the stump.

"But I—" Dominius started to say.

"Not today, dear," she said, patting his arm.

Donnie felt the skin on his forehead scrunch together as he watched the two of them disappear in a cloud of white mist. The Goddess gave him a soft dip of the head towards the forest at his back before she portaled the two of them away.

He slowly turned, following her general direction, and froze.

Chapter 27

Carolynn could see pure, white light filtering from a break in the vast forest just ahead. She pushed forward through the trees and brush, no longer mesmerized by the surge of energy she experienced every time she touched a bush or the bark of a tree. No, something deep inside urged her forward, quickening her pace. A voice whispered inside her head to go, to leave the safety of the forest and venture out into the unknown. Like a net had been cast out, and she was caught in it. As though an invisible string had been tied around her and something or someone was pulling her along the length of it.

As she neared the edge of the tree line, she became over-whelmed and frightened. The sudden harsh light blinded her for a few moments. She raised her hand, shielding her eyes as they adjusted, blinking hard. Slowly, she began to recognize she was at the edges of a rather large meadow set in the middle of the woods. The grass reached up to her knees and there were spots of orange, yellow, red, and blue wildflowers scattered throughout the soft green grass. The sight snatched her breath away.

She had never seen anything more beautiful.

Stepping farther out into the clearing, leaving the shelter of the forest behind, movement out of the corner of her eye caught her attention. She turned slightly to her left and was surprised to find three people standing out in the meadow. Two of them wore clothing that seemed to belong to another time, another world. She instantly recognized Sarena with her crown of auburn braids and stunning beauty, locking arms with a tall, thin man, handsome with eyes that spoke to his years. His eyes held her own, startling her as she jerked a step back. They were the exact same color as her own.

Carolynn looked to Sarena, eyes wide with a million questions racing through her mind when the Goddess winked.

Good luck, she heard the soft voice in her head merely a second before the two dissipated in a cloud of pure mist.

Of the third individual, all she could see was black clothing and a spine of steel, shoulders rigid, and raven black hair. She knew that hair, would recognize it anywhere as the rays from the sun struck it, reflecting greens, blues, and purples.

He turned towards her, the movement slow and deliberate, but that didn't stop her heart from stuttering in her chest, her pulse quickening at the sight of him. A sob caught in her throat as she raised her hand to her mouth, covering the noise. She wanted to run to him, to leap into his arms and never let him go, but his expression kept her feet planted where they were. His hands were clenched into fists at his side and released, repeating the gesture, anxious about something. Those marvelous ice-blue eyes were distant and dull, as though all hope had been erased. His hair was a mess, like he had been running his fingers through it repeatedly, and the color was drained from his skin.

Carolynn was afraid to be the first one to talk. Afraid that if she spoke, he might shatter into a thousand pieces, confirming that this was in fact a nightmare, a beautiful illusion, and that she really was dead. Or maybe it was a hallucination, her brain offering her some form of peace before her body finally gave out to the poison. She tucked a strand of hair behind her ear and took a small step towards him.

"Donnie?" she called out, voice raw and breaking.

The sound of his name, her voice, seemed to have shaken him out of some state. He rushed forward, closing the distance between them faster than she imagined, as though the wind carried him forward, and swept her into his arms. She buried her face in his neck, and he did the same, breathing each other in. A cry broke free as her fingers dug into his shirt, clinging to his shoulders, holding him tightly against her.

Where only moments ago he was a frozen statue, with nothing but the wind blowing through his hair to indicate he was real, now his body molded perfectly against hers. His arms wrapped around her waist, lifting her feet from the ground. She wrapped her legs around his waist as she wound her hands in his hair, feeling the silky strands between the tips of her fingers. She could feel his hands running down the length of her back, feeling her, touching her, as though he wasn't sure she was real and needed the reassurance. Hot tears rolled down her face as she took in his scent.

He was really here.

Donnie set her down, her feet back on the ground, but that didn't mean he let go. His hands came up, cupping her face, brushing her hair back, and whipping the tears away with the calloused pads of his thumbs. He kissed her eyes, her nose, before his lips finally found her mouth. It was quick and brief, but bruising. She kissed him back, dragging him forward as her hand gripped him by the back of his neck, the other hand digging into the fabric of his shirt at his hip.

They pulled away, taking in steadying gulps of air, resting their foreheads against one another.

"I was afraid I lost you. I didn't think I'd ever see you again," Carolynn said, her voice breaking.

"Even when the last star winks out and darkness comes for us all, I will find you," Donnie vowed.

"Am I dead?" she asked, afraid to look in his eyes for the truth.

"No," he said. Her palms didn't burn, didn't even sting. "You're going to be fine."

Even if he believed that to be true, that didn't mean it would come to pass. But if this wasn't a hallucination or a dream, how was he here? Where was here?

"Neila told me I'd been poisoned," Carolynn said, eyes closed as she took comfort in his hands running through the length of her hair and down her arms.

Donnie straightened, eyes searching hers. "You talked to Neila? How? When?"

"I woke up, but only for a minute," she said, shuddering as the memory of the intense fire consuming her body and then the black abyss she'd fallen into afterward flashed through her mind.

Donnie pulled her in closer, wrapping his arms around her back. She laid her head on his chest, hugging him.

"Is this all a dream?" she found herself asking as she caught sight of something human-like flying above their heads.

Carolynn felt his breath hitch against her cheek as though struggling with the decision to be honest or not. She could almost hear his thoughts, almost taste the turmoil roiling through him. She pulled back, tilting her head up, searching his face. She could tell what he had to say, what he thought, wouldn't be easy to take, may not even be easy to understand, but she needed to know.

"Tell me, please," she said, her voice softly pleading.

Donnie looked down, eyes holding hers as his lips pressed into a thin line. "It's all real."

Carolynn swallowed with some difficulty as she glanced around them. A place that seemed to be filled with magic and life beyond her understanding.

"I'm guessing we're not in Florida anymore?" she asked sheepishly, brow raised. She knew how stupid that sounded, how lame, but she couldn't work it out any other way.

"No," Donnie said flatly.

Still no tingling or pins and needles in her palms. He was telling the truth.

"Those people you were with. Sarena, she's really a God?"

Donnie nodded, slow and deliberate.

"How do you know her? How is any of this even happening?" she asked, the questions tumbling out of her faster than she could process. "If I'm not dead, then how am I here, but my body is back at Neila's?"

Donnie ground his teeth as he stood there. Was it a matter of him not being able to tell her? Or he just wouldn't?

"How do you even know Neila? I've never mentioned her before to you," Carolynn continued asking, their blissful bubble popping as she backed up a step. He didn't let her go, didn't remove his hands from her arms, but they did loosen, allowing her some space. "Why wouldn't you take me to a hospital if I was poisoned? My mom is a nurse, she could have helped. Does my mom even know what's happening to me or where I am?"

"No," he said automatically, face hard and unyielding. "She

knows nothing of your current state, and the humans would know nothing about the poison trying to kill you."

That word.

Carolynn could tell by the widening of his eyes and his stubborn jaw, he slipped up. Humans.

"I'm not a human," she said as a statement, no longer a question.

Donnie didn't answer, didn't speak. He didn't nod his head or tell her no. But his silence was enough. Deep down, she knew it all along, but having it confirmed, or as close as she'd ever get to confirmation, was a hard blow.

She swallowed hard, mouth dry and throat tight. "If I'm not human, then what am I?"

Did she really want to know? What were her options?

"Am I a monster?"

"No," Donnie said automatically, finally speaking. His hands came up to cup her face, thumb stroking her cheek, fingers pressing into the back of her neck, holding her firmly between his hands. "You are not a monster. I would know."

Carolynn tried to breathe through the emotion choking her, bubbling up from deep inside, her eyes stinging. She took in a deep breath through her nose and released it slowly. "Then what are you?"

Something tickled her legs, sliding up her jeans and wrapping around her waist. She glanced down between them to find silky, dark grey shadows wrapped around her, coming from him.

"I'm the monster," Donnie said, holding her gaze steadily, lips just barely parted. "I'm the creature that nightmares are made of and darkness hides from. I am Death."

Carolynn felt no stinging in her palms, no burning at all. He truly believed that of himself, that he was a monster. She gnawed on her lip, staring at him, waiting for him to say something, but he didn't.

"I don't believe you," she finally said.

"It doesn't make it any less true."

"You would never hurt me."

The moment those words left her mouth, she knew them to be fact. How could she ever have thought he would be the one who attacked her? How could she have not trusted him?

Donnie looked down at her, eyes hooded. There was no light

in his eyes, no smirk or dimple. No hint at teasing or playfulness.

"Just because I would never purposefully harm you, doesn't mean I wouldn't hurt others."

Carolynn could hear the threat behind his words. Could hear the promise in them. He would not hurt her, but he would hurt anyone who threatened her, and that did something, that caused a stirring in the depths of her body, awakening her.

"How much time do we have left?" Carolynn asked. She didn't know how she knew, but she knew she was on borrowed time.

His grip on her neck and face tightened, as though refusing to believe the inevitable. "You are not dying."

"Is there a cure?" she asked, hope budding inside.

Donnie swallowed, Adam's apple bobbing in his throat. "In order to save you, I have to lose you."

Carolynn's brow furrowed. "I don't understand. You don't want to be with me?"

His timing was a bit shitty.

"The poison has a cure, but its side-effects…" he trailed off, as though words were failing him. "My past is dark and terrible and violent and drowning in blood. Most of my deeds are unforgivable and not necessarily ones I regret."

Carolynn took in his words and the seriousness with which he said them, but didn't understand what that had to do with a cure. It couldn't be as bad as he was making it out to be, could it? But had she ever really known him to be dramatic? They had only known each other for less than a week. How much did she really know about him?

She shook her head trying to clear the questions that left her doubting them, herself, and him. "How does your past have anything to do with saving me? Do you have such little faith in me that you think I would just turn my back on you?"

Heat rose to her cheeks and chest as anger and hurt flooded her.

"Carolynn," he breathed, brushing his thumb along her skin.

Carolynn leaned into the touch, savoring her name on his lips when a liquid fire filled her veins. Her body was overtaken, consumed by a fire that had no beginning and no end. She opened her mouth to scream, but no sound left her. She felt paralyzed, unable to move or speak. She could see Donnie's expression turn panicked, eyes wide, and his mouth was moving, but she couldn't hear the words. Darkness surrounded her. Something brushed against her face and her back, enveloping her in its warmth, but she focused on those crystal blue eyes as she drowned.

Chapter 28

"**S**am!"

Sam stood in the kitchen, making sandwiches when he heard Neila's scream. He raced up the flight of stairs, taking the steps two at a time. His mind was racing as he pushed open the bedroom door.

Inside, Beth and Neila were on each side of the bed, panic etched in the worry lines on their faces. He spotted Shadow lying at the foot of the bed, making a soft whining noise up towards the body writhing in bed. Her clothes were soaked with sweat, hair sticking to her face, shoulders, and arms. She lay in the middle of the mattress, convulsing, limbs and head thrashing in the air.

"What happened?" he asked, trying not to sound as frightened as he felt.

"I don't know," Neila said, watching the girl. "One minute she was fine, and the next..."

Her voice trailed off. None of them knew what to do or how to help. They had never felt so powerless in their life.

"It must be the poison," Sam finally said. "Shadow, lie on top of her. We have to hold her down before she hurts herself." Or them, but he left that part unspoken.

Sam moved to the foot of the bed and grabbed a hold of Carolynn's feet, pinning them down on the bed.

Beth took the hint, doing the same on her side with Carolynn's arm, and Neila the other. Shadow climbed on top of the thin girl, firmly laying her large body on top of the girl's chest and torso.

"This can't be all we do?" Beth said, near hysterics. "We need to take her to the hospital. We have to do something. We can't just let her die!" Beth cried out, tears brimming.

The poor child was in a strange house, surrounded by strangers, watching her friend slowly die from a poison she'd never heard of.

"Beth, we're doing everything we can for her right now. Just take a deep breath," Neila said, trying to coax the girl out of a panic attack, but he knew her well enough. Neila was near to doing the same.

"Donnie, where the hell are you?" Sam shouted up at the ceiling, unsure if the bastard could even hear him wherever it was he went.

Donnie charged through the bedroom door, nearly ripping it off its hinges, and rushed towards the bed. "I'm here."

"Well?" Neila asked, desperation in her voice as she struggled to keep Carolynn's arm down.

Donnie looked to Beth, his eyes slightly glassed over as shadows rose from the floor, slithered across the bed over Carolynn and the wolf, towards the girl. Before Sam could shout or move, the shadows slid up her nose and down her mouth. He ran to Beth, catching her as her eyes rolled back and she lost consciousness.

"What the fuck?" Sam shouted.

"She's only asleep," Donnie said, not a single ounce of hesitation or remorse. "She can't be a part of this."

While Sam didn't approve of his methods, he couldn't disagree. The girl needed to be kept as far away from their world as possible. He moved her limp body to a sofa chair in the corner. He would move her to the next bedroom, but first things first.

"What did you find? Is there a cure?" Neila asked impatiently, voice rising.

"My blood."

Sam could have sworn the room dropped to freezing temperatures as everyone in the room stilled, taking in those two simple words.

Neila looked at him, mouth open in disbelief, eyes wide with fear.

"Absolutely not!" Sam roared, rage filling him.

"Sam," Neila pleaded, glancing down at the girl on the bed,

with hope and despair.

"No," Sam shook his head. "I will not have her living with everything you've ever done. All those wars and people you slaughtered, tortured, and maimed. She will carry those memories with her for the rest of her existence."

He knew his words were falling on deaf ears. Knew the bastard understood the consequences, that he might in fact lose her, and yet had still offered it as an option. Blood was sacred in their world. It contained an eternity of memories with it, and the fact that Donnie's blood was the answer filled Sam with dread and despair.

Donnie stood up, wind blasting Sam back as a gust erupted from him. "You think I don't know that?" the male snarled. "You think I want that for her? We don't have a choice; this is the only way."

"Says who?" Sam challenged and lifted his head in defiance. This could be some sick, twisted fantasy of his.

"Dominius."

That one name, of course. Sam's shoulders instantly fell as defeat coated him.

"Do it," Neila said from beside the bed. "Do it now, before she's too far gone."

She nudged the wolf off Carolynn's now still form and moved back away from the bed, away from the girl, and stood at Sam's side. Together, they watched as Donnie sat beside her on the bed, the mattress dipping beneath his weight. His hand came up to cup her face, brushing the hair back that was stuck to her skin. The gesture was intimate and gentle, something they never could have imagined.

Donnie reached into his pocket and pulled out something metal, flipping it open. The pocket knife gleamed in the light. The both of them flinched as he ran the sharp edge along his wrist, the smell of salt and iron permeating the air.

Donnie looked down at her. "I'm sorry," he whispered, before placing his weeping wrist against her mouth.

Sam felt bile rise to the back of his throat. His instincts screamed at him to stop this, to throw Donnie off of her and end this foolishness, but he stayed firm, slipping his hand in Neila's, clutching to her for strength.

Carolynn's mouth wrapped around his wrist and drank, taking

in the blood she needed. Donnie's shoulders spasmed, as though trying to keep himself contained. He pulled his wrist free, the wound already healing before their eyes. Drops of crimson dripped from her mouth. Donnie picked up the washcloth on the nightstand and dabbed at her lips, removing any trace of the substance. He rested the back of his hand against Carolynn's forehead.

"Her fever is already breaking," he announced to the room.

Sam and Neila audibly exhaled, as relief allowed them to finally breathe. She was going to be okay.

Donnie stared down at her. Eyes were still closed, still asleep, but she was at peace. Already, her temperature was going down to normal levels, and her breathing was strong. She was a fighter.

He caught movement out of the corner of his eye. Sam lifting Beth and taking her out of the room, but he didn't move. He took her hand in his own, so small, so fair and perfect compared to him. She was innocent, pure. If she stayed with him, that would change. He would corrupt her in some form or another.

"I know that look," Neila said. Somehow, she had moved to the other side of the bed without him realizing.

"Stay out of my head," he snarled, the threat clear. It was bad enough the Gods could see right through him; he didn't need her to see as well.

Neila chuckled, ignoring that her life had been threatened. "I couldn't even if I wanted to, but you're not as hard to read as you think you are."

"Do tell," Donnie said, sarcastic. As if he truly wanted her opinion.

"You think she won't choose you, or that if she does, you'll somehow be her downfall," Neila said.

Donnie shifted on the bed, uncomfortable beneath her green eyes. Maybe she was lying about not reading his mind.

"Did you think that maybe you two could be stronger together? A balance?" Neila suggested, brow raised.

Donnie didn't say anything; he didn't need to. Instead, he rubbed his thumb along her slender hand. Maybe he should leave. Would she remember their time in the meadow?

"Thank you," Neila spoke, breaking the silence. "For saving her life."

"I will always protect her," Donnie said automatically, voice like steal and fire, the wall through which any and all would have to break if they wanted to reach her.

All they could do was wait. Wait to see if the poison had caused any permanent damage. Wait to see what kind of reaction his blood would have on her. Wait to see what she remembered.

Carolynn could feel the poison lick through her veins. Her body convulsed uncontrollably, and there was nothing she could do. She could hear muffled voices far off in the distance but couldn't make out a single word, as though her ears were stuffed with cotton. She felt pressure on her chest, arms and legs. Someone was holding her down, touching her. The feeling of their skin on hers felt as though a thousand needles were being forced into her flesh, repeatedly stabbing her. She wanted to scream at them to get off, but no sound escaped her lips.

Couldn't they see they were hurting her?

The pain suddenly ebbed, transitioning into a dull ache. Her body quieted, and she felt lighter, no longer weighed down or assaulted by the poison. Her heart was beating slower, stuttering in her chest, barely moving blood through her body. This was it. She would never open her eyes again. She would never see her mother or Beth, go to college, or ride Tempest. She would never tease Shadow or fight with Spot. She would never touch him again or stare into those wonderous blue eyes.

A voice reached her in the void as she drifted. She could hear it more clearly over the other. It was deeper, echoing her heart. She couldn't remember his name, couldn't call out to him, but he was here. She knew he was. No, he couldn't be here. She didn't want him to watch her die, to say goodbye.

Carolynn lay still, praying death would take her swiftly. She didn't want this dragged out. Her consciousness slipped out of her body, and she knew this was it; this was her end. Slowly drifting away, something snagged her back. A smell. Something hearty and vital, something filled with death and life, past and present. Someone was moving her, raising her head.

Once again, that invisible tether around her heart pulled taut, holding her to this plane, to her body. She knew it was him holding on to her, refusing to let her go. Voices spoke around her, and she could have sworn she heard Spot, sounding accusing and angry, sad even. The words eluded her, unable to understand what they were saying, but the smell of iron and salt permeated up her nostrils. She knew the smell, knew what it was, but thinking was getting harder. Her mind was growing heavy, filling with a blackness that should have terrified her, but she didn't feel anything anymore.

She could feel herself begin to pull away, away from her body. A sense of calm overcame her, but it was all ripped away when she was forcibly slammed back into her body. A warm, sticky fluid was being forced in her mouth and down her throat. It was thick and vile, tasting of copper. Her mind was repulsed, but she felt her mouth open and her lips wrap around something firm and hard, taking more. The liquid spread throughout her body as her heart began to pump faster, harder, and more consistently. Everywhere the liquid touched, her body seemed to absorb it, taking it in as though it was life itself. Strength slowly returned to her. Whatever it was, was destroying the poison and healing her.

The miracle cure continued running its course, traveling through every inch of her. She could feel energy creeping back into her muscles and limbs. She knew the poison was nearly out of her system when the strange antidote finally reached her mind.

A brief image flashed.

Donnie.

Though not the Donnie she knew. This man was much darker and sinister. He stood on top of a bridge that was engulfed in fire. The flames grew brighter and stronger as it licked across the ebony night sky, the smoke choking out the stars and view of the city below.

Donnie's hair was different yet the same. It reached down to his shoulders in smooth, soft waves, though still as dark as a starless sky and disheveled. His eyes were still blue and as pale as the moon, but they weren't the light, tender ones that she caught staring at her, taking her in inch by inch. These eyes were daring and malignant, drinking in the mayhem and destruction around him as the bright flames reflected in his eyes. Those tender lips that she loved to kiss were turned into his devilish smile, but there was no dimple, no teasing. This wasn't sexy and flirting, it was terrifying and spelled Death. He wore a white tunic that hung loosely around him, billowing in the wind, with black linen trousers and bare feet.

What stood out the most was something dark that seemed to surround him. It was too prominent to be his shadows, and given the fact that it was night, that seemed unlikely. They stretched out on both sides of him, reaching nearly forty feet in width.

As Carolynn watched not only him but the landscape that surrounded them, memories and recognition began to fit some of the pieces together as she recognized landmarks. They were in London, England, at the London Bridge of 1212. Confusion settled over her. How could she recognize a place and time she'd never been? None of this looked familiar to her. The wooden structures certainly didn't exist in present-day London or any of the movies she had seen. But that wasn't the only thing that stumped her.

Why would she be dreaming of Donnie during an event that she never knew about? And why would she dream of a version him that existed eight hundred years before her birth?

Carolynn could feel every emotion and hear every thought as though they were her own. She could experience the joy he felt from the mayhem that was happening below. Men's, women's, and children's screams tore through the air as they tried to escape the deadly flames that consumed the bridge and spread to the neighboring buildings. The disorder and chaos excited him. The stench of burnt flesh overwhelmed him with such intensity he shivered with pleasure.

It was as though she was Donnie, his mind, his body, experiencing it in real time the way he had all those years ago. The structure beneath his feet—their feet—crumbled. The beams splintered, fracturing the foundation. Just as the bridge collapsed into the river, she thought for sure that he would fall as well and was shocked to find that not only had he not fallen along with the bridge into the raging river of the Thames, but that he was actually suspended in midair.

A low pulsing sound reverberated through her body, pushing against her ears. She gasped, closing her eyes in disbelief as she caught sight of them.

Carolynn opened her eyes, realizing she was no longer dreaming.

Chapter 29

arolynn blinked her eyes open, vision hazy and clouded. Her body felt heavy and groggy, but she could at least pull herself up into a sitting position—granted, slower than she would have liked. She glanced around the room and found herself back in the same bedroom she had slept in at Neila's. Shadow was sleeping soundly beside her legs, the weight and heat a familiar comfort.

Hey, Carolynn reached out to her wolf telepathically.

Shadow's grey eyes shot open, slightly disoriented as she found her. *Carolynn.* She sighed with relief.

Carolynn offered her a small smile, petting the wolf along the top of the head, scratching behind the ears.

You scared us, Shadow said, voice almost breaking.

I know. I scared myself, Carolynn admitted silently.

She glanced around the room and found Neila dozing in the armchair beside the bed.

"Neila," Carolynn said softly.

Neila opened her eyes lazily, blinking away the sleep. She sat up suddenly, throwing the blanket off that had been covering her. She wiped at her eyes, removing the gathering moisture as a warm smile lit her face. "You're awake. How are you feeling?"

Carolynn tucked a piece of hair back behind her ear and shrugged, the movement sore and sluggish. "A bit achy and tired, but okay."

Neila nodded as though that was expected. "You've been through a lot. I'm just glad you're okay."

"How long have I been out?"

"Almost two days," Neila said.

Carolynn couldn't help the surprise and shock that she was sure was plain on her face as her mouth hung open and brows furrowed. She had lost two whole days? It barely felt like a few hours. She glanced down and found herself wearing a wrinkled gray t-shirt twice her size and based on the familiar smell, she knew exactly whom it had come from. She ran her fingers through her hair and found it combed through, not the bedhead she had expected. Someone had cleaned her up and taken care of her. But who?

"Donnie?" Carolynn asked, glancing around. "Where is he?"

She remembered everything. Her dreams, Sarena, the green forest and that gorgeous meadow, her and Donnie's conversations, him admitting she wasn't human, all of it. While she had an insane amount of questions, mostly she just wanted him, to hold his hand and know they were alive. That she wasn't crazy.

Where was he?

The bedroom door opened wide. She sat up straighter in bed, heart pausing as her chest warmed, but whom she had wanted to see was not who was bouncing forward onto her bed. Beth was in an entirely different outfit than the one she remembered. Her tangled hair was pulled up into a messy bun. For the first time in what felt like forever, Beth wore no make-up or jewelry of any kind. Her best friend squealed as she took in the fact that Carolynn was awake and talking.

Beth pulled her into a bone-crunching hug, practically yelling in her ear, but she didn't mind. She was glad to be alive as she wrapped her arms around her friend and hugged her, patting her back.

"I can't believe your awake! You had me so scared. I seriously thought you were going to die," Beth said, voice high-pitched and animated. "You're not supposed to scare your best friend like that! At least not until we're old, with gray hair and wrinkly, saggy skin." She unwrapped herself and lay back against the headboard beside Carolynn.

"Agreed." Carolynn smiled, feeling a bit like her old self with Shadow and Beth. "I'm sorry for scaring you." She had more to say. Like how much of a sister Beth was to her and how much she appreciated the fact that she stayed by her side the entire time, but Beth didn't let her get a word in.

"Did you know that I am the bestest friend in the entire world? Because I am," Beth informed her.

"And how is that?" Carolynn raised a brow, unable to contain the smile over her friend's usual dramatic use of language.

"I have been covering your ass." Beth smirked. "I've been telling my dad that you are locked away with some boy. Better than telling him you're sick, 'cause he would drive to your house to check on you, and you know it." Carolynn nodded her head at that. Thomas was the only father figure left in her life, and he most certainly would have checked up on her to see if she was okay. While she wasn't particularly fond of the idea that Beth had made it sound like she had been secluded with a man for the last two days, it was better than the truth.

"And my mom?" Carolynn was almost too afraid to ask.

Beth grew unnervingly silent, averting her gaze. "Your mom has been a bit more difficult to manage."

Somehow, that didn't surprise her. Her mother was either one extreme or another. She was either extremely absent of mind and presence or overbearing and super observant, nothing between.

"And?" Carolynn prodded.

"I told her you've been at my house, but she's been insistent on talking to you," Beth said. "Somehow I've managed to keep her away, but I don't know how much longer she'll wait."

"Where's my phone?" Carolynn asked, looking around the room for a small, ancient flip phone.

Neila opened the bedside table drawer, pulled out the familiar device, and handed it to her. "Here you go."

"Thank you," Carolynn said, searching through her contacts, heart dropping at the number of missed calls and texts.

"Babe, are you sure you want to do that now?" Beth asked, sounding almost worried. "I can handle your mom."

"No, it's best if she hears from me. I can't have her come searching for me." Carolynn shook her head, eyes darting to Neila quickly. There was still too much she didn't know. The last thing she needed to do was involve her mother. "I have to do this."

Beth nodded along with Neila, both staying close. Shadow

laid her head in Carolynn's lap, offering a place to lay her hand, distracting her from the nerves buzzing in her stomach.

Carolynn held the phone to her ear as the phone rang twice before a frantic, feminine voice answered. "Carolynn Ranae, where the hell have you been?"

Carolynn cringed at the stern tone, swallowing hard. "Hey, Mom," Carolynn said meekly, glancing at Beth with wide eyes. "I've been at Beth's."

Crap, could she be any lamer? She should probably have gotten her story straight before calling.

"If you have been at Beth's, then why have you not called me back the last twenty times I've called you? Why have I only ever heard from Beth? Why did Thomas say he hasn't seen you in days?"

Beth's eyes were as wide as saucers.

Fuck. She was fucked.

"Would you like to try again?" Susana asked through the phone.

Carolynn glanced up at the ceiling, exhaling loudly. Neila's leg was jigging beside her anxiously, and Beth would most likely be in as much shit as she was when she got home.

We can just run away, Beth thought loudly.

As tempting as that was, it would solve zero problems.

"I'm sorry we lied, Mom," Carolynn said. Sticking as close to the truth as possible was her best bet.

"I understand you're going through a lot of changes, and that must be scary. But you cannot disappear for days without telling me where you are," Susana said, voice breaking.

Carolynn felt like an ass, an absolute ass. She had left her mother terrified, most likely thinking the worst. While the worst had almost happened, it didn't lessen her guilt.

"I'm sorry," she repeated, eyes burning. She really wanted her mom. Wanted to curl in her lap while Susana stroked her hair and told her everything would be okay, like she used to do when she had nightmares.

"Are you okay?"

Carolynn breathed in slowly through her nose, trying to combat the raging emotions inside. Shadow snuggled closer, licking her hand, and Beth burrowed down into the mattress, snuggling closer and holding her hand. Neila stood up from where she was and left the room quietly, offering them some privacy.

"I am now."

Susana seemed to pause for a moment, offering a solid minute's worth of silence as though processing those three words. "Where are you? I'm coming."

"No," Carolynn said almost too loudly. "No. I have to work through some things first. I promise I will be home tomorrow."

She could hear her mother sighing and could almost see her rolling her eyes and pacing their living room. "At least tell me your safe."

"I am." Carolynn nodded. At least as safe as she could be, whatever that meant.

"I love you, Star. You're my world," her mother said, sniffling quietly.

"I love you too, Mom," Carolynn said, before closing the phone. She brushed the back of her hand against her cheek, removing the single tear that had escaped her.

"Well, that was intense," Beth commented, trying to lighten the mood. "What are you going to tell her tomorrow?"

"The truth," she said automatically. "Or as close to the truth as I can get without her losing it."

Beth chuckled, before sobering up, giving her a suspicious side-eye. "So, are you going to tell me what's going? Why we're here at some stranger's house and not a hospital?"

Carolynn leaned her head back against the headboard, staring up at the ceiling. "I honestly don't have all of the answers. I have some guesses and suspicions, but I promise, once I know, you'll be the first I tell."

Beth smirked, squeezing her hand. "Damn straight."

The bedroom door pushed open, and a tall, dark figure stood masked in shadows in the frame, the hallway light at his back illuminating his silhouette, giving him an almost halo over his hair. He leaned against the wooden door, arms crossed over his chest.

Carolynn's breath caught, heart racing, anxiety spiking. She gnawed on her lower lip, gaze locked on those glacier-blue eyes. Moisture gathered as relief rushed through her, overwhelmed with racing thoughts and feelings she could barely sort out. She had been dying. She felt it, that feeling of letting go, drifting away, and she almost had, except that he saved her. No one had to tell her, she knew it was true.

She didn't know how, or what he did. But she was alive because of him. He had promised her in that meadow he wouldn't let her go, and he hadn't. He kept his promise.

"We'll give you two some space," Beth said, eyes flicking between the two of them. "Come on, you beast."

Shadow growled softly at her friend before reluctantly getting off the bed. *I'll be out in the hall. Call for me if you need anything.*

Carolynn gave her a brief nod without bothering to look away. She couldn't tear her gaze from him.

Beth walked past him, whispering something under her breath even Carolynn couldn't hear, but it got a light chuckle out of him. She almost frowned, curious as to what could have made him laugh.

Once the girl and wolf had left the room, it was just the two of them. Donnie stood frozen, still leaning against the door, legs crossed over each other, arms flexed against his chest. He was wearing a dark grey fitted tee and dark wash blue jeans, along with his typical pair of boots. Nearly identical to the outfit he wore in the meadow.

She couldn't stand the silence, couldn't stand the distance between them.

Chapter 30

"Come here," she finally said, patting the space beside her. Donnie seemed to hesitate, to pause, until he pushed off the door and walked forward, boots heavy on the floor. He sat down on the bed, mattress dipping beneath him. Carolynn took him in, his demeanor, his expressions, all of it. She could tell he was unsure, anxious, and nervous, but about what?

Carolynn reached out her hand and took the one in his lap, holding it tightly. He seemed to instantly relax, his shoulders loosening as though a weight had been lifted.

"You're here," she said, smiling sadly. Her eyes betrayed her as wetness streaked down her face.

Donnie's face fell at the sight of the tears, brushing them away with the rough pad of his thumb. "There's nowhere else I'd rather be."

She breathed out a sigh of relief, leaning into his palm as he cupped her face. She breathed him in, his warm scent instantly comforting her and calming her nerves.

Donnie stared, eyes fixed on her lips. "How much do you remember?"

"Everything," she said. "All of it."

Donnie hesitantly nodded, as though unsure what that meant.

"I'm sorry," she whispered, lips brushing against his palm.

"For what?" he asked, puzzled, brow furrowing.

"For not telling you what happened. For getting hurt and

basically accusing you. For nearly dying," she said, voice cracking and breaking.

Donnie hushed her, hand cradling the back of her neck, forcing her head back to meet his gaze. "None of this is your fault."

Carolynn gave him the faintest nod, as he held her like that a moment longer, throat exposed, her lips slightly parted as she stared up at him. Those eyes darted to her lips, and she could see the hunger in his eyes. She had been at death's door and had narrowly avoided it. His grip on her skin and hair made her blood sing. An electrical current raced along her flesh, electrifying and awakening every part of her, tuned specifically to him.

There had been a moment in that forest and in that meadow, where she didn't think she would ever have this. The ability to touch him, to speak to him, to feel his heart echo her own beat. There were still so many unspoken words between them. So much they had to discuss, so much she needed to know, but at this moment, all she wanted was him. The feel of his body beneath hers, his taste, all of him.

Carolynn locked eyes with him as she moved out from under the covers. His grip on her hair and on her neck never wavered. She paid little attention to the fact that she wore nothing but his shirt and pair of underwear beneath the covers as she moved above him on the edge of the bed, straddling his waist. He shifted beneath her, hand gripping her hips to steady her body. She sat down in his lap, the rough denim causing a delicious friction against her heat.

"Kitten," Donnie growled, stilling her hips. She hadn't realized she'd been shifting against him, against the hard length contained beneath the jeans.

The pet name that rumbled from him caused the bottom of her stomach to tighten and coil as excitement built. His hand ran up her bare thigh, gripping her hips, and pulling her body tight against his. She was hungry for him, starving for his touch and taste. She had nearly died and now craved life. She wanted to live.

Carolynn stared into those eyes, the eyes that captured her soul and stole her heart. Eyes that truly saw her for who she was and what she was and did not fear it. She could feel tendrils of dark smoke snake their way up her legs and down her back, stroking her, licking at her skin. She didn't have to look down to know his shadows were coming out to play. She didn't fear them, didn't think them monstrous or vile. She reveled in them and allowed them to touch and taste as they pleased.

The darkness brushed along her skin, nipples pebbling beneath the shirt. Her lips parted as her breathing came in quick, his hand still secured in her hair and her waist, keeping her from grinding onto him the way he knew she wanted to.

Was he afraid she wasn't ready? That she was too fragile? Too soon after her near-death experience?

She didn't have a chance to ask as he lost his patience and pulled her face down to his. It wasn't soft or tender, slow or careful. His lips were bruising and punishing, wild and consuming. It was as though he wanted to take her breath, her air, her being, and she would give it all. She opened her mouth, tasting and teasing, tongues battling as they drank each other in, but it did nothing to quench the fire that was building inside. His mouth molded perfectly to hers as his hands tightened on her, almost afraid she might disappear.

Carolynn wound her hands around his neck, cupping his face, gripping his hair. She felt alive in his arms and drunk off his touch. Her need and desire for him was intoxicating. She was ravenous— they were ravenous, something feral and primal overcoming the two of them. Something deep and connecting the two of them awakened, demanding more and more. She gripped the hem of his shirt and pulled it off over his head.

Running her hands over his shoulders, across the plains of his chest, and down the ridges of muscle coating his stomach left her mouth dry and parched. She wondered what his skin would taste like, imagined running her tongue up the length of his torso. To feel those dips and curves with her mouth. He was so fucking perfect.

She felt his hand shift from her hips to the front of her. She was finally free, released to move against him and feel that friction she so desperately needed. A moan slipped free at the sensation, but he devoured it with his mouth, taking her pleasure as his own. His hand slipped between the two of them, beneath the hem of her shirt, over the thin cotton of her underwear, and he pressed down. She bucked at the pressure, sucking in a breath as he circled around that bundle of nerves that were swollen and in urgent need of attention, of release.

Donnie pressed harder, rubbing against her clit as the pressure, deep and low, began to build. He moved from her mouth down her neck, sucking and nipping at the tender flesh. She tried to squirm, tried to move but those shadows wrapped around her, securing him to her, brushing along her breasts, her stomach, running up her thighs. The touches and the sensation were too much.

"Donnie," she called to him, leaning into his hair, gripping tightly onto his shoulders as she ground harder into his hand.

Those fingers dipped farther south, pushing her underwear to the side to find her heat slick with need. "Are you wet for me, kitten?"

Words were unreachable, intangible. She muttered something incoherent as he teased her opening, coating his fingers with her desire. He sunk one finger in, curling as he moved inside. She jerked against the movement, sinking farther onto his hand, demanding more. He pumped in and out, curling as he moved, hitting that sweet spot that shot fireworks behind her eyes. Her breathing became erratic and heavy as she began to pant. The pressure continued to build as she reached that peak that promised such a sweet release.

His thumb rubbed against her clit, causing a fresh wave of spasms. She was lost in a sea of pleasure.

"That's it. Cum for me, kitten," Donnie purred against her neck, pressing harder against that bundle in time with the curl of his finger.

Carolynn made to cry out as something within her exploded, causing waves of release to wrack through her body, but Donnie's mouth covered hers, kissing her, biting her lip as she came on his hand. She went limp against him, her body and mind spent. His arms curled around her, stroking her back, her hair, peppering soft kisses along her shoulder and up her neck.

Her eyes grew heavy as exhaustion settled deep inside of her. She felt them moving, felt him lift her in his arms, and lay her back down on the mattress, covering her with the blanket. His hand smoothed her hair back.

"Don't leave," she said, voice no louder than a mewling kitten. She hated how weak and small she sounded, but sleep was coming for her quickly.

"I'm never far," Donnie said to her.

The last thing she remembered was his fingers stroking her hair and a flash of obsidian iridescence.

Plumes of black smoke rose, coating the blue sky in a sheet of gray. A city was burning behind a wall of thick, tall stone. An army larger than any she could imagine flooded through the twin gates, swarming the unsuspecting citizens. They wore tunics made of a cloth that was unknown to her, possibly homespun, coarse, and jagged. She noticed they all wore skirts made of leather hide. Every man carried either a sword of steel or a plain wooden bow with a quiver full of arrows.

Their leather sandals kicked up clouds of dust. She could hear women screaming in the distance. The fear was visceral and ear-piercing, desperate and guttural, and it made her shiver, refusing to come to any understanding of what might be the cause of such a scream.

She was in the city, walking slowly through the streets past a large wooden structure that resembled a crude horse about the size of a two-story building. Someone familiar caught her eye, admiring the wooden horse. He wore the same tunic and skirt as the soldiers, except his was a darker hide. His tunic was much finer than most, and the skirt was smooth leather, properly tanned and shaped. The sword that he carried was not the same, dull steel as the other men that ran wild in the streets. His sword was branded with markings in a strange language up the center of both sides of the blade. The edges of the glistening metal were not chipped or dull. It looked ancient, yet newly formed, bringing back a feeling of déjà vu. She'd seen it before in her dreams.

The sword was coated in both dried and fresh blood, dripping off the sharp tip and falling onto the sandstone beneath his feet. He turned towards her, taking in the carnage, the death, and mayhem. A smile spread across his face. The light from the torches and burning buildings illuminated him. Every patch of visible skin was covered in soot and red dirt. Blood was streaked over his biceps, neck, and shirt. His black hair, half tied back with a leather strip, was slicked back with sweat, or maybe it was blood. But what caught Carolynn by surprise were his cold, ice-blue eyes, hungry and thrilled, looking for his next kill.

Carolynn was standing in the middle of Troy, Ancient Greece, the city burning, people being slaughtered in their homes, and Donnie stood in the midst of it. She watched as he sprinted down an alley, faster than humanly possible. She hurried after him and found she could somehow keep up. Her footsteps were silent along the sand-packed streets, keeping her back against the walls, hiding in the shadows. She thought she had followed him precisely through the streets but came to a dead end. The wall in front of her reached almost forty feet high. Her eyes rose up the length of the stone wall and was alarmed to find Donnie at the top of the terrace, fighting his next opponent stupid enough to take arms against him.

There was no staircase leading up, no footholds to be able to climb. But there he was, thrusting a sword through a soldier's chest with such a blur of speed she couldn't keep her eyes on his sword arm before he sliced through another body with zero resistance. It was as though he was cutting through butter

Her vision went dark. Donnie's look of determination and blood-streaked face faded from view.

Carolynn woke up to the sound of birds singing outside her window as the sun began its daily rise in the sky. She finally felt rested as the dream of Donnie in the middle of Troy faded, receding to the back of her mind. She squinted one eye open and found herself alone. Donnie was nowhere to be seen.

The bedroom window was open, allowing the sticky hot air to enter her room. Something small was perched on the windowsill waiting patiently for an invitation.

"Spot," Carolynn called softly, emotion choking her, She didn't know where he had been or what he had been doing the last few days; she only knew she missed him. There was so much left unsaid.

Spot glided into the room to perch on the nightstand beside her. Carolynn scooted on the bed closer towards him so that she could reach out and stroke his wing, delighted by the softness of his feathers. The barn owl rubbed his head against her arm, comforting not only her but himself as well.

"I missed you so much," Carolynn said, tears spilling from her eyes.

She couldn't remember the last time she'd cried so much. Probably her father's funeral. It felt odd yet strangely freeing.

I missed you more, Spot said. *But I was never far. I am always here.*

"I'm so sorry about the other day," she apologized. "I was horrible and rude, and I didn't mean what I said."

You have nothing to apologize for. I was wrong. I came off the wrong way. I just worry for you, Spot confessed, his feathers ruffling in the morning breeze that streamed through the open window.

"There's so much that's been going on. My powers have been changing. I've been having these dreams of this battle, people are dead, and—" She shuttered as she recalled the sword protruding through her chest. What if Sarena was right and they weren't just dreams but prophecies? "I'm scared."

Spot moved closer, claws clicking on the wooden furniture. *You've been having dreams?*

"Almost every night since my birthday, and they just keep getting worse. More detailed, more people, more violence," she told him, straightening up in bed. The words were tumbling out of her faster than she expected. She had been dying to tell someone, to explain everything. "When I was dying, I dreamt of a Goddess. She told me that my dreams were real. They were prophecies, and I shouldn't ignore them. My mom and Beth were dead in my dreams. Neila was there, and Donnie. But none of that makes any sense. What is happening to me?"

She remembered the meadow and her conversation with Donnie. He told her she wasn't human, and she knew he wasn't either, but he had called himself a monster. She didn't believe that, not for one second.

And your powers?

"They've been changing. I can still read minds, but Shadow was right, I burned a table with my hands, and after our fight, I blew up a fence. I was so angry, so aggravated, it just exploded out of me. And ever since I woke up, I've been having dreams of Donnie. Dreams of places and times I've never been or seen before. I feel like I'm going crazy," Carolynn said, running her fingers through her hair, her head pounding.

Carolynn thought she heard the owl sigh, but it wasn't in her head. She had never heard an animal make such a human sound before. She looked to the owl, brow furrowed, frowning. There was a strange tightening in her chest that she couldn't explain as nerves buzzed inside of her.

"Spot, what's going on?" she asked the owl. She could tell he wanted to say something, as unease rolled off of him in waves.

The owl shook his head, incredibly sad and guilt-ridden. *I never wanted any of this for you. This wasn't how it was supposed to happen.*

"What are you talking about?" Carolynn asked, curling her feet under her as though to stand, her anxiety increasing ten-fold.

Please forgive me.

Spot ruffled his feathers. Not in response to the wind or to satisfy an itch but he was molting. She had never seen a bird shed so many feathers all at once, but he wasn't just losing his feathers. He was quickly becoming larger.

Carolynn backed out of bed to the other side of the room. A wall hit her back as she moved to get away.

Spot was morphing, changing into a man. His wings turned into arms, claws into legs. His beautiful, white heart-shaped face shifted into that of a man with dark brown unruly hair and eyes exactly the same as her own.

Her hand flew over her mouth as she gasped, her heart stopping in her chest, and bile rose to the back of her throat.

No, this couldn't be. This wasn't happening.

It was Sam.

Chapter 31

"**W**hat the fuck?" Carolynn yelled.

What was she seeing? What was happening?

Thankfully, someone had put her into sweatpants while she'd been asleep, so she was no longer in just a shirt, but she still felt incredibly exposed.

The owl that she had known all her life, who had been there through every major, life-changing event, the one who had scolded, encouraged, and loved her, was a man? A man whom she thought she had only met just a few days ago?

Thankfully, he was clothed in a grey fitted tee and beige slacks. He seemed to know better than to try and approach her and stayed where he was across the room. As though he hadn't just given her a fucking heart attack.

"I can explain everything, just please sit down," Sam said, gesturing towards the armchair beside the bed.

Like hell she would.

"Fuck that! Who the hell are you?" Carolynn yelled. She thought she could trust the owl. Thought he was her friend and confidant. Was everything a lie?

"I understand you're upset—"

"Upset?" Carolynn laughed. She actually laughed, feeling rather hysterical and insane as her entire world was being turned upside down. "No, upset is going to the drive-through and finding your favorite food is no longer on the menu. Upset is your best friend canceling plans on you to hang out with her dirt-bag boyfriend. This, this is pissed and frustrated, and fucking confused. What the hell is going on here? Who the hell are you? Are you an owl, a man, a fucking fairy?"

"First of all, you will not curse at me. Second, I am the owl and the man; you've just always known the feathered side of me," Sam said, his tone authoritative.

"And you just thought to keep the fact that you can shift into a man quicker than it takes to microwave popcorn to yourself? Didn't think that was important information to share these last thirteen years?"

"I have wanted to tell you who I am from the very beginning, but it was imperative that I keep that part of my life hidden, to keep you safe."

"Keep me safe?" Carolyn scoffed. "In what world have I been safe? I have nearly died four times in the last week. Where were you during that? How would knowing who and what you are hurt me?"

"It's hard to explain—"

Carolynn scoffed again, rolling her eyes and shaking her head. "Why am I here, Spot?" She said his name with disgust. "Who even are you? And while we're on that topic, who is Neila? How do either of you factor into my life?"

"Will you sit down and let me talk?" Sam commanded, sounding exasperated.

Carolynn automatically took a seat, silently cursing her mind and body for obeying. Fuck, how had she not heard the resemblance, the identical tone and voice? Maybe 'cause she barely said two words to the man, that's how.

"Thank you," he sighed, rubbing his temples. "I understand how you might feel that I betrayed you. In a sense I did, but you have to understand I did what I thought was best. I looked after you the only way I could without drawing attention."

"Drawing attention to me?" Carolynn frowned. "From who? Who gives a crap enough about me to give a damn?"

"Oh, Carolynn." Sam sighed, sitting down on the edge of the bed as he ran his hands through his brown locks. "You are so precious and yet feared by so many."

Carolynn couldn't help the teenage drama as she rolled her

eyes, scoffing once again. That was the biggest crock of shit she ever heard, and she'd heard some doozies from her mother.

"Do you honestly expect me to believe any of that horse shit?" Carolynn asked, brow raised, staring him dead in the eyes, just waiting for him to declare this was some joke. "I was abandoned the day I was born. No one knows where I came from or who I am, so don't sit there and try to tell me I'm important to anyone, when my own birth parents left me."

Carolynn hated herself for the tears that were stinging her eyes. She felt like screaming, like punching through a wall, and breaking down on the floor sobbing. This past week had been nothing but a shit show, an emotional rollercoaster she had been waiting to jump off of, only for it to start again. When would the hits stop coming?

"Carolynn," he tried again, but she held her hands up to him, forcing herself to take in a deep breath before she did or said something she'd regret.

"Who are you really?" she asked again, forcing herself not to visibly shake as her nerves were shredded, her insides quaking.

"I'm an immortal, like you."

Carolynn stared at him as though waiting for the punchline, but it never came. They sat together in a moment of silence as she mulled over those few words that expressed so much.

Sam was actually claiming to be immortal, and that she was immortal as well.

He was cracked. He was literally insane. Maybe being a bird had dumbed him down. Weren't owls supposed to be wise?

"You're insane," she said, shaking her head. "I may not be human, but I am certainly not immortal. The other day proves just how mortal I am. I nearly died."

"The venom you were subjected to is from our world. It would knock most on their ass. It nearly killed you because you are still transitioning into your full powers. You haven't ascended yet."

"Wait, wait, wait." Carolynn held her hands up, staring at him as though he had two heads. Ascend, she'd heard that term before. "Our world? What world? And ascend? Ascend into what? I'm just a telepath."

Sam shook his head no. "Telepathy is a standard power for

people like us. It's the first to manifest. Yours just happened to manifest very, very young, and we don't know what other powers you may or may not have. There's never been another like you."

"What are you talking about, like me?" Carolynn was getting frustrated, feeling as though they were doing nothing but talking in circles. "Who are you? What are you? Is your name even Sam?"

"The name I was born with was Samonius, and I am a Demigod," Sam said, face completely serious.

This was starting to sound more and more familiar.

"You're telling me you came from a God and a human?"

"A Demigod is born from two Gods."

"Wouldn't that just make you a God?" Why was she even entertaining his psychobabble?

"Gods are made, not born. Demigods, or Demis, are born."

"But I thought Demigods were the children of mortals and Gods?"

"That is a common misconception. Gods cannot procreate with humans, just like a lion and a house cat cannot procreate. Gods are made; by whom, the heavens only know. But Demigods are born from two Gods. Usually not as strong, but still formidable and immortal, but only once they ascend by coming into their full power. If they make it that far. It's easier to kill a Demigod before their eighteenth birthday."

Carolynn's head was swimming as a migraine began to form behind her eyes. She rubbed at her temples, running her fingers through her hair, tugging at the roots. "Are you trying to tell me I'm the child of two Gods?"

Sam shook his head. "No, you are the child of two Demis."

That she remembered. Remembered reading about it in that stupid book Neila gave her. The book that depicted the Gods, showed Sarena and Dominius, explained Angels and creatures, and that stupid prophecy.

This time she laughed. "This is all a joke. I'm being punked." She glanced around the room, searching for hidden cameras. "Are you trying to indoctrinate me into some cult? That stupid book Neila gave me told of some prophecy, and you expect me to believe that it's about me?" Her mind was whirling from the implication, and she felt some part of her fracture as he dangled a kind of hope, some kind of understanding of where she came from and who she was, in front of her. "Why are you doing this?" she asked, voice small and fragile. "What you're saying is ridiculous and unfathomable. I'm no one. I'm just a girl who can talk to animals and rides horses. I'm no one."

Sam stood up with her, stepping forward as though to approach her but thought better of it and backed away. "You have never been no one."

"How would you know?" she asked, glancing around at the large room with the expensive furniture. "You're just some random guy who can turn into an owl and took pity on a lonely girl, which, by the way, is a tad creepy."

"It's not creepy," Sam said with a bit of annoyance.

"It kind of is." Carolynn pursed her lips, hands on her cocked hips. "Some random guy who can shift into an owl befriending a four-year-old girl sounds like a twenty-twenty special."

"I am not just some random guy."

"Then who the hell are you?"

"I'm your father."

Carolynn had to admit, she didn't see that one coming. Her mouth hung open, eyes widened, and then she frowned as she looked him up and down. She wanted to yell bullshit. Wanted to call him a liar, a fake, and a sick bastard to play this kind of game, but she couldn't.

Her mind was like a whirlwind. Everything she ever talked about with Spot—friendship problems, school drama, her first period. This whole time she was talking to her dad? He had been a part of nearly her entire life, and she never knew it. All those times she doubted who she was, where she came from, had those very same conversations with him, and he said nothing.

Then there was the physical evidence.

Those eyes. The exact replica of her own, and she'd seen them elsewhere as well. Didn't that other God Sarena was with have them as well? No, there was no fucking way. This wasn't really happening. Shapeshifting? Her father, her birth father, was a shapeshifter, son of a God. She was hallucinating; she had to be. Maybe the venom was still working its way out of her system, and this was all just some insane dream she was having.

You're not crazy.

Carolynn narrowed her eyes on the man in front of her. "Do not do that. Do not invade my mind and eavesdrop on my thoughts."

Anger boiled inside of her. Was he trying to prove a point or push her farther away?

"I'm sorry," Sam said, sounding sincere. "I'm not trying to make this any more difficult than it already is. I have wanted to tell you everything for the longest time. Did you think it was easy to watch you grow and not be your parent and raise you myself? It was torture, but I kept my distance because it was safer for you. If anyone had found out you were mine and Neila's—"

Sam cut himself off this time as the name slipped.

Carolynn couldn't help but chuckle, shaking her head and biting her lip, as a burning sensation blazed behind her eyes. "Of course. How could I not have seen it? How could I have been such a fool?" she nearly yelled. "You two must have had a great laugh behind my back."

"Carolynn," Sam tried and failed.

"So, what, you invaded and installed yourself in my life when I was just a child, but she couldn't be bothered until a week ago? Too busy?"

"Your mother and I—"

"No," Carolynn stopped him as disgust filled her voice. "You don't get to call yourselves that. You see, I have parents. Parents who taught me to ride a bike, walked me to the bus on my first day of school, went to my competitions, and took care of me when I was sick. Parents who raised me through the good and bad. Raised a kid who had the nifty ability to talk to forest creatures and read their minds, shit they don't make *How to* books on. Now, I may have lost one, and the other one is so stuck in her grief that she's barely around, but *they* are my mom and dad. They never lied to me or hid their identity, or tricked me into trusting them. They didn't abandon me at a fire station and pretend to be my friend!"

Hot tears streamed down her cheeks as her anger and frustration boiled over. The betrayal and deception cut deep, breaking her.

Carolynn ran out of the room and down the flight of stairs. She could hear him calling her back, hear him yelling for her to stop, but she ignored him and kept running for the front door.

"Carolynn?" Neila called, stepping out of the kitchen. A picture-perfect, turn-of-the-century housewife in expensive clothing and a floral apron.

Carolynn rolled her eyes in disgust. She couldn't deal with this. It was too much. She threw the front door open, blinded by the sun. She threw her hand up to protect her eyes, as she hadn't been outside and seen real light in days, but she didn't slow down as she began to run. She knew how to get home, so she set out, barefoot and wearing sweatpants and a t-shirt in the Florida summer heat. She pounded into the pavement as fast as she could until her legs were numb and she was sure her feet were bleeding.

Finally stopping, she took in her surroundings and found herself past the trailer park and at the end of town. Nowhere near home.

She stepped off the dirt road and into the nearby tree line, leaning back against a tree to catch her breath. Her feet were caked with dirt, gravel, and blood. She picked up her foot to examine the bottom and found gashes and shredded flesh. She winced at the gruesome sight before setting her foot back down. Now that she was still and the adrenaline was beginning to wear off, her feet felt as though they were on fire.

But none of that mattered. She didn't care that her feet were throbbing and injured as she sat down on the thick moss-covered floor and cradled her head between her knees and cried. She hadn't had such a gut-wrenching, hopeless cry since her dad had died. She was pissed and devastated, furious and disappointed. She wanted to punch the bark of the tree until her knuckles were broken and bleeding to feel some sliver of relief from the fury she felt boiling in her veins.

But that wouldn't change a damn thing.

It wouldn't change that Spot had essentially been a lie. Some stupid way to gain her trust and implant himself into her life. None of it felt real. Not his claim that she was an immortal kind-of God. Or that Sam and Neila were her biological parents, making every moment they'd shared corrupted, tainted somehow.

If any of what he said was true and she was a child of two Demigods, what did that make her? A freak? An anomaly?

She heard grass crunching a few feet away. She glanced up and saw Shadow slowly edging towards her.

Carolynn opened her arms wide, and the wolf rushed in, lying her head against her shoulders. She rhythmically stroked the wolf's black fur, soothing herself.

What can I do? Shadow asked.

"I'm just glad you're here with me." *And that I'm not alone,* but she left the last part unspoken.

They sat like that for a while. She didn't care about the time. Didn't care where she was or where she had to be. Didn't care that somehow the sun was already setting, and she had no clue what time or day it was, nor about the fact that she didn't even have a cell phone with her. The gnats were already buzzing around her, nipping at her skin. She nudged Shadow, who had grown silent and statue-like as they sat there. The wolf backed away a few steps, allowing her room to stand.

Carolynn was almost too afraid to examine her feet again. They were already swelling and painful, but she pushed herself up anyways, hissing as she went. Her feet felt like she was stepping on hot pokers repeatedly. She tried to ignore the sensation and took a step forward. Her knees buckled beneath her weight as she caught herself on the tree behind her.

If only she could clean them out, then they could heal.

You shouldn't be walking. Your paws are hurt, Shadow said, pointing out the obvious.

The wolf licked her hand gingerly, as though to soothe her. The feel of her rough tongue against her skin was somewhat comforting.

The run had helped to clear her head, but after crying for so long, she now felt exhausted and raw, like an exposed nerve. She could feel fatigue settling in, her legs shaking beneath her.

She just couldn't picture it. Sam and Neila, her birth parents. How could she even believe a word Sam said? Why should she trust them?

They did save your life, Shadow added somberly.

Carolynn glared down at her. "They also hid the truth from me," she retorted. Besides, she was fairly certain Donnie had more to do with saving her life than anyone else.

Samonius only wants to protect you.

Carolynn froze, the blows still coming. "I never said Sam's full name."

Chapter 32

This wasn't happening. Not her too.

Shadow seemed to freeze, realizing what she'd done.

Carolynn tipped her head back, chewing on her cheek as she inhaled deeply through her nose, taking in the humid, night air. She was drowning. She was literally drowning, trying desperately to cling to something, anything, to keep from losing it. Her hands opened and closed into fists, nails digging into her flesh to try and focus on the physical pain rather than her heart shattering.

Animals normally asleep were stirring in the woods, the trees. They were responding to her anger, her frustration, and her heartbreak as they crept, crawled, and slithered toward her.

The birds in the air, the mice in their burrows, the squirrels in the trees, and the foxes in their dens all began to gather. She knew she was projecting her emotions, hard and fast, pulsating from her skin, her pores. She was leaking and couldn't put a stopper in it.

She couldn't believe it. Shadow had known all these years, known who her birth parents were, known who Spot was all along, and never said a word. How many times had she talked to the wolf about her birth parents and the conflicting emotions she had about them? Shadow was supposed to be the one, out of everyone in her life, that she could trust, that she knew she could count on. Was her whole life a lie? Her world was shattering, and she wasn't sure if she could pick up all of the pieces. Everything she thought she knew was being blown apart, like dust in the wind.

"How could you not tell me?" Carolynn asked, choking back the bile that was threatening to make an appearance. "How could you keep this from me? Did you know about my heritage too? That I'm from some other world and descended from Gods? Or that apparently people were going to come after me?" Her stomach was clawing at her. She couldn't even remember the last time she ate. She wasn't sure if it was the sprint-a-thon after just barely surviving being poisoned or the overload of information she was receiving on a constant loop, but her body felt sick. Her head was pounding, her stomach twisting in knots and filling with acid. She rested back against the tree, no longer able to hold herself up.

I was charged with the duty of protecting you. Gods rarely choose my kind to assist them. When my pack was selected, I was offered to Samonius. My mother knew even as a pup that I would be best for the job. Sam took me to protect you, to be there for you. Spot may have always been Sam, but he was your friend first. Now is not the time to dismiss everything he has to say or offer. The attack at the house was only the beginning. They won't stop coming.

Carolynn had never heard Shadow talk so much in such a small amount of time. She couldn't believe what she was hearing. How had she been so blind? Was that all she was? A job, a duty, a responsibility? Did she regret having to spend every day with her? What a pain in the ass it must have been. To follow her around day in and day out.

Such a stupid child.

It has been my honor to be your guide, your familiar. I do not regret one minute of it. You are my responsibility, but you are also my friend, my pup.

A sob broke free as more tears left her. She didn't think she had any left, but there it was.

Her mind was on overload, and she couldn't think straight. She could hear a beating sound carried by the wind, paws skittering through the dead leaves littering the forest floor, scales slithering through bushes, the sounds growing louder and closer.

Carolynn?

Carolynn focused on the wolf, someone she now realized she hardly knew. She wiped her face with the back of her hand. "Just go away, Shadow. I don't want to see you," she said through gritted teeth.

Dozens of animals crept out from the cover of the trees and brush. They moved slowly, stalking towards Carolynn, providing a battle line on each side of her. Foxes, mice, deer, birds, owls, and countless other critters stood with her. Each one of them kept their eye on the wolf, as though she were the threat. Carolynn felt something bump into her side. She lifted her arm to peer underneath and found a large, adult buck. She wrapped her arm around his neck, leaning on him as he stood proudly at her side, head high. The agony in her feet was intense, and she had to bite her tongue to keep from crying out, but she forced herself to stand and push past the dizziness that surrounded her.

"I need you to leave," Carolynn said, not as strongly as she'd have liked, her voice wavering.

I am not leaving you. Shadow stood firmly, eyeing the gathering animals surrounding her.

Car lights brightened the road, illuminating the dark alcove she found herself in. The animals around her squeaked and yipped at the oncoming car, but did not move from their place beside her. Carolynn winced at the blinding lights, but she knew that car, knew the white racing stripes and teal blue paint. She sighed heavily with relief, almost overwhelmed by a fresh wave of tears as Beth pulled the Mustang to the side of the road.

The engine cut off before the car was even thrown into park. Her friend stormed out of her car, brown curls billowing around her.

"Where the hell have you been?" Beth yelled, feet stomping in the dirt. "I've been looking all over for you! Do you not realize you nearly died? You can't just take off, and—" Beth stopped short, finally looking up and taking in the scene unfolding around her. "What the hell kind of Snow White show did I walk in on?"

All Carolynn could manage was a shrug. The buck leaned further into her, as though sensing her growing fatigue and pain. She took extra care to avoid the large and pointy antlers. The deer helped her shuffle forward toward where Beth still stood beside the car. She hissed as the movement irritated the wounds along her feet, causing fresh hot tears to spill down her face.

Shadow made to move forward, to try and help in some way, but the animals around her stepped forward as well, blocking the wolf's path.

"Woah," Beth said, eyes wide as she witnessed the furry standoff.

"Please, Shadow. I can't deal with your betrayal on top of everything else. I need you to leave," Carolynn cried. She couldn't tell if her feet or her heart hurt more.

Shadow glanced around at the wall of fur, teeth, and claws standing between them. She backed away a step, conceding. *I will not be far.*

Carolynn watched as her wolf, her friend, slinked back into the tree line, blending in perfectly with the looming darkness. A piece of her heart vanished with the obsidian wolf, and she was unsure if she would ever get it back.

Without a word, Beth hesitantly stepped forward, eyes on the wild buck as she came to her side and wrapped an arm around her waist. Carolynn removed herself from the buck and leaned heavily on her friend as Beth all but dragged her to the passenger side of the car. It couldn't have been easy, given that they were roughly the same height and size, but she managed.

Carolynn sucked in a breath, holding the air in her lungs as her feet dragged along the ground, utterly useless. She could feel every grain of dirt, rubbing like sandpaper across her shredded feet. Beth opened the door and dumped her in the front seat, sliding her arm beneath her knees and lifting them carefully inside the car.

Beth didn't say anything during the drive home, but she could feel the constant side eye, as though she expected her to go comatose or have a breakdown at any moment. Carolynn was a bit surprised by the lack of twenty questions. She had never known her friend to hold her tongue, but then again, circumstances change. Maybe she looked worse than she thought. But what did thaw out her heart the tiniest bit, was the warm hand that held hers the entire drive home. Beth squeezed her lightly. A steady reassurance that she wasn't alone, and she wasn't. She always had Beth.

Images of her dream flashed through her mind. Her friend's dead body at her feet, eyes glazed over, body battered, bruised, and broken. She shuddered. She couldn't let anything happen to her. Right now, Beth was her lifeline, her tether to reality.

The trees blurred past as they drove down the dark roads of the town. Where was Donnie? He told her he wouldn't leave, but when she awoke he wasn't there. Wasn't there as her whole world crashed and burned. She felt numb and tired, forcing the day's events to a dark corner in the back of her mind, repressing the memories and heartbreak that came with them.

The car drove past the entrance to the trailer park and turned into the neighborhood. Carolynn could feel something pulling at her, a familiar, odd tug.

Beth pulled up to her house, lights illuminating the trailer and a figure sitting on her front porch, waiting.

Donnie.

Tears welled in her eyes as he stood, tall and dark, surrounded in shadows. Hers.

Beth turned off the ignition and got out of the car. She watched as Beth walked towards Donnie, the car's headlights still on. Beth must have said something to him as he was beside her door faster than she could blink, opening the car door. He bent down, eyes meeting before his gravitated towards her feet, as though sensing the injuries. She could have sworn she heard a growl emanate from him before he slipped his arms beneath her and lifted her out of the car.

Carolynn melted against him as his warmth seeped into her cold skin. She felt tears slipping free from her eyes as she buried her face in his shirt, gripping the soft fabric in her hand.

"Are you okay?" Donnie asked softly in her hair, lips brushing against her skin, sending a fresh wave of goosebumps across her flesh.

She shook her head, unable to make words. He seemed to take that as answer enough and walked with her towards the house.

Beth followed after them, racing up the steps to open the front door. She slipped past Donnie and forced her spare key into the swollen wood, shoving it open as it squeaked in protest. She held it open as Donnie walked over the threshold, bypassing the living room, and went straight for her bedroom. He made to set her down on the bed, but she didn't let go, clinging to his shirt.

Donnie sat with her on the mattress, settling her in his lap. Her feet dangled, still burning and stinging with pain, but right now, she just needed him.

"Tell me what's wrong? What happened?" Donnie asked,

brushing the hair back from her face, fingers grazing her neck.

"Everything. Everything is wrong," she said, shaking her head now bent in the crook of his neck.

Donnie gripped her by the base of her head and pulled her away, taking in her face, the swollen, red eyes, pale complexion, and dry cracking lips. "Who did this to you? Tell me, kitten. I'll—"

Carolynn shook her head again. "They lied to me."

"Who?" he asked, brows furrowing.

"Everyone," she said, voice cracking.

Beth came into the room with a bottle of water and pain reliever in hand. "Here babe, take these."

Carolynn automatically took the pills, popping them into her mouth, and took a big swig of the water, swallowing it down.

"Drink the rest," Donnie ordered, gaze hard and unyielding.

Carolynn obeyed, drinking the rest of the bottle, not realizing just how truly thirsty she was. Beth tried to hide the small smirk that was tugging at her lips as she took the empty bottle from her and set it on the nearby dresser.

"What hurts?" Donnie asked, keeping his questions simple and direct.

"My feet," Carolynn said, licking at her dry lips.

Donnie turned his attention to her feet that were caked in dirt and dried blood. His hand barely skimmed over the top of her foot as she hissed in pain. They were tender to the touch, even the A/C currently blowing was torture. He pulled his hand back, not willing to hurt her any more than she already was.

"Should we take you to the hospital? You might need stitches," Beth suggested.

"No," both Carolynn and Donnie said simultaneously.

"My mom is there, she can't see me like this," Carolynn tried to explain but could tell Beth suspected something else, given the odd look she was giving the two of them. "We just need to get the dirt and rocks out. Then they will heal on their own. They'll be fine by morning."

Beth snorted. "That's what you said about the cut on your hip and look how well that turned out."

"Well, this time I wasn't injured by a poisoned blade; it was my own stupidity," Carolynn retorted, glaring at her friend.

"Beth, can you go run the bath? It'll probably be the easiest way. Let them soak first," Donnie said.

"Sure," Beth drawled, turning on her heels and leaving them for the bathroom.

"She's just trying to help," Donnie said, keeping his voice low enough for Beth not to hear.

The sound of running water could be heard from the bathroom.

"I know." Carolynn sighed, leaning against him, her head resting on his shoulder. "Where were you? You weren't there when I woke up."

"I was called away. I apologize."

Carolynn snorted, smirking.

"Was something I said funny?" Donnie asked, eyebrow cocked, his features set in a serious manner.

"I think that's the first time I've heard you apologize," Carolynn noted.

Donnie made some kind of grunting noise that rumbled in his chest.

"Bath's ready!" Beth shouted from the bathroom.

Without warning, Donnie lifted her off his lap and carried her into the bathroom. She wanted to protest, tell him to put her down and that she was more than capable of taking care of herself, but she stopped. There was no way she could walk on her own.

Inside the washroom, they found Beth standing by the tub, an assortment of supplies laid out on the floor, including towels, peroxide, bandages, and tape. Donnie set her down on the edge of the tub, sitting beside her. He rolled up the bottom of the sweatpants to her knees before carefully lowering her feet into the water.

Carolynn didn't feel the heat at first, her feet covered in so many layers of dirt and grime. The water almost instantly became murky and dark as the blood and earth melted away. She made to bend over, to rub her feet and help the rest of the soil come off, but Donnie beat her to it. He took one foot in his hands and began to carefully brush away the remaining dirt, exposing the damaged flesh.

Carolynn looked away, clenching her teeth. She didn't want to see the damage, or how bad it was as he took a washcloth and continued to work out the small rocks, dirt, and other debris from the wounds.

"Are you going to tell us what made you run nearly ten miles out of town?" Beth asked, breaking the silence, coming up to stand behind her to rest her hands on her shoulders, offering a light squeeze and a distraction.

Carolynn swallowed hard as her morning replayed in her mind. Spot transforming into a man, learning of her heritage, and parentage. A small shiver ran through her, leaving her trembling.

Donnie froze, looking up from her foot. "Did I hurt you?"

Carolynn offered him a small smile. Surprisingly, whatever he was doing didn't hurt as bad as she thought it would. "No, it's not you."

Donnie's lips pursed, those ice-blue eyes turning a bit colder as though he was angry for some reason, before turning his attention back to her injuries.

"Sam and Neila are my birth parents," Carolynn finally said out loud. It was the easiest thing to explain out of everything she learned today. She watched Donnie continue his ministrations, methodically cleaning, and rinsing the cloth, not a single indication that what she said had been a surprise. He kept his face smooth and focused on the task in front of him.

Beth stilled behind her. "You're fucking kidding me."

"No, I am not," Carolynn said, wincing as a rather large pebble was pulled from her foot.

"Sneaky, slippery weasels," Beth cursed them. "I knew there was something odd about them. Aside from the fact that Neila could be your twin. But neither of them looked old enough to have a teenage daughter."

Donnie moved on to her other foot, cleaning it and removing the debris. He still hadn't bothered to look up, or show any reaction. That should be strange, right? Here she was, admitting out loud who her birth parents were, yet nothing.

She watched him carefully.

"It appears they don't really age," Carolynn said carefully. "Remember Spot?"

"Pretty barn owl? Yes."

"That would be Sam."

Still Donnie did not look up, pretending as though he heard nothing, eyes locked on her feet as though afraid to meet her gaze.

When he found her unconscious on the beach, he hadn't taken her to a hospital like most would have. No, he took her to them, to their house.

Carolynn continued, "Sam transformed from barn owl to man right before my eyes and told me I'm descended from Gods."

Beth sucked in a sharp breath, squeezing her shoulders in warning. Carolynn opened her mind to her friend, sensing her urgency.

What are you doing? You barely know him, and you're sharing all your secrets with him? She could taste Beth's outrage on her tongue like bursts of cinnamon.

"I don't think any of this is new information to Donnie," Carolynn spoke out loud. "Is it?"

Donnie paused in his ministrations, eyes finally raising to hers. Those blue eyes locked onto her, jaw ticking. "No."

"I feel like I'm missing something here," Beth said from behind her.

"So am I." Carolynn glared at him, feeling something crackle down her veins.

I need you to give us some space, Carolynn said telepathically to her friend. *I promise I will explain everything to you tomorrow, but I need a moment with him first.*

You better, bitch, or I will run your ass down with my car next time instead of saving it, Beth promised, leaning down and planting a kiss atop her head.

"I'll see you tomorrow," Beth said.

Carolynn caught the look her friend gave him on her way out, glaring daggers and promising violence.

Donnie pulled the drain on the tub, allowing the water to empty out. Blood and dirt disappeared in a swirl of black and red, erasing the evidence of her horrible night. He set her feet on the floor, no bandage, didn't even bother to reach for the peroxide, just set them down.

"Your feet are fine," Donnie said, still holding her gaze.

Carolynn arched a brow as she picked up one of her feet and examined the sole. They were completely unblemished. Not a single mark or scar to be seen. She knew she had done some serious damage to them when she'd caught a glimpse earlier. There were jagged edges and possible torn tendons. Not even she could heal that fast.

"Is healing one of your abilities?" Carolynn asked, no longer keeping up any pretense. What was the point?

"While it's not something I do often, it is common among my kind," Donnie confirmed. Either he didn't care that she knew, or he trusted her. Or maybe it just wasn't in his nature to lie. Either way, she felt it oddly unsettling. Should it be this easy? "In the same way that telepathy is common among yours."

Carolynn pressed her lips together, gnawing on the inside of her cheek. Guess the walls really were coming down. No more bullshit.

"Then why can't I see into your mind?" Carolynn asked, curiosity getting the better of her.

"Because I do not allow you to."

Carolynn thought that over. So, he was able to control who was allowed in and out of his mind. Guess he didn't trust her as much as she thought. Or maybe trust had nothing to do with it.

She pushed off the tub and stood, wiggling her toes in the soft bath rug. There was no pain, no indication that she had injured herself at all. It was amazing.

"Thank you," she said. It would have been a nightmare waiting for her feet to heal on their own.

Donnie simply nodded once, glancing down at the floor. She could see his shadows rippling around him, as though unsure and cautious. She desperately wished she could know what he was thinking.

Carolynn walked back into her bedroom with Donnie following closely behind. She sat down on the bed, scooting back and folding her legs beneath her. Donnie stood off to the side, putting distance between them.

That kind of hurt.

"So, you know Neila and Sam?" Carolynn asked, hoping to be able to put all of the pieces together.

"I've seen them around a few times, but I've never formally met them."

"Did you know they were my parents?" She bit her bottom lip, waiting for the answer.

Donnie met her stare, straightening against the dresser. "I suspected, given the owl's tendency to hang around. He was near you a lot more than you knew."

Carolynn frowned, something not adding up. "How do you know all of this? How do you know who they are? That Spot was Sam? How does none of this seem to faze you?"

"I've been around a long time."

She waited for him to say more, but he gave up nothing. She sighed with frustration, scooting forward on the bed.

"How do you know who they are and who I am?"

Donnie stared at her for a long moment, as though debating on whether or not to answer. She could almost hear the thoughts churning, feel the turmoil roiling through him. If only he would let his walls down, she could see and hear it all.

"It is my job to know the circumstances surrounding a target. Their history, their family, every aspect of their lives."

Carolynn blinked a few times, processing his words. She went from confused to flabbergasted, horrified to baffled. Target, meaning something to attain. She glanced at the book Neila had given her still sitting on her nightstand, recalling the few passages she had read. Was she truly that naive? Had she really been that blind and stupid?

Her eyes burned when she turned them on him, grey eyes marking him. She noticed a twitch of his jaw, his eyes softening as he watched her break even further before his eyes, but she ignored it. Was that all she was to him? The way he touched her, kissed her, how his shadows embraced her and caressed her, was that all some ploy to insert himself into her life?

"You've been watching me for a while?" she asked, voice cracking.

His Adam's apple bobbed in his throat. "I've been here for weeks. Watching you, learning everything I could about you."

"Why?"

"Because I was sent to kill you."

Chapter 33

Carolynn felt frozen, her mind ceasing all thought. She could hear her blood pounding in her ears. Even her lungs forgot to breathe as the air caught in her throat, mouth drier than the Sahara Desert. She stared at him yet couldn't actually focus, as though her brain wasn't connecting words to the individual. She couldn't have heard him right.

"You … were sent … to kill me?" she said, the words coming out fractured and disjoined.

"Matius had somehow learned of your existence and had ordered you to be terminated," Donnie said with a single nod.

Carolynn glanced back at the book beside the bed. "Matius, the King of Gods," she stated, remembering her instant dislike of the once fictional God, now apparently very, very real.

"Yes."

"Why? What did I ever do to him? What did I do to deserve death?"

"You were born," he stated simply. "Your existence challenges his rule."

"How?"

"I think you know how."

"The Prophecy," she whispered, glancing back at the book. Her mind couldn't process, couldn't take in the information and accept it as fact. It was too far-fetched, too extreme. She was a simple girl who worked on a farm. How could her existence be a threat to anyone, when up until a few days ago, she knew none of it existed?

She barely remembered the Prophecy. But what she did remember was something about the child of two Demis and ascension.

There was that word again. Ascending. Ascension. But into what, and how?

"Was any of it real?"

Donnie finally seemed to crack, his face furrowing into confusion as his brows scrunched, lips pressed into a thin line. "Was what real?"

"You," she said, looking back to him, staring into those fathomless, piercing blue eyes. Eyes that she could have gotten lost in for the rest of her life. Eyes that had seen her pleasure, lips that tasted her orgasm, hands that touched her in ways no one had ever dared. "Was all of it some ploy to get close to me?"

Donnie's jaw hardened, teeth grinding, hands flexing at his sides as though he was holding himself back. "Carolynn—"

"You came into my life, and for the briefest of moments, you made me feel alive. You made me feel like I wasn't alone anymore," she confessed. Something inside of her cracked, vibrating on a dangerous level. "Did you get off on getting me to cum for you? Making me feel for you, when all the while you were planning on putting a knife through my heart?"

Donnie finally broke free of whatever resolve had been holding him back and stepped forward, closing the distance, but she was faster. Carolynn got up from the bed and moved to the other side of the room, trying to put as much distance as possible between them. He whirled around, surprise lighting his face.

"Who are you?" She just needed to know. Needed to know this last confirming piece. "Or better yet, what are you?"

Donnie looked her up and down, as though sensing it building within her, but he spoke anyway.

"The Angel of Death."

Lightning cracked nearby, the sound nearly shattering their ears. The air was crackling with energy, at risk of catching fire with even the smallest of sparks. Her emotions were in control, and she knew she was unstable, but somehow, she didn't care. She thought she heard an alarming howl tear through not only the air but into the depths of her mind. The sound escaped her as soon as it appeared.

The Angel of Death. Donnie was the Angel of Death. The dreams of Troy and the London Bridge—they were memories. His memories. Somehow, she could see his past, and he had been right. They were dripping with blood and violence. Although, some twisted part of her wasn't all that bothered by it. She could have gotten past his history, his bloodshed, his craving for violence, but the very fact that he had made her feel, made her crave him... Now *she* was the Angel of Death.

"Carolynn?" he called to her.

Carolynn's soul-piercing grey eyes focused on him, like a viper, projecting her pain and fury, her agony and thirst for vengeance. She could see his hand twitch at his side, and she almost laughed. Did he think he could pacify her? Calm her down?

"You want to kill me," Carolynn said, pressure building, contracting, and expanding within her. "I won't let you get the chance."

"Carolynn, no—"

She didn't give him a chance to finish his sentence. A burst of energy expelled from her chest, rippling through the air, running currents along her skin and hair. A bolt of lightning left the center of her being and slammed into his chest, sending his body through her bedroom wall and into the living room. The air cracked as though being cleaved in two as shards of wood and plaster exploded.

Donnie lay in the wooden remains of the wall, winded from the impact as he struggled to sit up. Carolynn breathed heavily, chest rising and falling, struggling to take in air. Was she having a panic attack? How had she just blasted him through the wall without touching him?

Donnie was wrong all along. It was her that was the monster.

She glanced down at her hands, and fear flooded her. She backed away a step, as though she could escape, as though she could flee her own body. Currents of electricity rippled through her. Little bolts of lightning traced across the length of her arms and hands. She glanced up and found Donnie still here, still standing in the remains of her living room, eyes wide and terrified. But not for himself, for her.

Donnie's eyebrows drew together as his mouth opened to speak, but then paused. He moved a step forward through the debris and fragments of wood.

"Don't," she cried out, warning him back. She wasn't sure how he wasn't dead after that blast to his chest, but she wasn't sure if he could take another hit like that.

She couldn't stand the way he was looking at her with concern and worry, with affection and a desperate hope to help. She could almost feel his shadows touching her, coaxing her back from the edge, but all they did was remind her of the kitchen, his face between her legs, his lips on hers. How they tasted and touched one another. How she had never felt more safe or secure with someone than she did with him. How being in his arms felt more like home than the roof over her head.

Pressure built within her chest again, but this time it slipped from the tips of her fingers, forming a ball of electricity between the palms of her hands. Her body wanted her to release it, to expel it and unleash it upon the world, but she held it firmly, the blue and white ball of energy pulsating in her grip. It reacted to her touch, molding and contracting as she flexed her fingers around it. The ball weighed nothing, as though it was only air in front of her. She felt numb, cold even.

Movement caught her eye as the sound of wood scraping against wood distracted her. Neila pushed through the front door, shoving debris out of her way as she froze, taking in the scene before her. Her eyes surveyed the damaged wall, then flicked to Donnie, his once black shirt now charred and giving off smoke in some places, hair disheveled, and then she turned to her, glancing between the ball of energy in her hands and her face.

What she saw there, Carolynn didn't know, but Neila held her eyes, moving slowly towards her, stepping through the remains of her wall as though it was nothing more than a field of cotton.

"Donnie, you need to leave," Neila said, without breaking eye contact.

"No," he said, more growl than an actual word. "I'm not leaving her."

"Yes, you are," Neila said, moving around her bed. "Carolynn is feeling too much, and right now it seems to be because of you. If you don't want her to live with the guilt of blowing up this entire trailer park, then I suggest you leave. Now."

Carolynn swallowed hard, digesting her words. Could she really blow up the trailer park? Was that even possible? The ball sparked in her hand as though feeding off her anxiety and fear, swelling in size.

"Now, Donnie!" Neila yelled over her shoulder.

Neither of them looked to see if he actually left, too focused on the bomb between her palms.

Carolynn felt the ball of electricity and pure energy pulsate and bend, expand, and contract, as fresh waves of conflicting emotions surged through her. But she couldn't contain them, couldn't close the floodgates that had been ripped wide open. It swallowed her whole, devouring each and every thought and feeling that was boiling over inside.

"Carolynn," Neila said carefully, as though afraid to startle her, keeping her tone even and calm. She moved until she stood just in front of her, the ball of energy lighting up her face with bright white light.

"What are you doing here?" Carolynn managed to ask, refusing to even look up, afraid if she moved even a fraction of an inch, the bomb between her hands would explode. But Neila was here. Her birth mother was standing just in front of her. She couldn't think of all the times she imagined their first conversation as mother and daughter ever amounting to something like this. All the secrets and lies, the cover-ups and disappointment.

The ball sparked between her hands, growing an inch more.

"I'm here to help you."

"Help?" Carolynn laughed a bit manically. "What could I possibly need your help with?"

"I know you've been through a lot these last few days. You feel hurt, confused, betrayed, and I'm sure a bit lost, but I don't think you want to hurt anyone."

Carolynn felt the power between her hands pulsating strongly. Her gaze softened as she remembered sending him through a wall. The look of pain on his face, of concern—for her. The smoke coming off his shirt. She had electrocuted him.

"I don't want to hurt anyone else," she said, slowly raising her gaze to Neila, who looked at her with such affection that she began to almost instantly relax.

"That's it. Now I need you to calm your mind. Whatever emotions you're feeling, you need to take control of them, not them of you. Your emotions are what feed your power. The more intensely you feel, the stronger and more volatile you can be if you can't focus or channel that energy. You need to take it all in."

"What if I don't want to?" she asked, voice shaking. "What if it's too much for me to handle?"

"You are stronger than you know. Whatever your feelings, whatever you're dealing with, it is not beyond your control. Everything happens for a reason."

Carolynn nodded. She could do this. She closed her eyes, breathing steadily as she began to untangle the mess of thoughts and emotions within. She concentrated on her breathing first, making sure to focus on breathing through her nose and exhaling out of her mouth. The sound of her breath was the only thing she listened to, focusing on that. She could feel her pulse slow, coming down from the massive adrenaline rush to a steady, regular rhythm.

She sorted through her mind, focusing on more positive things in her life and shoving down the negative. The wind billowing through her hair on horseback. Beth's laughter and uncanny ability to be the light in her darkness. Her mother and how she used to braid her hair every night before bed. Her father sneaking her out of school so they could enjoy a day at the beach, just the two of them. Shadow and Spot, playing tag in the woods.

Carolynn could no longer feel the tingling sensation in her arms or the pulsing energy between her hands. She opened her eyes and no longer found electricity coursing up her arms. There was no ball of temperamental energy between her hands, just empty space. Instead, she found Neila's small hands laid atop hers, helping her to channel and focus her power.

Those emerald eyes were focused on hers, drooping wearily. Carolynn instantly dropped her hands at her sides, somewhat nervous, and put on the spot.

Neila staggered back a step before regaining her balance.

"Are you okay?" Carolynn asked, taking a step forward, ready to grab her in case she collapsed or lost consciousness.

"I'm fine," Neila smiled weakly. "I just need a moment."

"Here, sit." She guided her back to the bed until the two of them were sitting side by side. "Do you want me to get you anything? I'm pretty sure all we have is water, but it's cold; at least I think it is."

"No, I'm fine, really."

"Did I hurt you?" she asked, unable to hold back the question. She didn't think she had released any of the power, but then again, she didn't know what would happen to someone who was touching her when she was like that.

"No, of course not," Neila shook her head. "It's just when I touched you, I've never felt so much power from one being before. I was trying to help you channel your emotions and got a bit of a jolt."

Guilt immediately flooded her. "I'm sorry."

Neila glanced back behind the bed where the wall used to be, dividing the bedroom from the main sitting area. "Do you want to talk about it?"

Carolynn looked anywhere but at her and the mess at their backs. She didn't think she was ready to talk about it, but then again, Neila probably knew more about her messy relationship than she did.

"He and I had a chat," Carolynn said, refusing to say his name. Thinking it made her heart throb and vengeful thoughts cross her mind. She swallowed the feeling down, pushing it away. She refused let herself be overcome again. She had to get a handle on herself, on these new powers that seemed to pop up by the hour. She would not risk losing control again.

"He told you?" Neila asked, surprise written all over her face.

"I'm sure not everything, but it was enough." Carolynn fidgeted with the shirt she still wore, now streaked with dirt. It was his.

"May I say just one thing about him, and then we don't have to say anymore if you don't want to."

Carolynn breathed in deeply, and bobbed her head, staring at the carpet beneath her feet.

"While his intentions, in the beginning, may have been less than optimal"—Neila tiptoed around the fact that he did insert himself into her life with the sole intention of murdering her, but she let that slide—"the bond the two of you share, it's worth fighting for."

Chapter 34

"How would you know?" Carolynn scoffed, pulling at the end of the shirt. She wanted to change, wanted to get out of his shirt and stop smelling him. "Shouldn't you be telling me to stay away from him? Shouldn't your motherly instincts be warning me against him?"

She knew she was being a tad cruel, maybe even a bitch, but after the day she had, she earned the right to be a tad snarky.

Neila straightened on the bed, folding her hands in her lap. "Yes. My first thought when I saw him in town was to remove him permanently from your life. Sam and Donnie nearly came to blows when you were sick."

This perked Carolynn up. No one had told her any of that.

"But, once I saw him with you, saw the way he reacted and how protective he was, I came to an understanding," Neila said. "It may be difficult for you to understand, but Angels aren't the celestial beings lounging in the clouds full of light and goodness that humans like to depict them as. They are primal beings who give way to their nature, whatever that may be. I've known about Donnie and heard stories of him my entire life. Not once has he missed a mark and given up a target. He has a reputation for completing assassinations within twenty-four hours. But yours, he didn't, and I believe he couldn't."

"Why? He could have easily killed me at the club. Hell, he said he's been following me for weeks. I'm sure he had more than enough opportunities. Why didn't he?"

"Only he can explain his reasons to you, but I will say one thing. I don't think, even if he wanted to, even if he tried, he could ever physically harm you."

Carolynn looked out her window to the twinkling night sky. She didn't want to talk about him anymore. Even if what Neila said was true, he could still hurt her emotionally, mentally, and that was just as bad, if not worse.

"Your timing was a bit too on the nose," Carolynn finally spoke. "How did you know I needed help?"

Neila smiled, the sight annoyingly beautiful. "Shadow. She stayed close and could feel you psychically. Your pain. She called to me and Sam. I figured I would be the easier one to deal with."

Carolynn didn't bother confirming her suspicions. She didn't need to, as it was clearly obvious she didn't or couldn't see Sam, not yet, not for a while.

"I know Sam told you about us, and don't think he and I didn't have words about that. I wish I had been there when he told you, but I know he did tell you that we are your birth parents. I know it's been a lot all at once. I wish I had gotten to know you better before we told you, but time isn't really on our side right now," Neila said, brushing her hair back from her face. "But there are some things we need to discuss. There's a lot you still don't know, that you don't understand about us, where we come from, your powers, all of it, and I don't think we'll have enough time to go over it all properly."

"Because Matias is still after me?" Carolynn asked, turning to face her. Neila's eyes went wide with surprise, but she nodded in confirmation.

"Yes," Neila said. "What do you know about him?"

"Not much, just what I read briefly in that book you gave me. I know he's the King of Gods, that's about it."

Neila seemed to mull this over, carefully choosing her next words. "Matias is a tyrant. He's been in power since the dawn of time. No one really knows how long. But he's cruel and abusive, and there are a good number of Gods and creatures alike who would like nothing more than to see him removed from power."

"And these people think I can do that?" Carolynn frowned. "I'm barely of legal age, not to mention I have no clue how to control my powers that seem to keep multiplying. How could I be of use to anyone?"

"It's not just your powers that make you strong. It's your lineage and what you represent."

"You mean the Prophecy."

"That certainly sent Matias sniffing for you," Neila almost growled. She clearly didn't like the idea that something had tipped him off. "The Prophecy was told a little over a thousand years ago, and with that came a law. Demis weren't allowed to join. They were forbidden from forming unions and procreating."

"Matias tried banning Demis from dating each other?" Carolynn asked. If she didn't like the God already, she certainly like him less now. Separating groups of people never ended well.

"He did, and most obeyed. Those who didn't and were caught were punished severely." Neila slightly flinched as though a bad memory had resurfaced. "But some unions are inevitable and unavoidable. Sam and I were one of those instances. When we met, it was instantaneous, and we knew how much trouble that meant for us. But never in a thousand lives did we expect to be the ones to fulfill the prophecy. Demis having children is not common. It is hard for a God to get pregnant, let alone their offspring."

"How old are the both of you?" Carolynn couldn't help but ask, curiosity getting the better of her. She looked to be barely twenty, but Carolynn figured that wasn't the case.

"I was born nearly two hundred fifty years ago. Sam is about thirty years younger," Neila informed her. "Dominius and Sarena are close, have been for some time, so naturally we grew up together. It wasn't until we realized what we were to each other did we run. We've been living on Earth for almost two hundred years, hiding. When I got pregnant, we knew right away what it meant. We were still found by the occasional demon, but they never had the chance to report us, and we knew keeping you was not an option. Not when we were constantly fleeing and fighting."

Carolynn could hear the heartbreak in her voice, could feel the devastation of their decision, the longing, and the regret, but also the resolve. She made the only decision she could to keep her alive. To allow her to have a normal childhood, raised by two parents who gave her a stable and happy home. Something it sounds like Neila and Sam couldn't offer.

"Sam was able to keep an eye on you, make sure no one tracking you or discovering you were really ours. Everyone knows he's a shifter, but he can take any form, so it wasn't easy to tell who he was. There have been a few who came creeping and got too close, but luckily we were able to find them and remove them before it became a problem."

Carolynn listened to her words and tried to process it all. There had been beings or creatures already hunting her, and given the carefully chosen words Neila was using, she assumed that meant they were no longer breathing. The risk was too great. Her anger and feeling of betrayal dissolved the tiniest bit. She was grateful that they had been around, protecting her without even knowing it.

"If Sam was here as Spot, where were you?" Carolynn asked. She had only met Neila a week ago. Where had she been this entire time?

"I left shortly after I'd given birth to you," Neila confessed. "Sam and I, we were too noticeable together. If we settled down in the same area as you, together, we would have been found sooner rather than later. I wanted you to have as normal a childhood as possible. Or as normal as a child of Gods could have. I traveled around, tried to find ways to better hide you, hunting demons that had been sent down here to find us, to find you."

"What made you come back?"

"You. I knew your eighteenth birthday would bring changes, and I wanted to be here for you, to help you. I also heard rumors of an angel being sent to find a girl. There's only one angel they would send for a mission like that, and I knew that meant that somehow, they had found you. So, I came back and kept close watch."

"You knew the entire time Donnie was here for me? To kill me or bring me to Matias?"

"I suspected, yes."

"And you just let him live?" She didn't understand. How could a mother have essentially allowed her daughter to be stalked, to be tracked, and watched?

"You have to understand, he is not like other angels. If I had engaged with him, it would be catastrophic for this town. I stayed back, and I watched, but not once did he make any move or any inclination as to take you. Not once, and I just knew something was different."

Well, she had more faith in him than Carolynn did at the moment. She still didn't know if she was okay with any of it, but hearing Neila explain definitely eased the parts of her that were clinging to the rage and resentment. She didn't want to let it go, didn't want to give it up, but it was slowly dissolving away.

"Can you die?" Carolynn asked, realizing how blunt and tactless that was after saying it. "I mean, can you get sick? Sam mentioned we're immortal."

"Well, I think immortality is a bit of an exaggeration, but we do age extremely slowly. A Demi can live for a couple of thousand years. But we can die. We're not easy to kill, and we don't really get sick, not the way humans do, but if a fatal blow is struck, yes, we die," Neila explained. "But you, I don't know. You could age like a Demi and have some preclusions to injury, or you could be closer to a God. They don't get sick or die or age after a certain point. No God has ever been killed, but the tale is only a God can kill another God."

"But I was poisoned, cut by a knife. Wouldn't that mean I'm a Demi? And if I'm the child of two Demis wouldn't that make me weaker?" Carolynn asked, confused by all the inner workings of this new world she was being thrown into.

"Not necessarily. Not with the Prophecy in play, and given the level of powers that have already manifested you are more a God than a Demi. You haven't finished your Ascension, so you are still prone to injury and poisons. You don't understand just how vulnerable you are right now," Neila's lips pressed into a thin line, shaking her head.

"What does it mean to ascend? How do I do that? When does it happen?"

"Ascension is a bit different for any Demi, but it typically happens not long after their eighteenth birthday. It's when the bulk of your powers are awakened. For some, it's as simple as feeling a deep emotion and turning into a cat, like Sam. For me, I was angry, angrier than I had ever been, and my power kind of exploded out of me. It knocked out everyone in a ten-foot radius.

But for you, it could be a combination of things. The fact that it hasn't happened yet, only tells me you have more powers to discover first. They can still manifest even after your Ascension, but it's the body's way of adapting to your power, evolving to handle the energy that you contain."

Carolynn bobbed her head as she struggled to take it all in. It wasn't necessarily an answer, but it was better than what she had before, which was nothing. She appreciated Neila taking the time to explain everything, and while she could understand the circumstances surrounding her birth, it still didn't relieve her of the hurt and betrayal from Spot, Sam, or whatever she was supposed to call him. It didn't excuse Shadow either, but that was a different matter altogether.

The sound of a doorknob turning had both of their heads swiveling towards the front door. Carolynn stood up, immediately followed by Neila, who instantly put out an arm, pushing her back. Carolynn pushed the arm down, hearing the thoughts of the person on the other side of the front door.

"Shit," she hissed, stepping around her bed and into the remains of her wall. How was she going to explain any of this? And with Neila here?

"Carolynn?" Susana called out, taking in the splintered wood and plaster littering her living room. She turned towards the wall that should have been there and instead found fractured beams and most of the wall gone. "What the hell?"

Chapter 35

Carolynn's mind scrambled as she tried to come up with some kind of explanation. "Hey, Mom. I can explain."

Susana's brown eyes were wide, taking in the scene before her. "I'm waiting."

"Right, well, you see, I was working on my exercises, and I was trying this new flip and I got carried away," she lamely said. She didn't even know the last time she had practiced any of her tumbling or fighting skills, but it was the best she could come up with.

Susana sighed heavily, rubbing her temples. "How many times have I told you to practice outside?"

"Only about a thousand."

Susana made a small noise that screamed, *how were they going to fix this?* "You know you're cleaning this up and paying to have the wall replaced, right?"

"Absolutely." Carolynn tried to force a smile.

"Now, are you going to explain where the hell you've been the last few days? Lying to me and Thomas about your whereabouts? I didn't know we were keeping secrets," Susana said, flinging her bag onto what was visible of their couch.

Carolynn moved forward, stepping over a large chunk of her wall. "It's hard to explain."

"Why don't you at least try."

How in the world was she supposed to explain any of this to her mother? The mom who thought she was an alien, for shit's sake. What would she do if she learned she came from Gods? Like real, flesh-and-blood Gods.

Carolynn fumbled for words as her mother stared at her, waiting, her brow raised, and lips pursed. The expression that screamed 'bullshit'. Her mother could smell it a mile away.

"I—" Carolynn tried and failed.

"The truth, Carolynn." Susana stared her down.

"I got hurt," Carolynn finally said sheepishly.

"Hurt?" Susana frowned. "You don't get hurt."

"Yeah, I know we thought that."

Susana seemed to finally take notice that there was a stranger in their house as she turned towards Neila and froze, looking stunned for a moment.

Carolynn flicked her gaze between the two of them as each of them showed hints of recognition. Susana then looked between Neila and her, as though fitting an inexplainable puzzle piece together.

"Mom?" Carolynn called Susana. What was going on? What was she witnessing?

"You," Susana finally said, eyes still fixed on Neila. "I—I didn't think I'd ever see you again."

Carolynn's brow furrowed, taken aback. "You two know each other?"

"I didn't think you'd recognize me," Neila said, averting her eyes.

Neila and her mom had met at some point, that was plain, but had her mom known who her birth mother was all this time?

"You're not a face that's easy to forget. Aside from the fact that you haven't aged a day since I last saw you eighteen years ago," Susana said, eyeing her from head to toe. "You're my daughter's birth mother, aren't you?"

Carolynn's mouth fell open, heart racing in her chest. She felt disoriented and a tad dizzy. For just five minutes, could there not be some new revelation?

Neila simply nodded once in confirmation.

"Mom," Carolynn said, voice small. "You knew who my birth mother was this entire time?"

Susana finally looked at her, eyes softening, tilting her head. "No, Star. I didn't. But the two of you standing beside each other, I feel stupid for not putting it together before. You could be sisters."

Carolynn glanced at Neila. They were the same height, same build, same delicate nose, same hair color even minus the black streaks in her hair, but Carolynn's eyes, the chin, even the way she stood slightly slouching, that was Sam.

"How do you two know each other?" Carolynn asked, still not understanding how any of this was real. It's like she was stuck in some bad daytime drama.

"Can we sit first? My feet are killing me after standing all day," Susan said, already shuffling towards their dilapidated table, which was still intact.

The three of them gathered around the small table. Susana leaned back in her chair, rubbing at the soles of one of her feet. Neila sat straight, hands in her lap, as though anticipating something, while Carolynn sat with her hands folded on the table, waiting for someone to explain.

"Would you care to start?" Susana asked Neila, brow raised.

Neila nodded before turning to Carolynn, inhaling deeply before she began. "It was close to my due date when I met your mom. Sam and I, we had been running for so long—well, I got sick. I'd never been sick before, but suddenly I couldn't stop vomiting. I felt weak and tired. I grew dehydrated very quickly."

"All I remember is this man with eyes just like yours running into the ER with this very pregnant woman in his arms, begging for help," Susana told her.

The corner of Neila's mouth pulled into a half-smirk, as though reliving the memory herself.

"I thought you said we don't get sick," Carolynn asked Neila.

"We don't, not like humans do, but my body was reacting to something. It turns out I was in labor, and you were siphoning my powers."

Susana leaned forward, elbows resting on the table. "So, she gets it from you? The telepathy?"

Neila glanced at her for permission. Carolynn nodded.

We can trust her, she told her.

Neila seemed to accept that as enough of an answer. "She gets it from me and Sam, her birth father."

"It's genetic," Susana said, coming to terms with the odd

conversation they were having.

"Yes, it comes from our parents," Neila said carefully. "But when I left her at the fire station, I never imagined it would be you who adopted her, but I am grateful. You helped us that night. Made it so I was strong enough to deliver, and you didn't ask any questions, even after we told you you couldn't take any blood."

"It was definitely a strange request. Usually, only addicts refuse to have their blood drawn," Susana said.

Carolynn nodded her head absently. She wasn't sure what to think or how to feel anymore. Anytime she felt like she had her feet on stable ground, the rug kept getting pulled out from underneath her.

"But why are you here now?" Susana asked Neila. "Why have you come back after all this time? To take my daughter?"

"No, I would never," Neila shook her head.

"Then what am I missing? Did you just come to tell her who she was and where she came from, which, by the way, no one has told me? So, why now?"

Carolynn started to say no, started to deny anything going on that could remotely put Susana in danger. She didn't want her mom involved, not at all. Her dream, the nightmares, it was all too real. She didn't want her mom anywhere near their world, but Neila gripped her hand, giving her a tight squeeze.

You have to tell her. Otherwise, she will think the worst. Trust me.

Carolynn could see the sympathy, the empathy written on Neila's face. She swallowed hard, a knot forming in her stomach as her anxiety rose. She reached out with her one free hand and grabbed her mom's, looking into those blue eyes. "Mom. There are some things that have been going on, that I need to tell you."

Carolynn tried to keep herself from shaking, her body overrun with nerves as she went into detail about the last weeks' worth of events. She told her about the mishap with the saddle. Were it not for her reflexes, she very well could have broken her neck. She told her mom about the break-in at the house. Her mother nearly blew a gasket, but it was learning that she had been injured and poisoned that brought tears to her eyes. She explained all that she had learned the last few days, where she comes from, and how her powers have been changing and growing. She even told her about the dreams that started the night of her birthday, and how they prophesized Susana and Beth's death, leaving out the part about her own demise. She didn't react to Neila's surprise or outrage over the last part. But she didn't go into detail about Donnie, leaving him out almost entirely.

That was private and no one else's business.

She paid close attention to her mother as she spoke. The change in posture as her shoulders drooped and straightened as the events of her story changed and fluctuated. The slight parting of her mouth to the thin displeased line she was familiar with. But mostly the saddening of her eyes, the disappointment, and the hurt.

Carolynn leaned back in her seat, fidgeting with the end of her shirt as she waited for someone to say something, anything.

Susana brushed away the tears that had leaked from her eyes and sat up, leaning on the table. She laid her hands out, palms up, gesturing for her to take them. Carolynn laid her hands on her mother's, holding on tightly.

"I am so sorry you've had to go through all of that on your own and didn't think I was strong enough to tell me," Susana said, voice breaking with unbridled emotion.

"Mom," Carolynn tried to tell her it was fine, tried to tell her she was okay, but the words caught in her throat.

Susana looked between Carolynn and Neila, slowly coming to terms with everything she had been told. "So, the two of you are Goddesses?"

"No," they both said simultaneously.

"My mother is a Goddess, but I am a Demi, not as strong as a true God," Neila explained.

Carolynn tried not to point out the fact that she hadn't mentioned her dad. Unless she didn't know who her father was. Susana looked to her for her own answer, and she shrugged.

"We don't really know what I am."

"And these dreams you've been having"—Susana swallowed—"they show I'm dead?"

How could you not have told us about them? Neila intruded on her mind.

It's not like I've had the time, Carolynn retorted. *I've been a little busy lately trying not to die.*

Still, you should have told us. We could have done something sooner.

Like what? Lock them away?

"Are you two talking to each other through your minds?" Susana asked, eyeing the two of them.

"Sorry, Mom," Carolynn apologized.

This was all too weird, but she was shocked by how well her mother seemed to be handling it. She really was doing a lot better than she had given her credit for.

"Why didn't you tell me about any of this before? I think it would have been pertinent information to know that someone or something is hunting after my daughter." Susana glared at her.

"But my dreams –"

"If it's my time, then so be it. But that doesn't give you the right to keep things from me. You're my daughter, it's *my* job to keep you safe. Not the other way around." Susana then looked to Neila who instantly sat proud. "Is that why you came back? To protect her? Or is there something else?"

Carolynn wasn't sure if Neila was reading her mother's mind or what, but she began to shake her head.

"I didn't come here to take her from you, if that's what you're insinuating. She's your daughter, and you raised her beautifully. I only came because around our eighteenth birthday is when powers truly begin to develop, and I had heard a rumor that she had been found," Neila explained. "I'm only here to help."

"You should have come to me the moment you felt she was in danger," Susana said sharply.

Carolynn was slightly surprised by her mother's tone, claiming her territory and going all mama-bear.

"Humans do not survive in our world," Neila said, not giving her an inch. "We thought it was best to keep those who knew about her to a minimum. You being involved only puts you in further danger."

"As you said, she is *my* daughter and that was my call to make," Susana said firmly before turning back to Carolynn. "No more secrets."

Carolynn nodded in agreement. "No more secrets."

Neila glanced towards the front door, as though someone had called to her. "I should be going. I do apologize for the overload of information. It wasn't my intention." Neila stood up from the table, making her way to the door, but she turned back. "Thank you, Susana. For everything."

Carolynn turned around in her seat to say something, 'thank you' maybe, but found the door already closing behind her. She turned back to her mother, skin itching with curiosity. She wanted to get into her head, see what she was thinking, how she was handling it all, but fear restrained her. Too afraid of what she might find.

It was her mother that finally spoke.

"Maybe we should leave. Go somewhere far away, where no one can find us." Susana sounded desperate, they both knew it, but Carolynn shook her head.

"I don't think it's that easy. I barely understand any of what's happening. My powers, who else might come looking for me. I don't think running away will solve anything. Besides I can't just leave, Beth is in danger as well. Then there's Neila and Sam. They'll be found out and killed for even having me," Carolyn tried to explain, tried to get her to see that it wasn't as simple as her running away. But there was another option. "I think maybe it's you that should leave."

"I'm not leaving you behind." Susana stood up from the table, biting her nails.

Carolynn knew she would be stubborn, but she had to see reason. "You can't stay here. They're going to come after you to get to me. I can't—" She choked back a sob rising in her chest. She blinked back the tears that were threatening to spill and hardened her jaw. "You can't be here when they come. I can't watch you die."

"My place is here with you," Susana said, her hand grazing her shoulder as she pushed her hair back. She felt hot tears roll down her face. "You are the best thing I've ever done, and I'm sorry I've been so shitty lately, but I want you to know how proud I am of you, and if I do die, you need to know it wasn't your fault. I wouldn't take any of it back."

"Mom." A small sob escaped her as she angrily wiped away her tears.

"Losing your father gave me some clarity." Susana offered a weak smile. "Life is cruel, but it's also wonderful and beautiful.

When you love and allow yourself to be loved, you accept that loss is inevitable, because it is, and that's okay."

"I won't lose you," Carolynn promised.

Susana grinned, leaning in and kissing her on the forehead. "Of course you won't."

Carolynn watched as her mother left her alone in the kitchenette and closed her bedroom door behind her. She took in a deep shuddering breath. All she wanted was her pillow and food, but she highly doubted there was anything edible in the house. She couldn't remember the last time she grocery-shopped. There might still be a pop tart in her nightstand.

She glared at the remains of her wall scattered throughout the living room, grimacing at the large chunks of wood. Sighing, she went to the kitchen under the sink and pulled out a black trash bag. Flicking the bag open, she bent over, picking up the smaller pieces that didn't need to be carried out separately and shoved them into the bag.

Images flashed across her mind as she cleaned, replaying over and over in her mind. Donnie's look of confusion and hurt as she blasted him through the wall. The concern and empathy she could feel from him as he tried to get closer, even at the risk of his own life. Hell, maybe she was giving herself too much credit. She probably couldn't kill the angel even if she wanted to. Not that that was a bad thing.

Hauling the bag over her shoulder, she carried it outside to the back of the house where the garbage bins were housed. As she threw the trash into the bin, she could sense she was being watched.

You look better.

Carolynn whirled around to find Spot—or better yet: Sam in owl form—perched on the railing of the back deck. She felt her heart sink at the sight of him. She was completely drained and emotionally exhausted. She did not have the energy for him.

"What are you doing here?"

I wanted to check on you.

"Well, you came, you saw, now you can leave." Carolynn gestured for him to go, to scurry or fly off to Gods know where. Just anywhere but here.

Carolynn, Sam warned.

She knew she was being rude, and it wasn't typical behavior in their relationship, but that was before. Did he really expect for nothing to change? That she would just learn who he really was and everything would be fine? He was out of his owl mind.

"What do you want from me? It's been a shit, no good, very bad day. I've had it up to here with info dumps and long-lost relatives. I'm tired and hungry, and I just want my bed," Carolynn sighed. She was ranting, she knew she was, but could he really blame her?

Look on the table.

Carolynn frowned, turning around to the patio table where she found a take-out bag from the diner. She cautiously walked over to it, for some off reason expecting it to explode or shapeshift into a bat, something. But all she could do was smell the greasy cheeseburger it contained. Her stomach growled loudly. She side-eyed the owl, pursing her lips.

"How did you know?" Carolynn asked sheepishly.

I know you, he said simply.

Carolynn pulled the burger out of the bag and peeled back its wrapping, the heavy scent making her mouth water. She bit into it and nearly moaned. Damn, she was starving.

"We're not okay," Carolynn said aloud. "But this helps."

The owl snorted, ruffling his feathers. *Get some rest. We will talk more tomorrow.*

"Yay," Carolynn said sarcastically as she continued to devour the fast food and watched as the owl took off into the black, moonless sky. She stood there eating, watching as his white form disappeared into nothing more than a speck.

She threw her trash away into the bin before heading back inside. The remains of her wall were left in chunks around the room, and it could wait till tomorrow, as she was dead on her feet. She walked into what remained of her room and found a black wolf sitting on the floor at the foot of her bed. She stopped short.

Carolynn sighed deeply, hanging her head back, staring up at the ceiling. "How is it that you always appear after all hell breaks loose?"

Luck, the wolf offered sarcastically.

"Or shit timing," she retorted. "Look, I don't want to talk anymore tonight. I just want sleep."

Fine.

Carolynn waited for Shadow to say more but she didn't. Instead, she curled up on the floor, tucking her nose beneath her tail, and closed her eyes. Carolynn quickly stepped into her closet and changed out of the dirty clothes into an oversized tee that hung just long enough to cover her butt. She climbed into bed, grateful there was no dust or debris on her comforter as she snuggled beneath the cover, sinking into her pillow. The bed shifted as Shadow came up to lie beside her. The wolf snuggled up to her side like they always slept and Carolynn relaxed further into the bed as the familiar smell of her fur coaxed her to sleep.

Lightning streaked across the sky. Wonderfully beautiful men and women fought against each other in a great clearing. The sound of metal swords clashing against each other drowned out the calls of battle and screams of pain. A man with her eyes, Dominius, transformed into a great lion and lunged for a hooded figure. Two women fought side by side with blades and daggers. Sarena and Neila moved as though they were dancing, steel catching the sun high in the sky as the swiped down anyone in their paths. A dragon tore through the clouds, ripping apart angels that dared to approach.

Carolynn looked down at her feet. Her mother lay below her, still and unmoving in a pool of crimson, her throat slit from ear to ear. Her face had an expression of shock, her eyes wide open and glazed with death. Beth lay close by. Brown bouncing curls lay across her face, body mangled and broken. Her beautiful face was covered in cuts and bruises, as though she had been brutally tortured to death.

Donnie was fighting in the crowd. Fighting his way towards her, his sword in hand, dripping with blood. He was struggling to reach her against a surge of angels pushing him back. She looked down at her own hand to find a heavy blade in her grasp. She felt too tired, too weak to even try and lift it, her body feeling heavy and aching all over as if she'd been thoroughly beaten. She was sore and could feel her skin was crusted over with dried rust-colored blood. Light bounced off a piece of metal nearby, catching her eye. She looked up at the sword aimed for her throat.

Carolynn jolted awake, sitting up straight. Her breathing was heavy and erratic, her cheeks wet and eyes crusted and sore. Her ears were still ringing with the echoes of a faraway battle.

"Damn it," she whispered.

Chapter 36

Carolynn blinked her eyes steadily as her vision came into focus. She stared up at the ceiling, knowing full well she'd never be able to fall back asleep. She sat up slowly, rubbing the sleep from her eyes, and stretched out her stiff muscles. She felt sore and tired as though she hadn't slept at all. Glancing down, she found Shadow still snoring beside her.

Moving quietly out of bed, she headed for the bathroom. Inside, she began to methodically run her brush through her hair in a steady rhythm as she worked out the snags and kinks. She went through her normal routine and got ready for work.

She heard Shadow moving off the bed as she pulled on her riding boots. She took one final look at herself in the mirror and adjusted her necklace so the clasp was in the back.

You're going to work? Shadow asked, head slightly cocked to the side.

"Yes. I haven't been there in days thanks to my near-death experience," Carolynn said, putting her hair up into a high ponytail. "I need to get back into the rhythm of my life."

She slipped her phone into her back pocket, grabbed her wallet, and looked through what once was her wall. Last night came back to her in pieces. Her injured feet, Donnie healing her faster than anything she'd ever seen, learning his true purpose here, infiltrating her life, her hea— no, she stopped those thoughts before they could finish. Nothing good could come of it. It didn't matter that she craved him like an addict, or that she could almost feel his touch, his hands in her hair, on her skin, between her legs. An aching began to build there quicker than she would have thought.

She needed to get a grip.

Carolynn stepped out of her bedroom, avoiding the larger pieces of her wall that were still strewn about the room, and stopped mid-step, surprised to find her mother sitting at the dinner table, sipping on a cup of coffee and eating a plate of eggs and toast.

"Mom?"

Susana looked up from the depths of her mug and smiled. "I made breakfast."

Carolynn paused. This was certainly out of the ordinary. She couldn't remember the last time they had breakfast together and sat down across from her. "Is everything okay? Why aren't you at work?"

"I called my supervisor and took some time off. I don't go back for another two weeks."

"Why?"

"Because it's been made abundantly clear to me that I've been a shit mom. My daughter is off galivanting with Gods and nearly dies, and I had no clue," Susana said pointedly. "I want to spend time with you, and I need to be more present."

Carolynn cast her eyes down guiltily. While she was thrilled to have her mom home more, now really wasn't the best time to start bonding. "I'm actually on my way out."

Susana seemed to finally take notice of her attire. "You're going to work? Is that wise?"

"I haven't been there in days. I have to get back. Besides, I won't hide. I need to live my life."

Susana nodded as though understanding the need to get back into routine, back to normalcy. Hell, it was what she did right after Dad died.

"That's fair," Susana said. "Do you need a ride?"

"No, that's okay. I enjoy the walk," Carolynn smiled, grateful for the offer. "Do you have plans for today?"

"I'm just going to hang here. Do some shopping, find someone to come replace your wall." Susana raised a brow at the chunks of wall still in the living room.

"I will take that out before I leave."

"You better, you rascal," Susana chided, hiding a smile behind her mug.

"Yes, ma'am." Carolynn laughed, getting up from the table. She gave her a quick peck on the cheek, before swiping a slice of toasted bread off her plate. She grinned as she shoved the toast in her mouth before bouncing towards the living room.

Carolynn picked up the last remaining chunks of wood still on the floor. Shadow came along and picked up a rather impressive slab of plaster. Carolynn shoved open the front door with her shoulder, yelling goodbye through the toast still hanging in her mouth as Shadow followed her out, kicking the door closed behind them.

Concentrating on the loose floorboards beneath her feet, she carefully took the steps down one at a time and tossed the wood into a pile on the side of the house.

Maybe they could have a bonfire or something.

Grumbling as she noticed her leggings were covered in dust, she brushed herself off with one hand while munching on the now soggy bread, when she stopped in shock as she finally took in her surroundings.

The toast, now forgotten, fell to the gravel driveway.

"What the fuck?"

Carolynn stood, mouth gaping open, eyes widened as she stared at a midnight blue Chevy Camaro Coupe parked in her driveway. She glanced around the property, twisting and turning each way, waiting for someone to show up with some kind of explanation, but there was no one. She circled around the car cautiously as though she expected it to transform, which didn't seem to be too far of a stretch given that she had witnessed an owl turn into a man. Shadow sniffed at the car cautiously. There was no one inside, and no rational expectation as to why in the world it would be in front of her house.

She carefully opened the car's driver door. It was unlocked. She stood there waiting like an idiot, expecting an alarm of some kind to go off, but nothing happened. She slid into the driver's seat, the leather immediately conforming to her body. The new car smell was overwhelming with a hint of lemon as though someone had recently wiped it down. She ran her hands over the steering wheel.

The dash held a ten-inch screen with a fully operational navigation system. It definitely seemed to carry all the bells and whistles.

Damn, it is a nice car, she couldn't help but think. It must have cost a pretty penny; that was certain.

This thing had to belong to someone. She popped open the glove compartment and inside found the owner's manual, two sets of key fobs, and the title and registration to the car. She read over the title and recognized her own name on the paper.

"What the fuck?" she repeated again, only this time louder. "Someone bought me a fucking car!"

Shadow stood beside her on the driveway, wedged between the open door and her as she shoved the title paperwork in the wolf's face.

Please remove that before you give me a papercut.

"Who the hell would be dumb enough—" Her words trailed off as she thought about it. She wanted to scream, wanted to find that bird and wring his neck, bio-dad or no. She slammed her head back into the leather headrest, internally screaming.

You're giving me a headache. Shadow winced.

"They bought me a car! Did you know about this?" she asked, ignoring the wolf.

They don't tell me everything.

"Well, they certainly talk to you more than me," she grumbled, tossing the paperwork back into the glove compartment and slamming it shut. "This is insane. I'm giving it back. I didn't ask for this."

But you need a car, Shadow commented, as though it made perfect sense.

"Not like this." Carolynn shook her head, staring at the beautiful, sleek lines of the vehicle. "I wanted to earn one, buy it myself. This makes me feel cheap. Like I can be bought."

Well, can we at least use it for now and give it back later? We're going to be late.

"I'm not driving this!"

Use it or lose it.

Carolynn glared at the wolf. She hated it when the wolf was more practical.

"If I'm driving this car, then you're staying home."

I stay with you. I'm sorry about yesterday and not telling you, but you can't—

Carolynn cut her off. "It's not about that. I'm not punishing you." She shook her head. "I need you to stay with Mom while I'm gone. I can't be in two places at once, and if she isn't going to work, she's all alone here. I need you to stay and look after her."

Shadow seemed to consider it for a moment before nodding her large head. *I will stay.*

Carolynn let out a breath she hadn't realized she'd been holding and smiled. "Thank you."

Shadow backed away from the car, pushing the door shut carefully with her front paws. Carolynn pushed the start button, and the engine purred to life beneath her feet. She tapped gently on the gas pedal, and the engine roared defiantly as the brakes held it in place. She couldn't help the smile that crept across her face or the laugh that escaped her as Shadow mentally scolded her. She put the car in reverse and as she backed away from the house, she watched Shadow's beautiful fur slink into the tree line, blending in seamlessly with the darkness. A lump formed in her throat for some unknown reason, and she shook it off as she pulled out of the driveway.

The drive to the stables was a smooth one as she took the backroads where no one would bear witness to her blowing the speed limit, the trees and fields a blur. The car was magic, driving effortlessly through the bends and turns. Carolynn secretly hated that she had to give it back, but she did.

Carolynn drove the Camaro up to the house, parking beside Beth's Mustang. As she stepped out of the car, she could already see Beth nearly running from the stables. Her friend's face was a mixture of confusion and astonishment. Her brown hair was billowing in the wind behind her, her brown eyes wide, and her mouth hung open awkwardly.

"Where the hell did you get that?" Beth asked, jabbing a finger at the car. "Did you steal it?"

"I found it," Carolynn said, slamming the car door shut. How absurd for her to think she'd steal such a conspicuous car.

"You found it?" Beth asked in disbelief, hands propped on her hips. "You don't just find a car. You find a kitten, or a sweater, or even twenty bucks on the sidewalk, but not a car."

"It's from Neila and Sam." There was no other explanation needed.

Beth paused as she took that in. Her mouth formed an O until the shock wore off. "Well, shit, can they be my new mommy and daddy, 'cause I'd love me a car like that."

"This is so not the time for a joke."

"Who's joking? Look at the bright side: no more walking everywhere. No more calling me for rides. While I enjoy all the bonding time, being your taxi was *so* high school."

Carolynn raised a brow at her friend and had the strong urge to smack her upside the head. "Thanks for the love and support."

"Anytime, bitch." Beth laughed. "But seriously, what's the problem?"

"Aside from the fact that the parents I didn't know about until yesterday just bought me a car that I didn't ask for? It's too much; it's going back," Carolynn told her, leaving the car behind and heading for the stables as she yelled over her shoulder. "And don't think I won't remember that you have now called me a burden for driving me around."

"You know I'm kidding," Beth called, running to catch up. "But why are you giving it back? It's so shiny and pretty."

"Because I'm not someone they can buy, and I don't need a pity car," Carolynn said, stomping her feet down the aisle to her office.

"I get it, they're inserting themselves in parts of your life you didn't ask for," Beth said, holding her hands up in surrender. "Now, are you going to tell me what else has your panties all in twists?"

Carolynn froze at her desk, mid-shuffling through mail as her friend's words sunk in. Was that what she was doing? Throwing a tantrum, having a fit, acting out? She wanted to hit something, wanted to throw herself so deep into work she forgot the world around her, but she didn't think there was enough horse shit to shovel in the entire state of Florida that would help her forget her problems. She perused through the mail instead.

"Okay, or you can just *not* answer me. I get there's been a lot of shit for you lately. Birth parents, nearly dying, finding out you are some Goddess, and who knows what else. It's not like we've really had the time to chat, but you see, the problem is, if you don't tell me something, then I'm going to start overthinking and believe it's something that I did. Except that I know there's nothing I could have done wrong, seeing as how you were in a coma for two days, and I've barely seen you since. So rather than let me overthink, why don't you throw me a bone, any bone?"

"You don't think any of those issues you listed is enough to cause me to be in a mood?" Carolynn asked, barely looking up from the latest veterinarian bill. Thomas was going to have a heart attack.

"For me, yes. For you, she who walks on water and barely bats a lash at most mortal issues, no." *Damn, can Donnie just screw her already; she needs to loosen up.*

Carolynn flinched at her friend's thoughts flooding through her mind unwarranted and unprovoked. She rolled her shoulders back, feeling tension gather there as she tried to repress last night, tried not to think about him and that creeping sadness and loneliness that accompanied it.

Beth seemed to take notice, eyes widening as though it was her that was the mind-reader and not the other way around. "What happened with Donnie?"

Carolynn visibly flinched again, putting the mail down on the desk a bit harder than necessary. "What makes you think something happened? I'm fine." She noticed how flat her voice sounded as the words left her mouth.

"Carolynn, I'm your best friend. I know you."

"I really don't want to talk about it."

"Well, that's too bad, cause I do," Beth pushed.

Carolynn slammed her hands down on the desk, causing it to lift off the floor for just a second. "He informed me last that he's the fucking Angel of Death and was sent here to kill me. Are you happy now?"

"What? How am I just finding out about this now?"

"Maybe it's because it's not something I desperately wanted to discuss."

"Fuck," Beth hissed, chewing on one of her fingernails. "Has he ever tried to hurt you?"

"What?" Carolynn asked, not really hearing her.

"Well, has he ever tried to hurt you?"

"Does that really matter? He told me he was sent here to kill me; shouldn't that be enough?"

"What exactly did he say?"

Carolynn rolled her eyes. She should have never said anything. "I don't remember."

"Now I know you're lying," Beth said, still pushing and prodding.

"Beth, I need you to drop it. I don't want to talk about this," Carolynn said, her blood rising as that pressure continued to build. She could feel her control slipping as she remembered him, how stone-faced he was as he confessed to her, and how apologetic he looked after she blasted him through the wall. She could feel the energy building inside her once more, and she quickly tried to steady herself, taking in even and slow breaths.

"You know I can't drop it. What did he say?" Beth pressed.

Fuck!

"Beth, that's enough!" Carolynn's self-control evaporated. She could feel the ball of energy expelling from her body, aiming itself for Beth. Without a moment to consider what she was doing or what was even happening, the energy had left her.

Beth's eyes widened at the sparking ball of electricity emanating from Carolynn's body; that is, until she flung herself down on the ground, effectively ducking. She flung herself back up on her knees and stared wide-eyed at Carolynn.

"What the fuck was that?" she screamed, looking to where the ball of light had gone and seeing a hole the size of a soccer ball now punched through the wooden barn wall.

"Fuck, are you okay?" Carolynn asked, breathing heavily as she stepped toward Beth.

"You just tried to kill me!" Beth hollered.

"Will you lower your voice," she hissed, "and stop being so overdramatic. I don't think it would have killed you, just knocked you out for a bit."

"Oh, like that's so much better," Beth grumbled, standing up and dusting the dirt off her jeans. She glanced back at the hole in the wall and whistled. "When did that new power develop?"

"Last night," Carolynn admitted, cocking her head to the side as she could see the main house through the hole. "When I used it on him."

Beth looked back at her, eyes sympathetic. "I'm sorry I pushed."

"I'm sorry I nearly killed you."

"You just said it wouldn't have!"

Carolynn shrugged. "I don't know how any of this works."

"That's real comforting."

"Carolynn?"

Both girls jerked towards the door where Jason stood, leaning against the door frame.

Carolynn tried to smile, rubbing her palm at her chest where the energy had escaped, feeling an ache there. "Jason, come in."

"I'm gonna head out before I really do end up dead," Beth joked, kissing Carolynn on the cheek.

Carolynn tried not to visibly react to her friend's words, but her dreams instantly resurfaced.

We'll talk later, she heard her friend think.

Beth. Carolynn called to her, forcing Beth to stop mid-way out the door. *Don't leave the house tonight.*

Beth frowned, brows furrowed, but she didn't complain, didn't question it, just simply nodded. *Okay.*

Carolynn turned back to Jason, ignoring the questioning look, and sat down at her desk across from him. She noticed a yellowish stain around his eyes, and a small lump on the bridge of his nose, which looked to be a tad crooked.

"What happened to your wall?" Jason asked, tipping his head to the perfectly symmetrical hole.

"Accident," Carolynn answered coldly. "What happened to your face? Did you walk into a pole?"

"Miscalculation. It won't happen again." Jason smiled. "I heard you've been sick. I hope everything is fine."

"Perfect. Just a touch of the flu."

"Glad you're better."

"Thank you."

"I asked Beth where you were staying, wanted to send you a get-well bouquet but she's very protective of you," Jason said casually, picking hay off his shirt.

"The feeling is mutual, but I appreciate the thought," Carolynn replied, getting an odd feeling, like oil over water.

Carolynn watched him as he slowly rose from the chair. She

leaned back in her seat as he moved to stand beside her desk, hovering over her. She didn't like the height difference and didn't like how he was dominating her space. She was about to stand up and reclaim her authority when he leaned in, and she panicked. Was he trying to kiss her? But he pulled a straw of hay from her hair and flicked it on the floor. How the hell did that get there?

"I'm glad you're alright," Jason said, just before turning and leaving the room.

Carolynn felt dazed and peculiar as she watched him go. She pushed herself out of her chair when something caught her eye.

Lying on her desk was a long-stemmed red rose. The color of the petals was like nothing she had ever seen before. It was so deep and rich in color it was almost black. The smell of the rose was enchanting, mesmerizing, so rich in flavor it nearly made her dizzy. She glanced back up at the doorway where Jason had left.

How had she not noticed him carrying it?

She glanced back down at the rose. The longer she looked at it, it really did look black, reminding her of Donnie, his hair, his clothes, how he oozed darkness. She could still feel his shadows, brushing against her skin, caressing and stroking her.

Anger flared inside. Anger and hurt and a soul-crushing pain she didn't know was possible. Pressure built within her again. She had to get out of the barn, had to get away from buildings, animals, and people, before she hurt someone else.

She ran and ran, ignoring her name being called, ignored the whinnies of the horses, and just ran.

Chapter 37

Carolynn walked down the road, her feet aching. She wasn't sure how far she'd been running or exactly where she was. She should turn back at some point, but what was she going back to? Where would she go? She wasn't even sure where the hell she was. Somehow, she had missed the sun setting and moon rising. How the hell had it gotten so dark so fast? Was she losing time? Had she been that deeply engrossed in her own thoughts and emotions she lost the entire day?

She couldn't go back to the stable, too many horses and an unsuspecting barn help. She couldn't go home and put her mother at risk. Not when she was so volatile, so at risk of losing control. Already she could feel that energy, that pulsing, electric ball, writhing beneath her skin, desperate to be released, to be let free.

A brisk, forceful wind blew her hair forward, tickling her neck. The air had been dead the entire time she'd been outside, and something dark and warm brushed against her legs and along her hip, which could only mean one thing, one person.

She tried not to react, to not outwardly shiver as those shadows seemed to skim over her, as though checking her for any visible wounds, but they couldn't see the ones inside. She tried not to react to his scent as it enveloped her, wrapping her in its warmth and instant comfort that told her she was safe. How was that even possible? Safe with him?

"Why are you here?" she finally spoke without glancing up at him as he kept pace alongside her.

"I wanted to check on you. You shouldn't be out here by yourself."

"How long have you been following me?"

"I technically never left," he admitted. "That was a nice car they gave you."

Donnie's deep voice sent a shiver down her spine. She wanted to reach out and touch him, take his hand, feel his warmth, and soak it into her skin, but she pushed them into the pockets of her leggings instead. She needed to get a grip.

"Some people would call that stalking," she retorted sarcastically.

"I'd call it keeping you safe," he replied coolly.

"Safe from who, you?" Carolynn asked, stopping to look up into his face. There were no street lights on this road, only the light offered by the crescent moon in the sky, which wasn't much, causing his ice-blue eyes to be much starker and contrast against his pale skin and dark hair and clothes. It hurt to look at him, hurt to see the concern in his eyes, in the set of his mouth.

Was it real?

Donnie stared straight again, his posture stiff and shoulders back, and continued walking, forcing her to keep up. "There are other creatures out here that want to hurt you, to capture you," Donnie said, "but I am not one of them."

"How can I trust that?" Carolynn stopped dead in the middle of the road again, forcing him to turn.

"I saved your life, for fuck's sake. I risked any kind of future with you in order to save you," Donnie said in one quick breath, rubbing his temples.

"What does that even mean?" Carolynn frowned. "How does saving me risk anything?"

He turned on her quickly, eyes hard and unyielding. "Because I had to give you my blood, and an Angel's blood contains every memory of everything they've ever done, good or bad."

Carolynn's mouth hung open as she put the pieces together. "Troy and the London Bridge," she whispered, recalling the life-like dreams she knew were too detailed to be a dream, but that's because they weren't. They were memories. His memories.

Donnie leaned back on his heels. "So they've started already."

"I've had a few dreams." Carolynn nodded. "But why would that change anything? Why would your memories risk whatever it was between us?" She watched as he visibly flinched at the past tense she used. She didn't mean it, not really, but she took a sick pleasure in seeing the reaction.

Maybe he did care.

"Do you think I want that for you? Do you think you'll be able to look at me after witnessing the things I've done, the people I've murdered? The joy I took in killing and maiming humans for the last two thousand years?" His eyes were bright and feral, and if she looked close enough, she could have sworn she almost saw the flames from Troy deep within.

"You think you can just decide how I will handle that? How I will have to make peace with your past?" Carolynn asked, voice rising. How dare he assume! "You came here to kill me, for fuck's sake; to take me away and let Matius do Gods knows what with me. How can I trust anything you say?"

Donnie's hand shot forward faster than she could see. He gripped her arms in a death-like grip, not hard enough to hurt or bruise, but just tight enough so that she couldn't move, couldn't escape. He dragged her forward, towards him, until their chests were touching, and she could feel the rise and fall of his chest, his ragged breathing. He was angry.

"I told you I was here for you, you, the silly human. You're the one who chose not to believe me," he growled, actually growled in her face.

"Like I was supposed to know that you were here to kidnap me!" she shouted back. "And I'm not human, am I? So don't call me one."

Donnie lifted her off the ground until only her toes touched the pavement and their noses were touching. "Haven't I proven on more than enough occasions, I will not hurt you; that I would do anything for you."

"Was any of it real?" She had to ask, had to know, and silently begged him to lie. Because if he said it was true, it was all real, there was no going back. There would never be anyone else that could come close to him.

"All of it," Donnie promised, voice softening, holding her gaze, those blue eyes telling her far more than his words did.

Carolynn's heart stuttered in her chest. Her ears rang as her heart rate quickened and blood ran fire through her veins. "Prove it," she whispered, her lips brushing against his.

She didn't care that this was stupid. Didn't care that maybe it wasn't wise to fall for the Angel of Death, but they were past that. Past reason and rationale, past common sense, and common decency. All she could hear was her blood pounding through her veins, for him. All she could think of was that he was touching her but not in any of the places she needed to be touched. All she wanted was for this to be real. For him to want her almost as badly as she needed him.

This was dangerous. He held too much power over her mind, her heart, and body. This might very well end in a rain of blood and fire, or at the very least with a sword through her chest, but if she only had a few days left to live, it would be with him. That, she would never, could never regret.

Donnie stared down at her for a moment, eyes searching, before he finally crushed his lips against hers, pressing them into a searing kiss she was certain would be imprinted on her soul for the rest of eternity. She opened her mouth for him, tasting him, teeth and tongue clashing and fighting. She wound her hands around his neck and in his hair, gripping onto the roots and pulling. His hands released her arms, only to grip her at the waist and hoist her up against him, forcing her to wrap her legs around him.

She pressed herself hard against him as they devoured each other, tasted, and teased. She could live off of this, off of him. The taste of him was something she could never dream up or be rid of. He was her own special drug.

She pulled back, catching her breath, and rested her forehead against his. She had to know, had to see.

"I want to see them," she said, her voice soft and raspy.

Donnie seemed to freeze, to pull away, but she held on tight. She wouldn't let him pull away, not anymore. They were beyond secrets now.

Carolynn pulled her head back only enough to look him in the eye, to see into those ice-blue eyes that were wide, the pupils barely the size of a pinprick. She was seeing fear, true fear. Was he afraid she would judge him? That she would think any less of him? Maybe there was a difference between knowing and seeing, but she had to see them. Had to know it wasn't just in her head. He was an Angel, right? That came with very specific parts.

She didn't know what changed his mind, but he nodded his head once before his shoulders shook and a gust of wind blew the hair back from her face.

Even in the dark, they were giant and magnificent and stole the breath right from her lungs. She gasped, mouth going dry, eyes widening as she took in their width, their beauty. Her fingers tingled, itching to reach out and stroke the feathers that were as long as her forearm. There were thousands of them layered over one another, secured to the strong wings that grew from his shoulder blades. Each of them contained their own tiny rainbow, reflecting shades of green, blue, purple, and pink.

"Donnie." She breathed his name in wonder, unable to tear her eyes from them. "They're beautiful."

A calloused hand cupped her cheek, bringing her attention back to him. His eyes were bright, and for the very first time since the night they met, he looked relaxed, like he was finally himself. An Angel.

Her Angel. Her Angel of Death.

"*You're* beautiful," he corrected, his voice rough and raw.

Carolynn swallowed hard, her heartbeat rising, filling her ears and drowning out the noise of the forest around them. She licked her lips, feeling parched but not for water, and she watched with a deepening hunger as he tracked her tongue. She bit her lower lip, smirking.

"Can I touch them?"

Donnie's brows scrunched, eyes still staring at the lip caught between her teeth. "What?"

"Can I touch your wings?" she asked again.

This time he did look at her, once again hesitant and unsure.

"Unless you don't want me to," she said, trying to take it back. He was already sharing so much with her, she didn't want to push him.

"It's not that," he sighed, eyes darting between hers. "No one touches an Angel's wings except for their mate. It's intimate."

"Oh," she said, her mouth stuck on the word. Mate. Did he have someone else?

"There is no one else." Donnie tightened his grip on her waist, her neck, forcing her back to here and now, with him.

"Can you read minds too?" She chuckled.

"Sometimes I wish I could read yours," he admitted. "But no, I can just see it on your face."

Carolynn nodded her head, glancing back at his wings again. "Go ahead."

Her eyes widened, brows raised. "Are you sure? I don't have to."

"There's no one else in any world I'd want touching my wings, apart from you."

Carolynn understood the underlying message easily enough but tried not to dissect it just yet, her hands ready and eager. With one arm, she released her grip from his neck and reached out over his shoulder. The crest of his wings was taller than him, but she didn't need to reach very far as he pulled them in tighter, closer to her. Her fingers made contact, and Donnie instantly shuddered beneath her as she stroked the downy soft, velvety feathers. They were more luxurious than anything she could have imagined as she ran her fingers along the arch of the wing and back down the layers of plume. She felt him tense beneath her, going rigid as she stroked up and down the small section of wing she could reach.

"If you keep doing that, we are going to end up in a much more compromising position," Donnie said through clenched teeth, veins bulging in his neck and something hard pressing through his jeans and against her core. "And I can't promise I'll be gentle."

Carolynn slowly pulled her hand back, watching him closely. His eyes were almost completely black, feral. She felt warm and hot all along her skin, and something was building deep in her belly. She squirmed against him, trying to ease that ache, but his hands tightened on her neck and waist.

"Kitten, I'm trying very hard to be a gentleman. I don't think you want your first time against a tree, but you're making it extremely difficult," Donnie growled, the sound sending a delicious shiver down her spine. "Now, be a good gir—"

Carolynn cut him off, pressing her lips against his, hard and demanding. She didn't want to talk, didn't want to explain or hear any more about their fucked-up worlds. She just wanted him, to feel his hands, his tongue, his lips. She wanted it all, and she didn't care if it was in a bed, against a tree, or on the forest floor, she just wanted him.

His hands gripped her shirt, almost as if he was warring with himself between taking it off or shredding it, but instead, he let it go and went farther south, cupping her ass and squeezing her hard into him. Carolynn moaned into his mouth as his surprising length rubbed against her clit, as his lips traveled across her jaw, down her neck, and across her chest. She tilted her head back, her skin afire everywhere he touched and kissed, her brain turning to mush when she heard a faint scream.

Donnie must have felt her tense as he stopped, pulling back, struggling to catch his breath. "What is it?"

Carolynn turned her head towards the wind, trying to focus, trying to concentrate. Was it a trick?

But she heard it again, this time stronger, more desperate, and in pain, sending a psychic shock to her system. Her heart sank, bottoming out as bile rose to the back of her throat. Her heart rate kicked up, adrenaline spiking.

Donnie tensed beneath her, like a coil ready to spring. "What's wrong?" he asked, his voice suddenly more commanding and serious as all thoughts of pleasure were erased.

Pain pierced her chest, her neck, and face. She cried out, flinching from the assault and curled into him, as the psychic attack battered her, but it wasn't her body that was being victimized.

"Carolynn, you have to tell me what's happening," Donnie demanded, pushing the hair back from her face.

"My mom," Carolynn cried, tears streaming down her face as the pain became worse. Someone was hurting her mother. "We have to get to my house."

Chapter 38

Donnie didn't miss a beat.

Pushing off the ground in a powerful leap, he took to the sky, his wings beating effortlessly as he launched them into the air. This wasn't how their first flight should have gone; it should have been magical and intimate, awe-inspiring and breathless. Instead, hot tears streamed down her face as she was assaulted by more attacks, and physical pain that wasn't her own. Her scalp burned as though someone or something was yanking her hair out by the roots. She whimpered, curling further against his solid body, burying her face in his neck. His arms wrapped tighter around her as his wings beat harder behind him, propelling them further faster.

What would normally have been at least a half-hour drive took them only minutes flying. Before she knew it, Donnie's feet landed softly in the overgrown grass that adorned the front yard. The trailer was dark, with no lights to be seen. Even the sliver of light offered by the moon shied away.

Carolynn scrambled out of his arms as he reluctantly let her go. Her feet hit the soft ground, and she felt frozen in place as her eyes finally adjusted to the darkness. Her breath caught in her chest as she noticed the stubborn front door, famous for sticking no matter the weather, now hung by a single hinge.

Without a moment's worth of hesitation, she darted for the house. She could hear Donnie calling her back, but she ignored him as she raced up the steps and swung open what remained of the front door. She stopped short as her feet met the familiar carpet, and the scene before her nearly caused her heart to stop.

She could feel him come up behind her, could feel his presence, his desire to shield and protect her, but only took the slightest comfort from it, as what was left of her house caused her heart to shatter. Her hand flew to her mouth as she tried to muffle the cry, her eyes widening, pupils expanding in the darkness. Her home was almost unrecognizable. Furniture was tossed upside down; it had been thrown around like a ragdoll. Their television was shattered on the floor, and pictures that had decorated the walls hung loosely or were missing entirely.

She attempted to take a step further into the house but an arm blocked her path. She glanced up at Donnie. His wings were nowhere to be seen as he stepped forward.

"Stay," he ordered as he moved through the remains of her house, inspecting each room for any intruders that might still be lingering. His boots crunched, stepping on wood, glass, and random pieces of furniture.

For once, she listened and stayed in the frame of the door, listening for any hint of life, any movement.

Was this her life now? A never-ending battle.

Everyone she loved was in jeopardy, their lives at risk because of her. She finally moved forward, stepping further into the living room. The couch was no longer where it once was. Instead, she found it lying upside down through her mother's bedroom wall. Something crunched beneath her foot. She lifted it up and found her mother's usual coffee mug that read *bite me* now broken beyond repair, coffee staining the carpet even further.

A sob choked her at the sight. Where was her mom?

Carolynn took in the mess of her home. The kitchen cabinets with broken or missing doors barely hanging from the ceiling, and missing in some places, the walls busted and knocked down. This was her childhood, the home where she was raised her entire life, and it had been violated in the worst ways. What was once her safe place was now shattered and broken.

She made her way towards her room, or what was left of it. Clothes were strewn around, and nearly every piece of furniture was destroyed and broken, leaving nothing to salvage. She stepped over a rather large piece of wall. The loveseat had removed what had been left from the night before, propped against her bed.

Carolynn froze as she heard a whimper. Something moved under the loveseat. She leaped toward the couch, slipping on debris, scrambling to the furniture. She reached beneath the worn fabric and lifted, bending her knees, when she felt the weight completely removed. Donnie lifted the couch as though it weighed nothing and tossed it over their heads to the other side of the room in a loud crash.

A black form twitched on the floor as the weight of the furniture was gone. Carolynn couldn't see anything, couldn't make out a single detail, and her body responded to that deficiency. Her hand lifted, palm up, her desire manifesting in a bright white orb that hovered above them, illuminating the entire house, and banishing the darkness.

"Shadow!" Carolynn cried, dropping to her knees beside her friend.

Shadow lay on the floor, her body contorted into an odd angle at the spine. Deep gashes covered her body as though large beasts had attacked her, matting her fur with blood. Part of her ear was missing, and something dark trickled from her nose.

Carolynn choked back bile as dread flooded her. A sob tore through her as she fought the urge to scream, hot tears streaming down her face. She knelt beside the wolf, trying not to jostle her as she lifted her head into her lap, running her hands over her body to try and stop the bleeding, but the wounds were no longer weeping.

"Shadow," Carolyn said again, trying to rouse the wolf. "Shadow, can you hear me?"

Donnie knelt beside her, placing his hand on her back.

Carolynn shook him off as she shook the wolf. Her friend made no sound, no movement. "Shadow, wake up! You can't be dead; you have to get up!" she cried and noticed a faint rise and fall from her chest.

Carolynn glanced around the house frantically, catching Donnie's eye. They had to get her help, had to get her out of here, but he gave a hopeless shake of the head. She wouldn't make it. She could already feel the wolf's life slipping through her fingers.

"Shadow, you can't die," Carolynn pleaded. "Please don't leave me."

I'm sorry I failed you. Shadow's voice was faint, barely a whisper, and fading.

"No," Carolynn breathed, sniffling loudly, tears scattering as she shook her head. "You could never fail me. You're my best friend. You've always been there for me. I'm so sorry about the way I acted. I'm so sorry."

I love you, pup. You've been the best human friend a wolf could ask for.

Carolynn cried harder, barely able to see, but she didn't need to see as she felt Shadow release her last breath, her chest remaining still, frozen in time. The wolf went limp in her arms, head falling back as the life in her was snuffed out. Her gray eyes, the same shade as Carolynn's own, rolled back, and she was gone. She held onto the wolf tighter, burying her face into the wolf's neck, and sobbed, breathing her in one last time.

"Please," she begged. "Please don't go."

She pulled Shadow farther into her lap, the blood soaking through her clothes, rocking back and forth. She hiccupped, holding her tightly. Her mind was blank, and she felt numb to the bone, like she was floating and watching everything from far away.

"Carolynn," Donnie called to her quietly, hand resting on the small of her back, rubbing small circles into her skin. "We need to leave. They could come back."

"We can't just leave her," Carolynn said, her voice thick.

She slid her arms underneath the body and cradled the wolf against her chest. She stood up from the ground with Shadow in her arms and walked outside. She didn't notice the wolf's weight. She knew it had to be heavy, but she barely felt it as she walked towards the edge of the woods surrounding what used to be her home. She could feel Donnie just behind, twitching at any noise and movement.

Carolynn stopped just a few feet into the woods where the ground looked to be clear of debris and brush. She placed Shadow's limp and lifeless body gently on the dew-soaked grass, still wet from the day's humidity. She stepped back, Donnie standing beside her as she took his hand, intertwining their fingers.

She looked at her friend, for the last time ever, and cried, tears slipping down her cheeks.

Carolynn closed her eyes as the energy of the trees, the earth, and the forest life surrounded her. She could feel life pulsating, stirring in the ground and all around. It was almost like the forest she'd been in, where Sarena had left her in that other world. This wasn't as intense but just as much full of life. Her chest felt heavy as sorrow overcame her, and she remembered the countless hours, days, and years she'd spent with the wolf. Chasing each other through these very woods. This was where Shadow was born, and it would be where she was laid to rest.

She opened her eyes as a white light filtered through her closed eyes. Sunrise was far off. Had a car approached? But they were too deep into the woods for it to be so bright.

Glancing down at herself she noticed her skin reflecting a light as pale as the moon, illuminating the space around them. Donnie's eyes reflected silver, wide and in awe. A wind picked up around them, tossing her hair around her shoulders, brushing along her flesh, her face. The hair on her arms and neck stood, as moving figures enclosed around them.

Shadows crept out of the darkness, surrounding them on all sides.

Wolves. Dozens of wolves gathered, varying in age and color, from pups to elders, from stark white fur to reddish brown and black. They all stood silent, watching her, mourning their sister, friend, and mother. One of the pups stepped forward with eyes identical to Shadow's, nudging her paw.

A fresh torrent of tears ruptured, pooling into the earth. The ground shifted beneath their feet. Donnie pulled her back by the hand he still held as roots from the surrounding trees lifted themselves free of the soil. Shadow shifted as they wrapped around her body in intricate knots and swirls, encasing her in a beautiful tomb.

Carolynn watched as her friend was pulled beneath the surface, dirt covering her. A sob tore free, knowing it would be the last time she ever saw her wolf, but then she gasped, taking a step back into Donnie's body, his arms wrapping around her waist as she witnessed deep, rich purple tulips sprouting from Shadow's final resting place, the petals peeling open in full bloom, releasing a sweet, floral smell.

Carolynn smiled sadly, somehow knowing the flowers would be in bloom all year.

"How did you do that?" Donnie asked, lips brushing against the arch of her ear, not even bothering to hide his shock.

"I don't know," was all she could think to say, and it was the truth. She didn't know how she used any of her powers, they just seemed to react to her will, her emotions.

The wolves in unison raised their muzzles, noses lifted to the sky as the largest of them, a pure black Alpha with one white paw, let out a heart-piercing howl. Each member of the pack joined in the mourning song of grief, as they cried for their pack mate.

A shiver ran down her spine, gooseflesh pricking across her skin. She could feel the pack's sorrow as though it were her own. She lost her best friend, but they had lost their family, their blood. The Alpha cut off the cry, ceasing their call. He looked to Carolynn, dipping his head as a sign of respect before slipping back into the forest, the rest of the pack following.

The small pup that had nudged his mother's paw glanced back, looking at her. Carolynn offered him a soft smile as she watched him scamper after his litter mates.

Donnie tugged on her hand, pulling her away from Shadow's grave and back towards the house. She clung to it as though it were a lifeline. Maybe it was. Her only grasp on sanity as the night's events settled over her.

"We should leave," Donnie repeated the same sentiments from earlier.

"To where?" she asked, voice raw and thick.

"Sam and Neila's, until we can figure something else out." Donnie looked out over her head, still keeping watch.

She could only nod, barely hearing or processing what he was saying. "My mom's not here."

Donnie finally looked down, taking in her state. "I know. We'll find her."

Carolynn nodded. Yes, they would.

"I need to get a few things before we go," she said, already heading back into the house. Donnie followed closely behind her, grumbling something unintelligible under his breath.

Inside the house, she pushed the coffee table out of the way, removing large chunks of wall and cabinet as she climbed her way into what remained of her bedroom. It was trashed. The mattress was shredded, and clothes were ripped apart as though someone had been searching for something. She finally pulled her hand free of his as she headed for her closet. Grabbing a duffle bag off the floor, she shoved what little clothes were salvageable, items worthy of what the next few days might entail, and placed it on the bathroom counter.

Carolynn glanced in the mirror, barely recognizing herself. Her shirt, pants, and arms were streaked with blood. Her hands were sticky and red, with crimson flakes fluttering to the floor with every movement. Not even her face was untouched, her hair wild and manic, and a single streak of red across her cheekbone. She tried to quiet the panic she felt building and rising inside. She couldn't lose it just yet. She had to stay focused.

She turned on the sink, not caring that it was frigid, and began washing the blood from her hands, arms, and face, scrubbing it all off until she felt raw. Drying herself off with a towel and ensuring she got every bit of blood removed from her skin. She peeled her clothes off and threw them in the corner, knowing that is where they would forever stay. Changing into a set of clean clothes, she began to brush her hair, her mind still blank and unable to process.

Shadow was dead, and her mother was gone, but gone where?

Carolynn stepped out of the bathroom, wearing black cargo pants, a tank top, and boots. She noticed a bag beside a silent Donnie, standing near the edge of the bed. She glanced around the edge of the mattress, expecting her wolf to come around and appear, but her heart died just a fraction over the fact that she knew she'd never see her alive and well again.

She ignored the heartache and the desire to simply curl in on herself in the middle of her bedroom floor and cry until the earth swallowed her as well. She stepped towards the bag and peered inside, finding some random keepsakes, pictures that weren't ruined of her, Shadow, Beth, and her mom, and a couple of other knickknacks, mostly from her mother's room.

Did he too realize that this house was no longer her home? That she could never and would never feel safe or secure as she did that morning. Her life here was shattered and irreparable.

"Where would they take my mom?" she asked, zipping the bag closed.

She watched as his eyes flitted to the ceiling, suggesting somewhere other than here.

Right. Of course.

"How do we get there?"

"I don't think that's such a good idea. If you go there, you're dead."

"And if I don't, my mother is most certainly dead," Carolynn reminded him, recalling her dreams. Her stomach bottomed out. Her dreams. The very one where not just her mother was gone, but—"Beth."

Chapter 39

"We have to go," Carolynn said, panic clear in her voice as she slung her bag over her back and Donnie did the same with the one he carried.

Donnie reached for her hand, already charging for the front door. Her hand slid into his, fingers intertwining, as they raced down the front steps. Her feet had barely left the wooden porch before he swept her into his arms. She could feel his body vibrating like something was itching to be released. With a single breath, his wings were fully extended, pulling in tight before he leaped into the air in a single, powerful leap.

Carolynn watched them beat against the wind, defying gravity as he swiftly flew them over the trailer park. Her house disappeared into nothing but darkness beneath them. She curled into him, not wanting to look back at her home, which was nothing more than pieces of wood and four walls.

The air stung her skin as they flew higher into the clouds, his wings pumping gracefully and with precision. He was magnificent to watch as the wisps of atmosphere surrounded them. She just prayed to whatever Gods cared to listen that she was getting to her in time.

They landed with ease on the fresh-cut lawn beside the stable, hidden in the shadows. Donnie's wings folded in, disappearing the moment he flexed his shoulders and set her down.

Carolynn glanced at the house, reaching out with her mind,

searching for her friend, but all she could hear was her parents, arguing about something petty, no doubt.

"She's not in there," Donnie said, keeping his voice low as he stood at her back, his breath fanning the side of her face.

"How do you know?" she asked, still searching the big house for any trace of her friend.

"Her scent is stale towards the house. She came down here recently," he nodded to the barn doors which stood ajar.

"Her scent?" she questioned, stepping towards the stable cautiously. "Never mind, I don't want to know."

The fact that he could tell the difference between Beth's scent and the horses around them was a tad disturbing. She could only imagine what she smelled like to him if his sense of smell was that good. What did they make Angels out of, bloodhounds?

The stable was eerily quiet. There were no horses shuffling in the hay, or even tails swishing. She went into the office. What could have been so important that Beth felt the need to come down here? She flipped the light switch on, but nothing. No buzz of electricity; it was just dead. She glanced over her shoulder, where Donnie hovered, protecting her from the rear, his ice blue eyes the only thing visible in the darkness, and they were taking everything in. Did he have built-in night vision too?

She didn't have special Angel eyes, and if the lights were dead then she had to make her own light. For the second time that night, she created her own ball of sunshine and tossed it up towards the ceiling, where it froze in the air, illuminating the room. Her eyes adjusted to the sudden brightness.

Carolynn moved towards the desk and found the papers she had organized and cataloged strewn about across the wooden surface and on the floor. Her chair was knocked over on its side, and the rose Jason had left was lying on the ground. She bent over to pick up the rose, but Donnie beat her to it, carefully plucking it from the floor, as though it may shift into a serpent and bite him.

She made to call him out, to say something about his overprotective crap, but stopped when she caught him sniffing at it hesitantly.

"There's poison in this rose," he said, sniffing it again to be sure, "and blood. Someone touched one of the thorns." He dropped it to the floor, and she watched as his shadows slithered out of him, slinking along the floor until it enveloped the black rose. She observed as the shadows encased the flower and when they pulled back, left nothing but dark ash.

She froze at the sight, realising those lovely shadows that had touched and caressed her so tenderly, were in fact deadly in their own right. Backing out of the office, she went back out into the stable aisle, her little ball of light trailing her from up above as Donnie stuck to her like her own personal guard, her shadow.

The horses were still too quiet.

Carolynn approached Tempest's stall and found the mare wide awake, nostrils flaring, ears pinned back until she recognized her. The horse seemed to sigh in relief, approaching the door.

You shouldn't be here, the mare warned.

Carolynn rubbed her hand down the front of the horse's face, scratching up by her ears. "What happened here? Have you seen Beth?"

He took her. He took Beth, Tempest said quickly. *She tried to fight him, but he was too strong. I wanted to save her, wanted to help, but I was held still, frozen.*

"Who took her?"

Donnie stiffened at her side.

That boy you hired, Tempest said.

Carolynn frowned. Jason? There was no way. How? Why?

I knew he was trouble from the moment he got here, Tempest continued before she could ask. *Always watching you, he was. You and Beth. He was trouble.*

"Wait, stop." Carolynn held up a hand, her mind racing. "Jason took Beth?"

A deep growl emanated from Donnie, his eyes nearly black and hooded. Carolynn glanced up at him, brows furrowing.

Did he just growl?

"What's wrong?" she asked.

"I should have known," was all he said, hands flexing at his side.

He was always slinking around, following you. Whenever you weren't looking, there he was, watching you. Like a predator with its prey.

"And you never thought to tell me?" Carolynn asked her horse. How had all of this been going on, and she knew about none of it?

She glanced at Donnie once again and knew exactly why.

I thought it was the mating ritual for humans, Tempest said, swishing her tail. *It's not so different from this Angel here. He watches you just the same.*

Donnie seemed to glare at the horse, eyebrow raised, as though he could actually hear what she was saying. "Did she say something about me?"

"Wait, you know he's an Angel?" Carolynn wasn't sure she heard her correctly.

"Animals can usually sense otherworldly creatures," Donnie informed her, as though she should have already known that little fact.

Tempest bobbed her head. *Some of us can even see the wings. They're very pretty. Like millions of rainbows.*

"She said your wings are pretty." Carolynn side-glanced him.

Donnie puffed his chest, that dimple coming out to play as the corner of his mouth pulled up into a shit-eating grin.

"How come you never told me?" Carolynn asked her horse, feeling slightly off. How was she the last to know everything?

Shouldn't that be his business to tell?

Carolynn grunted, crossing her arms over her chest. She needed to focus. This wasn't about Donnie or Jason at the moment. Her mother and now Beth we're missing, and she had no clue where to even start looking.

"When did Jason take Beth? How long ago was it?" Carolynn asked.

Not long after we were fed dinner. He dragged her past my stall. She looked like she was sleeping. She smelled oddly sweet, like Mrs. Morgan's flowers.

The rose.

"Jason took Beth, and she's been poisoned." Carolynn turned to Donnie.

Donnie made that same noise again, primal and feral, promising death and violence. It sent an oddly delicious shiver down her spine and deep into her belly.

"I should have known he'd make his move," he said, almost to himself.

"What are you talking about?"

Donnie looked down, meeting her gaze. His eyes slightly lightened but were still rimmed with black. Were those his shadows?

"He was sent here for the same reason I was."

Carolynn threw her hands up in the air. Of-fucking-course he was. "Is there anyone left in my life not trying to kill me?"

I'm not. The mare stated.

"Technically, I've never tried," Donnie retorted.

Carolynn shook her head, pinching the bridge of her nose. "That was a rhetorical question."

Donnie grunted, rolling his eyes.

Carolynn ignored that. "So, they have both my mom and Beth, but why? What would they want with them? Why take Beth?"

"Why else?" Donnie shrugged, as though the answer was obvious. "For leverage."

Chapter 40

Carolynn flung the door open, with Donnie close behind on her heels. He was refusing to let her out of his sight and deep down, she didn't mind. She got a slight thrill and jolt of excitement over how protective he was. It felt good to know he was in her corner, looking out for her. Even if it was all for nothing, right now, it meant the world to her.

The foyer was the same as she remembered, bright and white. The crystal chandelier suspended from the ceiling casting light into every corner of the room.

Donnie slammed the door shut behind them, dropping her bag that he still carried onto the floor, just as Neila nearly sprinted into the room, eyes wide and body tense. Was she expecting a fight?

Carolynn could only guess how they looked to them. Donnie's eyes were still nearly black, on edge, and twitching at every sound and movement. He wasn't taking any chances. Whereas she was just tired. Her eyes felt swollen and sore, her body run down yet wired, like an exposed nerve. Opposites were conflicting inside. She wanted to curl into a ball and lose herself to her grief and loss, while another part of her wanted to scream and fight, taking vengeance on anyone who had ever threatened her and her family. She wanted to find the person who took Shadow away from her and make them pay with their own lives.

"Carolynn?" Neila called, sounding surprised to find her in their foyer.

Carolynn tried to force a smile, but she couldn't muster the energy. She went to open her mouth and say something but movement out of the corner of her eye drew her attention as Sam descended the staircase quickly, clearly surprised to find her here. His grey eyes flicked to Donnie at her side, and they narrowed immediately.

Hostility. Check.

Sam looked at her, eyeing her up and down as though expecting to see or find something. "Carolynn, what are you doing here?"

"Not to say that you aren't welcome," Neila added, giving Sam a warning look. "We just weren't expecting you."

Carolynn tried to brush off the annoyance that was already brewing beneath her skin at Sam. She couldn't help the reaction he brought out in her, but she also couldn't afford to be rude. Not now, not with everyone she loved at risk. She felt Donnie move in closer, stepping into her side more closely as he rested his hand on her hip, pulling her in against him. She leaned slightly into his tall frame, tucked beneath his arm, and took as much of his strength as she could.

She steadied herself, finding her voice before it had a chance to crack. "I need your help," she admitted. "Someone has taken my mom and Beth."

Neila and Sam collectively froze, the words slowly registering. She watched carefully as Neila's face went from surprise to shock, and then hardened into something fierce and cunning, something general-like.

"Who?" Neila asked, her voice calm and rigid like a boulder in a blistering storm holding firm.

"Oriel's son," Donnie answered at Carolynn's side.

Concern flickered across both of their faces. Sam and Neila exchanged glances, communicating amongst themselves. Carolynn waited patiently, though slightly peeved that they weren't discussing whatever it was aloud.

"Who is Oriel?" Carolynn heard herself asking. The name sounded familiar but she couldn't recall who or what it meant.

"He is the God of Death," Sam answered, finally breaking whatever was happening between him and Neila to look at her. "Ruler of the Under Realm."

"What could he want with my mom and Beth?" How did this God fit into her story?

"They are the people closest to you," Neila said, nearly repeating the same thing Donnie had told her earlier.

Leverage. They were the bait.

"What does Oriel want with me? I thought it was Matias who was after me, who wanted me dead." Carolynn asked glancing up at Donnie.

"Oriel is just a puppet. Matias's lap dog," Donnie informed her.

Sam snickered, but it quickly became a grunt as Neila's elbow collided with his ribs. Carolynn's lips pressed into a thin line as she tried to contain a smirk. He deserved that and worse. Donnie's hand tightened on her hip, fingers digging into her hip. She gripped his side, fisting his shirt in her hand.

"Matias is the one behind all of it, there's no doubt about that," Neila said, eyeing Sam in a way that promised a serious talk later. She gestured for them to follow her into the living room, the same room she had been offered muffins. "Matias is afraid of something he doesn't understand. Someone he perceives as a threat to his rule. Whether it's founded or not means nothing to him."

Carolynn sat on the couch as Donnie sat in the armchair across from her, giving him perfect visibility of the front door. Neila sat beside her, hands folded in her lap.

"He means to kill me," Carolynn spoke aloud the words they had been tiptoeing around. Neila visibly flinched while Sam solemnly nodded. She tried to ignore Donnie's hands gripping the armrests of his chair, impressed that the material held against the strain. "Matias is the King of Gods, right? What kind of threat could I possibly be? If he hadn't sought me out, I would have never known about this world, about my heritage, and been none the wiser."

"He doesn't feel he can take that chance. Your powers, your potential, are unknown, possibly unmatched. You could overthrow him, remove him from power, and he can't stand to lose that kind of control," Neila said with venom, jaw hardened and set.

"Do you know him?" Carolynn asked. Aside from the obvious that he was trying to kill her daughter, she got the feeling there might be history. "Have you ever met him?"

"No," Neila shook her head adamantly. "Thank the Gods."

Carolynn glanced to Sam, who was leaning forward in his chair, as though needing to be closer to Neila, support her for something. But without even having to read his mind, anger rolled off of Sam in waves, but it wasn't directed at Neila. He was angry *for* her.

"Am I missing something?" she asked aloud, glancing to Donnie for assistance. Was there yet another piece of her life she didn't know about? But Donnie seemed just as puzzled, straightening in his chair, looking at Neila in an odd, speculating way.

"No." Neila continued shaking her head, which led Carolynn to take that as a yes.

"Neila," Sam said, whether in warning or to get her to open up, she didn't know.

"Just tell me," Carolynn almost pleaded, almost let them hear the desperation in her voice. She was tired of the secrets. Look where all of it had gotten them. If she had known about any of this sooner, she could have done more. She could have protected her mom, Beth, she could have saved Shadow. "I've had enough of the secrets."

"Neila, you don't have to," Sam said, eyes only on her, his wife, mate, whatever they were to each other.

Neila glanced back over her shoulder to him. Carolynn watched as she swallowed hard as though holding back some kind of emotion. It wasn't until she turned to face her, did she see the unshed tears sparkling in her emerald eyes.

"We owe her the truth," Neila said, holding her head high. "All of it."

Carolynn looked to both of her birth parents as she waited for Neila to speak, but what came out of her mouth was something she could never have anticipated.

"Matias is my biological father."

Carolynn stared at her, waiting for her to admit this was all a joke. That she didn't really just confess that the God that had been hell-bent on keeping her from ever existing, not to mention trying to murder her, is in fact her grandfather?

This was some sick, twisted, fucking joke.

"Bullshit," Donnie spat, leaning forward in his seat. "Matias has never sired any children. He's made sure of that."

Carolynn didn't want to know what he meant by that last bit, but she was waiting for an explanation.

"Matias doesn't know I'm his," Neila said sternly, expression hard and sad. "My mother hid me until I was old enough to fend for myself. I've lived on Earth all this time to hide from him."

"Sarena and Matias were never in a relationship. I would have known," Donnie said, sounding as if he was questioning his own words.

Neila shifted in her seat, eyes darting around the room. "It wasn't consensual."

Carolynn's heart sank, and she watched as Donnie's face fell in despair and then morph into anger. Even though his hands were drenched in blood, and death followed him throughout history, it seemed he drew a line at sexual assault, and for that she was grateful.

"Sarena never said—"

"No one ever knew," Neila told him, cutting him off. "Except for Dominius. He helped my mother afterward, and then when she had me, he gave her sanctuary, the one place Matias wouldn't dare trespass, and she raised me until I was able to leave."

"No one is blind to Matias's crimes," Sam broke his silence, glaring at Carolynn's Angel. "We know what he's done to any potential offspring. They don't survive their mother's womb."

Carolynn's stomach rolled as nausea rose up her throat. This world that they lived in was full of violence and unthinkable cruelty. How could any of them stomach it?

"That's why he's been trying to prevent your birth, from you ever existing by putting the ban on demigods mating. If he kills his own children before they take their first breath, what do you think he would do to a potential threat in another world?" Neila said, explaining their situations perfectly.

"What's with this mating business? I don't know what it means where you come from, but here it's very primitive and results in babies," Carolynn rose a brow. That word kept popping up more and more.

"It's similar for us, but in our world, your world, couples mate for life," Neila said simply. "For some it's a choice, for others"—she glanced between her and Donnie—"it's fate. It's not something one enters into lightly. It is a commitment that goes beyond life and death."

That was new information Carolynn pondered over. Mating for them wasn't about the physical act, but the eternal bond, a promise that went beyond vows. She glanced at Donnie and found him watching her, ice-blue eyes taking her in. Was that what they were?

Images flashed in her mind as her dream resurfaced. Him walking across a battlefield with a longsword in hand, Beth and her mother dead at her feet. She had to get to them. Had to try and save them.

"I won't let anything happen to them," Carolynn said softly, staring down at her hands neatly folded in her lap. She could feel their eyes on her, tracing over her skin, but she was afraid to look up, afraid she might break.

"Carolynn, you can't go there," Donnie said, as though he could hear her very thoughts.

Carolynn glanced up at him curiously. It was as if he knew exactly what she was thinking. She shrugged, shaking her head. "I won't let them die. I can save them."

"Who said anything about them dying?" Sam asked frowning.

Carolynn looked to Sam and Neila, her eyes dancing between the two of them. "I dreamt of this. Of Beth and my mom in some other world, dead at my feet. Sarena told me not to ignore my dreams. I've had them too many times to be a coincidence."

Sam straightened as Neila shifted on the couch, gnawing on her bottom lip.

"What else was in these dreams?" Sam asked.

"A battle, a big battle. Everyone was fighting. Angels, creatures, even a dragon. You all were there as well, in the thick of it." She looked to Donnie and found something she recognized from her dreams; determination, the same look he had when he struggled to reach her in the battle.

"And what were you doing?" Neila asked softly, studying her face.

Dying. "I don't remember," she said, looking out at the large bay window that overlooked the rose bushes illuminated by the porch lights.

"What is that?" Neila's voice rose as she pulled back the hair from her neck.

Carolynn's hand instantly came up to cover her skin, pulling it back to find flakes of rust in her hand. Dried blood.

"Whose blood is that?" Neila asked, tone straightforward and as tough as iron.

"Where's Shadow?" Sam glanced around, as though only just realizing her usual companion was nowhere to be seen.

Carolynn bit the inside of her cheek hard to keep from crying, tried to keep the burning in the back of her throat from overrunning her. She dug her nails into her palms, refusing to break. "She's dead." Her voice was barely louder than a mouse, but she was heard just the same followed by a deafening silence. She was almost certain she could hear the gnats buzzing outside on the lights.

Sam looked as if he had been physically slapped, eyes wide and slack-jawed. Neila's eyes instantly welled with unshed tears.

"How?" Neila asked in disbelief.

"She was trying to protect my mom, and they killed her," Carolynn said, holding her gaze with her own.

Neila looked to Sam, for guidance or support, she didn't know, but Carolynn watched the two silently communicate.

"What do we do?" Neila asked him.

"We try to change the future," Sam said with a sigh.

Carolynn exhaled quickly, releasing the breath she hadn't realized she'd been holding. "Great, so when do we go?"

"You're not going."

Carolynn turned to Donnie, startled by the calm death in his voice, leaving zero room for argument. He was staring at her coldly, his ice-blue eyes firm and unyielding. Did he seriously expect her not to go? This was her mother and best friend they were talking about! Of course she would go.

"What do you mean, I'm not going?" Carolynn asked, rage flashing in her eyes. "I don't think I asked for permission."

"It's too dangerous," Donnie said flatly, as though she wasn't really considering the risks. "You would be playing right into their hands."

"I have to go. This is my mom and Beth we're talking about. I am not sitting this out while you all go and risk your lives."

"Which is why you can't see this rationally," Donnie argued. "You are too close to this."

Carolynn looked wildly at Sam and Neila, finding little to no support. "You're telling me that you're all going to go there to try and save them, and I'm supposed to sit here and do nothing? Pretend like everything is normal?"

"Can't you see that we're just trying to protect you?" Neila asked.

"Isn't that why we're in this mess in the first place?" Carolynn flung at her. Neila flinched at the words, and Carolynn regretted them the moment they left her mouth, but it didn't make it any less true. She couldn't stop the torrent of word vomit. "If I had known what I was from the beginning, besides a freak, none of this would have ever happened. If I had the proper training instead of being the loose cannon that I am, then maybe I wouldn't be some vulnerable girl that needs protecting."

"And if we hadn't given you up, you would have never known your parents or Beth. You would have had a life of constant running, hiding, never being able to settle down and have a real home. Living in constant fear is no life for a child. Which is worse?" Sam asked.

"At least they wouldn't be in danger because of me." Carolynn knew her voice gave away her defeat. She slumped back into the couch cushions, keeping her eyes fixed on the hardwood floor, afraid to make eye contact as the pressure behind her eyes grew.

"Carolynn, this isn't your fault," Neila said, reaching out to her with a hand.

Carolynn pulled back out of reach. "Then whose is it?" she asked in barely a whisper. She swallowed hard, taking in a steadying breath. "Is it ok if I stay here for the night? My house, I can't go back there."

"Of course." Neila nodded. "You can stay in the same room you were in before. You're always welcome here."

Chapter 41

Carolynn had managed to swipe both of her bags from Donnie as she headed for the stairs. She could hear the others still in the living room discussing names of people she had never heard of, as she took the steps two at a time. She pushed open the bedroom door and flipped on the light switch. For a moment, she squinted against the fluorescent lighting. The bed was perfectly made, not a single crease to be seen. She dumped her bags on the floor at the foot of the bed and shut the door.

The dresser along the wall across from the bed had been wiped clean. Not a speck of dust to be seen. Curiosity getting the better of her, she opened one of the top drawers. Inside were shirts of varying colors and prints. She pulled out one of the first items of clothing her fingers touched and held it up. It was a black T-shirt that was pinched at the waist, in her size.

"Isn't that my color?"

Carolynn clutched the shirt to her chest, her heart bottoming out as she spun around to find Donnie standing in the far corner of the room by the balcony window. Her eyes were wide, and she was fairly certain a heart attack was a possibility as her heart raced beneath her breasts. She quickly shoved the clothing back in the drawer and pushed it closed.

"I didn't hear you come in," Carolynn said out of breath, glancing at the balcony door that was securely fastened shut.

"I didn't use a door."

She glanced back at the bedroom door, and he was right: it was still closed, and he was about as far away as he could get from it. She pursed her lips, suspicious of how he managed to get inside without touching either of the doors that would have provided him access.

"You ever going to tell me how you do that?"

"Maybe one day."

If they had any days left went unspoken. He was about to leave and try to save the only family she's ever known. What if he didn't come back? What if he—

Before she could even finish the thought, Donnie was in front of her, his hand cupping her face, his thumb pulling down her bottom lip that she hadn't realized she'd been chewing on.

"Whatever your thinking, don't," he said, voice deep and velvety.

Goosebumps raced along her skin, and an ache began to grow.

"I thought you said you couldn't read my mind," Carolynn said, voice soft and breathless.

His other hand cupped the back of her neck, forcing her to tilt back and meet his gaze. Those blue eyes were like molten ore, igniting a fire she wished he would feed.

"I can't, but I am getting better and better at reading you," Donnie said.

She wasn't sure she believed him, but her brain was turning into mush as dark tricks of light began to curl around them, wrapping her in their warm embrace.

"When are you leaving?" Carolynn asked. She needed to know. Needed to know how much time they had left.

"Soon," he said, that singular word fanning across her flesh with a single promise. His hand tightened around the back of her neck, forcing her to tilt further back, exposing her vulnerable throat.

"But not now," she breathed.

Donnie shook his head no as she placed her hand against his chest and felt the comforting beat of his heart. She inhaled deeply, further pressing her chest against his as she took him in. The warm tint to his pale skin, his obsidian black hair, those mesmerizing blue eyes that saw straight into her soul, didn't see a monster or a freak, but a woman. She didn't care about his initial intentions when they first met. She didn't care about his past being drenched in blood. She knew who he was now, and that was someone that would go to the end of the world for her. Someone who would shield and protect her, always.

A slight shiver ran down her spine as something rigid pressed into her lower stomach.

"Are you cold?"

Carolynn looked up into those pale blue eyes and shook her head no.

"What is it?" he asked, cocking his head to one side as he pulled her in even closer, eliminating any space left between them.

She could scarcely breathe as her pulse raced, but this could very well be their last night, their only night together. She wouldn't waste it.

"I don't know if I could survive anything happening to you," she said, her voice barely above a whisper as she licked her dry lips, sucking in the bottom one between her teeth.

Those icy eyes turned into white fire as they watched her mouth, but his hand around the back of her neck softened, thumb pressing just under her jaw in a firm yet tender gesture.

"Even when the last star winks out of existence and darkness comes for us all, I will find you." Donnie narrowed his gaze, voice like iron and steel, sharp and unbreakable.

The back of her eyes stung as her throat became thick. She took in an unsteady breath as she parted her lips. "I—"

Donnie didn't let her finish before he descended on her, mouth crashing against hers. She tasted him with her tongue, teeth, and lips. He tasted just like honey, sweet and smoky, something she would crave and desire, need and hunger for the rest of her days. It didn't matter if she had all of eternity left, as long as he was at her side. She moved her hands from his chest and wrapped them around his neck, rising up on her tiptoes, pressing firmly into his body.

A low growl from deep in his throat vibrated against her, and it caused a flood of warmth between her legs so powerful she clamped her knees together. She gripped his hair, pulling at the roots as their hunger grew. Those powerful shadows of his dug into her back, twisted around her waist and grazed over her ass while his hands still held her face, pulling on her hair, grazing the tips of his fingers down the column of her neck. He pulled the hair tie from her hair, letting it fall loosely around her. His mouth moved away from hers, running down her jaw as he tipped her head back, nibbling on her collarbone only to lick his way back up her neck and suck on her bottom lobe.

Carolynn let out a breathy moan as her skin ignited, electricity shooting through her as his touch sent her ablaze. "Donnie," she panted.

"Yes, kitten?" His words purred against the hollow of her throat, nipping her tender flesh.

She shivered once again at the pet name. The growing tension between her thighs was nearly unbearable as she pressed herself into his rigid length straining against the denim of his pants. She needed him, wanted him. All of him.

Carolynn took a step back, the shadows instantly releasing her, coiling themselves around their master as he stood there, eyes questioning. Those perfect lips were swollen and red and his creamy skin was slightly flushed. His chest rose and fell but he didn't appear as winded as she felt, her head spinning. She was almost certain there wasn't enough oxygen in the room. Decidedly, she pulled her shirt over her head and tossed it to the side of the room, not bothering to see where it landed. Instead, she held his gaze as those wintry eyes darkened, watching her hands move behind her back where she unclasped her bra, allowing the thin straps to slide off her shoulders as it went to the floor.

She stood there for him to look. She didn't cover herself or shy away. He was a two-thousand-year-old Angel. He had probably seen thousands upon thousands of women naked, but this was their first, her first, and she would not hold back now. She watched his Adam's apple bob in his throat, taking in a shaky breath.

"Kitten, we don't have to—"

Carolynn took a step forward, effectively silencing him as her hips swayed. "I want you. I want this."

That seemed to be enough for him as those shadows of his ripped free and pulled her forward, pressing her breasts into the soft cotton of his shirt. The contact alone against her sensitive nipples almost had her hissing. Donnie's hands gripped her waist as she felt her feet leave the wooden floor. Her legs automatically locked around his hips, arms entwining around his neck as she clung to him. They kissed harder and more urgently, biting and nipping each other. She needed to feel him, all of him, needed to feel so full until she was sure she'd burst.

Carolynn felt him move and sit on the edge of the bed. She sat back on his lap, slipping her fingers beneath the lining of his shirt, grazing his hip bones with her fingertips. She pulled the shirt up and over his head, tossing it behind them. She leaned back, admiring the body made by the Gods, designed just for her. She didn't care who he had been with before, just as long as she was the only he ever thought of moving forward. She placed her hand on his chest and pushed him back onto the bed. Before he could say something cocky, she placed her lips on his left pectoral first. He hissed between his teeth. She ran her tongue along his flesh to the other pec, nipping as she went.

"Fuck," Donnie rasped, jaw clenched.

She moved down his chest and across those rippling abs, tasting every ridge, dip, and line. Salt and smoke filled her mouth, but she wanted more. She ventured further south, but just as she reached that beautiful V, she felt herself being lifted and flipped around, now with her back on the bed. She let out of breath of air as her mind tried to catch up.

"My turn," Donnie growled, the color of his eyes nearly completely eliminated. He was hungry and tonight, she was his feast.

Donnie kissed her hard, bruising and punishing, before he went to her left breast, taking her nipple in his mouth and sucking deep. Carolynn's back arched off the bed, pressing herself further into his mouth, but he would have none of that. Those shadows slithered up the bed, took her hands and pinned them above her head, removing any leverage or purchase she may have had, forcing her flat on her back. She pouted, glancing down at the stupid dimple showing even with her breast in his mouth. His teeth teased her, rolling the sensitive nub until it stung before he licked the hurt away. His hand came up to knead her other breast, rubbing the nipple between his fingers, pinching until she squirmed. Her breathing was labored and loud, her sounds pathetic and desperate, but she didn't care. Her core was throbbing painfully, and soon he would find out just how ready she was.

"That's my good girl," he praised, kissing down her stomach. Those fingers deftly undid the fastenings of her jeans and pulled them off, panties and all. Donnie stood up, staring at her sex, weeping and swollen. He breathed in deeply, as though he could smell her from where he stood. "Fuck, baby."

Carolynn whimpered, trying to squirm, to move from the shadows' hold, but they held firm.

Donnie made a tisking sound, and the shadows retreated as he stared at her wet sex, unbuckling his pants and stepping out of them. Carolynn tried not to panic or stare too obviously, but the hard erection was difficult to miss. Her mouth dried as she was suddenly unsure if he would fit.

"As much as I'd love to feast on your pretty pussy until you dripped off my chin, I don't think I can stand another minute of not being inside of you," Donnie admitted before moving forward on the bed and settling between her legs.

Carolynn almost cried with relief. She needed to feel his fullness, feel him move and fill her. "Thank the—"

"No," Donnie said forcefully, stilling above her as he slipped a hand beneath her head and squeezed the back of her neck until her breath caught and she exposed her neck to him, those eyes devouring her as they held her gaze. "They have nothing to do with us. It's just you and me, kitten. I will kill every fucking one of them if they lay even a finger on you."

"And I would burn the worlds to the ground for you," Carolynn promised.

That earned her a wicked smile, that devilish smirk coming out to play. "I promise I'll go slow."

Carolynn swallowed hard, her heart racing, the tip of his swollen cock already pressing against her entrance. "Only at first."

He traced a single finger down the hollow of her throat, eyes locked on her racing pulse. "I don't know what I did to ever deserve you."

Carolyn reached up and pulled him down as her legs wrapped around his warm, lean body, bringing him closer. His cock pushed inside, stretching her. She closed her eyes at the stinging, burning pain. He was too big.

Donnie held himself still.

"Kitten, open your eyes."

Carolynn breathed in slow, steady breaths, and she opened her eyes to find him staring down at her, and what she found—the smoky honey she could almost taste on her tongue—overwhelmed her, filled her lungs and heart.

"That's it, baby. Stay with me," Donnie coaxed her as he began to move, burrowing himself deeper.

Carolynn breathed through it, holding his gaze. A sort of panic began to fill her, almost sure he couldn't go anymore, that he would surely tear her, but the burning began to turn into a different kind of fire. Her muscled began to relax as he seated himself to the hilt, pressing into a spot she never knew existed, that left her brimming with heat and lightning.

She needed more, needed to move. She tilted her hips up, arching her back just slightly off the bed, causing Donnie to hiss as though he were in pain. She froze.

"Fuck, kitten. I'm trying so hard to be good here," Donnie swore, teeth bared.

"I don't want you to be good," Carolynn heard herself say. "I want you to be yourself."

His brows furrowed slightly as he took her in. Maybe she was the only one to give him permission to be himself. He was the Angel of Death. Her Angel, and she wanted all of him. No more holding back.

Carolynn thrust her hips up again, causing his jaw to clench and a delicious friction to elicit a moan from her. She needed more.

Donnie bent down and stole the breath from her lungs in a searing kiss that had her halting mid-thrust. Her arms automatically went around his neck, pulling him closer as they kissed. Would she ever get enough? Was there even such a thing as enough? She didn't think so. Not with him, not like this. Not with his tongue down her throat, his teeth on her neck, and his dick buried deep inside. He was the Angel of Death, and he was hers.

Donnie pulled out until only the tip remained, only to push back in, stretching her all over again. Carolynn let out a sound she didn't recognize as pleasure shot through her. He pressed his forehead to hers as he moved within her, at first slow and controlled, with deliberate and powerful strokes that quickly turned to a punishing frenzy. She held on tightly as he gave her body what it wanted, what it had been craving since the moment they met. Their bodies moved together, grinding and gripping onto one another. Something powerful, final, built deep within as her breaths became shallower and more labored. Her mind was turning to mush, thoughts were no longer possible.

"I'm gonna cum," Donnie warned, his voice wild and rough, straining to hold onto some sort of control.

Carolynn's own orgasm was just within reach as he pounded into her, slamming their bodies into the mattress. She called his name, almost like a prayer, asking for something.

"Cum with me, kitten," Donnie coaxed as he thrusted once more, a primal and animal-like roar tearing from his throat. But she could barely hear him.

Not over the noise in her own head as the universe exploded around her. Stars in the heaven shone with such intensity she was sure the night sky was now a brilliant white as pleasure tore through her body, ripping apart every cell only to piece them back together with his essence and life. A tether locked into place between them; she could feel it like a string, impervious and eternal.

"Carolynn."

The sound of his voice, in awe and in shock, forced her eyes open, and what she saw shocked her. The room was truly alight as though the sun had been contained in that very room, but it wasn't a star that was the source. It was her. Her skin, still joined with his, was glowing so brilliantly he was shielding his eyes. She took in steadying breaths as her orgasm still rang through her, leaving her spent and limp.

Slowly, the light began to fade, and Donnie rolled them onto their sides, cradling her body against his. Her eyes grew heavy as sleep gnawed at her. She was sure he spoke, words soft, but the intention clear.

"You were always mine."

Carolynn opened her eyes sleepily, waking from a dream so real and life-like she was almost certain she hadn't slept at all. She propped herself on her elbows, taking in her surroundings. The room was still dark as she could see the glittering night sky out the window. Glancing down, she found her body covered by a thin, white sheet and already knew beneath it, she didn't have a single stitch on her. She glanced beside her on the bed to find Donnie lying on his back, one arm propped behind his sleeping head. Her gaze raked down to his bare chest, the sheet only covering him from the waist down.

He looked so peaceful, worry-free. Something she had never seen on him waking. There were no creases on his forehead, no scheming, worry, or anticipation of attack. She didn't think he could be any more beautiful.

She felt a touch sore between her legs as she stretched her body. There was a smarting ache deep in her core that she was certain wasn't pain, but a different sort of throbbing. She glanced over at him quickly and sighed. The bond that had snapped into place only a few hours ago was still there. It wasn't visible to the naked eye, but she could feel it, like a threaded cord linking the two of them together. She had no clue what it meant.

Silently, she slipped out from underneath the sheet, her bare feet hitting the cold wood floor. Her skin was covered in gooseflesh immediately as she stood naked in the dark room. She somehow managed to find her clothes strewn about the room, and as she was zipping her boots closed, she heard the sheets rustle behind her.

Carolynn turned around to find Donnie observing her dress, face unreadable. Color flooded her cheeks as she pulled her hair to one side and stepped closer to the bed, sitting beside him. He was propped on his elbow, watching.

"Where do you think you're sneaking off to?" he asked, voice cold and unpredictable.

Carolynn tried not to flinch at the lack of warmth, the lack of trust even after what they shared in this bed. "I'm sorry."

Before he could question or demand to know what she was doing, she bent down and kissed him one last time. A tingling sensation ran across her lips to his, passing through his body. She could feel him tense beneath her, taste the shocking panic as he realized what she was doing, but she held fast until he drifted off into a deep slumber and fell back against the pillows.

Carolynn pulled back, cold wetness staining her cheeks as she pressed her fingers to her lips, savoring the warmth and memory of his mouth. She wanted this night, the few moments they got to have, to be the last memories she had when the time came. She flicked a tear off her cheek as she watched the hurt and shock on his face fade away into an expressionless slumber.

She didn't really know if she could pull it off, if it was even possible, but at this point, she wasn't sure if there was anything she couldn't do.

Gently, she brushed a strand of hair off his face, allowing her hand to rest against his skin a moment longer and committing it to memory.

"I love you," she quietly whispered and without looking back, she left the room, closing the door firmly behind her.

Chapter 42

The smell of dry hay and manure. The endless pastures, green grass and horses grazing. The feel of worn leather and gliding in a saddle as a horse's muscles rippled beneath her.

A cloud of dirt surrounded her leather boots as her feet landed on solid ground. She glanced around and found herself standing just outside the barn doors of the Morgan Stables.

Carolynn patted herself down, assuring herself she wasn't missing any parts, and she had really made it.

Yep, all in one piece. Teleportation, check.

She barely even had time to process the influx of powers that were at her disposal. That would have to be worked through later. She had a job to do defying fate and all.

The air tasted charged on her tongue, almost warning her to turn back and leave immediately. She kept quiet, her steps soundless as she moved through the double barn doors. Straining her ears, trying to catch any kind of sound that would alert her to another presence, she felt something. First stall on her left.

Carolynn froze mid-step, her hands balled into fists, ready at her side. "I thought I smelled a rat."

A chuckle came from the darkness as he stepped out of the stall and into the aisle of the stable. He was in his usual attire, shirt, dark wash jeans, and boots. His blonde hair was tousled, as if all he did to it was run his fingers through. He had his hands shoved in his pockets as he casually leaned against the doorframe of her office.

Even under the cover of night and barely any light, she could still see his sapphire eyes.

"I have to say, I'm surprised you showed. I didn't think you'd have the guts," Jason taunted without a hint of emotion.

Carolynn crossed her arms over her chest, digging her feet into the floor. "Really? Then why would you be here waiting?"

"Because all humans are the same. You're predictable. I take something you care about and you come running. It's sad how vulnerable you all make yourself." He shrugged.

"You forgot one thing." Carolynn rose a brow as his furrowed. "I'm not human."

The corner of his mouth pulled into a half-smirk, making her stomach twist and nausea overwhelm her. It was sinister and worrisome, making her skin crawl.

"Where is my mom and Beth?" Carolynn asked, steeling her spine.

"Safe."

"I think you and I have very different versions of safe," she said, spitting the words. "Safe does not entail kidnapping women from their homes, drugging them, and dragging them to another world."

Jason pushed off the frame, stepping forward into the tiniest bit of light offered by the sliver of moonlight coming through the window in the roof. She caught the smell of burning wood and sulfur, stinging her nose. She took an involuntary step back as he moved in closer towards her, only to hit the stable wall. He stopped short before her, leaving only a few feet between them. One more step would close any distance, and she would smash his face if he even tried.

He smirked playfully, eyeing her up and down. "You are a beauty. It's too bad that Matias wants you so bad. We could have had fun," he said, reaching up to touch her hair.

Carolynn grabbed his hand, twisting it with a sharp jerk that had him spinning. She bent the wrist at an unnatural angle up and into his back. Something cracked. Jason yelled out and struggled, but she held firm to the arm lock she now had him trapped in. She tilted her head to the side in case he decided it was best to try and headbutt her. She did not fancy a broken nose.

"I suggest you keep your hands to yourself. That's for Shadow, you fucking prick," Carolynn warned, pushing him away forcefully.

"What does your wolf have to do with any of this?" Jason asked, silently cursing as he cradled his broken wrist.

"Like you don't know," Carolynn yelled, rage running through her veins. "You killed her when you broke into my home and kidnapped my mother."

"Hey, now," he stumbled back, eyes wide. "My only job was to get Beth. I had nothing to do with your mom or your wolf."

Carolynn didn't want to believe him, didn't want to let her rage thaw and cool, but she felt no pins and needles in her hands, no sign that he was lying. She watched as he babied the wrist, already bruising and swelling. "You're going to want to get that looked at. Looks nasty."

His face was red with fury, but from one moment to the next he flipped a switch and was his usual, casual self. "Okay, maybe I deserved that," he said flippantly.

Carolynn ignored him. She didn't have time for this crap. The longer they dragged this out the more likely Donnie would find her. "I'm going to ask you one last time, preferably before I do something that I can't take back."

She held her hand out in front of her and allowed her anger, her pain and sorrow, grief, and loss to consume her. As though a spark had been lit, a flaming ball of oranges and yellows hovered above her hand. It was beautiful in a dangerous and psycho sort of way. It didn't burn, but she could feel the heat coming off of it. The flame tickled her skin as she teased it with her fingers and tossed it in the air, catching it for dramatic effect. His hesitant step backward told her it worked.

"Where are they?"

Jason staggered back another step, holding his one good hand up in surrender. "Let's calm down. If anything happens to me, there's no telling what will happen to sweet Beth."

She almost lost control of the fireball in her hand as her heart stuttered in her chest at the sound of her friend's name. She squeezed the ball of fire between her fingers until it was no more than wisps of smoke. She closed the distance between them and grabbed him by his shirt, fisting the material in her hand.

"Where are they?" she screamed in his face.

Jason didn't move, didn't even flinch at the crackle of lightning across her knuckles. Instead, he pursed his lips, an eyebrow-raising in mockery. "They could be in multiple places by now."

Like an ice-cold knife slipping between her ribs and puncturing a lung, she flinched back, taking in a sharp breath of air. Something snapped within her like a rubber band. She raised her fist, aiming for his jaw but was halted when a hand wrapped around hers, fingers curling around her tight fist.

"Now, now, none of that." He clicked his tongue at her, shaking his head as a show of disappointment. "I don't need another black eye from you."

Carolynn frowned, pulling her arm free from him. "I think I would remember punching you. It would have been a fond memory."

Jason scoffed, rolling his eyes. "I'm almost offended you don't remember our little scuffle," he said, eyeing her up and down like she was a piece of meat. "You put up one hell of a fight. I have to say I didn't think you had it in you."

Carolynn stared at him, puzzling his words together.

"Since you look confused, I'll give you a hint," he said, leaning in. "That flashlight of yours nearly gave me a concussion."

Carolynn shoved at him, forcing her palms into his chest, and added a touch of power for emphasis. Jason stumbled back, trying hard not to land on his ass. "You fucking bastard."

A ball of fire materialized in her hand at her side.

Jason stumbled back another step, still clutching that broken wrist to his chest. "No hard feelings, darling. I was just following orders. When a God gives you a command, saying no is not an option. It's do or die," he said, as though breaking into her home and attacking her with a poisoned knife was as transactional as buying groceries.

Her mind wandered to Donnie. If following a God's orders was so serious and life-threatening, what had made him go against his own orders? Why spare her?

"You stabbed me! I nearly died!" Carolynn yelled, her voice shrill and cracking with emotion as the memory of the pain, drowning in its poison as it consumed her mind and body, overwhelmed her. She shook her head, trying to shake that feeling of being trapped, unable to breathe or move.

"That was—unintentional."

Carolynn seemed to pause at his choice of words. She could have sworn she heard a twinge of sympathy and guilt in his voice behind the bullshit bluster. At this point it didn't matter if he was sorry or regretted his actions. She was running on borrowed time.

She sighed heavily, pinching the bridge of her noise as exhaustion settled in the crook of her neck. "Look, I just want my mom and Beth. They are innocents in all of this. I came here to try and find you so you could take me. I'm offering myself in exchange."

Jason's brow rose in surprise, lips slightly parted. "You would turn yourself over for two mortals?" he asked in disbelief.

"They're my family," she said. There wasn't anything she wouldn't do for the ones she loves. But given the fact that he looked at her as though she suddenly sprouted two heads, he clearly had no idea what she was talking about, and that left her heart aching.

"Your funeral," Jason mumbled as he moved to stand beside her.

Carolynn watched as he still clung to his broken wrist, now swollen to twice its normal size. Sweat beaded on his forehead and she knew he must be in a lot of pain. She noticed him wince as he went to reach for something in one of his front pockets.

Damn it, she silently cursed to herself.

"Give me your hand," she said, aggravation dripping in her voice. She didn't wait for him to offer it or even give him a chance before she took the broken wrist and wrapped her hands around it and closed her eyes. She imagined bones piecing themselves back together and projected her power through her hands.

A soft snapping sound could be heard as the wrist popped back into place. A small whimper left the boy in front of her, but she ignored it as she released his hand. He rotated the newly healed wrist and seemed surprised by the fact it was now perfectly fine.

Jason looked at her frowning, mouth tilted down. "Why would you do that?"

She shrugged. "I can't have you passing out on me."

Jason ignored her comment. "How many powers do you have?"

Carolynn shrugged her shoulders once again, unwilling to answer him. "Are we leaving or what?"

He glared at her as though expecting a different answer or even payment, but she held his gaze, giving him nothing. He pulled out a thin golden chain from his jean pocket. Dangling on the end of it was a stone, the likes of which she had never seen before, set into a gold cage. It seemed to cast a faint glow even in the darkness.

"What is that?" she asked, eyes fixed on the unknown stone.

Jason rubbed the pendant between his fingers. "This is called Adala. It's a native stone from our home realm, Aros. It's the only way for Demis to travel back and forth to Earth."

"It's beautiful," she whispered. "How does it work?"

The corner of his mouth pulled up into a half smile. He placed the stone in the center of his palm, holding it out for her to see. The other hand reached out and grabbed a hold of her arm, pulling her in closer.

"Focus on its center," he instructed.

Carolynn watched as his eyes pierced the depths of the stone with fierce unwavering concentration as he said barely loud enough for her to catch. "Aros."

She suddenly felt a harsh tugging sensation, as though gravity were pulling at every molecule in her body, twisting and tugging in every direction possible, remaking her from the inside out. The world became a pristine white, clean and endless. Her stomach rolled with nausea. Her body felt weightless, yet as heavy as a cement truck. She was positive her head would explode from the pressure until her eyes began to focus and color filled her vision. Her feet landed on solid ground, jarring her bones, knees aching and teeth clenched so hard she was sure she had broken a tooth.

The scene before them was dark. Glancing up at the sky overhead, she saw it was black, filled with threatening clouds as red lightning flashed, casting a blood-colored light. The ground was made of rocks and debris from the surrounding ruins. It looked like she was standing in what used to be a city of some sort but had since been destroyed and left to waste away. There was a heavy smell that hung in the air, raising goosebumps on her skin, immediately reminding her of death and stinging her nose. Her pulse picked up, causing her anxiety to spike, and sweat gathered at the nape of her neck. Every part of her was tense, like a tightly coiled spring.

She would not show fear here.

Jason began walking between the crumbling buildings, leaving her to follow behind. She took in the ruins around her, what looked to be houses that lined the streets. She stared into a glass-less window and saw a dark figure watching before it quickly moved, causing the remaining curtain to flutter. Carolynn picked up her pace and caught up to him, as she found herself lagging.

"What is this place?" she asked, spotting dozens of charred skeletons scattered among the rubble.

"This is my home."

Carolynn almost laughed at what she assumed was a joke, but judging by the stern set of his jaw and hard eyes staring straight ahead, she knew it wasn't and kept the giggle to herself. She glanced around at their surroundings once again and shuddered.

"I thought you were from New Jersey."

"Have you never heard of a cover story?" he asked, sneering at her out of the corner of his eye. "I was born and raised here. Earth is just a distraction. This is my father's domain."

As she attempted to process what he was saying, she noticed Jason was beginning to disappear slowly down into the earth as though it was swallowing him whole. She hesitated as she observed his legs, then his torso disappear before her very eyes. Slowly, inching her way forward, she realized there was a staircase in the middle of the rubble descending beneath the ground. She exhaled as she reached out with her foot, checking for the next step, relieved to find solid foundation below.

Carolynn caught Jason glancing back over his shoulder, ensuring she was still following. She took in a steadying breath and slowly trailed after him.

The staircase seemed to go on forever as they continued to descend lower, much deeper than she could have imagined was possible. There were roots hanging from the ceiling, sticking out of the cracks and spider-webbing through the stone walls and ceiling. She noticed something was protruding from the wall and stopped, curiosity nagging at her. She allowed the tiniest bit of fire to gather in her palm, and what she saw flooded her with fear and nearly had her hurling on the steps. She threw a hand over her mouth to keep from screaming, the fire completely extinguished and forgotten.

"Most who come down here never leave," Jason said from in

front of her, nodding at the skull that was permanently embedded in the wall, hollow and jaw wide open as though whoever it had been had died screaming.

They were descending into what she now realized was a mass grave. She tried her best not to lose her nerve. She didn't care what she had to do, she was not dying in this depressing shithole. All that mattered was Beth and her mother.

Jason continued going down and down, and Carolynn scrambled to keep up. The sound of her rapid heartbeat and the tapping of her boots on the stone steps were loud enough to drown out any other possible sound. She knew they had to be nearing the end of their hellish descent when the air started to become less stale. She could just start to make out a faint glow of light ahead. They rounded a final corner as her feet left the last step. Blisters rubbed on her heels from the leather boots but she pushed the discomfort aside as the shock of her surroundings hit her like an icy blast.

"Is this the underworld?" she asked, her voice hushed and low as she took in the vast cavern they now stood in, with stalactites hanging from the ceiling a hundred feet above their head, the tips razor sharp. Stalagmites rose in large columns scattered randomly throughout the realm, the stone a deep, blood-red color.

Jason glanced back at her with a knowing half-grin that was answer enough.

Carolynn stared off into the endless space with fathomless shadows where she could have sworn dozens of small creatures blinked at her. The ceiling above them was covered in the same red stone, with cracks letting loose roots that dangled dozens of feet down. Columns as wide as her trailer made out of some kind of compacted dirt reached the ceiling, holding the massive cavern together. Bleached bones jutted from the handmade cement, sticking out at awkward and eerie angles. She turned away from the empty eye sockets of hundreds of skulls watching her.

Sweat was running down her temples from the oppressive heat that was rising from the stone ground. It seemed Hell gave Florida a run for its money.

A hooded figure was heading for them. It was tall, nearly two feet taller than her. She stood straighter, shoulders back as it approached. Out of the corner of her eye she caught Jason tensing.

It stopped a few feet away from them. The hood concealed his face, masking any human-like feature the darkness may have contained. If there was a face behind the hood, she couldn't tell. The cloak he wore looked older than should have been possible. Frayed holes decorated the eaten fabric with various shades of black and gray scattered throughout. It dragged behind him in the dirt, gathering rocks and debris as he walked.

Carolynn took a step forward, steeling her spine, and stared straight into the darkness of its face. "Who are you?"

"I am Oriel, the God of Death," a voice that sent shivers of terror lancing down her back and rose the hair painfully on her neck said. "And it is a pleasure to meet you, Carolynn."

Chapter 43

That voice sent trembling vibrations through her bones. Carolynn clenched her teeth to keep them from rattling loudly. She pushed forward into his mind, something she had always sworn she wouldn't do, but this was a God. She would do anything she could to survive. As she tried to see inside his head, she found nothing but a black fog.

"Where's my mom? Where's Beth?" Carolynn asked, projecting her voice, echoing off the stone walls.

Oriel turned his back to her, not bothering with a response, and walked back the way he came. Not requiring an invitation, Carolynn followed after him with Jason on her heels soundlessly beside her. She could feel the stable hand's tension, the anxiety, and the stress like it was her own. She didn't know who or what she would be if she had been raised in this death pit with a father like the God in front of her.

Jason was a Demi, like her. Did that mean he was telepathic as well? Were all Demis and Gods able to read minds?

They rounded a corner through a double-column archway. The heat was stifling, perspiration causing her hair to stick to her neck and face like she was basking in an overheated sauna, and bit back the urge to fan herself.

There was barely any light to see where she was going, making her feel overwhelmingly claustrophobic. She was determined not to let them see any weakness as she stubbornly set her jaw and breathed in slow and steady breaths through her nose. It looked as though they were entering some kind of dungeon. The sides of the hall were lined with cells fortified by iron gates. Some cells were as big her the trailer she grew up in while others were stacked on top of one another, small enough for a house cat. As they walked through the row of cells, she could have sworn she saw fist-sized scales glistening in the dim light.

Her eyes went wide as saucers. "Where are you taking me?"

Silence was her answer as he continued on and she followed. They came upon a set of wide stairs, and surprisingly they were ascending. A weathered door sat at the top of the stairs, chipped and flaking, yet it seemed to shimmer as though reinforced by some type of magic.

Oriel stepped aside, long sleeve beckoning her to enter.

Carolynn stared at the door and took in a deep breath as she pushed the door open and stepped inside the room with absolutely no light, no fire, just utter, pure darkness. The exit creaked loudly as it shut behind her, leaving a loud ringing in her ears as it slammed closed. It was cold in the room, which was a slight relief from the sticky heat. The room smelled heavily of mold and mildew. She could hear a faint dripping sound somewhere as water leaked onto the stone. She looked all around but couldn't see a thing.

Silent cursing went off in her mind in a voice that wasn't her own. She recognized that foul language, and a whimper came from nearby.

"Beth!"

Someone was moving, fabric brushed against the wall as metal clanged together. "Carolynn?"

Carolynn cursed under her breath as her shoulders sagged with relief and her stomach twisted. What was she doing in this shithole? What had they done to her?

She couldn't see in this Gods forsaken darkness, when suddenly she remembered. She held her hand out in front of her for the third time in the last twenty-four hours and created a small ball of sunshine, throwing it up into the air, where it held suspended over her head. She closed her eyes against the sudden burst of light, hissing as they adjusted to the brightness. Slowly, as they adjusted, she made out a frail shape in the far corner of the room.

Carolynn sprinted across the enclosed room, sliding on the stone floor as she knelt beside her best friend and wrapped her arms around her. Her chest seized when she found Beth was nothing more than skin and bones. Her friend's lungs wheezed with each breath, struggling and wet. She pulled back to get a good look when she took in a horrid gasp, hands instantly covering her mouth in shock.

Beth's face was riddled with bruises and shallow cuts. A deep, pus-filled gash ran underneath her right eye. Her once warm and vibrant brown bouncing hair was knotted and matted to her head, covered in filth and blood, and she smelled like piss.

How could all of this have happened in just a few hours?

"Beth," Carolynn cried, wet warmth running down her face. "What have they done to you?" She choked back the bile rising in her throat. She wanted to just sit there and cradle her friend, reassuring her everything would be okay, but how could it? She wanted to scream and fight, cry and hurl. Her best friend had been tortured, beaten, and Gods know what else. All because of her.

"You shouldn't have come. They're going to kill you," Beth said. Her voice, once light and airy, the voice that had always brought a smile to her face, was hoarse and dry, filled with a hopelessness that crushed her.

Carolynn shook her head. "I don't care about me. I couldn't just leave you down here." She gently placed her hand against the side of her friend's face, careful not to press too hard against the purple bruised skin. The cheekbones of her face were stark in the light. She had to do something, had to fix this, and she could.

She had been able to fix Jason's wrist, she had to at least try to relieve some of her friend's discomfort. She wasn't sure if she could remove the infection or repair severed nerves, but she would try anyways to help her as much as she could. The palm of her hand warmed and buzzed against the sunken skin. She watched as the bruises lessened and the purple-blue bruises transitioned into a faint pink tone. Beth wasn't completely healed, but already she looked better and seemed to be able to breathe a bit easier.

"Who did this to you?" Carolynn asked, trying not to sound too winded as her bones ached and a fire pain shot down her spine. Apparently healing intense injuries had some repercussions.

Beth took in a deep steady breath. "I don't know. There's never been any light in here."

"How could this have happened to you in just a few hours?"

Beth scrunched her face and slightly winced, touching the still visible cut beneath her eye. "What are you talking about? I've been down here for weeks."

"Beth, you've only been gone about twelve hours."

Her brows furrowed, confusion plain. "I don't get it."

"Time must move differently down here." Carolynn looked around the room, taking in their surroundings. From what she could tell, it was a plain empty cell with stone walls, floor, and ceiling covered in a green, wet slime. It was a miracle her friend hadn't succumbed to pneumonia. "We have to get out of here."

Carolynn took notice of Beth's hands wrapped in metal cuffs, chaining her to the wall. The cuffs had rubbed her wrists bloody and raw, ringed in an ugly purple color, blistered and torn. Beth must have twisted and pulled on them for hours on end. She bit back the overwhelming desire to hit something and instead focused on escape. Fury flooded her veins as she reached for the chains, and the metal sprang open at her touch.

Beth pulled her hands to her chest, rubbing at the sore wrists, bringing the blood flow back to her fingers.

"What's with the new powers?" Beth asked, brow raised.

"They seem to keep popping up," Carolynn said with a shrug. "Have you seen my mom?"

Beth's quizzical brow was answer enough. She felt her heart drop into her stomach, but she swallowed down the disappointment and fear.

One thing at a time.

"They took her too?" Beth asked.

Carolynn nodded. "Can you walk?"

"I think so," she said, reaching out for Carolynn's offered hand.

Beth stood up shakily, her knees giving out before she could get her feet under her. Carolynn wrapped her arms around her friend's frail body, supporting what little weight she had left.

"How do we get out of here?" Beth asked.

Carolynn helped her friend support herself against the wall before walking over to the door she came through and reached for the iron handle. The moment her skin touched the metal she was blasted back, her body flipping through the air, slamming into the wall beside Beth. A deafening crack resonated through the room; dust and dirt fell from the ceiling, covering them in a thick layer that had Beth coughing. The air had been thoroughly removed from her lungs as her head smacked into the stone floor, and she slid down the wall onto the ground. Her back felt as though someone had taken a flaming torch to her skin. She was pretty sure her arm was broken, and she could feel something wet running down the side of her face.

Flashing lights behind her eyes blinded her, and her ears rang as if the bells of Notre Dame were inside her head. She tried to take in a breath and immediately regretted it, as it felt like daggers were being forced down her throat and into her ribs and chest.

"Fuck! Are you okay?" Beth yelled, stumbling towards her.

Carolynn held up her good arm, signaling to give her a moment. She lay there on the cool, damp floor, face down in the red stone. She could feel a wet pool, warm and sticky, gathering next to her face. Shit, she must have cut her head, which would account for the splitting headache already forming. She tried to move the broken arm and felt relief as it moved. She didn't think the arm was actually broken, just severely bruised, most likely dislocated. Panic and terror began to rise within her, but it felt disconnected, like it didn't belong to her. She flipped over onto her back, biting down on her lip as the motion made her want to vomit what little she had in her stomach. She tried to sit up on her elbows, blinking away the stars that seemed to be moving, when she felt it again, panic and terror, and a slight tugging on that bond.

She flung her hand to her chest, gripping at the thin fabric of her shirt as she realized it wasn't her panic or terror she was feeling. It was his. He was here, somewhere in Aros. Could he have felt that impact, her injuries and pain? Was that what this was? Her mind raced as she could only imagine what he must be thinking.

I'm okay, she screamed down the bond, unsure how any of this was possible, let alone worked.

Carolynn struggled to get up off the floor, shaking her head and trying to rid herself of the ringing in her ears and brain. She stared at the door, loathing that piece of wood. The back of her head burned fiercely, and her good arm automatically reached up, touching a tender spot on her temple near the hairline. She felt a deep, long gash and winced. It didn't seem to be bleeding anymore, and she was glad there was no mirror around to see the damage. She had to get out of here, now. She had to find her mom, needed to get to Donnie.

The fucking door must be protected by some kind of shield.

"How do we get out?" Beth asked meekly.

Carolynn glanced at her friend and felt an anger so fierce rise within her, it erased everything else. Erased the pain and fear. Beth had never sounded so frail, so beaten and hopeless. She wanted to erase every being and creature that had a hand in breaking her friend.

Without answering, Carolynn channeled her anger and pain and aimed for the door as she felt a release of power expel from her body, channeled through her outstretched hand. She noticed a ripple through the air like a stone behind dropped into a still lake. The blast of energy collided with the door, causing more dirt and dust to fall from the ceiling. The wooden door was now bent in the middle, but it wasn't enough.

She thought of her mom being taken, Shadow dying in her arms, and Beth's frail beaten body. Another wave shot out, a blue-tinged bolt of power shot from her hand. The door buckled, shuddering at the impact as a solid crack snaked up the wood, but it still held. She rolled her shoulders back, biting her lip to keep from crying out over the pain in her arm and body. She remembered Donnie in her dreams, fierce and beautiful, wielding his sword and cutting down anyone in his path. He was an Angel, her Angel.

The tip of a sword protruded from her own chest.

Carolynn screamed as twin bolts exploded into the door, blasting it open. Wood split the air, stone fragments exploded shrapnel all around. She stared at the now gaping hole not just eliminating the door but a good portion of the surrounding wall.

Exhaustion weighed her down as the power that she used left her depleted, but she pushed it down, ignoring it all. Carolynn wrapped her around Beth's thin waist as both girls struggled to hold each other up. She walked over the threshold and left the cell with the thick crack spiderwebbing from a single point of impact on the back wall behind them.

"Someone probably heard that," Beth whispered, stating the obvious.

An alarm sounded, loud and shrill, like a dying animal, magnified to the point where she was positive her ears were bleeding. It stopped them in their tracks just as they reached the last step, overwhelming them both. Carolynn struggled to push forward as the noise felt like nails raking through her mind.

They clung to one another as they hurried down the long row of cells until she remembered something. She stopped at one of the first cells she had passed when she had initially walked through. The cell door was about as tall as a three-story building and wide enough to allow two full-grown elephants to pass through.

Carolynn touch the cell door hesitantly, praying she wouldn't be blasted back a second time that night. She met no resistance, no hint of magic or power as she laid her hand on the lock.

Unlock.

A mechanism clicked, releasing the door. She pushed the sliding cell door open, grinding her teeth as her body protested the movement and strain on her already bruised and battered body. The little ball of sun that still hovered over their heads wasn't enough to see into the depth of the cell that went back much further than she had anticipated or even thought possible. It was dark and endless, and who knew how deep the cave went. She pulled Beth back away from the entrance as tendrils of smoke billowed over the stone floor, gathering around their feet.

Carolynn and Beth backed away, tilting their heads up to the point that if they leaned back any further they would end up sprawled on their backs. The ground trembled beneath them like a slow beat of a drum. The dragon came into view as she stepped out of the cell. She was larger than anything they could think to compare her to. She had amber-colored eyes the size of a dinner plate. Her long snout was decorated with sharp long fangs pressing into the gums. Her neck was long and serpent-like, incredibly muscular with spikes running down the length of her spine. Her wings were folded at her sides. The scales were a brilliant gold color that reflected the light of Carolynn's little ball of sun in vibrant yellows and oranges. They both stood silent in shock and awe, mouths gaping open.

The dragon lowered her head until she was at eye level with the women. A forked tongue flicked out of her mouth, tasting the air. Her eyes narrowed intensely on Carolynn.

You, Goddess who freed me. What is your name?

Carolynn swallowed hard over the booming, authoritative voice in her head. "Carolynn."

I am forever indebted to you, Carolynn, the dragon said, dipping her head as a sign of respect.

A clanging sound could be heard further down the hall, boots pounding against the stone floor.

"Do you know how to get out of here?" Beth asked, glancing nervously towards the hall entrance, shaking with fear.

Carolynn wrapped her arm tighter around her friend and was slightly surprised, not realizing Beth had heard the dragon as well.

The dragon tilted her head at Beth as if only just noticing the human at her side. *It has been a millennium since I was first imprisoned in this wretched place, but escape has never left my dreams. I am surprised you survived this long, human child. Your lungs are strong.*

Carolynn forced herself not to flinch at the fact that this dragon had heard her friend being tortured, her friends screams loud enough to penetrate the thick brick walls and make it down here. She inhaled sharply as guilt slammed into her. "You wouldn't have happened to see an older woman taken down here as well? Blond, short hair?"

No other humans have come down here. The dragon lowered her belly to the ground, flattening herself on the stone floor. *We should leave. The guards will be here any minute.*

Beth needed no further encouragement as Carolynn helped her onto the dragon's back, placing her legs carefully around the sharp spikes. She sat behind her, close enough to where she could be sure Beth wouldn't slip off. As soon as they were on, the dragon began to move. For as big as she was, the dragon's movements were smooth and fluid, not at all what she had expected.

They left the dungeons behind and entered the great room she had first been introduced to in this pit of hell. Hooded figures rushed towards them from all directions. There were hundreds of them, each wrapped in their own decrepit brown robes and carrying a long spear. They were closing in, raising their weapons.

Hold tight.

The dragon expanded her wings to their full extent, the wingspan massive and impressive. The thick, leathery wings knocked over the acolytes as she stretched them out and began to move them, gathering momentum and air. She sprang off the floor in a ground-shattering leap and launched herself into the air.

Carolynn barely had enough time to grab onto Beth ensuring she wouldn't fly off as she tightened her thighs around the creature's thick neck. Who knew a decade of riding horses would pay off on a dragon?

They were both hunched over the dragon's neck, holding on as tightly as they could, when they noticed they were ascending fast toward the ceiling. Both girls ducked their heads, bracing themselves, but the hard impact with the ceiling never came. Where she had expected to be suffocated by dirt and entangled in long dead tree roots she was instead greeted by a blast of fresh air stinging her skin. She breathed it in deeply, taking in gulps of air. While she had only been down there for a few hours, it had felt much, much longer.

Lifting her head, she found that they were no longer down in the Underworld but instead flying over the graveyard Jason had first brought her to. She briefly wondered what had happened to him.

They flew high over what she assumed was Aros. They were several hundred feet in the air, gliding swiftly along the air currents. In each direction she looked, she saw a different landscape. Back behind them was the graveyard, dark and unwelcoming. To their left was an endless forest, housing a numerous variety of trees, lush and green, the canopy nearly brushing the clouds as swarms of birds crested over the treetops. To the right was a great river winding in and out of valleys and rolling hills. Ahead of them were mountains with snow-capped tops and rocky cliffs.

Carolynn could have sworn she saw something move ahead in the clouds, but it disappeared as quickly as she saw it.

They dipped forward as the dragon began the descent towards a green valley. The dragon's wings beat heavily against the air, reverberating through her body as she slowed their speed, her claws touching down on the soft, fertile land. Carolynn forced her stiff legs to move as she slid off the dragon's back, helping Beth down once her feet were firmly on land. Her friend already looked much better now that they were out of that dank dungeon, but the pale and sallowness of her skin had her worried.

"Thank you for getting us out of there. If not for you, I don't think we would have made it," Carolynn said gratefully.

You would have found a way, of that I am sure. The dragon pulled her wings in tight, ready to take off.

"Wait," Carolynn called out, the dragon halting mid-launch. "I didn't get your name."

Zafrina. If you ever have need of me, you only need speak my name. The dragon lifted off into the air.

The girls staggered back, buffeted by the giant wings. They watched as she flew away, disappearing amongst the clouds. Carolynn and Beth stood there watching the magnificent creature, when Carolynn suddenly got the sense they were no longer alone. She spun around quickly, hands up in defense as a current of electricity rippled over her skin, awaiting release, but she hesitated.

A woman was walking towards them. Her white, satin dress brushed against the plush green grass as it swept around her. Her rich auburn hair was lifted by the breeze, billowing behind her, and those emerald green eyes were fixed on her, lips pursed and jaw set with worry.

"Sarena!" Carolynn called out the moment she recognized the Goddess, lowering her hands to her side.

"You shouldn't be out in the open like this," Sarena scolded, eyes flitting to their surroundings nervously. "Someone could report you to Matias."

"I'm pretty sure he already knows I'm here, seeing as how we just came from the dungeons of hell," Carolynn said matter-of-factly.

Sarena rolled her eyes. "You truly have no understanding of the dangers you face here."

"My mother is in this realm somewhere, and I intend on finding her no matter the danger," Carolynn informed her.

"How do you two know each other?" Beth asked, glancing between the two of them.

"He has Neylara?" Sarena asked, face turning ghostly white.

"Neila? No, she was fine last I saw her. No, someone took my mom, Susana," Carolynn said, trying to ease the Goddess's fear.

Sarena's features slightly relaxed as the fact that her daughter was not in her assailants' hands, but only by a fraction before she looked at her with unwavering concern.

"If he has your mother, it's already too late. He never gives up what he takes."

With the exception of her, it seems, but Carolynn kept that last part to herself, not willing to bring up the Goddess' traumatic secretive past.

Carolynn shook her head, not caring what she said. "I have to save her. I won't leave her here."

"You don't understand what he'll do to you," Sarena pleaded, voice shaking and eyes wide with terror.

Carolynn swallowed hard as the memory of her dreams resurfaced, the blade piercing her heart. "I know exactly what he's capable of."

Sarena frowned, brows pinched and mouth slightly gaping, but before she could say anything further, Beth startled.

"You're Neila's mom!" Beth exclaimed, as though putting the final piece together. "She's your grandma."

Sarena glanced around nervously, shifting on her feet. Carolynn pulled Beth in tighter, hushing her. "Not here," she warned.

"It's so obvious. The three of you look so damn alike it's scary," Beth pointed out, ignoring the warning looks.

"I should have known the minute I saw you. You and Neila could pass for twins."

Carolynn snorted, surveying the Goddess. The same body, hair, and even the eyes were twins to Neila. "That's why you helped me when I was dying. You brought me here to protect me, didn't you?"

Sarena nodded. "Yes. It's forbidden to involve ourselves in mortal affairs, but the circumstances are unusual."

"I'm also not a mortal," Carolynn pointed out.

Sarena smiled sheepishly, the corner of her mouth pulling into a dazzling smile that must have ensnared thousands of men. "Well, yes, there is that technicality. I'll take you both back to Neila. You can't stay here."

Carolynn shook her head adamantly. "I'm not leaving, not without my mom. I managed to save Beth, and I intend on her staying out of their hands. Now I have to try and save my mom."

Sarena clasped her hands in front of her, skin tight over the knuckles as she worried them together, chewing on her bottom lip nervously.

Was that where she got the nervous habit from?

"Donnie is already here somewhere, I can feel him getting closer," Carolynn said, hand automatically grabbing for her chest where the bond tugged at her incessantly.

Sarena eyed her curiously, gaze flicking from her chest to her eyes. "You had sex with the Angel."

It wasn't even a question.

Carolynn nearly choked on the air she was breathing as her heart stuttered in her chest. Beth turned on her like she had sprouted two heads, mouth gaping open.

"What?" Beth nearly screamed. "I get kidnapped and you go and lose your virginity?"

"Can we keep our voices down?" Carolynn hissed, her face going hot and beat red. "It wasn't planned."

"But you completed the bond?" Sarena asked, as though she could see the thing which was now tethered between her and her Angel.

"I don't know what that means, but I feel something now that wasn't there before," Carolynn said, offering the Goddess the best kind of explanation she could muster.

"Interesting," Sarena mumbled, lips pursed in thought.

"Like I said, Donnie is here looking for me, and he can't find me before I have a chance to find my mom," she said, ignoring the torrent of thoughts coming from her friend. "There's going to be a big battle by the end of the day, and I can't have Beth anywhere near it. Sarena please, I need you to get her out of here and somewhere safe."

Sarena considered her for a moment before she nodded solemnly.

"Go with Sarena, she'll keep you safe," Carolynn said, brushing the matted hair back from Beth's face.

"I don't want to leave you," Beth said quietly.

"If you stay here, we're both dead," Carolynn said frankly, and that was the most truth she could offer her.

Sarena grasped Beth by her arm and tucked her into her side, but Carolynn reached out, taking the Goddess' hand before she could disappear. "Before you go, there is something else I need from you."

Sarena stared into her eyes. Carolynn could hear the muttering from within the Goddess' mind as Sarena exhaled loudly, knowing full well she wouldn't like the request that was about to be made.

Chapter 44

Carolynn pushed through the dense shrubbery, twigs and thorns scratching her skin and tearing what was left of her clothes as she continued down the path Sarena had guided her to. Luckily the Goddess had done as she asked and gotten Beth the hell out of there. Sarena wasn't too thrilled to tell her where to find Matias, but she knew well enough that if she didn't provide the information, Carolynn would have found a way.

She was coming up on Matias's compound, which looked more like a palace than the military-like structure she had imagined. Getting closer to the side entrance she had been informed would be the easiest access point and her best chance of avoiding the guards, she took in her surroundings. A small creek bed with crystal clear water rushing over smooth rock caught her eye. She bent down beside the cool liquid and cupped her hand in the frigid water, raising it to her lips. The water was sweet and refreshing as it washed down the sticky dirt and grime caking her throat. She took a few more gulps before taking herself in from the reflection of the water. Her face was painted in a mix of dust and blood. A deep, nasty two-inch-long gash ran down the side of her face along the hairline. Her hair was tangled and matted, tearing free from its confines. She freed her hair from the braid and plunged her head beneath the shockingly cold water. It sent a crippling shock down her spine all the way to her toes but she stayed under washing out her hair and scrubbing at her face until her lungs screamed for oxygen. She pulled herself out of the frigid creek.

Water ran down her back and chest, soaking what was left of her torn shirt. She tried to squeeze out the excess water from her hair and replated it once again, throwing the braid back over her shoulder. Standing up from the creek bed, her skin was covered in gooseflesh as the wind glanced off her wet skin. She surveyed the arm that had been crushed against the wall during her little impact, the one she had originally thought to be broken. The sight of it nearly had her throwing up the bile in her stomach. It was purple and blue from shoulder to wrist and lifting it was nearly impossible.

She suddenly wished Donnie was with her. He would know what to do, how to complete this mission. But she knew it was best she was taking this risk alone. She couldn't worry about his safety along with her mom's; it would be too much. She straightened, trying her best to ignore the lingering pain in her arm and head, squared her shoulders, and continued to the palace. As she grew closer, she could start to make out the grey marble walls through the veil of greenery. Surprisingly, it was more modern than she had thought, in an ancient Greece sort of way with the tall pillars and arches. It contained various levels, ranging from two to five levels depending on the tower and wing of the palace, and the roof was made of an iridescent glass-like material. It was stunning.

Carolynn carefully made her way to the edge of the forest, ducking behind a wide oak that could easily conceal three people. She had made it to the west wing of the palace. There were no windows that she could see, only solid slabs of marble for walls. To the left at the far end of the wall was a screen door swinging open and closed as servants came and went. The help was carrying various items in and out of the compound from baskets of clothes to bowls of fruit and freshly baked bread she could smell from where she stood. There was a guard stationed outside of the swinging door, seemingly monitoring the flow of traffic. He wore a plain white tunic and loose-fitting pants, feet bare on the cobblestone-lined path. Oddly, he seemed familiar to her.

Carolynn began to move soundlessly through the shrubs, making her way closer to the door, when she froze at a voice.

"Michael!"

Carolynn ducked behind a large rose bush, keeping out of

sight. She watched from behind a thick vine as the guard—Michael, she presumed—left his post and went inside. She glanced around the area and found a large outdoor kitchen nearby, containing countless bowls of food. Servants were busying about, preparing and carrying them inside. She dashed out from behind the bush, grabbed a bowl filled with various colored berries, and placed it on her shoulder in hopes to conceal the nice slash down her face which she was almost certain would scar. Keeping her head down, she quickly opened the screen door and entered what looked to be the kitchen. It was larger than any she had ever seen. One wall alone contained only ovens.

She maneuvered around the work stations and servants, seemingly blending in among the hustle and bustle of the kitchen. She approached the only door leading into the main part of the palace and quickly ditched the bowl on the nearest counter, slipping out of the kitchen into a seemingly deserted hallway. She looked down both ends of the hall and headed in the direction towards the center of the estate. Voices were moving her way from an adjoining hall. She grabbed the handle of the nearest door, found it unlocked, and slipped inside.

Quietly closing the door, she pressed her ear to the wood, listening carefully to the voices growing louder with each second. She quickly turned and faced the room, finding herself in what looked to be a study. Books lined each of the walls and a large formal desk sat in the middle of the room. She hurried over to the desk and noticed the surface was bare. It was plain and unused. She slid open a drawer and found it empty except for a single, double edged blade. She rolled her eyes at the weapon. Of all the things to be in a desk.

Carolynn picked up the dagger. It was light and sturdy in her hand, evenly balanced. She pulled back the leather to reveal the blade. It was recently sharpened and no more than nine inches long. On the hilt lay a single large gem, one she recognized instantly by its signature glow. Adala. She slid the dagger back into its sheath and tucked the blade into her waistband at her hip, tugging her shirt down over it. She tiptoed back to the door and cracked it open enough to see two large males walking down the hall in her direction.

"Damn, that human can scream."

The other male chuckled. The sound left her feeling gross and unclean. "It'll be over for her soon."

Carolynn pushed the door shut before pressing her body against the wall, holding her breath as their voices grew more distant. She squeezed her eyes shut as she inhaled deep and calming breaths, attempting to stave off the hyperventilating she could feel creeping in. She couldn't afford to lose it now.

She opened the door once again to find the hallway empty. They were gone. Leaving the safety of the study, she walked down the hall once again, walking the way the guards had come from. Maybe they had just come from her mother. Maybe she was close.

Carolynn reached out with her mind, searching for her mother's familiar imprint. She came across dozens of individuals residing and working within the palace and slipped past each of them, not recognizing a single mind. She pushed herself further, farther than ever before until she found a mind she recognized.

She found her!

Susana was crying. She was hurt, barely breathing, but she was still alive.

Carolynn took the next right, the palace composed of nothing but endless and winding hallways, a tight and confusing maze meant to bewilder any intruder, but she followed the sound of her mother's voice in her head, taking it as a good sound as it got louder the closer she got.

I'm coming, Mom, she called to her, making yet another left.

Carolynn?

I'm here, Mom! I'm coming! Carolynn picked up her pace, continuing down corridor after corridor. She was almost there, her mother's mind becoming clearer.

No! You have to turn around! Get out of here! It's you they want! Her mother's voice screamed in her head.

Carolynn ignored her mother's pleas and took what she knew to be the last turn, smacking face first into two guards. They stood before a closed door decorated with rune-like markings. Her eyes widened as she took a step back, the guards mouth pulling into taunting smirks that promised violence.

One of them she recognized as Michael from outside the kitchen as he stood in front of the door, barring her way to her mother. Up close, his brown hair was cropped short. He had light hazel eyes, and his face was all sharp angles. She noticed the tone of muscle beneath his white tunic and was instantly reminded of Donnie.

They were Angels, she realized.

"We've been waiting for you," Michael said, voice calling to her like honey to a bear.

She was trapped. Her one arm was pretty much useless. She could barely lift it, let alone use it for self-defense. Who knew what kind of skills they possessed, given what she'd seen Donnie been able to do, let alone what powers they had. She looked the two guards up and down, assessing them. They were similar in build and size, large and hard looking.

Fuck it. She wasn't being taken without a fight.

Carolynn kicked out with her foot, landing a solid blow to Michaels knee. He went down hard on the marble floor, yelling out in pain. She spun around and back-kicked the other guard in the face, knocking the wind out of him as blood spurted from his nose. Michael stood up, recovering quicker than she'd have liked, and he ran for her. She sidestepped him, tripping him in the process. He went stumbling into the wall. The other guard swung back around on her, nose broken and face drenched with blood, fury plain in his black eyes. He charged, fists flying, aiming for her head. She barely had time to duck, his knuckles scraping over her head. She came back up, and with her good arm she punched him in the gut.

She felt someone tackle her from behind, knocking the wind from her lungs as their full body weight pinned her to the ground. She landed hard on the marble floor, body screaming in protest as she lay flattened between the hard ground and the Angel on her back. The impact jarred her already broken body and she bit into her cheek, drawing blood. She felt the body on top of her shift positions as the other guard came around to help him get her arm, pinning them to her back. A scream escaped her as the dislocated arm grinded against the empty socket, fire lancing down her body. One kicked her swiftly in the side, shutting her up effectively. The air fled her body as she heard a loud audible crack. There went a rib or two.

One of the males dug a knee into the middle of her back as they secured her. Tears fell from her eyes unwillingly as her shoulder tore tendons and muscles. Cold metal fastened around her wrists, cutting off the circulation. The metal gave her a weird jolt racing up her arm and throughout her body leaving her cold and hollow, senses dulling. Something in the cuffs dampened her powers.

She felt that now familiar tug on her chest and her heart sank. No, no, no. He couldn't come here, not like this.

Stay away! She begged him, pleading with the universe that he could somehow understand her.

Hands gripped her hard beneath her arms, lifting her off the ground. A small yelp of pain tore from her lips as they pulled on her dislocated shoulder. Sweat beaded on her forehead as she bit harder on her tongue, struggling to take in a solid breath.

The other guard spun her around to face him. She spit blood into his face, landing on his cheek. She watched his smile turn into rage before he raised his hand, backhanding her across the cheek.

Her head whipped to the side, nearly giving her whiplash. She would be surprised if a bruise wasn't already forming, but she'd be damned if she let them see any more weakness from her. Her lip was now split. She could feel the wet warmth dripping off her chin onto the pristine marble floor. She looked up into his black eyes and glared, challenging him.

The male looked as though he wanted to her hurt again, use her until she really did scream, but Michael cut in.

"That's enough. Put her in the room until he calls for us," Michael ordered. It seemed he was the Angel in charge in this dynamic.

The Angel didn't seem to like the order, but he obeyed anyway. Opening the door, he tossed her inside to a dimly lit room.

Carolynn collapsed on the floor, face meeting a hardwood floor as she coughed hard, jostling her shoulder again.

The door slammed shut, but she barely heard it over the pounding in her head and the mind-numbing pain dulling her mind.

"Carolynn?"

Carolynn could barely move, barely respond. She groaned onto her side, arms still secured behind her back.

"Oh, my baby," Susana cried from the corner of the room, inching closer.

Carolynn felt cold hands roam over her body, feeling for injuries and wounds she knew she had a plenty. She cried out as her mom touched her shoulder, unable to help the hot tears pouring from her.

"You stupid, foolish girl. Why did you come? Why didn't you listen?" Susana cried, helping her into a sitting position.

Carolynn swayed as she tried to stay upright, her vision growing blurry and dark in some spots, exhaustion weighing heavily on her.

"I couldn't leave you here," Carolynn said weakly. It was the only answer she had.

Susana sniffled and Carolynn couldn't bring herself to see her mother cry, so she hung her head instead.

"I'm sorry, Mom," Carolynn said, voice cracking. "I'm sorry for all of this. I'm sorry this is happening to you. I'm sorry you're at risk because of me."

Susana shushed her, cradling her like she used to when she was younger and had awoken from one of her night terrors. "Oh, my baby," she repeated. "I would do anything for you, you know that, right?"

Carolynn cried, burying her face in her mother's shirt.

"Let me take a look at you," Susana said, pushing her back to get as good of a look at her as she could in the dim lighting.

Susana turned her head this way and that, examining the long cut down her head. She moved on to the shoulder that was dislocated and most likely permanently damaged given the odd angle it was now in.

"Your head needs stitches, it's a nasty gash, and your arm definitely needs surgery, you have torn ligaments that a single popping back into the socket won't fix," Susana assessed.

But without saying it, they both knew nothing was going to happen with any of her injuries. There was no help, no sutures, no surgery.

"Are you okay? Have they hurt you?" Carolynn asked, trying to see her mother, make out any bruises or visible damage.

"I'm okay," Susana assured her. "Just a few bruises. The girls I fought back in high school could hit harder."

Carolynn tried to laugh, but all it did was jostle her arm. She bit back the pain as she took in a deep, unsteady breath. While she appreciated her mother's humor, she knew these Angels' strength was unmatched, and she was silently glad she couldn't see much of the damage to her mother. She wasn't sure what that kind of rage would do for either of them.

The handle of the door jingled as the door swung open. Michael stood in its doorway.

Susana held her close, trying to put her body between her and the Angel, but Michael only seemed to have eyes for Carolynn.

"You, back to your corner," Michael said, voice smooth like velvet.

Susana, without protest or resistance, stood up and walked back over to the far corner, leaving Carolynn alone and slumping down on the floor. She watched as Michael's black boot stepped closer until she could smell the leather, wafting up her nose along with a hint of cinnamon.

Strong, firm hands gripped under her arms and hauled her to her feet. Carolynn cried out, knees buckling beneath her.

Michael's eyes narrowed on the odd placement of her shoulder and the black and blue bruising peeking out beneath the sleeve of her shirt.

"You're hurt," the Angel said, stating the obvious.

"No shit, dipshit," Carolynn spat, vision darkening around the edges.

She just wanted to sleep, to curl into a ball on the floor and close her eyes, drifting off into oblivion.

Michael rolled his hazel eyes at her rudeness and moved a hand, hovering it over the damaged arm. Carolynn felt a warmth itching along her skin. Her mind became clearer with each passing second, until an audible snapping tore a scream from deep in her throat. White-hot pain lanced through her but then was gone the next instant.

Sweat covered her brow and lip as her face furrowed in confusion. Glancing down to her shoulder, she attempted to move the arm and found little to no pain.

"You healed me," Carolynn said aloud, surprise audible in her voice. "Why?"

"I didn't heal you entirely, just enough. We can't have you passing out before the fun starts," Michael said, face blank and impassive.

The other Angel, now, she could believe he would find torture and maiming others enjoyable, but Michael, she didn't believe it for one second.

"Can all Angels heal? Is that a common power for you?" she asked, unable to contain her curiosity.

Michael pulled back, eyeing her suspiciously. "You know about us?"

"I know more than I'd like and not enough," Carolynn said honestly. "Donnie is your brother, right? You two look a lot alike."

Michael's eyes widened at the Angel of Death's name, his lips pressed into a thin line. "What do you know of my brother?"

"I know he's here, and he's coming for me." She didn't know why she was telling this stranger any of this, but it was as though she couldn't stop the words from leaving her mouth. "If you can, try and keep him away. I don't want him to see me like this. I don't want him to watch me die."

A puzzled expression contorted his features just as another male body filled the door way.

"They're ready for her."

Chapter 45

Michael glanced back over his shoulder and nodded to the guard waiting, before shoving Carolynn forward out into the hallway, where three more guards waited. She tried to look back into the room, to see her mother one last time, but the door was closed behind them before she could say a word.

Carolynn was taken through a maze of halls, enough that she could no longer keep track or remember where they had come from, let alone where she had started from the kitchen. The walls were bare. There were no portraits, no decoration, nothing save for solid, white marble. They came upon a set of stained-glass French doors, tall and wide enough to fit Zafrina through. Her mouth gaped open at the opening and its sheer size. The palace was definitely much larger than she had anticipated. As they grew closer, the doors opened by themselves, allowing them entrance.

They proceeded inside a large receiving room, definitely big enough to hold a ball accommodating the entire population of the small town she grew up in. Dozens of chandeliers were suspended from the glass ceiling, reflecting light throughout the large space. It was almost too bright. With the glass ceiling, the crystal chandeliers, and the white marble floors, it was all overwhelming and did nothing for the pounding in her head as she squinted her eyes. Every inch of the wall was made of the same stained glass as the door, showcasing vibrant gardens on the east side and a rocky outcrop leading to the winding river she had seen from atop the dragon's back. It was grand in all its splendor, dazzling and beautiful in such a hellish situation. She silently wished she wasn't in this predicament and had been able to learn of her heritage, and her people; had the chance to explore this world, instead of wishing it would all burn to the ground.

Through the blinding light, she noticed there were specific shapes carved into the stained-glass windows and found that each panel contained different images, as though showcasing some specific event or multiple. If only she had read more of that book Neila had given her, she may have recognized some of them, but now they were nothing more than beautifully rendered art. The floor beneath her boots was pristine and smooth, with no visible flaws or imperfections.

At the very end of the hall was a large man standing in front of a metal wrought throne. He was a heavily built man who looked as though he had eaten one too many cakes, but beneath the extra layers, she could see the hard and strong man he had once been, that she had recalled from Neila's book. His black hair was curled around his head and hung past his shoulders, matching the thick and full beard. His clothing was simple yet elegant and reminded her of her Angel. He wore a black silken tunic and matching trousers secured around his waist by a belt that held a long sword at his hip.

Carolynn swallowed down her fear at the sight of that sword, forcing back the nerves that threatened to leave her a trembling mess as she recalled the tip of it being forced through her back. She had saved Beth; the future was already changed. Nothing was certain. Her stomach was tied in knots, and the growing hunger pains did nothing to help the building nausea. She forced herself to stand up straighter and gritted through the pain. Even though Michael had somewhat helped her shoulder, it didn't change the fact that it was still sore and aching, not to mention the broken ribs or other numerous cuts, bruises, and fractures she had sustained in the last few hours.

This man would not intimidate her. Remembering what Neila told her about Sarena, she wanted to throw a fireball right at his face. Disgusting pig.

She felt a sharp shove in her back as the guards behind her urged her forward. But what she saw almost had her choking on the air she breathed, eyes going wide. Those eyes, Matias's eyes, were the very same color as Donnie's.

"You must be the girl who has caused me so much trouble," he said, his voice light and humorous, yet somehow charming. The voice did not match the man standing on the dais.

"Am I supposed to know who you are?" she asked flippantly, throwing in a bit of that teenage attitude she was known for at home. Probably wasn't the wisest thing to do, but fuck it, she was already in deep shit.

He glared at her harshly. "I am Matias, King of the Gods." Anger seeped into his voice.

Carolynn grunted, pursing her lips, as though the title was meant to impress her. Her split lip cracked open, drawing fresh blood.

Matias eyed her carefully, squinting those eyes at her. "What is your name, girl?"

"Carolynn."

"Carolynn," he repeated, as if tasting how it felt in his mouth. The sound of her name on his lips nearly loosed her stomach and her bowels. "I have to say, I don't see what all the fuss is for. My Donnie should have had no problem in dispatching you, and yet he didn't." He cocked his head to the side as though to better assess her.

Carolynn kept her mouth shut, raising her head just an inch, stubbornly refusing to give him anything.

"Now, what was it?" Matias asked aloud. "Were you constantly surrounded by people? My Donnie is always cautious and avoids exposure. There's no way you outsmarted him. Contact with him has been cut off since he left, but that's not all that unusual either. So why didn't he kill you?"

Carolynn rose a brow, and a small smile tugged at her split lip. He really had no clue. A laugh bubbled on her lips, turning into a full-blown manic giggle.

Matias snarled, lip curling up in fury. "What is so funny?"

"You really have no clue, do you?" Carolynn laughed.

"What don't I know?" he growled.

"Donnie and I are mated," Carolynn said, using the term she had heard Sam and Neila use. Though she didn't quite understand its meaning, she got the impression that it was serious, even more than marriage and vows. Maybe it had something to do with this bond Sarena mentioned.

Matias roared, his face was bright red with anger, his nostrils flaring. "You lie. That's impossible. Donnie can't love; none of the Angels can. They have no souls."

Carolynn snickered. Donnie had a soul, and she didn't give a shit what this monster thought, and she didn't let her mind or her soul linger too long on the love aspect. They hadn't said it aloud to each other, and if that was why their bond had been created in the first place, she needed to hear it from him first.

"Is that why he couldn't stay away from me? Why he followed and protected me, saved me even from drowning? I can see it in the way he looks at me. The way he touches me. The way we—"

He moved faster than she could process, his fist smashing into the side of her head, sending her sprawling down onto the marble floor. She didn't have her arms and hands to catch herself from smashing into the marble floor so she curled her body, landing on her injured shoulder, most likely dislocating it once again as the impact had her vision go dark for a split second. She could feel something tugging in her chest, like a piece of paper tearing. If she didn't have a punctured lung yet, she did now. The wound on her head had reopened and was bleeding, leaving her in a small puddle of her own blood. The crimson color was startling against the brilliant white marble. She coughed as she tried to catch her breath; blood sprayed from her mouth and coated her throat.

Not good.

Her head was spinning, and her ears were ringing once again. The side of her face hurt like hell, and tears stung her eyes. She tried to roll and sit herself up, but she couldn't move. Everything hurt. Her broken ribs were grinding against one another making breathing extremely difficult as each breath caused a sharp pain.

Hands slid beneath her arms, gently raising her to her feet. She twisted her head to see who it was. Michael. He was watching her strangely. She ignored the look and turned back to Matias, who stood before her. Assuming by the satisfied look on the God's face, she must have been a sight to behold. She stuck her chin out stubbornly, spitting blood at his feet.

"I will kill you," Matias promised, lips peeled back, revealing pearly white teeth. "But first, I will break you."

From behind, she could hear the large French doors opening. She tried her best to turn her head back and look, wincing as she did. Two guards walked in side by side, and between them, dragged by her arms, feet trailing behind and blonde head hanging limply, was her mother. Carolynn felt her feet move without thought, trying to get to her, but Michael held her tight, dragging her back until her back was pressed against his chest. Someone else, maybe another guard, had come up beside them, hands gripping her shoulders, and slammed her down on her knees. Her body no longer registered the pain, couldn't process or think of anything else but her mother.

Carolynn struggled against the hands on her shoulders, keeping her pinned down on her knees. The more she resisted, the more they dug their fingers into her flesh. A hand wrapped in her braid, yanking her head back.

The two guards dragged her mother closer, stopping about ten feet away. She wasn't sure if her mother was even breathing, as her body was slumped over.

"Mom!" Carolynn yelled.

The sound of her terrified scream caused Susana to stir. She slowly raised her head, eyes blinking sleepily as her dull blonde hair fell back to reveal her face. It was badly bruised, with a broken jaw and nose. Susana tried to offer her a supportive smile but flinched at the pain.

Carolynn continued to struggle. "What did she ever do to you? She did nothing wrong!"

"That's where you're wrong," Matias laughed, bending down until their eyes were level. He reached out a meaty hand and brushed the hair from her face. Carolynn jerked away violently from his touch. "She raised you. She loves you, and that is enough for me."

Carolynn shook her head, tears and blood scattering. "Why? I didn't even know any of this existed. You could have just let me live my life in ignorance."

"I would never take such a risk, but soon none of this will matter anymore. Soon, you will be a distant memory."

"Please let my mom go. You have me now. I'll do whatever you want," she begged, glancing from the God to her mother.

"It's okay, Star," Susana said, her voice raspy and broken. "It's going to be okay."

"Your mother was only kept alive long enough to get you here, but now—" Matias made a motion to the guards, signaling them.

A knife reflected in the light from the windows as it slid across her mother's throat faster than she could release the blood-curdling, guttural scream. Everything was in slow motion. Her mother's look of surprise. The blood weeping from the fatal wound. Matias snickering, eyes alight like he enjoyed the show.

The guards released their hold on Susana's shoulders, dropping her face first onto the marble floor. A deep crimson red pooled on the ground, growing in size by the second as she bled out. Her mother's face was blank, eyes still wide open.

Carolynn screamed in horror, fighting as hard as she could. If she could get to her, if she could just put her hands on her, maybe she could heal her, save her. She could feel her power awakening, struggling against the cuffs, building inside. It was strong, heavier than anything she'd ever experienced. The metal cuffs released, snapping off as electricity raced along her skin.

Something blunt hit her on the side of her head, and her world went dark.

Chapter 46

Leaves slapped against her face, scraping what was left of her skin. Dirt gathered in her boots, collecting through the tears and holes in the leather as they dragged behind her along the forest floor. Her hair caught on branches as they passed, yanking at her scalp. She had completely lost feeling in the arm that had dislocated again; the other one was just as numb from the tight grip the guards had on her.

Her head throbbed, face aching and eyes sore as she adjusted to her surroundings, blinking away the black spots clouding her vision.

Where was she? How did she get here? But then she remembered.

Brilliant red on white, her mother's wide, horrified eyes as the chilling metal cut into her throat. Carolynn's whole body went cold with shock. Her mom was dead, and she had done nothing. She didn't save her.

Mom was dead.

Carolynn allowed her body to go limp, head drooping, hanging between the guards that carried her.

The warmth of the sun beat against her bruised and bleeding skin. Unable to restrain her natural gravitation to the rays, she looked up into the light. They emerged out of the woods through a break in the trees. She squinted against the sudden brightness and discovered that they entered an open clearing, the grass dead and bare. Overhead, threatening clouds were gathering and lightning danced in the sky. Déjà vu overwhelmed her, coating her throat in bile. She choked back the vomit as the scene from her dream unfolded before her very eyes.

Matias walked ahead of her, surrounded by his own guard, Michael stationed on his right. She was carried by two guards and had accumulated a protection detail of her own. Through the wall of tall males, she could see a large following had gathered below the dais they now stood on. The crowd was a giant mix of Gods and creatures, varying in size, shapes, and colors. Some she recognized as centaurs, griffins, and nymphs, but there were plenty she had never seen or heard of before.

The guards dragged her to the front of the erected platform, forcing her down on her knees, showcasing Matias's prey to everyone in attendance. She glanced out over the crowd and tried to swallow through her dry, parched mouth that still had traces of blood.

This was her nightmare.

Donnie pushed through the crowd that seemed to double in size by the minute. He had spent the last day tormented out of his mind, feeling every hit, every punch, and attack that had been inflicted on her. He could feel through the bond that she was still battered and broken, growing weaker by the second, but he had been unable to find her. That was until he heard whispers about a gathering. A gathering hosted by Matias, and he knew. Matias had her.

He had never felt such rage before, an uncontrollable thirst for violence and vengeance. He had imagined the hundreds of ways he could make a man beg for death, plead for a swift end, but he would not be so generous. He would enjoy every moment of torture to any single person who laid a hand on her. She was his, and no one would survive his wrath. He was death. He was the bringer of death, and it seemed as though some required a reminding of that fact. His sword was a welcome weight in his hand as he regripped the pommel. The metal sang to him, thirsty for blood.

The crowd moved around him. He knew his temper was leaking, permeating the air around him, strong enough for the Gods and creatures in attendance to taste, to shrink back in fear. Good. They should fear him. He knew Neila and Sam were somewhere nearby. They had realized Carolynn had slipped out soon after he did. Knocked him out cold with her power. Treacherous little vixen. Who did she think she was to leave him behind like that? To think she could do this on her own? He wanted to scold her, to shake her and yell that she was a naive fool, but another part of him wanted to fuck her, bury himself so deep inside as he whispered in her ear how fucking brave she was, how fearless, and fuck if that didn't make his cock throb.

Damn woman.

Donnie watched as guards, his brothers, dragged his mate out from the tree line and onto the stage. He watched as she struggled to lift her head, and the sight of her nearly had his knees buckling and him vomiting whatever was left in his stomach from yesterday. Vengeance boiled his blood, and rage was his fuel as his shadows slithered from his grip, coiling around him, threatening everyone in attendance. The creatures and Gods that were closest backed away as darkness gathered at his feet and wrapped around him. He could see the blood cracked and dried on her face from a gash down her hairline. A split lip on that beautiful mouth dripped fresh blood. Her shredded and torn clothing revealed a dislocated shoulder riddled with bruises and the odd angle from which it hung. Those were only the wound he could visibly see. Those stunning silver-grey eyes were red-rimmed and swollen. Tear streaks stained her face, but she didn't look sad. She looked the way he felt. Pissed the fuck off.

He wanted to destroy every Angel, every brother who dared touch what was his. He wanted to torture them until they screamed, begging for the end, only to feed them to the pit demons and watch as they were eaten alive. He struggled to restrain himself and his shadowy companions. If he acted now, she would be killed on that spot.

"Thank you all for gathering," Matias spoke, his voice carrying out over the crowd, silencing all. He took a single step forward beside the guards who kept Carolynn on her knees. A growl almost tore from Donnie's throat right then and there. "This is a very special day. One we have waited millennia for. Today we will end the false prophecy. Today we will be free of the threat to our world."

Donnie glanced around the crowd. Most of their faces were

riddled with disgust, others were horrified. Carolynn was barely of legal age, still a child to most in the eyes of the ancients. The sight of her was not being received as well as Matias had hoped.

"Can we get this over with?" Carolynn spoke, her voice strong and brave, shocking not only Matias but the crowd watching. To some, her voice might be recognizable as she sounded much like her grandmother. To others, her speaking was an act of clear defiance, something not often seen. "You're boring me, and I have better places to be. Things to do, places to see."

Some in the crowd smirked at her courage. Others snickered at the insult of her still having her tongue. Donnie's grip on his sword tightened.

"Patience, girl," Matias snapped, slapping her across the face hard enough to knock her head back.

Donnie flinched as his cheek stung, as though he had been hit as well. He made to step forward, made to fly to her and hack the King's head clean from his shoulders, when a hand gripped him by the shoulders, holding him back with surprising strength.

Donnie whirled on whoever dared to stop him but froze, frowning at the God beside him. It was Dominius. Sam's father and Carolynn's grandfather. Those silver eyes bore into the stage and his brother who ruled them.

"Not yet," Dominius said under his breath, quiet enough for only him to hear. "If you go now, you both die."

Donnie gritted his teeth. If it was anyone else that had dared hold him back, he would have already relieved them of their head, but Dominius, the Truthteller, his word was the future. Not listening to his advice would be foolish.

Matias straightened his shirt and smiled at the crowd. "This girl is not who some of you thought her to be. She is dangerous and has the ability to destroy us all. Today, you will witness the end to this foolish prophecy, and we can move forward in peace and prosperity."

Carolynn spat blood on the ground in front of her, holding her head high as crimson spittle dripped off her chin, holding the eyes of the entire crowd. She was fearless in the face of death. Donnie didn't think he could have dreamed of a stronger female and wasn't sure what he ever did to deserve such a feral, courageous creature. He puffed his chest slightly, that devilish smirk he knew she secretly loved came out as he swelled with pride. That was his mate. A bond he never knew could be possible for a monster like him, and she was all his.

A good portion of the gathering murmured amongst themselves. From the few words he could pick out, it wasn't going Matias's way, and judging by the glare in those eyes of his, the King of Gods knew it.

"Her existence is a threat to us all! Unchecked power will lead to our destruction. The fact that there has never been another like her should be cause enough to terminate the threat," Matias preached to his congregation. He gripped Carolynn by her tangled braid and tipped her head back exposing her throat. He raised his sword, the one Donnie hadn't noticed him holding, and pressed it to her throat, metal kissing skin.

A single crimson tear slid down her neck. Donnie jerked forward but Dominius still had a tight grip on his shoulder. His heart raced in his chest, eyes bulging, his shadows prepared to decimate anyone who came near. He knew the damage Adalon steel could do. Its wounds would leave a scar that would never fade. He was about ready to toss Dominius into the crowd, Truthteller be damned, when a voice he recognized froze the blood pulsing through his veins.

"This ends now, Matias."

The crowd gasped, searching for the Goddess the voice belonged to. Carolynn's stomach clenched tightly, her pulse racing. She knew that voice, knew who it belonged to, as dread seeped into her soul. She forgot all about her battered body and the sword pressing into her throat as she looked out and found Sarena.

From the opposite side of the clearing emerged a small group of no more than thirty. At the head of the group was Sarena with Neila and Sam at her side. Each member of the group carried an assortment of weapons. Some wore metal armor, others preferred the freedom of loose clothing. Each looked formidable in their own right.

Neila and Sam had eyes for her only. Neila's were silver lined, hand clasped over her mouth as she took in the state of her. Sam looked as though he was ready to burn the world, not giving a damn about the consequences. But Sarena, the beautiful Goddess, was fixed on the King and the blade he still pressed to Carolynn's throat. Carolynn whimpered, trying to pull away, but his grip tightened on her hair, and the cold sting of steel cut into her skin.

"Sarena," Matias called to her. The way he said her name twisted her gut and almost had her gagging. "It's been an age since I last had the chance to look upon you. You haven't changed one bit."

"Oh, but I have, my King," Sarena said, mocking the title. "I would like to introduce you to my daughter, Neylara. Mother to the girl you are poised to kill."

Matias froze for the briefest of moments. Carolynn could feel his grip on her hair loosen and retighten as though he was processing the Goddess's words. "You never had a child. I would have known."

"I gave birth to her two hundred forty-six years ago," Sarena said with a knowing smile.

Carolynn couldn't see the King who stood just slightly behind her and to her left, but she could taste his shock, like acid exploding on the back of her tongue. The sour taste of disbelief. Clearly, he had not forgotten the night he had raped the beautiful God, ultimately turning the wheels of the prophecy he lived in fear of. While she couldn't see his expression, she could see Sarena's, and it was one of pure satisfaction.

"I see you have finally put it together, but let me explain to the rest of your court, your realm, whom you claim to have only the best of intentions for." Sarena pursed her lips before turning to the crowd, who had already circled towards her, offering her their full and undivided attention.

It was clear by the way they watched her, and felt for her, she was most beloved. Carolynn didn't know what she was up to; she only hoped that it was enough of a distraction.

"You all know me, know who I am and what I stand for," Sarena began. Already the crowd nodded, praising her for numerous deeds Carolynn could only hear whispers about. "Over two centuries ago, Matias had begun to court me, but I refused. We have all heard enough stories about his conquests and those he takes to his bed. I refused to become another trophy for him to collect. Matias did not take no for an answer. He raped me."

The crowd hushed, shocked into silence. Tears leaked from Carolynn's eyes as she watched the Goddess bare herself to the crowd, to her peers and friends, as she stripped herself of her deepest, darkest secret.

"But that night he didn't only take something from me, he gave me something as well. He gave me my beautiful daughter Neylara. I know most of this comes as a shock to you all. I did well concealing my child to save her life. You all could not know of her existence. I knew in my heart, our King would never tolerate a possible successor, given that she is his only heir," Sarena looked to her, a sad smile on her lips. "That is, until Carolynn."

"Lies!" Matias hissed, spit flying from between his teeth.

"It is our grandchild you hold at the edge of your sword, Matias," Sarena said, exposing the King for the entire realm to see.

The crowd began to shift on their feet, looking between the two Gods wearily. Most looked vengeful, hands moving towards swords already strapped at their hips. Others seemed to sense the brooding tension and looked ready to flee at a moment's notice.

"I do not have nor do I recognize any heirs," Matias spat, regripping Carolynn's braid, causing her to hiss in pain.

"I do not recognize you as my father, just the bastard who forced himself on my mother, but that is my daughter you threaten," Neila said, stepping past the Goddess, twirling twin blades in her hands that reflected the lightning streaking in the sky above them.

"And who is the unlucky father of this abomination?" Matias asked, lifting her head higher by her hair.

"She is mine," Sam said, stepping forward to stand beside Neila, resting a hand on her shoulder, the other cradling a hand-carved bow.

Matias startled. "Samonius?"

Gasps echoed through the crowd; for what reason, Carolynn didn't know. She was missing something. But the voices in the crowd, the people that came to witness her execution, were growing loud and angry. While some still looked at her like fresh meat waiting to be slaughtered, licking their lips as though they could taste her blood, most were growing restless, throwing disgusting and traitorous looks at the King.

Matias could feel the tide turning on him as he let go of her hair, pulling his sword away from her throat. Carolynn sagged back on her heels, hands still bound behind her back, her throat stinging where the sword had sliced into her flesh.

"This is a necessary sacrifice," the King said, not quite sure if he was trying to convince the crowd or himself. "She will be the end of us."

"The correct reading of the prophecy is that she will overthrow you, not the Gods. Just you," a voice rose above the murmurings of the crowd as a tall man resembling Sam quite perfectly came to materialize at his side. Dominius. "Do not think us fools by feeding us lies. This is all about your love for power, brother."

Carolynn jerked at the relation. Dominius and Matias were brothers? She was going to be sick.

"You may be my equal in power, Dominius, but you are *not* my blood," Matias spat, taking the God's opposing side as a clear sign of betrayal.

God politics was causing her head to spin as Carolynn found an odd sense of relief. She wasn't a product of incest. At least that was something.

She took in the opposing group with her birth parents at its front and her grandparent's strong support; she couldn't be prouder. A small glimmer of hope began to take root until she nearly choked on her heart, her soul spasming in her chest when she heard him.

"Let her go, Matias."

Chapter 47

Carolynn could have sworn her heart literally ceased beating as his voice carried out over the two-hundred-something crowd. She glanced out, and there he was standing in the middle of it. How had she not felt him so close? Did the cuffs not only dampen her power but their bond? Or was she that out of it she couldn't distinguish him or her pain?

The mass of creatures and Gods stepped away from Donnie, leaving him to stand in the center on his own. He stood there in all his beautiful terrifying glory, with his ancient sword in hand, and those shadows billowing in a nonexistent wind. His black iridescent wings were tucked in behind him. Guess there was no reason to hide their existence here. Those silver-blue moonlight eyes found hers and expressed so much all within the blink of an eye that she cried out, leaning forward on her knees. Her heart and soul were pulling her towards him, demanding to be near him. If it wasn't for the two sets of hands gripping her by the shoulders and pulling her back, she would already be at his side, cuffs or not.

"Donnie, my son. I'm so glad you could join us. This child has told me some concerning things about your failure of a mission. Would you care to explain yourself before our court and your brothers?" Matias coolly asked, calling him out before the masses.

Carolynn struggled against the hands holding her, keeping her firmly on her knees against the unforgiving wooden platform. If they touched him, if they tried to hurt him, she would destroy everyone in this fucking clearing.

"I failed at nothing. It was my choice not to kill her when I came to the realization she was not the threat you made her out to be," Donnie said casually, his voice ringing clear across the field.

"You were mistaken if you thought my command was a choice," Matias gritted out, glaring at the Angel of Death, face beet red.

"You are correct in not giving me a choice, and yet I made one," Donnie said, declaring his side in all of this.

A part of her beamed. He was choosing her before everyone he knew. The other part wanted to thrash him for putting himself in danger.

"You traitorous bastard," Matias spat. "How could you choose this abomination over your own blood?"

"Rude," Carolynn grumbled under her breath.

"She is my mate, my soul bond. Harming her would be like cutting off my own arm. It is not something I am willing or want to do," Donnie said, those ice-blue eyes finding hers.

The back of her eyes stung at his admission, and she finally found that bond that led her directly to him and sent one single thought down that link. *You're mine.*

And you are mine.

Carolynn's eyes widened. She heard him. She could actually link with him.

"Traitor!" Matias roared, the sound reverberating off the ground and air.

The air rang with the sound of swords being pulled from their sheaths, wings beating in the wind, and lightning cracking across the sky. Half of the crowd turned on the other half, fighting breaking out from within. Dozens of Angels hiding within the clouds fell from the sky, attacking those on the ground, aiming for him. Donnie disappeared under a mass of flesh and feathers as his brothers overwhelmed him. Neila and Sam broke off from their group, gunning straight for her, but were cut off by a large number of Angels and Gods alike. She watched Dominius take the form of the greatest lion she'd ever seen, and lunge for a tall figure cloaked in a tattered, ancient robe. Oriel.

She caught sight of Sarena fighting hand-to-hand combat against a man with four arms, brandishing a sword in each hand.

Her moves were precise, and her speed left her as simply a blur. Sam held the opposing group back, putting arrows into anyone who attempted to overwhelm their small group. He was concentrating on the sky, firing arrows into Angels that tried to breach their ranks. Carolynn searched for Neila in the mass of bodies, finally spotting her tucked away in the center of the fighting, blocking attackers with her sword from all sides. It was a sight to watch her fight. She could see she had a cut above her right eye and blood dripped from her nose, but those emerald green eyes were wild with the adrenaline of the fight.

The sun began to shine through the clouds, casting a golden hue. Carolynn looked up towards the sky and saw that it wasn't the sun, it was Zafrina. The dragon was descending fast towards the ground before tossing her wings out to slow her speed, just before she plucked an Angel up by its wings with her razor talons. The Angel in her claws was a woman with a nasty looking mace. Zafrina flew her out over the river and dropped her into the racing rapids below, wings sliced through.

Carolynn thought she could make out Donnie's black hair and wings, his sword flashing through anything and everything coming within reach of his ancient sword. She wanted to yell, tell him to leave, when she felt herself being torn away, dragged back from the fighting. Hands gripped under her arms, pulling her backwards off the dais and out of view from the chaos. She kicked out, flailing her legs trying to connect with the nearest guard, when she made contact with a shin. His stumble was enough for her to roll to her knees and stand. They seemed surprised by her flexibility and nimble moves, distracted just long enough for her to sweep the legs out from underneath the next guard. Someone slammed into her back, almost driving her face down into the ground. She stumbled but managed to get her feet back under her and spun around, landing a spinning back kick and sending her attacker back on his ass.

In that second, that brief respite, she decided right then and there that this would not be the end of her story. She had to fight. Had to stay alive and survive this. Had to get back to him. She felt her powers awaken, as though that singular choice broke free something vital and pivotal. An acceptance. An awakening. Her

Ascension.

A blast erupted from every part of her as power—magic—flooded her. Her eyes snapped open.

Electricity raced across her skin in a single, powerful current down to her hands into the cuffs around her wrists. They clicked open, releasing her hands. There were three guards circling her as she glanced around at each of them. She noticed they had somehow made their way back onto the dais, in full view of the crowd that was still doing their best to tear each other apart.

The guard in front of her lunged forward. She sidestepped him, driving her elbow into the center of his back. He went down hard, planting face first into the wood platform. The guard to her right threw a knife that she barely missed as she rolled forward on the ground, ignoring the stabbing pain in her side and useless arm. She bounced onto her feet, slid the knife she had tucked into the band of her pants out from under her shirt, and stabbed it into the belly of the guard. He fell to the ground, clutching his bleeding abdomen.

The last guard, Michael, threw himself at her. Reflexively, a wave of electricity rolled across her skin. Michael didn't have enough time to pull back. His hand connected with her arm, which sent him flying twenty feet back into the crowd, disappearing from view.

Carolynn spun around, the hairs on the back of her neck raising in warning, and found Matias. The remaining guards were fighting off those daring to near the dais. Matias held his sword in one hand, watching her carefully. Carolynn spotted a sword lying unclaimed on the ground next to an unconscious guard. She darted for the blade and picked it up before Matias could block her. The weapon was heavy and definitely too big for her to wield, but she would have to make do. She gripped the hilt with both hands, pushing back the agonizing protest of her dislocated shoulder. She ignored the bellowing voice in her head that told her she had no business sword fighting, but circumstances offered her little choice. She had learned hand-to-hand combat growing up, not fencing.

Matias charged for her, sword raised high. She managed to get the sword up in time, blocking the blow. The force of the hit jarred her to the bone. She gritted her teeth and lunged for him, swinging wildly. Matias jumped back in surprise, reassessing his opponent. He attacked again, and she blocked, parrying the blow before striking out and getting in a solid hit. They both managed to get in a few blows. Carolynn's confidence grew as they danced, striking and feigning, lunging and dodging, but she was tiring quickly, and he could see it. She was slow to parry his next hit, and the tip of his sword sliced into the top of her thigh.

Carolynn dropped to one knee. She didn't have much blood left to lose, as her vision swam with black dots. She couldn't get the sword up in time to block the next swing. His sword knocked hers from her grip, sending the blade sailing through the air and out of sight.

Matias's sword raised over his shoulder, the lingering sun glinting off the steel. The world went quiet around her as she watched the blade slice through the air, plunging down to her chest. She closed her eyes in anticipation when she felt herself thrown to the side, slamming into the earth.

Carolynn screamed as cold metal sliced through skin and breast bone, plunging all the way through to her heart until it severed her spine. She grabbed at her chest, trying to get the weapon out, but found nothing there. Wide-eyed and manic, she frantically threw herself up onto her hands and knees, looking around for the source of that pain.

Donnie stood where she had been just moments before, with Matias's sword plunged deep into his chest, the God's hand still holding the pummel. The King's eyes were wide with shock and horror as he pulled the sword free with a sickening wet sound. Donnie collapsed onto the ground, blood seeping from the wound and staining the dead grass.

Carolynn's blood ran cold as she stared at her Angel in utter shock. She could feel the hole in his chest as if it were her own. This wasn't supposed to happen. This wasn't how it was supposed to go down. She saw it, she saw all of it. It was her that was supposed to die. She looked up to Matias, his wide-eyed expression matching hers as he looked down at the damage he had done, that he had caused. Her mind went numb, blank, filled with pure, golden red flame.

No! "No!" She screamed aloud and telepathically, her mind, soul, and heart shattering as she let out a psychic blast that stunned the creatures and Gods still fighting into silence, rippling for miles and miles. She threw herself at the King, surprising him with her speed, and thrust her hand into his chest, breaking through skin, tendon, and bone. She could feel his beating heart in the palm of her hand, the warmth of his lifeblood, and she squeezed. His lips quivered, but he didn't make a sound.

A guttural, animal-like sound tore from her throat as she tore the bastard's heart from his chest and admired the black, withered organ in her hand. She glared at the King just as his entire body erupted into ash, leaving behind only dust fluttering to the floor.

Carolynn looked back at her hand. The heart and blood were already gone, as though it had never even happened.

She threw herself to the ground beside Donnie. She could hear voices all around, some shouting, others crying. There were people gathering around her, some familiar, but none of them mattered.

"Donnie, can you hear me? Stay with me." She pressed her hands to his chest, trying to staunch the bleeding. He didn't move and didn't even seem to recognize the pressure on the wound.

His eyes flittered open. They were pale and unfocused. "Carolynn?"

"I'm here, baby. I'm here. Don't leave me," she pleaded, tears streaming down her face. She brushed the hair back from his eyes. "You're going to be okay, you hear me?"

"I'm sorry I didn't find you sooner. I didn't protect you," he whispered breathlessly, blood seeping from the corner of his mouth.

"Hush, it's okay. I didn't give you much of a choice, leaving you like that." She smirked, sniffling loudly.

Donnie tried to laugh, but it got caught in his throat, turning into a cough and bringing blood to his lips. "I wanted to thrash you for leaving me like that."

"You still can; you just need to hold on," Carolynn cried. Blood no longer seeped from his wound, and his skin was growing cold. "Someone get some help!"

He swallowed shallowly. "I wish I could stay."

She squeezed her eyes shut briefly as a sob escaped her. "You can't leave. Not now. Not after I've just found you. We have so much left to do. We're supposed to be forever."

"We are forever." A solitary tear slipped from his eyes. "I love you."

"No, Donnie. Don't leave," she sobbed as the tether that linked their souls snapped, his chest falling one last time. The bond that bound her to him recoiled, shattering her heart and fragmenting her soul. His beautiful wintry blue eyes fluttered closed. "Don't leave me."

Carolynn laid her head against his chest, gripping at the fabric of his blood-stained shirt. She sobbed into him, screaming at his lifeless body. She sat up to take one last look at him and before her very eyes, his body began to dissipate, disappearing into the earth. The only evidence of his body was the soiled clothes left behind. She searched out with her hands, not believing what her eyes were seeing, and only came up with chunks of dirt and grass. She pounded her fists into the ground, screaming her soul away.

Chapter 48

"**S**hould we take her to the hospital?"

"So, she can be treated as a psych patient? Absolutely not!"

"What else can we do? She hasn't moved or said a word, not since—"

"I know, Neila. She just needs time."

"We healed her body, but her heart…" Neila started saying. "It was more than just love for them, you know that, right? You felt that psychic blast; we all did." Her voice shuddered in memory. "I can't even imagine. What if she can't come back from this?"

"She has to."

It had been a week since Aros. Since her life had been twisted, gutted, and ripped apart. She lay in her bed, curled around herself as she could hear them arguing outside her door. They had been doing it off and on since they had come back. Neila and Sam had been standing in the hallway for quite some time now, but for how long exactly, she didn't know. Time had been a lost concept for her. She didn't remember how she got back or even left Aros.

The last time she had been in this bed had been with—no, she couldn't think about that yet. Each time a memory with him crept up on her, it brought on a new wave of pain she didn't even know existed, threatening to drown her. She wanted nothing more than to give up and join him in the afterlife, whatever or wherever it was. Somehow, she knew she would find him waiting for her, but she almost smirked at the scolding she knew would await her. She couldn't do that, he would never want her too. He would want her to keep living.

Carolynn slowly got up from the bed, peeling back the covers. Her joints were stiff from laying still for so long. Her entire body was sore and cramped, one giant bruise. They had managed to clean all of her wounds, realign her shoulder, bandage her ribs, and heal the minor cuts, but most of her damage was beyond their expertise. It was something her body had to heal naturally. The cut on her head and thigh had needed stitches, and the cut on her throat was slow to heal. She would forever carry the scars, inside and out. She limped over to the window, staring out the glass into the rose garden when something dark and shiny caught her eyes. Wedged between the wall and the dresser, Carolynn bent down, wincing at her ribs as she pulled out a leather jacket. Emotion choked her as tears filled her eyes. Gripping the leather tightly, she leaned into the worn fabric. His scent still clung to it. Tears slipped from her eyes as she hugged the jacket tight to her chest.

Carolynn opened the bedroom door and found the hallway now empty. Hobbling down the stairs, she heard voices coming from the kitchen. She stopped outside the swinging door when she heard her name and paused to listen.

"You know what this means, right?" She heard Sam, his voice full of worry and concern.

"She's only eighteen. They can't expect this from her," Neila protested.

"She doesn't have a choice. The law clearly states—"

"I don't give a damn about the law!" Neila yelled, startling her. She didn't think she'd ever heard the Demi yell. "Do you think that girl is fit to rule Aros? She's just a kid who's lost more than anyone I know. They can't expect this of her. Not right now. She needs time."

"She doesn't have time," Sam continued. "She killed Matias, and right now, there is a vacuum in Aros. She has to fill it, or someone else will."

"She's not a God," Neila stated.

"Dominius told me she has fulfilled the prophecy. She's not a Demis."

Carolynn didn't want to stand on the other side of the door any longer. It was time she partook in these conversations regarding her future.

"Then what am I?" Carolynn asked, startling them both from where they stood.

Neila was sporting a few of her own gruesome bruises, a nice shiner, and a golf ball size bruise along her bottom jaw. She looked exhausted.

Sam immediately moved to Carolynn's side, offering her his arm to help support her towards the kitchen island. She allowed the help as her limp was obvious with the slash on her thigh, and her broken ribs made movement difficult.

"We don't have to talk about this right now. You've been through a lot," Sam said, as though she needed a reminder.

The sympathy and pity lacing his voice cut her deeper than any knife. "I need to know."

Neila tried to smile, but only half of her face was able to accomplish the gesture before she winced, cradling her bruised jaw.

"You're a God," Sam finally said.

"Bullshit," Carolynn said automatically, her brain unable to find another more suitable word or phrase.

"We don't know for sure," Neila tried, but Sam's glare stopped her.

"Yes, we do," Sam corrected. "We all felt it, your Ascension, and killing Matias was more than enough confirmation. Only a God can kill another God."

Carolynn had heard that before. She didn't feel like a God, not that she knew what that should feel like in the first place.

"Do you have the keys to my Camaro? Is it here?" Carolynn asked, glancing around the kitchen for her keys.

Neila looked at her as if she sprouted two heads. "Honey, did you hear us?"

"I heard you," she said nodding, not really listening. "My keys?"

Sam stepped forward, leaning on the counter in front of her. "You shouldn't be driving."

"Then can someone please drive me to Beth's? I need to see her. See that she's okay," she said, knowing her voice sounded a bit desperate, but let's face it, she was.

Carolynn hadn't seen her best friend since she left her in Sarena's care that horrible day. They told her that an Angel had healed her partially, but once she arrived home, her parents essentially put her under house arrest, forcing her to recover at home from what she told her parents was a car wreck. She needed to see her, needed to see her friend alive and breathing. That something good had come out of this hell.

"I'll take you," Neila said quietly. She picked up the keys off the counter behind her, jingling them in her hand.

Carolynn followed after her, limping slowly behind her into the three-car garage. She recognized the Camaro beside the Audi and winced as she lowered herself into the car. The drive there was quiet. Neila didn't try to make small talk, and Carolynn didn't offer to fill the silence. She stared out the window, watching the world fly by.

They pulled into the driveway. The house looked the same as it always had, one of the main constants in her life. Carolynn sat in the car, staring at the front porch much longer than she intended to. Taking in a deep breath, she forced herself to open the door, leaving Neila without saying a word, and shut the door behind her. She walked up the steps and knocked on the front door. Pretty sure it was the first time she'd ever done that. Normally she would have walked right in, no permission necessary, but these weren't normal times.

Thomas opened the door and gasped at the sight of her. His hands flashed out and before she could flinch back, he pulled her into a crushing embrace. Carolynn bit her lower lip, enduring the hug. He quickly released her as she let out a low hiss of pain.

"I'm sorry. Beth had said you two were in an accident, I just thought she had gotten the worst of it," he said matter-of-factly, gesturing towards her face and what was visible of her body. In a not-so-subtle way, he was pointing out that she had received the worst of it, but that she wasn't so sure of. She'd have preferred for Beth not to have gotten hurt at all. "I'm so sorry about your mother. She was an amazing woman."

Carolynn nodded her head solemnly, her face cold and distant. That was the other part of their cover story. Her mother had died in the car crash. "Thank you. Is Beth upstairs?"

"Yes," he said quickly. "Go on up. I'll bring some tea."

Carolynn nodded in thanks as she forced her feet to move towards the stairs. She took them one at a time, trying not to overdo it with her leg and lungs. The last thing she needed was to tear her stitches. She finally reached the second floor and pushed open Beth's door. Her friend was lying back against the headboard with a Cosmo magazine opened on her lap. Her hair had returned to its lustrous chestnut color, and the bruising on her face was already a fading yellow. Her skin was no longer sallow and thin, but it's normal pink and lively color. She was still pretty thin, her bones sticking out more than they used to, but she looked so much better. The cut under her eye was healing nicely. She'd be lucky enough to only have a thin scar, barely noticeable. Her wrists were bandaged, covering the blisters and scarring left from the manacles.

Carolynn couldn't contain the small sob that worked its way up her throat. She was relieved to find her friend alive and healing. She was relieved that it hadn't all been for nothing. She was devastated that day had cost Beth so much.

Beth looked up, startled to find Carolynn in her bedroom. She smiled wildly, ecstatic to see her friend until she noticed her broken, shattered face. Tears welled in her friend's eyes. She held her arms out to her, tossing the magazine to the floor.

Carolynn climbed into the bed, curled up against her best friend, and cried.

Chapter 49

Several Months Later

Carolynn stood in the small clearing near her old house, standing in front of the patch of purple tulips and the neighboring bed of poppies. She kneeled down beside the two graves.

Neila and Sam had made sure to bring her mother's body back with them, laying her to rest. They held a small ceremony for her, burying her beside Shadow. Her father had been cremated when he passed. This seemed like the most appropriate spot for her, where Shadow could watch over her in the next life.

Carolynn plucked a poppy from the ground and twirled it between her fingers, trying to find the words she had come here to say.

"Hey, Mom," she started and instantly felt foolish for talking to a grave, but Sam and Neila had encouraged her to say goodbye, insisting she needed closure.

They weren't wrong.

This was her first time being back here, the place she had grown up. The last few months had been spent in Adalon, but those months had felt like a year. Time moved differently there.

"So much has happened," she said, her voice catching. "So much I want to tell you. So much I needed you for. Things I just needed my mom for." She angrily wiped the tears off her face. "I miss you so much. I'm so sorry I couldn't save you. I tried. You have to know I tried."

Carolynn stood up, throwing the poppy down on the earth. She felt annoyed with herself. She was still angry, angry for a lot of things, and a lot of reasons. She was mad at the world but mostly herself. This was stupid. She went to turn away when movement in the brush caught her attention.

She waited for the animal to show himself when a large, black wolf stepped out of the brush and walked hesitantly towards her. She knelt down on one knee, extending her hand for him to smell. The wolf sniffed her hand, licking her fingers in submission. He couldn't be more than a year old. He was all black, except for his large, white paws. He was big, even by wolf standards, and his eyes were light grey, just like hers.

"Your Shadow's pup?"

I am Kai. The oldest of my mother's last litter, Kai told her, sitting back on his haunches, proudly puffing his chest.

"Named after your grandfather. What an honor." She smiled, the first true smile she'd had in a long while. "You look just like her."

Grandfather says the same.

Carolynn nodded. "I was just visiting her," she said, motioning towards the bed of tulips.

Yes. I've been waiting for you to come back.

"Why?"

I wish to serve you the way my mother did, he informed her. *I'd like to help you and offer my protection.*

Carolynn smiled, an idea taking root. "There is something you could do for me."

Heidelberg, Germany

Sirens rang in the air as the police sped past. Drunken laughter filled the streets. The smell of stale beer and cigarettes wafted through the air. The Hauptstrasse was overwhelmingly filled with city goers out for the night. The castle ruins on the hilltop looking over the Rhine Neckar were illuminated brightly for all to see. The shops were closed for the night. The only places open for business were restaurants, bars, and clubs full of drunken teens and loud, burly adults.

An elderly couple holding hands and strolling down the cobblestone street looked sideways at him. He dashed into the nearest ally, bumping into a rowdy teenager with an open bottle of liquor in hand. The teen cursed at him in German as he fled down the street. He found an empty alleyway and slid down the side of a brick wall, huddled beneath a black trench coat he had managed to steal. He felt a tap on his shoulder and jerked away, facing the person with his hands up in defense.

"Woah, it's okay. I'm not going to hurt you." A tall brunette stood against the bitter chill, dressed for warmth and a night out.

"What do you want?"

She held her hands up, showing him she meant no harm. "I just want to help," she said slowly, bending down to his level, balancing on the tips of her shoes. "What's your name?"

Thankfully, she asked the one question he knew the answer to. "Donnie."

This book has been a major labor of love. It has been in the works for 12 years, since I was a nineteen-year-old kid in college with her husband deployed to Guantanamo Bay living with her parents and dreaming of a badass Angel and his Goddess vixen. Since then I have had four children, traveled Europe as an Army Wife, divorced, and remarried, but Donnie and Carolynn have always had my heart. This book has been sitting on my computer untouched for almost eight years, when finally, I felt settled enough in my life to dust it off and finish Stars Ascending to where I could feel proud of it as a thirty-year-old woman. My writing from twelve years ago has definitely changed and I wanted it to reflect that.

I have had amazing support from my friends and family through this very long process. Kathleen and Brianna, you were my very first cheerleaders, my sound boards, and my will to continue even when I felt like I was going insane. If not for you there may not even be a book. Thank you for pushing me to follow my dreams or for encouraging me to keep going. I don't know if you will ever truly understand how much you mean to me.

Aunt Denise, Grandma, and Aunt Pam, my first three proof readers during that very first draft. Your excitement and sorrow over the ending was the real boost I needed to know I did something right. Its not a good book if it doesn't break your heart just a little.

Katlynn, you and your mom were the reason I actually finished writing. You encouraged me to keep going and to find that ending within myself... or maybe it was the yelling at me to finish so you could finish reading, either way, thank you!

To my Book Friends! Stef, Chloe, Sib, it has been an amazing 4 years of know you amazingly talented and creative women who inspire me every day. Thank you for all your love and support and all the smut!

Marjorie, this book would not be what it is without you. Thank you for taking the chance on me and putting the finishing touches on it.

My children, Carolynn (she was named after the creation of this book!), Aiden, Evelynn, and Cameron, for teaching me what it is to be a mom and that in order to succeed I must sprinkle fairy dust and dream of unicorns.

Richard, my love, my heart. You have taught me what true love is. Love is worth fighting for and I wouldn't want to be on this crazy ride called life with anyone else.

Stars Forgotten is the next book in the Stars Ascending Series.

✦ Will Carolynn find Donnie?

✦ What happened to his memories?

✦ What is next for Aros and Carolynn as Queen of the Gods?

✦ Stars Forgotten coming May 2024

Did you enjoy Stars Ascending?

If you enjoyed this book please leave a review or comment where you purchased the book. Thank you for your support.

About the Author

Heather Smith has been crafting stories for as long as she could remember. It wasn't until she was fifteen that she wrote her first novel of which she had no intentions of publishing. Stories has shaped her and was always known for having her nose stuck in a book, preferably fantasy.

Currently, she is working on multiple series, all fantasy genres. When she isn't writing about fantastical worlds, she resides in Spring Hill, Florida with her four children and husband, and spends her time attending school events, working, and loving on her fur babies.

Find more information at:

www.heathersmithauthor.com